D1371714

Also by Moacyr Scliar
Published by Ballantine Books:

THE STRANGE NATION OF RAFAEL MENDES

Translated by Eloah F. Giacomelli

MOACYR SCLIAR

BALLANTINE BOOKS • NEW YORK

Library of Congress Catalog Card Number: 87-17598

ISBN 0-345-34861-3

Manufactured in the United States of America

First Ballantine Books Edition: January 1989

OLD AT DAYBREAK

WHAT TIME IS IT? WHAT TIME IS IT?

It's six o'clock.

Six o'clock in the morning and everything is fine. Time, so to speak, flows slowly; History, so to speak, follows its course—and the urge to urinate is driving me crazy. No, not crazy. Nothing could drive me crazy at this point in my life, not even this wild urge to urinate. True, I do feel discomfort on account of my full bladder; but at least I have a bladder, at least I can hold in the urine. Which at the age of seventy-two is quite something, isn't it? I am the master of my bladder. I challenge it, and except for some occasional leakage, I always get the upper hand. It doesn't control me, this clepsydra, this organic timepiece that inexorably keeps filling up. Time, yes, now that's something that controls me; but not its agents. Does my bladder fill up? I empty it. Not as quickly as I would like to, but I succeed in emptying it. I should go to the bathroom now. . . . But I don't feel like getting up. I spend most of the day lying here. It's true that today is a very special day; if I were younger I would be jumping out of bed eagerly, singing. But I'm too old now, even for the special days, which are few and far between, by the way. Besides, this is such a good bed. So prodigal of surprises. Under the bedcovers I find everything: crumbs of the cookies that I ate yesterday, and the day before yesterday, and last week, cookies being invariably part of my meals, always taken in bed. And there are books here as well, and newspaper clippings, and letters that I've written and never mailed; some dirty clothes, empty bottles, a knife, some twine. . . . A survival kit. If the city were to be invaded by the waters again, as happened in 1941, and if the floods were to transform this bed into a boat, I wouldn't be a desperate castaway; I would have the means to survive both physically and spiritually. Enough to keep me alive until the waters entrusted me to some Mount Ararat.

It's not a boat, though. It's a bed. The bed that my wife

3

and I picked in a small store in Bom Fim, almost fifty years ago. *Give me your warmth, my beautiful girl, give me your warmth, which is balm to my sorrow.* Beautiful, hardly; kind, yes; gentle. When she fell ill, I was struck by the certainty that she wouldn't live much longer, she was much too frail. She died in the Public Charity Hospital, notwithstanding Dr. Débora's efforts to save her. A very serious case—and very uncommon, too, according to that kind lady doctor. My wife wasted away until she died. She left me with a young son, whom I raised with sacrifice, and he too died when still a young man, what a pity. A victim of the rat race, too eager to rise to the top quickly. Had he been more moderate, had he spent the day—or the morning at least—in bed, he might perhaps have survived. Even though he would have had to live on crumbs.

She understood me, my wife did, and life in her company was good. Lying on this very bed, surrounded by books and sheets of papers, I would work ceaselessly on my historical research. What I earned then was a mere pittance, but she never held it against me; on the contrary, for as long as she was able to, she provided for the household by making artificial flowers and knitting pullovers for a store. Then all of a sudden, there she was, in my arms, dead. She died and the days went by.

And now, what time is it? Hm? What time is it?

Ten past six. I've been awake since four o'clock, ruminating thoughts. Things happen while I lie here: wars and coups d'état, cases of people coming suddenly into a fortune, and devastating love affairs. But me, I'm old and I'm lying down. If I got up, it wouldn't be to take over power, but to urinate. I'm aware of my own limitations. Yes, I'm an educated man; I've studied a great deal, which, however, hasn't done me any good. Not until today, that is, because today I intend to change things; the historical moment has arrived. I'll seize this opportunity, one in a lifetime. I won't be a fool like that descendant of Jonah's who, wanting to identify himself with the prophet, used to plunge into the waters of Lake Tiberiades, and remain underwater—intensive training it took!—for a long period of time, waiting for the gigantic fish that would come to swallow him. One day this man, while submerged, raised his eyes and what did he see through the clear waters? The soles of two feet walking on the lake. Did he think that it was Jesus walking toward a transcendent destiny? No. He concentrated on examining the skin on the soles of those feet. A smooth, rosy skin; from this the man inferred that the walker must be someone given to contemplation, someone so much above reality that it was possible for him to walk on water. Jesus, a contemplative? The man was mistaken. It was neither the first nor the last error in a long line that has come down to our times.

To whom am I speaking? To God? I don't know. I don't know whom I'm speaking to, but I speak as a person of commanding knowledge: I'm an educated man, an historian. I don't hold a university degree, of course; I'm self-taught. I know more about History than many a university professor. Nobody knows more abot the *cristãos-novos*, the New Christians, as the Christianized Jews became known, than I do. Nobody has studied their genealogy so thoroughly. I've returned to the biblical roots of these strange individuals, hybrids of Christians and Jews.

It's true that this knowledge hasn't done me much good. . . . It has made me neither rich nor famous. I've tried to profit from my knowledge—but without success. At least until now. At least until today, until this very hour.

What time is it? What day is today? How is the weather? What is the exchange rate on the dollar? Has Franco died yet? Who has died? What kind of pain is this in my chest, or in my belly, or in my hand, or in my head?

Why ask? Why ask so many questions when time keeps running out, faster and faster? And by the way, how much time do I have left? Little? How much is little? Months, years? Minutes? How many minutes?

The morning dawns, as usual; and, as usual, there are questions. What else can a solitary old man do but ask questions? Questions, questions. Always.

Today, however, it is going to be different. Today I'll get an answer to my tortured questionings. In the rough sea of anguished uncertainties, peace and tranquility will finally reign. A speck of order will be introduced into chaos because now there is a plan, a program, an objective; a goal: ten thousand dollars.

Money is the answer. The answer is money. A short, distinct, definitive answer—dollars.

A man is going to pay. Although innocent, he'll pay. Innocent? He can't be all that innocent: if he's going to pay it's because he's not innocent. And he'll pay. He doesn't

know yet that he will, of course; at the moment he is unaware; he dreams. At the moment he lies asleep, like many
other citizens of Porto Alegre. Soon, however, he'll wake up,
and then the countdown will start. By the time the sun goes
down today, the goal will have been reached: ten thousand
dollars. Funny: I've never laid eyes on a dollar bill, I don't
even know what one looks like. But there's no need to. All I
have to do is ask. No, not ask—demand. I'm glad I'm
convinced of this fact: I can demand. They owe me a lot of
money, at least ten thousand dollars. Even more, for sure; a
minimum of ten thousand. Dollars. I'll demand. Rafael Mendes
will pay.

What time is it? What day is today?

It's six-fifty—Monday, November 17, 1975. The parcel is
now probably being delivered. The parcel for Rafael Mendes.

And Rafael Mendes? What does he see upon waking up?

RAFAEL
MENDES

THE EYES OF THE PROPHET? HM? THE EYES OF THE PROPHET? No. Neither the eyes of the prophet nor the bonfires of the Inquisition, nor the caravel, nor the decapitated head of Tiradentes, none of this does Rafael Mendes see upon opening his eyes. And yet it was a night of adventures, of love affairs and of betrayals; a night of fire and of blood, of wine and of annato; it was a night of harps and of drums. It was a night that lasted for centuries. And from which he might never have awakened: for in the last of a succession of terrifying dreams and nightmares he was being attacked by a knight in medieval armor who kept tightening his iron gauntlets around his neck to the point where he could no longer breathe; to the point where—although aware that it was but a nightmare—he felt he was dying. He was saved by the pale dawn; the first flash of light of this day woke him up, startled, gasping for breath, drenched in sweat. But alive. And the first thing that he does upon being reborn is to look at the clock.

Six-fifty. With his hand still shaking, he pushes the alarm button in before the small electronic clock goes off. Then, with a sigh, he lies back again. Little by little he calms down—a serious matter these nightmares, these ghastly apparitions. Where do they come from? Rafael doesn't know, he doesn't have the vaguest idea. By and large, he used to sleep well and it was even hard for him to wake up—on the day of his university entrance exams his mother had to splash him with cold water in order to wake him up. But now—now everything has changed. He doesn't sleep much, he doesn't sleep well. But why not? An acquaintance of his who also suffers from nightmares speaks of *anxiety*. *Anxiety*. Yes, but is there anyone who doesn't feel *anxiety*? Is there anyone who doesn't worry every now and then about a promissory note in the bank—or speaking more broadly, about the meaning of life, about death? Everybody feels anxiety. Rafael Mendes doesn't think that he's any more anxious than the average man of his age, thirty-nine.

Helena lies asleep beside him. Helena, who used to suffer from insomnia, who used to complain of anxiety—Helena is asleep. Asleep and even snoring. It's true that hers is not a normal sleep, it's sleep induced by the pills that the doctor prescribed—she does sleep, however, and sometimes won't get up until ten o'clock. It's not that Rafael begrudges her her sleep. Helena *has to* sleep, she has earned sleep; she's been through quite a lot, poor thing. Because of their daughter: *What will become of her, Rafael? Of our Suzana?* Rafael tries to reassure her; she shouldn't worry so much, she shouldn't take matters to heart so much; yet, the fact is that he too worries about their daughter. She's probably the cause of his nightmares. Although she doesn't appear in them, she must be the reason behind them. Suzana and everything else, of course, but mostly Suzana. Helena used to take things in stride. Even in moments of adversity—of which there were many, God knows there were—she remained stoically calm, bearing the hardships with exemplary resignation. Now, this state of affairs with Suzana. . . . It has really upset Helena. Ever since this trouble started, she's been unable to eat or sleep properly; she has fits of crying; she's been going from doctor to doctor; she has consulted psychologists; and under the pseudonym "A Distressed Mother," she even wrote a letter to a newspaper. A letter that the editor described as being *anguished*. A letter that was given prominence by being printed in boldface and which, except for its last paragraph ("Hoping this will receive the traditional welcome," etc.), was published in its entirety. A letter that, however, did not receive a response worthy of it. "Nobody is willing to help me!" she cries out in moments of utmost distress. "Nobody!"

And not even in her sleep can she find rest. Which is substantiated by the way her face screws up in pain at intervals. She must be dreaming about Suzana. What else could she be dreaming about, poor thing? The bonfires of the Inquisition? The decapitated head of Tiradentes? Maybe. It's possible that married couples share the same nightmares; but this wouldn't be fair. The bonfires of the Inquisition? Why? Isn't Suzana causing her enough heartache as it is? Poor Helena.

With pity, and with tenderness too, he gazes at her. He loves her. He is sure he does, or almost sure. To be perfectly honest, he doesn't really know what it means, this thing called *love*. If he were pressed to come up with a precise definition of this feeling, he would hesitate. It was with admiration that he once overheard one of his office workers saying: "I love my wife almost as much as I loved her on the day we were married; some twenty percent less, maybe, but I still love her." A mere subordinate, yet cocksure about his feelings, cocksure about many things. Unlike Rafael, who doesn't feel sure. Not at all sure. And with each new day—a day like this one now breaking, for example—he grows less confident; less and less so by the hour, by the minute. It's six-fifty-five. With a sigh, he pushes the bedcovers aside, gets out of bed, goes to his daughter's bedroom.

Empty. Even before entering her room, he was sure that's how he would find it, and yet, up to the moment of opening the door, he was still hoping he would find her there, asleep. Cradling the plush cat in her arms, just as she used to when she was a little girl. The plush cat is now hanging by the neck from the chandelier.

As it has been for the last three months. The maid, horrified, wanted to take it down. Suzana wouldn't let her. It was a symbol of oppression, and its punishment well-deserved, she explained. Which didn't make any sense to the maid, the daughter of farmhands in the interior. And ever since, the maid has refused to set foot in the bedroom. Which suits Suzana just fine: she doesn't want anyone tidying up her things. This accounts for the amazing disarray: clothes strewn over the chairs and on the desk, lying in a heap in a corner; books and records scattered everywhere. On the walls, torn posters: a Guevara, an Einstein sticking out his tongue, a Christ with the caption JOIN THE NEW ESSENES. That's the sect she belongs to: a group of young people, some living in communes, others not; all of them believing in a primitive form of Christianity mixed with paganism. Christ, they claim, has a double identity—male and female. As a man, he attracts women with his purity, with his gentleness; under the form of a beautiful woman called Sophia he entices male proselytes. Through copulation with her they reach truth—orgasm standing for Passion, death, and resurrection. The ancient Essenes lived in communes, true, but they would remain chaste until they reached a certain age; the contemporary Essenes use sex as a form of initiation. The New Essenes? The old indecencies, that's what it amounts to, mutters Rafael. How disgusting, how stupid. What bothers him the most in this bedroom is the smell, a mixture of incense, alcohol, mustiness, marijuana. Enough to make him dizzy. Abruptly he gets out of the room, closes the door behind him, returns to his room, goes into the bathroom, turns on a switch and—there is light. Bright light: several lightbulbs shine in this spacious bathroom, reflecting themselves on the chrome-plated metals. Pure light, abundant light; such things, trivial though they are, touch Rafael Mendes. Darkness instantaneously chased away thanks to light! Thanks to the anonymous workers who at this very moment are moving about silently and diligently in a distant hydroelectric power plant!

In spite of everything, this country has vitality, energy; it's a country of contrasts, an irritating country, yet a great country, no doubt about it. And with this thought he takes off his pajamas, steps into the shower stall, and at one stroke, turns on the cold-water tap. The jet of water hits him violently, he has to stop himself from stepping out of the shower, but anyway, that's what he wants—a stimulating, ice-cold shower. Then, turning off the tap, he grabs a towel and vigorously rubs himself dry (a piece of advice from his Latin teacher in high school: Boys should take a cold shower and rub themselves dry vigorously with a rough-textured towel. His towel is not rough; anyway, the Latin teacher is already dead, and so are many of his former teachers). He feels better. Not *well*, not one-hundred percent well, yet better. As his employee would put it, twenty percent better; but how close to feeling really well is he? Not close at all. If only Suzana. . . . *I'd better shave and listen to the news.* He turns on the radio.

ARE YOU READY FOR THE GREAT ADVENTURE OF YOUR LIFE? asks the announcer in a grave voice, which is, however, neutral, devoid of excitement, of promises. The question remains unanswered: The radio goes silent, the station is off the air. A power failure. An event not entirely unexpected, yet unexpected enough to annoy Rafael Mendes: Such exorbitant rates they charge us, these people at the Electricity Company, they charge the highest rates in the world and look at the service they provide. A real ripoff it is. In the United States, in Europe, the person responsible would have long been fired.

ARE YOU READY FOR THE GREAT ADVENTURE OF YOUR LIFE? The question keeps reverberating in his ears. What kind of adventure could that be? A voyage around the world in a flimsy caravel? An outer space exploration? An expedition to Africa? A meeting with a mysterious woman? A plunge into the past in search of childhood ghosts or even historical roots? The probing of the future in a daring exercise in perspective? No, of course not. More likely a plot of land by the seaside. Or a new car model. The station is back on the air, and the announcer is apologizing; it was indeed a power failure, he informs his listeners with no apparent grudge. But without saying what kind of great adventure it is, he moves on to the next commercial, and soon the news is on.

Preparations for the establishment of the Petrochemical Pole are underway. Rio Grande do Sul can no longer remain an essentially agricultural State, somebody, a politician, declares; we have to enter the industrial era even at the price of causing some harm to the environment. A Federal Decree putting into effect the National Alcohol Plan has been made public—and again someone makes a statement: We cannot remain at the mercy of petroleum, we must become self-sufficient in energy. West Germany's Minister of Foreign Relations arrives in Brazil to put into effect our nuclear agreement; Brazil announces that it will resist any pressures against this agreement; and yet another statement: It is, somebody says, our last chance (last chance of what? It's not clear). Water in gasoline causes the crash of a Cessna in Minas Gerais—two dead and two wounded. In São Luís, the explosion of an oxygen container kills thirteen people and leaves twenty wounded. In São Paulo, the implosion of the thirty-story-high Mendes Caldeira Edifice takes place. The Government will grant homeowners a twelve-percent rebate on their monthly mortgage payments to the National Bank of Housing; someone, a labor leader, voices his opinion that even so the dream of owning a house is becoming less and less real for millions of Brazilians. Petrobrás will ask a financial consortium headed by the Libra Bank for a one hundred-million-dollar loan. Ford launches its luxury models for 1975. It is hot: Yesterday the temperature rose to 37 C. Commenting on the decision made by the Brazilian Government to establish diplomatic relations with Mozambique at the embassy level, a spokesman declares: Brazil is a sovereign country that follows its own independent line of foreign politics; besides, we have interests in common with the Third World countries, which like us, are fighting a severe international crisis. Uleanto won the Great Bento Gonçalves Prize for 1975.

Next, a commercial, soon followed by the last news item:

Generalissimo Franco remains in a coma. Gosh, mutters Rafael. He's not in the habit of talking to himself; but like all the citizens of Porto Alegre, and like everyone else, generally speaking, he can't help being amazed at the dictator's stamina. Why doesn't this fiend die, everybody wonders (or at least he imagines that everybody does). Not that he's particularly interested in this matter; he isn't; he doesn't like Franco, he doesn't have any particular regard for the Spanish caudillo, but—he's a human being. Anyhow, human or not, it doesn't matter. What does matter is the fact that there was nothing in the news about the financial market. Proof that the rumors haven't reached the media yet. Fortunately, Rafael thinks to himself, relieved. He finishes shaving, turns off the radio, goes to the livingroom, sits down on an armchair, and lights a cigarette. He shouldn't, not so early in the day: The doctor has already advised him to cut down on smoking, there's something wrong with the T-wave of his electrocardiogram and the chest X-Ray doesn't look too good, either. Top executives can't afford to get ill, says Boris, halfway between a joke and a veiled warning; although Rafael doesn't like his tone, he agrees that top executives have to stay healthy and maintain a high level of energy, so he has cut down on smoking, and he has his first cigarette only after the morning coffee. Today, however, he's making an exception. Because of the nightmare, or because of Suzana, or even because of Franco being in his death throes, whatever the reason, he feels restless, and only a cigarette can help. Besides, the maids haven't brought in the coffee yet. Disgraceful. There are two of them and they can't even handle the work that Helena handled all on her own when they lived in the small apartment in Floresta. If Helena knew about this. . . . But no, Rafael doesn't want her to get upset about a trifling thing. Anyway, the maids are now moving about, and Rafael can hear them talking in the kitchen. Curiously enough, they are discussing Franco. Isn't it something, says one of them, the way this man is hanging on. Right, replies the other, these old folks are really strong, not like us who can be knocked down by any slight breeze. Well, reasons the first maid, it can't be much fun, hanging on to life like that, we have to make room for other people. The second maid—who always agrees with the first one—agrees again, and adds another well-considered statement, to wit, what kind of life is that, thrown on a hospital bed, unaware of what's going on around him, relieving himself in bed—that's no life. And what is life?—Rafael feels like asking. You who are so smart, come on, tell your boss here what life is! They know nothing, no, they don't. They don't even know how to brew coffee properly.

He stands up, opens the door leading to the balcony, then steps outside. He loves this balcony; it's the one place in the house where he can feel better. Because of the beautiful view that unfolds from there: Not as magnificent as the enthusiastic advertisement claimed ("Spectacular apartment with a gorgeous view, located in aristocratic urban neighborhood," etc.), but the view is beautiful, anyhow: the hills, the river. A small strip of the river—and what else would he want to see from there? A beach, the vast ocean, the shores of Africa, who knows? The apartment is spacious, comfortable (besides being, as Boris remarked at the time when Rafael first bought it, right for his social position). He likes the apartment, he likes Porto Alegre, a city he doesn't know much about. That it was founded by sixty Azorian couples in the eighteenth century he learned in elementary school; but he learned very little else about it. The little he learned, however, is enough for the current exigencies of his existence. Sixty couples: all he needs to know.

It's not the city that occupies Rafael's mind now, it's his daughter. Where in the world is she? He doesn't have the slightest idea. When it comes down to it, he doesn't have the slightest idea about anything relating to Suzana. Which leaves him perplexed rather than hurt. How did this all come about? How did the little girl that he used to rock to sleep become transformed into this stranger he can't even communicate with?

"Good morning, Senhor Rafael."

It's one of the maids, a little mulatto girl with a pert face. Although Rafael dislikes her, he doesn't say so; he doesn't want to make things any more difficult for Helena. Poor thing, she's already got plenty of problems: The last thing she needs is to have to go hunting for another maid, a species that's becoming more and more rare, even in this city of Porto Alegre, where all these girls from the interior converge in search of opportunities and guiltless sex.

"And Dona Helena?"

Trying to vex me, she is, this little hussy. She knows that Helena sleeps late in the morning, and yet she has to ask.

"Later."

"I see. And Suzana?"

"Dona Suzana," he corrects her dryly.

"What?" Her face wears an expression of surprise.

"Dona Suzana, do you hear? All right, you may leave the coffee here."

Crooning to herself, the maid walks away.

For a few moments Rafael Mendes sits staring at the stainless steel coffee pot in front of him; a dark drop hangs from its spout. Spellbound, he watches it: Will it fall? It does. It falls and a dark stain forms on the white tablecloth. The sight of this stain brings to his mind something that happened to Suzana once. She was two years old when he and Helena finally managed one evening to go out for the first time. Until then it had been impossible, his mother refused to look after her grandchild, saying she wasn't a babysitter; finally, they got hold of someone reliable, an old servant who used to work for Helena's mother—a fat, quiet woman who had difficulty breathing; she suffered from high blood pressure. But she was extremely devoted to the little girl, so one evening they decided to go out for dinner and then take in a movie. They returned home late. Upon opening the apartment door they were horrified at what they saw. Suzana was sitting on the floor, very quiet. Before her, lying face down in a pool of blood, was the servant—dead. She'd been dead for hours, according to the doctor they sent for; she must have felt suddenly indisposed, and as she fell down, she hit her head. And Suzana? What had happened to her during all that time? Impossible to find out. An incident long relegated to a catalogue of obsolete things. Except that such things will haunt you. They always do.

Rafael Mendes raises his eyes and looks at the front door.

(Later he'll wonder what made him get to his feet and open the door. In retrospect, he may come to the conclusion that it was a presentiment, but this explanation will neither satisfy nor reassure him, because he doesn't really believe in presentiments. After all, there are plenty of people who, moved by strange presentiments, rise to their feet, open the door—and find nothing. But if it wasn't a presentiment, what was it then? Yet another unknown factor to increase his perplexity.)

He rises to his feet, walks to the door, and with an abrupt gesture, opens it. *There is* something.

There is a box in front of the door.

A cardboard box, old and tattered, crudely tied up with

some grimy string. Who placed it there? wonders Rafael, intrigued. It couldn't have been the maids; they know their boss dislikes untidiness and wouldn't leave things lying in the corridor of the building. Moreover, the box is for him, Rafael; his name is written on the lid in big, carefully traced letters. Both his name and address.

Rafael Mendes's initial reaction is to open the box. He even steps forward—but stops short, suddenly suspicious: What if it is a trap? A . . . bomb? A box-bomb?

Ridiculous. A bomb? Why? Who in the world would send him a bomb? Who would go to the trouble of plotting an attempt against the life of a man who is interested in nothing but his work and his family, a man who hasn't harmed a soul, a man who, in addition, suffers from nightmares that wake him up gasping for breath? As far as he knows, he doesn't have any enemies. And he stays away from politics; as a matter of fact, he doesn't understand a thing about politics and doesn't even want to. Now Boris, yes, he has connections in the two national parties—the National Renovating Alliance and the Brazilian Democratic Movement, he has financed electoral campaigns, he must have made political enemies—not to mention other enemies, and there must be quite a few of them. But that's Boris's problem, Rafael doesn't want to get involved, notwithstanding his own high position in the firm (for how much longer Rafael will manage to keep himself apart from certain, let's say, scabrous matters is another story. But this is not what is at stake at this moment. At this hour in the morning, in this place, and under these circumstances).

Rafael knows nothing about the underworld of crime. He hasn't engaged in any shady deals; the brokerage business doesn't preclude the occasional wheeling and dealing, but thre has never been anything amounting to embezzlement. He merely tries to survive, that's all. Like everybody else, he too is caught in the rat race. He fights to keep himself afloat, he keeps flailing his arms, his legs, and if in the process some-one gets hurt, it isn't on purpose—and it certainly wouldn't warrant a bomb. At least not a bomb *this* big.

Neither does he have any dangerous connections. Once he met a man in a bar, and this fellow, an elderly mulatto with a carioca accent, after saying that he had been a member of former President Getúlio Vargas's Department of Journalism and Propaganda, began telling him some muddled story about the killing of Indians in Rio Grande do Sul. If I'm bumped off, the man said, write to the newspapers and tell them everything. A rather strange situation; but they were both drunk, and anyhow, the incident took place a long time ago; Rafael couldn't have been more than thirty years old at the time.

Could the box be the result of one of Suzana's mix-ups, somebody with a grudge against her, a rival group perhaps? Possible, but rather unlikely. The left-wingers she's been hanging around with, or used to, are basically fun-loving types, who speak of rivers of blood but wouldn't harm even a fly. Anyhow, as far as Rafael knows, his daughter is now going through a mystical phase, and mystics don't send bombs.

However—whether or not it contains a bomb—how did the box get there? Who brought it? Who succeeded in walking across the lobby, where day and night—and at no small cost to the condominium (not that Rafael minds, though it's expensive)—there is always a doorkeeper who even carries a weapon? He goes into the kitchen (a *modern, spacious kitchen)* and under the questioning eyes of the maids, he picks up the intercom phone. The doorkeeper answers.

"Yes, Senhor Rafael."

"What's this box in front of my apartment?"

The man hesitates:

"I put it there, Senhor Rafael. It was too early, I didn't want to wake you up. I was just about to. . . ."

"Who brought it?"

"To tell the truth, Senhor Rafael, I wasn't here when it was delivered. It was the other doorkeeper, he's off at six o'clock, who received it. He said that a young man had come with a box for you."

"And this young man—did he say who sent the box?"

"No."

A pause. From the kitchen Rafael can see the box through the half-open front door.

" Senhor Rafael . . ." begins the doorkeeper, embarrassed. "I'm sorry, sir, but when I took the box upstairs to your place, it burst open. I did my best to tie it up, but I must say that it opened."

"And what's inside?"

"Some clothes and books . . . I'm sorry."

"That's all right, young man. This can happen."

He puts the receiver down, suddenly relieved, euphoric

even; he could say to the maids, Imagine, darlings, somebody sent me a box and I was afraid to open it because I thought it was a bomb—a bomb, imagine! But without saying anything, he makes for the front door, and picks up the box. Heavy, but not too heavy. Nothing that would strain his heart or his backbone. With some difficulty, he places the box on the balcony outside the living room. Getting a knife from the table, he cuts the string. And he opens the box.

CLOTHES, JUST AS THE DOORKEEPER HAD SAID. OLD CLOTHES: old shirts, old pants. Two old suits in an old-fashioned style—dating back to the thirties or forties. A Panama hat. A Borsalino cap. Bow ties—three of them. A pair of shoes with woven vamps. And oddly enough, a pair of combat boots of the kind soldiers used to wear a long time ago. Taking these articles out of the box, Rafael carefully stacks them in a pile on the balcony.

At the bottom of the box he finds some old, yellowed books, most of them historical texts: *The Inquisition in Portugal and in Brazil, The Sugarcane Cycle,* among others. A notebook with annotations. Inside Rafael finds a photograph. An old snapshot taken by an itinerant photographer; the caption reads: *Porto Alegre-Rua da Praia—1938.* It shows a couple, the man holding a child on his lap. . . .

For some seconds, Rafael gazes at the photo; then his eyes brim with tears. The little boy in the sailor suit is himself. And the man in the white linen suit, smiling shyly, is his father, Rafael Mendes, who in 1938 walked out on his family never to come back.

The door opens.

"Hi."

Rafael turns around, startled. It's Suzana.

Beautiful, his daughter. Rafael has to admit that she is beautiful, despite his displeasure at seeing how grubby and slovenly his daughter has become: her hair dishevelled, her dress tattered, her feet in rawhide sandals—not to mention the cigarette dangling from the corner of her mouth. She's beautiful despite her slenderness and small frame, despite her stooping posture. As beautiful as Helena; the same beautiful mouth and big dark eyes. Eyes now staring at him with an expression of insolent defiance.

Defiance? Yes. But there's also weariness on her face. Weariness and a certain perplexity. The same perplexity that Rafael sees on his own face when he looks at himself in the mirror upon getting up in the morning. And wasn't it perplexity too that he saw in the eyes of the little boy in the photograph?

"What's that?" asks Suzana, pointing to the snapshot.

"None of your business," Rafael replies, quickly putting the photograph into his pocket. Irritated; irritated and aggrieved; it's the same aggrieved irritation that his mother could barely conceal whenever he asked about his father. "Besides," he adds, "don't you think that I'm the one who should be asking the questions? Where have you been?"

She sighs.

"So here we go again. It's going to start all over again, the same old fight. Why, Father? I could say it's none of your business where I've been, but then you'll say that you're my father, that you have the right to know whose company I keep, and I'll say I'm now eighteen years old and can damn well choose my own company, and then you'll say that as long as I live here and eat your food I owe you explanations, and I'll say you can stick your food up your ass, and then you'll be furious and tell me to hold my tongue, and I'll say no way and then I'll run to my room, slam the door shut, throw myself upon the bed and start crying while you remain here muttering 'how shameless, how shameless.' No, Father. We're not going to watch this rerun again, are we? Maybe we could try to change ourselves, what do you say? Why don't you begin by telling me about that photograph? Why don't you try to tell me everything? Hm, Father?"

He doesn't reply. He keeps staring at her in silence.

"All right," she says. She goes to her room, slams the door shut. Rafael plops himself into an armchair. In a daze. It's eight o'clock and so many things have already happened to him since he managed to extricate himself from the gauntlets of the warrior. He tries to sort out his thoughts, to make sense of things—without success, for he's far too disturbed. Fortunately, the maid walks in; fortunately, she reminds him that the coffee is getting cold; fortunately, he comes to his senses. After all, it's Monday, and he has to go to work, he has to earn a living, there are all these bills to pay, the mortgage, the condominium fees, the maids' wages, the supermarket, Helena's psychiatrist. He sits down at the table: it's important to eat, even if he's not hungry. At least a slice of bread, a cup of coffee, a small one, but with milk and sugar—he can't go to the office on an empty stomach, it would make him dizzy, trigger palpitations, the doctor has already warned him about such things. Before sitting at the table, though, he carefully folds the clothes, puts them back, together with the books, into the cardboard box. He carries the box to his study and locks it in a cabinet. As for the photo and the notebooks, he puts them in his briefcase. He'll examine them leisurely in the office, away from the prying eyes of the nosy maids.

He sits down at the table, turns on the radio. The last chords of a soothing melody, and soon afterward the announcer repeats his previous question: ARE YOU READY FOR THE GREAT ADVENTURE OF YOUR LIFE? in the same grave, emotionless voice. It refers, as Rafael had suspected, to a plot of land you can own by the seaside, a place near the town of Laguna, in the state of Santa Catarina. A dream place. The sea breeze, the charming landscape, etc., everything yours for low monthly payments. Rafael pours himself some coffee, takes a sip. Cold. Even so, he drinks it.

Another newscast. Generalissimo Franco remains in a coma, and the doctors have given up any hopes of saving him.

Franco, Spain: his father. In 1938 Rafael Mendes abandoned everything—family, friends, his medical practice, his government job—to go to Spain, where a civil war was raging. Why? He has never found out; his mother is tight-lipped about this subject. Understandably so, but the fact is that she is tight-lipped. When Rafael was a child, she used to tell him that his father had gone away on a trip and that he would come back one day (like King Dom Sabastião returning to the Portuguese people?). Later she told him that his father had fought in the war and had been killed. And she would say nothing else:

"I don't know, Rafael. I don't know why he had to get mixed up in it."

"But was he a communist?"

"No. He was never involved in politics."

"Was he upset at the time?"

"No. A bit eccentric, perhaps; but I wouldn't say upset."

"But then. . . ."

"I don't know, Rafael. I just don't know. It was the war, that's all. Many people were . . . idealists."

Other people, both friends and acquaintances of Dr. Rafael Mendes's, were equally evasive. The old bacteriologist Cuvier de Souza, known in the medical circles as *Dr. Microbe*, once talked to him at length about his former classmate at the Faculty of Medicine:

"He was a very kind man . . . I liked him a lot. Do you know that the two of us were the very first people to test penicillin in the state of Rio Grande do Sul? Penicillin which I produced, my friend, in a lab I had at the far end of my backyard!"

But when Rafael Mendes wanted to know about Spain, the doctor became reticent:

"Well, such things do happen. Who knows what was going on in his head. Or in anyone else's mind, for that matter."

Then slouching over the microscope, he changed the subject:

"Bacteria. . . . They've always fascinated me, ever since the day when I first looked at them through a microscope. It's a whole world, my friend. A world of tiny creatures that live, flit about—and don't talk. Talking is not always necessary."

Disconcerted, Rafael took leave of him. And as time went by, he stopped asking questions; he had resigned himself to the fact that it would be impossible to throw light upon this mystery—until the moment when, opening the door, he came across the box.

COULD THIS BOX HAVE BEEN SENT FROM SPAIN? COULD it be that Franco's imminent death had encouraged the anonymous guardian of his father's belongings to ship them to Brazil? But if this were the case, who was the bearer? Who in

Porto Alegre saw to it that the box got to Rafael Mendes without any advance notice?

Picking up a crust of bread, Rafael pierces it with a toothpick, into which he then inserts a small piece of the paper napkin. And behold, a hull, a mast, a sail—the small boat is ready. Rafael pours coffee on the saucer and there he places the tiny vessel to sail away. Blowing upon it, he creates a favorable breeze; the tiny boat glides away but soon keels over and sinks in the dark liquid. Sighing, Rafael looks at his watch. It's late, he must be going.

He goes into the bedroom, finishes dressing; Helena stirs in bed. "Where did I go wrong?" she murmurs. "Tell me Rafael, where did I go wrong?"

Poor Helena. Raised in a straitlaced family—her father was a Lutheran minister—and given to hard work and to the pursuit of virtue, she just can't comprehend her daughter's metamorphosis. From a gentle, attentive girl into a rebellious, wild beast: How did it happen? Helena has good reasons to feel hurt; she was always a good mother, she did everything she was supposed to do. She breastfed her daughter at regular hours, kept her tidy and clean, taught her to follow good hygienic habits; helped her with her schoolwork, gave her some sensible advice when she turned into an adolescent. The result of all this? Rebelliousness. Rebelliousness and uncleanliness. Rebelliousness, uncleanliness and licentiousness. Weird ideas. Atrocious behavior. Vices aplenty. A constant stream of foul language, even in the presence of guests. Venereal disease—who knows? Who knows what's been happening to this girl?

The worst of all is the idleness. Suzana doesn't *do* anything—she doesn't study, she doesn't work, she doesn't even have a hobby like playing the piano or sewing. And to Helena, nothing could be worse than laziness. Not nowadays, not since the sleeping pills, but until recently she would get up early in the morning to go shopping at the supermarket, at the fruit stalls; she would look after all the needs of the household, leaving nothing to the maid (having two servants is something new—Rafael's decision, which she but reluctantly accepts). She still looks after her husband's clothes, and if it weren't for the tremor in her hands, she would darn the holes in his socks too—before marrying him she had taken sewing lessons. A fine woman.

And Suzana? She mocks. She sneers. Soon after joining

this sect, The New Essenes, she started taunting her mother: "Christian! Some Christian you are! What are you willing to do for Jesus? Would you fuck an atheist if that's what it takes to turn him into a believer?" "May God forgive you," Helena, shocked, would mumble. "May He save you because there's nothing I can do anymore to help you, except pray and pray a lot." "Phony prayers!" Suzana would reply. "Jesus doesn't want your prayers! You pharisee!" She has now toned down her hostility toward her mother; she ignores her, which is much worse. Poor Helena.

Rafael sits down on the bed by his wife, and leaning over, kisses her on the face. Again, he thinks: *My wife, she's beautiful.* Still beautiful, despite the expression of contained suffering. Beautiful. There are other women more beautiful; more intelligent, more funloving, more sensual. But Helena is *his* wife. This really counts. A lot. She has been important to him ever since they first met at a dancing party.

A mutual friend had introduced them to each other:

"Helena, I'd like you to meet Rafael; Rafael, Helena is the daughter of our pastor. You may dance with her, but see that you treat her with respect. And no necking!"

Rafael had laughed then, but ever since he met her, he has always treated her with respect: Throughout the two years of courtship, the two years of engagement, the nineteen years of marriage. To him, love and respect are intertwined. Boris, who is a bachelor, often remarks with a tinge of mockery mingled with a certain admiration:

"I asked you to work for me, Rafael, because any man who stays married for such a long time is bound to be faithful to the company he works for."

He is faithful. He's had a fling or two, of course; more out of need than wantonness. Since the problems with Suzana began, Helena has lost interest in sex. "I'm sorry, Rafael, but I'm not in the mood, I just can't," and so he was forced to turn to someone else; nothing serious, however. Because there are things that carry more weight than sex. Like spending nineteen years together, struggling and suffering together—this carries weight. Even if there is no love, there's still friendship. There's tenderness. It's with tenderness that he now sits gazing at his wife. Such a kind woman. So affectionate, so attentive. No, she couldn't have failed as a parent. If someone has failed, it's him, Rafael. There must have been an occasion when he failed—or many, perhaps. How many?

Two, three? One hundred and twenty? In what way did he fail? By beating his daughter? To the best of his recollection, he has never beaten her. Some light spanking, for sure, but that's not damaging, it's even recommended by modern child psychology, according to what he has heard. Did he yell at Suzana? But who hasn't yelled at their kids? It's unlikely that he inflicted traumas upon his daughter by yelling at her, or by using a sharp tone of voice, or by frowning at her. It must have been something more serious. Something like the incident that occurred on that winter night.

It was a freezing cold night, and the *minuano*, the cold dry wind that blows from the southwest, was hissing furiously. Around midnight, Suzana, who was then three years old, woke up crying. She was afraid of the wind. "Go and bring her here," said Helena; Rafael, sleepy, didn't want to get up, so Helena went to the child's room, picked her up and put her on their bed between the two of them. Suzana laughed, happy. All three of them were laughing, frolicking, singing children's songs. Meanwhile, under the blankets—

Under the blankets *things* were happening. Rafael's foot kept searching for Helena's foot, his hand on her thigh. *I want you,* he whispered, his voice cracking with the sudden, violent desire. He turned off the light, and moving over his daughter, he lay on top of his wife. "Not now," she protested feebly, "the child is awake, Rafael, this is crazy." He, however, wasn't listening, he was already entering her: a quick, nervous act of copulation. Then still panting, he slipped back to his side of the bed.

Groping about, Helena found the light switch. "Don't," he whispered, but too late: in the raw brightness created by the lightbulb he saw Suzana's eyes fixed on him. There was no accusation in her gaze, not even sorrow; perplexity, maybe, but not the innocent perplexity of children, it was something else, something disturbing. Disturbed, he got out of bed, went to the small living room of the apartment and there he remained smoking, shivering with cold, determined not to go back to bed until his daughter had fallen asleep. Once in a while he peered through the door—and there she was, staring at him. "Oh, shit," he kept muttering, overcome by guilt and embarrassment. Guilt, embarrassment, and irritation as well; he was sleepy, he had to get up early in the morning. Finally the little girl fell asleep and he could slip back into bed. "I told you so," murmured Helena, still upset, "I told you we shouldn't have done this."

Could this incident have been the cause of everything? Could it have been the seed, which after being latent for a long time had finally germinated to grow into this carnivorous plant of hatred? A good metaphor—but does it correspond to reality? Helena believes it does. After talking to psychologists and to her own psychiatrist, she firmly believes that this incident was the cause of everything. Rafael, initially skeptical about such interpretations, is now beginning to think that she might be right. A childhood trauma, it could well be. Otherwise, how to explain this transformation in the girl, a transformation that makes her seem possessed? A trauma. It could well be.

And if he assumes the blame for his daughter's strange behavior, shouldn't he also assume the blame for his father's behavior, a behavior no less strange than his daughter's, and for his mysterious disappearance? What did he do to make his father leave home so abruptly? Did Rafael make fun of him, did he irritate him with his shrill screaming? Did he spill soup on his books? (His father had a huge library, a haven he repaired to whenever he could, there to submerge himself in reading. What did he read, that kept him so engrossed? Rafael has never found out: Soon after his father's disappearance, his mother sold all his books to the owner of a second-hand bookstore. When Rafael was a teenager, he was once stopped on the street by an elderly gentleman who asked him if his father was still interested in genealogy. "My father is dead," Rafael replied, and he walked hastily away so that he wouldn't cry in front of a stranger. He ran home, locked himself in his room, and cried for a long time; then he wiped his eyes and consulted a dictionary. He wanted to know the meaning of genealogy.) So? What had he done to displease his father? Did he cry a lot at night? Suzana would bawl all night long, keeping him awake. Rafael, at that time, was trying to finish an evening course in Economics; always tired, he would nod off in class. The teacher would wake him up: "What have I just said, Senhor Rafael? What did I say about Marx's mother?" Rafael didn't know. He knew absolutely nothing about the fact that Marx's mother had demanded that her son stop talking about capital and that he start doing something about earning the said capital. His classmates would grin. Rafael ended up dropping the course. But he didn't walk out on his wife and daughter; he continued to work hard as a real estate salesman and he didn't make much money. After meeting Boris, his life changed. But it was then too late to go back to college. He sacrificed a career because of his daughter. They have sacrificed many things, Helena and he. But apparently they haven't absolved themselves from the mistakes they've made, from the traumas they've inflicted.

And on his father—what kind of trauma did Rafael inflict? It would be more logical to think that it was Rafael's father who had inflicted a trauma upon Rafael as a result of a trauma his grandfather had inflicted upon his father, and so on and so forth in a succession of traumas transmitted from generation to generation; a distressing picture it is, but isn't this just like the history of humanity? Julio, who used to work with him at the office, had always maintained that it was; but Julio had been a depressive who ended up killing himself, who knows, maybe to interrupt an anguishing sequence of events that affected his life. Now, is Rafael so powerful that he can inflict traumas on both his daughter and his father? Can he generate traumatic waves that might be transmitted with reverberations to the past and to the future, upward and downward, leftward and rightward? Rather unlikely. Besides, not everything was a trauma. Not where Suzana was concerned. They have a photo album that bears witness to the beautiful moments: Helena, at the maternity hospital, breastfeeding Suzana; Rafael pushing Suzana in a stroller; Rafael on all fours with Suzana riding astride his back; Rafael on the beach, building a sand castle for her. And the pictures taken at birthday parties, with all the children in their clown hats standing around the table, and the birthday cake with two small candles, four small candles; seven, ten; and also all the other pictures showing Suzana in school, at dancing parties, during a trip to Rio (the Sugar Loaf Mountain, the Corcovado); and also a snapshot that caught her unawares as she stood by the window, a dreamy expression on her face. Many pictures; many moments. Good moments. Good pictures: As Rafael bettered himself, he kept upgrading his photographic equipment. He was paid a good salary, they lived comfortably. . . .

Suddenly Suzana changed. The artless smile gave way to the mocking, bitter expression; the childish remarks to the ironic observations; the peaceful family life to the almost daily fights. A sudden transformation—as sudden as the transformation that Rafael imagines his father underwent. Why?

Could it be that Suzana inherited something of her grandfather's character, a predisposition to sudden instability? Could this be something genetic, inevitable?

There is no time now for any further lucubrations; it's eight-fifteen. Kissing his wife once more, he gets to his feet, puts on the jacket, picks up the briefcase, and leaves. He takes the elevator down to the underground parking lot, where at that hour there is already much activity: The roar of powerful engines echoes in the spacious precinct, cars pull away, the tires screech on the cement. Rafael walks toward his parking stall. He greets a neighbor: A top functionary at City Hall. Another neighbor: The manager of a large pharmaceutical laboratory. A third one, a doctor, waves and comes over to him to talk. He is still young, this doctor (a neurologist, it seems), and usually cheerful; there is, however, an undisguisable tone of anxiety in his voice as he asks:

"What are these rumors flying about, Rafael? People are saying that the situation of your finance company is not good—is it true?"

Rafael reassures him: of course not, everything is fine, it's only the market that has been a bit jittery.

"I bet it's the franc. Not the Swiss franc, the other one. The franco with one foot in the grave," he quips.

The joke falls flat; the other man forces a smile: "Well, Rafael, I have quite a bit of money invested with you people, see that you don't let me down, you'll tip me off, won't you, if things are really on the skids. I want out before it's too late."

"Don't you worry," Rafael assures him. "I'd do anything to help out a neighbor."

Saying goodbye, Rafael gets into his Opala and starts the engine. The doctor also gets into his car, and waves to him: "You won't forget, will you, Rafael?" and drives away. Rafael, too, pulls out; after leaving the parking lot, he drives up a quiet street until he gets to the Avenida, then plunges himself into the stream of cars. The usual traffic jam, with horns blasting in the air. Rafael whistles softly. No use losing his temper. What for? To have a heart attack, an ulcer? Not worth it. Besides, his schedule is flexible. He's no longer a mere employee who has to clock in at a regular time. Now that he's an executive, he doesn't have to quit or start work at any fixed time.

The man in the car next to his, a battered Corcel, stares at him with a threatening scowl. Why? Is this man, like the neurologist, another suspicious investor? Rafael doesn't know him, has never seen him before. There was a time when he knew almost all of the clients of the finance company, but since the expansion he no longer has contact with them, he now deals only with documents, with balance sheets. Maybe the man is indeed an investor. Then again, maybe not: there are so many people who go about scowling for no reason at all. So many people ready to pick a fight with anyone. If Rafael were to scowl back, the man would probably ask: *What are you staring at me for? Don't you like my face?* And Rafael would have to (what else?) retaliate with an insult, and the man would then open the door, step out of his car with an iron bar in his hand, and Rafael would have to open the glove compartment and take out the gun . . . except that he doesn't have a gun. Luckily: This way he won't get mixed up in turmoils, he has enough problems of his own to harass him. The traffic starts moving again, the Corcel turns into a sidestreet. Luckily.

He turns on the radio. Another newscast (there's no shortage of them, for sure, at this hour). But it's the same news he's already heard: Franco remains in a coma. He'll remain in a coma, for sure, until Rafael gets downtown, and until the following day, and the following, and the following, generation after generation. . . . That's a good idea for a book, he thinks to himself. He's not much of a reader, he has neither the time nor the inclination to read; however, here's a novel he would like to read—the story of a man who, despite being in a coma, still wields power.

Next to him now is a big cattle truck. Twenty or thirty or forty steers travel behind bars—to the slaughterhouse, surely. They seem perplexed, the poor animals (what's happening? what happened? what's going to happen?). Rafael is reminded of something Boris once told him about his relatives in Europe, who were taken to concentration camps like cattle to the slaughterhouse. A fate Boris, born in Brazil, had escaped. As a matter of fact, Boris would even have somehow escaped from a cattle truck like this one transporting him to his annihilation. Initially—for the first couple of kilometers—he might be perplexed or frightened; soon, however, he would find a way to reverse the situation. By bribing the guards, for instance. By offering them partnership in some business enterprise—say, public transportation. ("Why transport people to their death? These are passengers with a one-way ticket, passengers who don't pay for their tickets. A much better deal would be to transport workers and farmhands to the fields.") Guards and prisoners would escape with the truck, already transformed into the first vehicle of a large fleet that would eventually cover Europe, the Americas, and Africa. Boris is shrewd. Rafael has no doubt about it. He'll find the means to get over the problems besetting the finance company. But how, Rafael doesn't know.

He stops for a red light. A girl comes up to him, gestures to him to roll down the window (he always keeps the windows up—as a precaution against assaults). She must be Suzana's age, and dresses like his daughter: a long tunic, rawhide sandals, necklaces and bracelets. And the same dishevelled hair. A member of The New Essenes, for sure. "Jesus loves you, darling!" she shouts, holding a brochure out to him. Even without looking, Rafael knows what it is: a comic-strip story about an atheist ("I didn't believe in anything. All I wanted was money and power"), who is converted ("I returned to the arms of my sweet Jesus") and who finds happiness (". . . and now I'm happy"). So that's what Suzana does: She accosts drivers, calls them *darling*. The shamelessness. And why is she home, sleeping? If at least she got up early in the morning, like this girl. But no, she'd rather sleep in the daytime and go out at night. The shamelessness.

"I'm not interested," he says dryly.

"It doesn't matter, darling." The girl smiles; it's a somewhat forced smile, but a smile nevertheless. "Jesus still loves you. And I love you too. A kiss."

Taking hold of his head, she kisses him on the face, almost on the mouth. Then laughing, she steps back, and walks toward the car behind his. Embarrassed, he smoothes down his hair, glances around him. The truck driver is grinning:

"Why didn't you take advantage, buddy? The chick was giving you the come-on and you missed the chance! You're a real fool, man."

The light turns green, Rafael, irritated, drives off revving the engine; he cuts in front of a sports car (what do you think you're doing, hey oldster, yells the driver, a young man wearing sunglasses), the traffic now flows freely, he passes car after car, still irritated, such shamelessness, such shamelessness.

Downtown, he leaves the car in a parking lot. He'll have to walk a few blocks to the finance company. So much the better. The walk will calm him down a little.

Carrying his briefcase, he walks along Rua da Praia. It's a beautiful day—that's something: a beautiful day—and he strolls down the street. It's a luxury he can afford, there's no need for him to hurry: less haste, more speed is what Julio used to say—poor Julio. Not so these office boys in their gaudy shirts, or these salesgirls with folded arms and a bewildered expression on their faces as they walk toward their place of work, the Lojas Brasileiras or Lojas Americanas or Casas Pernambucanas, or some other department store; or unlike these plainly dressed gentlemen heading for their offices or government bureaus. As he saunters along Rua da Praia, he searches for a familiar face; to greet someone on this street is almost a need, it would be a solace, particularly on this morning, a morning so replete with threatening omens.

But Rafael doesn't recognize a soul. He no longer knows anyone. The city has grown, there are no streetcars anymore on Rua Borges de Medeiros, no photographers at the entrance of Galeria Chaves. And no paperboys hollering out the headlines as they run down the street. Instead, there are now newsstands exhibiting, in addition to newspapers *(Franco remains in a coma)*, brightly colored pornographic magazines. And the café once located in this old building, the café where he used to be a regular, is now a video arcade, and despite the early hour it's already jampacked. A group of young people stand admiring the skill with which a boy with an Afro wields an electronic weapon. The agonized repeating howls of the bear he's shooting mean the boy must be a good marksman. Rafael is familiar with this game, he's seen it played at another such establishment in Camboriú, a town in the state of Santa Catarina: The beast is shot at, it turns around, it's shot at again, it turns around—endlessly, relentlessly, until a sudden silence signifies that the player has used up all the shots entitled by the token he'd inserted into the machine; with a bored sigh he drops the weapon. Rafael walks on but soon stops again in front of a show window displaying adding machines. Now, that's something he likes; he knows everything about adding machines, he keeps himself well-informed about every new model that comes on the market. And these *are* new models, state-of-the-art machines. He'll come back at another time to talk to the manager and find out about prices. Now he can't, it's getting late, and he hurries away. He arrives at the headquarters of the finance company. An old but respectable-looking building, utterly unlike those buildings so common downtown, with their maze of large and small rooms housing companies that are often mere fronts for dens of racketeers, drug traffickers, and drug addicts. Boris knew what he was doing when he chose the *Dom Furtado de Mendonça Edifice* for the headquarters of his finance company. Boris always knows what he is doing.

Rafael gets into the elevator. He greets a company employee (arriving late for work, is she? No, she probably went out on an errand and is now back), who smiles at him obsequiously. And the elevator operator greets him effusively, then comments on the beautiful day: in his opinion the good weather will hold, the days will become increasingly more beautiful, will probably reach an almost unbearable level of beauty—an excessively radiant sun, a tremendously blue sky. No more clouds. Rain? Don't even think of it. Were Rafael to suggest, however, the possibility of losses that could be caused by the drought, the elevator man would immediately correct himself and say it's going to rain, it won't be long before it starts. A nice fellow, this old man; usually garrulous, yet unassuming. He's a black man. Whenever he talks about his ancestors—one of his favorite topics, by the way—he remarks that many of them were slaves. He mentions Palmares, a hideout for runaway slaves in the seventeenth century, and recalls his grandmother eulogizing the *Lei Áurea,* the law that abolished slavery in Brazil. His grandfather worked in the fields from sunrise to sunset, but he operates an elevator, forever marveling at this wonderful technology: "You press a button, and it starts working." Besides, he is in contact with important people, businessmen as well as beautiful women who leave a subtle scent in the elevator cab. Sometimes matters whispered about in the elevator have hit the headlines. He has already said to his wife that he could make a fortune with the things he knows; however, he admits that he hasn't mastered the art of piecing together a coherent picture from fragments of information; he hasn't been initiated into this game of power and money, which is full of unknown factors. Slavery still casts its shadow upon him. This, though, doesn't prevent him from saying at the moment when they get to Rafael's floor: "I've heard that the company is going down the tubes, Senhor Rafael." There's no time now to clarify the implications of this remark, made in a casual tone; nor to find out the reason behind the new way of addressing him, the reason why the *Doutor Rafael* of a few days ago gave way to the *Senhor Rafael*. The elevator doors open, others are waiting, he has to step out. He gets out, followed by the woman employee.

So people are already talking, he thinks to himself as he walks down the corridor. Even the elevator operator is talking, and if he is, it must be an open secret, probably the talk of the street, what's astonishing is that the newspapers haven't reported it yet (right below FRANCO REMAINS IN COMA: *Rumors about Situation of Finance Company Shake Stock Market*). Maybe it will hit the headlines tomorrow. Maybe there's already something on the radio.

"Good morning, Doutor Rafael."

The doorman, deferential, holds the large glass door open. On the wall opposite the entrance, right above the head of the pleasant, smiling receptionist, is the name of the company, *Pecúnia S.A.*, written in letters of burnished metal. Three thousand and six hundred square meters; three floors decorated by the famous Ballestra, of São Paulo. The image of strength and sobriety that Boris has always wanted his business enterprise to project is evident in the hardwood panels, the crystal chandeliers, the marble, the red carpets. The company emblem, designed by a heraldry expert, alludes to Boris's family name, Goldbaum: It depicts a gold tree against a blue background, with the legend *Arbor Aurea*. Something Rafael has always thought rather tacky, but the clients apparently go for it.

Walking past the reception area, he enters the waiting room; except for Boris's office, which has a private entrance, access to all the directors' and managers' offices is through this room. This large room (approximately ten meters long by eight meters wide) is known as the Coin Room. One of Boris's ideas: Near the farthest wall, dangling from ceiling-suspended metallic strings, are huge reproductions of ancient coins—the smallest one being nearly half a meter in diameter. The cruzado, the doubloon, the talent, the louis d'or, the penny—they swing in currents created by hidden fans, casting whimsical reflections about the room as they swirl in the spotlights aimed at them. (There's a rumor, which Boris hasn't refuted, that he owns several other collections of the same coins, in a smaller size but minted in gold and silver.)

In the middle of this room stands the main attraction, again a reminder of Boris's family name: The gold tree. Small, with a thick furrowed trunk and sparse foliage, it resembles a bonsai. Hanging from the branches are half-open pods containing seeds like the ones found in bean pods, except that these are metal seeds and glow intensely in the spotlights. "Gold?" the visitors wonder, amazed. Boris has always left them wondering; they *must* be gold, though. Proof of this belief is the fact that the tree is kept inside an unbreakable glass dome. Embossed in gothic letters on an acrylic plaque is—by way of explanation—the history of the Gold Tree. "The Gold Tree," the inscription informs, "is one of the three trees mentioned in the Bible, the other two being the Tree of Life and the Tree of the Knowledge of Good and Evil. Unlike the first two, the Gold Tree was not in Paradise, but somewhere in the vast territory that stretched to the east of Eden, where it waited for dauntless and enterprising men to find it. The Gold Tree," the inscription goes on to explain, "derives its name from the powerful tropism of its roots toward this most precious of metals. Avidly searching for subterranean lodes, the roots infiltrate themselves into the hardest rocks. They solubilize the ore by secreting a certain liquid and then they absorb the ore; after circulating in the sap, the liquified gold is then deposited into the seeds in the pods, and eventually they become grains of the purest gold, their shape perfectly spherical. Although the Gold Tree can live for millennia, their total number nowadays probably doesn't exceed ten. This is because the adventurers that come upon them are interested only in seizing the seeds in order to sell them. What they do not know is that these seeds, surprisingly enough, are capable of germinating, thus generating—after a long period of time—new Gold Trees. Wisdom, patience, discernment are thus richly rewarded." As a matter of fact, the family name Goldbaum was adopted by Boris's great-grandfather in Europe under the conviction that a name or a family name can condition one's destiny. In this case, the conviction came true: Boris does have his Gold Tree. Or if not the Gold Tree, the material possessions that gold can buy: real estate property, cars, land. He has even invested in art: Adjacent to the Coin Room is an art gallery with paintings and sculptures by famous Brazilian artists, and even a small Frans Post—not a widely known painter, but unquestionably the painting is an authentic piece of work by this Dutch master. A good collection worth several million dollars. However, what has made Boris Goldbaum famous throughout the country—he has even been profiled in the TV program. *Fantástico*—is the Coin Room. The guest book has the autographs of distinguished visitors, among them, the Minister of Finance and the Minister of Projects. In the financial circles, the whole thing is regarded as an eccentricity, if not a publicity gimmick, but Boris says that the Coin Room is intended as some kind of homage to the all-time great financiers. Among them, he particularly admires the Rothschilds, to whom he claims to be distantly related. To verify the existence of this family connection, he had German genealogists do some research, which although far from finished, has already cost him a fortune; the initial findings, however, are encouraging—the experts believe that Boris's great-grandmother might have been a cousin of the first Rothschilds. It is the founders of the dynasty that Boris would dearly love to have as ancestors. He's not interested in any of the more contemporary Rothschilds: The barons who live in castles in France, who devote themselves to horsemanship, to philanthropy, to the cultivation of certain exclusive varieties of grapevines—these don't interest him at all. The Rothschilds he admires are the first ones, the five brothers. In every major European capital, each brother laid the foundations upon which a financial empire was to rise. Of the five, Boris's favorite is Nathan of London. In sharp contrast to his elegant brothers, Nathan was pudgy and unattractive. With his hands stuck into his pockets, he would stand by one of the pillars—Rothschild's pillar—in the London Stock Market. From there he would follow the bidding, and it was there that he pulled off the coup that was to increase the wealth of the family overnight.

Thanks to the speed with which his brothers' agents moved across Europe, he had been informed about Napoleon's defeat at Waterloo even before the British government knew anything about it. So what did he do with this valuable piece of information? Did he rush into buying English bonds and shares? No. On the contrary, he began to sell them, thus triggering a run on the stock market. *Rothschild is in the know*, the speculators thought, *if Rothschild is selling, it means that Napoleon has won*. The price of bonds and shares kept plummeting; then, at the eleventh hour, Nathan Rothschild made one final bid and everything was his for a

ridiculously low price. A huge fortune made in a matter of
minutes.

What a master stroke, says Boris with a sigh. That's art,
my friend, pure art. It takes a genuine dramatic talent to pull
off something like that. Full control of one's emotions is
essential. The face: impassive, stony. The voice: steady,
confident. The eyes: fixed. The trace of a smile, a tremor in
the voice, a fleeting glitter in the eyes, and all is lost.

In those days, Boris goes on, the stock market was an
adventure, it was life itself. Not anymore. Nowadays, it's the
telex, the computer. Of course, personal abilities are still
important, but intensely developed awareness, quick reasoning, a deep genuine knowledge, no longer count. Among the
Rothschilds, it was Amschel, the founder of the dynasty, who
first gave signs of having this special talent. He started out as
a coin dealer. He would carefully keep his collection of
ancient coins in small cases lined with velvet; to collectors,
he would then send beautiful gothic-lettered catalogs illustrated with pictures of his coins. It was this passion of his that
brought him and Wilhelm, the Prince of Hanover, together as
friends: power now allied to money. With the prince's approval,
he opened a small money-exchange house, the *Wechselstube,*
where the currency of all the German feudal states could be
exchanged.

Mayer Amschel Rothschild was not avaricious. He realized
that money had to circulate. However, it wasn't without pain
that he disposed of his coins. Before handing them over to a
buyer, he would cast one last lingering gaze upon them,
trying to fix in his mind the stylized drawing of a tree, the
firm profile of a prince, the fancifully embossed number—a
five, or a two, or a seven.

Boris has a portrait of Mayer Amschel, painted in the style
of the Dutch masters. It depicts him as an old man, together
with his wife, Gutele.

Boris has contradictory feelings about the matriarch of the
Rothschild clan. On the one hand, he respects her: He can
feel in her not only the age-old strength of Jewish mothers,
but also an additional component—the firm determination of
a Roman matron, could that be it? The end result was this
woman's remarkable ability to lead her children along the
road to victory. On the other hand, her presence in the
Rothschild clan irritates and even repels Boris. It seems to
him that the ship that so dauntlessly braved the treacherous

sea of international finances could well dispense with a female figure. Money is a man's business. Only men possess the capacity for abstraction necessary to discern the face of the Goddess of Fortune in the numbers hastily jotted down on scraps of paper. To women, money represents merely the ordinary: a home, food, clothes. At best, jewelry, and not always real: low-carat gold, flawed diamonds. Costume jewelry. Boris definitely doesn't take women seriously. He acknowledges that the women's movement has made progress; in his publicity campaigns he addresses the female sex—*Women investors, at the Pecúnia you are given special consideration*—but that's about it. This Boris, whom gossip columnists refer to as *our most eligible bachelor* wants women only in bed, and then for a short period of time: a week, a month—until the moment when they start mentioning marriage. Then, gently but firmly, he sends them packing.

Of course, he pays a price for this attitude. There are investors, and good ones too, who won't entrust their money to the Pecúnia because they disapprove of what they consider frivolous behavior. And even Boris's own family puts pressure on him to grow up and get married. His mother and sisters are always phoning to tell him about various charming, intelligent—and even wealthy—young ladies. But Boris doesn't want to hear about them:

"I've already got all the charm I need, Mother," he shouts over the phone: The old woman is practically deaf. "I said that I've already got all the charm that I need! That's right! And all the intelligence too! And money I have too, Mother! That's right! I'm loaded with money!"

Boris doesn't like his mother and sisters too much; of his father, however, he has fond recollections. His father was a communist tailor who would spend his meager earnings on books. He knew Marx by heart and was able to answer such questions as: Can you quote paragraph two, page three, of the German edition of *The Eighteenth of Brumaire?*—and: Karl's first dog was called Toddy; what was the name of his second dog? His father was a first-class tailor, but had no personal ambitions. On the contrary: He hoped one day to use his expertise to finally get even with the bourgeoisie. He had even devised an incrimination scale based on the various kinds of fabric favored by the bourgeoisie: English cashmere indicated a ruthless despoiler (the sentence: death by hanging); S-120 linen, a bribetaker (the sentence: execution by firing squad); radiant alpaca wool, a crafty politician (the sentence: imprisonment in a cage for public exhibition) and so on. "Thank goodness," says Boris, "that my father died before he saw his son rich. He would never have forgiven me for my silk shirts; I'd get a life sentence, at the very least."

RAFAEL GREETS HIS SECRETARY AND GOES INTO HIS OFFICE. Big, not as big as Boris's, but much bigger than the offices of the other directors; after all, Rafael is a trusted man: His rank is reflected in his desk (hardwood), in his chair (with a high back, not as high as Boris's, but still quite high, with five centimeters of the backrest protruding from his head), in the telephones (five of them, including a red phone for direct access to Boris), in the comfortable armchairs, in the thick carpet. The pictures on the walls are not worth millions like the ones in Boris's art gallery but they are signed by the most prominent painters in the arts community of the southern part of the country.

Rafael sits down, places the Samsonite briefcase—a gift from Boris, who purchased it on New York's Fifth Avenue—on the desk. A beautiful briefcase—solid, dependable, really impressive; it's true that for a while Rafael fantasized about this briefcase: a fantasy about opening it one day and finding a rattlesnake lying on his papers; but that's already in the past. His fears are now of a different kind.

He opens the briefcase: There's the notebook. He takes it out, puts it on the desk, sits staring at it.

An old notebook with a torn, stained cover. The kind that school children use for their homework and that adults sometimes like to use. Heaven knows why. Out of a yearning for their own childhood, perhaps.

No, Rafael doesn't recall seeing this notebook before. But then he hardly remembers anything from his childhood; it's amazing how other people can recall so many things from their first years of life; he can't: It's as if he were looking at the past through opaque glass. Shadowy forms, nothing but shadowy forms. Slowly he leafs through the notebook. A journal? No, more like a record of scattered annotations, phrases and words that a person jots down almost at random, for reasons known only to him. As for the handwriting, he can't say if it's his father's. As a matter of fact, he has never seen much of Rafael Mendes's handwriting, except for his signature. Besides, there's nothing unusual about this handwriting he is now looking at, quite ordinary it is, in the lilac ink popular in his father's time. A graphologist would probably be able to disclose a little more about his father's character, and even throw light upon the reasons behind his abrupt departure ("Your father, although a physician, was really a potential warrior. Notice the way he crosses his T's with a violent stroke—like someone wielding a sword. He had an uncontrollable vocation for action—these curlicues, don't they look like smoke rising from a burning city?" "Could this description apply to a revolutionary?" "Yes. A revolutionary. Why not? Trotsky's handwriting looks pretty much like his. Are you familiar with the life of Trotsky, sir?" "No, I'm afraid I'm not very interested in such matters." "Neither am I—please, don't get the idea that I'm a subversive or something like that. I happen to be familiar with Trotsky's handwriting because I have a book with a specimen of his signature. There is a resemblance between the two signatures, I can assure you.") On the surface, none of the annotations makes much sense. What does it mean, for instance: *The Prophet Jonah—glass?* And what or who is *Maimonides? The Inquisition:* This he knows what it is, of course, and ditto for *The Dutch Invasions.* Both must be related to his father's interest in History; ditto for *Colombo and Palmares,* the colonies established by fugitive slaves; but *the treasure of the Essenes* is again a mystery (a legend? something like the legend of the Gold Tree?). And there are also small drawings: ancient weapons (a bow and an arrow, an apple, a halberd), escutcheons, flags that Rafael has never seen (but what does he know about flags, anyway?). Finally, the following verses:

Matato está el fijo del rey, malato que no salvaba,
siete dotores lo miran, los mijores de Grenada.
Siete suben y siete abajan, ninguno le face nada
ainda manca de venir el de la barba envellutada.
Calentura fuerte tiene, las tripas tiene danadas.
Tres horas de vida tiene, hora y media han pasadas.
En esa horica y media—hasedle bien por su alma.

And the words of a lullaby:

> *Duerme, duerme, mi angelico,*
> *hijico chico de tu nacion.*

In Spanish: Meaningful to someone who went to Spain. But what kind of Spanish is this? It doesn't resemble the kind spoken nowadays in Buenos Aires, for instance, the kind of Spanish Rafael is familiar with from several visits to that city. He has never heard anyone recite this poem, nor has he ever seen it in print anywhere. It seems to be a Spanish dialect, but where is it spoken? In which *nación?* Why did his father write down this particular poem? What does it mean? Rafael heaves a sigh. The notebook hasn't really been of much help. At least the photograph helped him recall his father, the face he had forgotten; when he was a teenager he used to imagine his father as having the face of a soldier photographed by Robert Capa, a photograph Rafael had seen in a book about the Spanish Civil War. A dramatic photograph: Hit square on the chest by a Falangist bullet, the man is falling backward, his arms wide open: his right hand still holds the rifle, but the weapon is now useless because he is about to die, no doubt about it; and because he died, Rafael appropriated that man's face on which pain and surprise were stamped, and superimposed it upon his father's face. Now Rafael no longer needs this borrowed face for he has a face, although it is old and out of focus; a face but still no answers. To sum up, what does he know about his father at his hour, on this day? That he was a physician and a humanitarian—which he learned from an old lady, one of the many old ladies who entrusted their savings to the Pecúnia: "Your father was very kind, Doutor Rafael. I consulted him once; very charming and kind he was; a bit eccentric, but kind."

Eccentric. That's what his mother also says, her husband was eccentric. Yes, but what does she mean by *eccentric?* That Dr. Rafael was crazy? That he was different? And why different? Because he didn't say much? Because he read a lot? True, he did read a lot. According to the owner of the secondhand bookstore who bought Dr. Rafael's library, he had amassed a large number of fine history books. Mostly Braziliana, but also some World History. And in a large cabinet with glass doors he kept a collection of assorted curiosities: ancient maps, astrolabes, sextants, telescopes, compasses, retorts, hourglasses, clepsydras.

His mother hadn't wanted to keep any of it; she offered all those objects to an antiquarian: "Take everything." "But I'm rather embarrassed, ma'am, they are real treasures." "I don't care. Take everything." "Wouldn't you like to think it over, ma'am?" "Take everything. Or I'll throw them away." "For heavens' sake, please, don't do that! I'll take them." He did. And of his father's belongings there is nothing left.

Yes, that's about all Rafael knows. There are some memories, too. . . . Dim images . . . Sensations . . . A mustache brushing gently against his face when he was a little boy . . . A deep baritone voice singing a lullaby . . . But it's difficult to recall such things clearly.

There's a knock on the door. Startled, Rafael hastily puts the notebook away in a drawer and locks it.

"Come in."

"Excuse me, Doutor."

It's the office boy coming in with a long computer printout: the balance sheet showing the transactions of the previous day. Still upset, Rafael thanks him. The young man stands looking at Rafael:

"Are you feeling all right, Doutor? Is there anything you need?"

Rafael thanks him: No, he doesn't need anything. He's fine, a slight headache, that's all. It will soon go away. The young man, however, still lingers at the door. Finally, he is bold enough to ask:

"Doutor Rafael . . . Is it true what they are saying?"

Rafael looks at him, surprised.

"What? What are they saying?"

"That this company is about to close down."

He takes one step forward:

"Look, Doutor Rafael. If it is true, I want to let you know, sir, and Senhor Boris too, that you can count on me for anything at anytime. Senhor Boris—"

He stops abruptly, wipes his eyes.

"Senhor Boris has been like a father to me. He got me this job, he helped me buy a small house out there in Alvorada, he paid for the medicine that my wife had to take when she was ill. I'm deeply grateful to Senhor Boris for everything I have, Doutor. Really grateful."

Rafael stares at him, surprised. This man, deeply grateful

to Boris? That's news to me! Well, well, was Boris then helping this insignificant, boring little man, so insignificant that Rafael can't even think of his name, and so annoying that people call him Sticky? That's news, disconcerting news; it shows that he doesn't really know Boris as well as he thought he did, despite their long acquaintanceship. Definitely, there are things that the computer printouts don't tell.

"All right, St— All right, young man. Thank you for your concern. It's quite comforting to know that we can depend on such dedicated employees."

As soon as the man leaves, Rafael unfolds the long printout and begins to peruse it. He does his own calculations; for the next half hour he presses the keys of the calculator with annoyance, at times cursing under his breath. When he is finished, he flings the mechanical pencil on the desk, leans back in the chair. It's worse than he thought. The crack, which began to widen a month before, has become a huge hole. The situation is now unmanageable. The fears of the neurologist, of the office boy are well founded; the Pecúnia is indeed in the red. The deficit, just taking into account the bills of exchange without coverage, amounts to thirty million dollars. Besides, there are all those floating checks, and the bank loans, and the fat payroll. "I have the highest rate of profit potential in the market," Boris has often boasted, and indeed he has, but this situation has its price too, and then there is the matter of the disastrous mismanagement of the company, and all those parties given to entrepreneurs and investors—the whiskey and the champagne in bottles carrying the emblem of the Pecúnia, the Gold Tree. It's all over now.

Picking up the red phone, he dials Boris's number. "He's not in yet," his secretary informs. "Let me know as soon as he comes in," says Rafael. He can barely control his annoyance: Here's the ship springing leaks everywhere and Boris doesn't even put in an appearance. He might be the financial wizard people say he is, but he is intrinsically irresponsible. Like Suzana. "Oh, shit," he mutters.

He rises to his feet, paces about the office; he opens a cabinet, takes out a bottle and a glass, pours out a shot of whiskey, then sits down on an armchair, sipping the drink while looking at the view absentmindedly: The heart of the city, the shimmering river, a freighter slowly sailing away. I wish I were on that ship, he thinks. Traversing the sea. Toward some far-off region.

The phone rings. A woman's voice, husky, sensual.

"It's me. Celina."

Celina Cordeiro. Ex-Miss State of Rio Grande do Sul, ex-wife of a wealthy industrialist, a well-known socialite. Boris hired her as the company's public relations person: Her job consists in making contacts with various people, in finding potential investors, such as wealthy farmers; she's very good at what she does. Rafael's admiration for Celina is independent of the affair he's having with her. An educated, intelligent woman with class. No longer as beautiful as she was in the days when every newspaper carried her picture; she was in a car accident that marred her face; the scars, despite several plastic operations, are still visible on her beautiful, altered face. But she still has a gorgeous body, and in bed she's an ardent lover. Her affair with Rafael has obviously nothing to do with love; it's part of a plan, but so far she hasn't made any demands on him. They usually meet at noon, at a very convenient place—a kind of hotel located downtown, a place with an interesting detail: Access to this building is either through a door that opens onto a tranquil side street or through a tobacco shop. A tobacco shop! The elegant gentleman seemingly looking for fine tobaccos is actually on his way to a tryst. He is not interested in the pipes with fanciful bowls. Nor is he interested in the amber cigarette holders; nor in the Cuban cigars, the cigarillos, the table top models of chrome-plated cigarette lighters; nor in the pocket knives, the daggers with etched blades; nor even in the lottery tickets. This gentleman is about to discreetly enjoy a minor affair of the heart. Without glancing at the shop owner, who leans on the counter reading a newspaper, Rafael draws aside the velvet curtains at the back of the small store, walks down a narrow, dark corridor, reaches an inner, Spanish style courtyard with a small public fountain: a peaceful, picturesque place right in the heart of a city that grows at a vertiginous pace. Another corridor starts from this courtyard leading to three apartments set aside exclusively for the use of a few, selected customers. Celina prefers the apartment in the middle, the one with mirrors.

An artist in sex, this Celina. With her, it's never the same: There are always new positions, new techniques—for she has studied the subject thoroughly: Under the name of her dead sister Cornélia, she gets all the books she needs to keep herself up-to-date from a mail-order catalog, or else, disguised behind dark glasses, she buys them from newsstands located in distant neighborhoods. She is an expert in the Oriental modes of copulation (these people are really well versed in this subject. Who would have thought so by looking at them, slightly built, with slanted eyes); one mode she particularly fancies requires that the man and the woman do it on a horse galloping across a vast meadow—being a city dweller, though, it's unlikely that she'll ever find the opportunity to try it out.

"There's no need to identify yourself, Celina." He tries to make a wisecrack: "This aphrodisiac voice of yours—"

"It's been a long time since we last talked, Rafael."

The tone of voice is aggrieved; contained, but bitter.

He makes excuses:

"I'm bogged down with work, as you know. I haven't had time to see you."

"It's not as if I were living on some other planet. . . . Oh, forget it. I've got to talk to you, Rafael. Today."

"Today, Celina? But I can't today, I'm really awfully busy."

"All right," she says, with impatience. "Then it'll have to be over the phone. I want to know everything there is to know about the situation of the Pecúnia, Rafael. Tell it like it is. In black and white."

Ah, so that's what it is. She too has got wind of the situation. Which is not surprising, considering that even the elevator operator and the office boy are already discussing the matter. Rafael tries, senselessly, to sound unconcerned: "Now then, Celina, it's just a rumor. We've had some problems with cash flow, but this—"

She cuts him short—and her tone of voice is now ominous, threatening:

"Let me tell you something, Rafael: You can't bamboozle me, do you hear? Don't think that you and Boris can take me to the cleaners. I happen to know that the Pecúnia is hanging by a thread, and everybody is saying that the government is about to step in, and that you and Boris are decamping, heading for Paraguay. But I'm warning you: If you're actually thinking of pulling off this swindle, I want compensation, Rafael. Substantial compensation for everything I've done for you, and I've done a lot, as you well know. I demand an indemnity, I want a year's salary as severance. Otherwise I'll raise a howl. I'll spill the beans, and you know that I have plenty of friends in the press who can concoct some really scabrous story. And I have connections in the area of security too. I'll smear you, Rafael. You'd better believe me."

Rafael reassures her, saying there's nothing in the rumors; the company is going through a difficult phase, but has the means to weather the difficulties; it's not true that the government is going to step in; on the contrary, the government is interested in preventing any panic in the stock markets, something like this would only tarnish the image of the country abroad, and frighten away the foreign investors.

"Watch out, Rafael," she says, still rather suspicious. "Watch out. You I can trust, you're a decent guy. Boris, however—"

"Don't worry about Boris."

"All right. We'll wait and see."

She hangs up. Almost immediately another phone starts ringing. It's Boris's secretary: He won't be in this morning; he wants Rafael to have lunch with him at his house; his chauffeur is at Rafael's disposal.

"All right."

Typical of Boris. That's how he settles everything: with a lunch or dinner invitation, with a small intimate party; with a phone call to Rio, or to Brasilia, or to New York, or to Zurich; with a tip, substantial or not; or with a gift, expensive or not. Resigned, Rafael folds the computer printout, opens the briefcase—and it's then that he sees the piece of paper. A leaflet, now yellowed; it must have been among his father's belongings:

"Read to the end! You might find it useful! The occult sciences—genealogy—chiromancy—graphology—astrology—phrenology—sensibility to electromagnetic waves—telepathy—spiritual healing. Genealogy is a positive science. Who was your father? Who was your grandfather? Our ancestors determine our fate—the living will always be, and increasingly so, governed by the dead. Bring us your old photographs—letters—notebooks—family documents. By consulting Professor Samar-Kand you will be able to find out about the most important facts of your life. Alchemy too Cabala, the science of numbers. Porto Alegre has never seen anything like this. Unheard of in the metropolis of the pampas. Modern Tarot cards. If you are disheartened, spiritually upset, if you are faced with dishar-

mony in your blessed home, with bad business deals,
with lawsuits, with separations, or if you are having
difficulties in succeeding in life, etc., don't forget:
Professor Samar-Kand has the solution.''

Followed by an address. But what is this? wonders Rafael,
intrigued. What kind of nonsense is this, the occult sciences?
Did his father have anything to do with this?

He turns the leaflet over and, oh, yes, there it is: a message. It seems that this professor something doesn't have any
stationery for he had to use the back of the leaflet to write his
message:

"Dear Senhor Rafael Mendes. These things belonged to
your father. I have some other objects and papers that might
interest you. Please get in touch with me." Rafael heaves a
sigh. Now he knows: There is someone in Porto Alegre who
can talk to him about his father.

Who is this professor? The leaflet suggests a con artist;
could his father have been in any way involved with a con
artist? But he can't make suppositions based on a leaflet;
besides, con artist or not, he intends to seek out this man, so
he had better wait before passing an opinion on him. Moreover, there's a far more pressing matter right now: He must
talk to Boris. He picks up the briefcase and walks toward the
door. The phone starts ringing. It's not the red phone, it's the
one on the PBX system. With his hand on the doorknob,
Rafael hesitates. Finally *(shit!)*, he turns back and answers the
phone. "Your wife," says the secretary. He heaves a sigh;
and then he sighs again (how many times has he already
sighed this morning?).

"Okay, I'll take the call."

A click, a silence, and soon after:

"Hello! Rafael? Hello!" says Helena, sounding anxious.

"Yes, it's me, Helena." Rafael tries not to lose his temper. "It's me, you can talk. Is something wrong?"

"Ah, Rafael," she says tearfully, "this telephone of yours
is so complicated! Rafael, what will become of her, Rafael?
Tell me, what will become of her?"

"But what happened?" asks Rafael, torn between impatience and alarm.

"She didn't sleep home last night, Rafael. Again. She
didn't come home until early this morning, the maid told me.
Did you know that she came home only this morning?"

"Yes."

"And why didn't you tell me, Rafael? I'm her mother, Rafael, I've got to know about it!"

"Listen, Helena." Rafael tries to remain cool and collected, somebody has to. "You were asleep, and you know what the doctor said . . ."

"What the doctor said!" She blows up. "I don't give a damn about what the doctor said! I want to know where my daughter spent the night, Rafael."

"Probably with those friends of hers, the ones from the sect—"

"Sect, my foot! They haven't seen her for a month, they keep phoning all the time, asking about her!"

"Then—"

"Then what, Rafael? We've got to know what's happening to her, Rafael! I'm afraid she got herself into a jam, Rafael."

"What do you want me to do?" says Rafael, already annoyed.

"What do I want you to do?" She's now shouting. "Rafael, for heavens' sake, you're her father!"

"Listen, Helena, I can't talk to you now, an urgent problem has come up and I have to see to it. But I'll find a solution for this situation with Suzana, I promise you, Helena, I will."

"You will, Rafael?" She's in tears. "But how, Rafael? How?"

"Leave it to me, Helena. I'll find a solution somehow, I've already told you."

Silence.

"Helena?"

"Yes, Rafael. I've heard you. Bye now, Rafael."

"Bye, Helena. I love you, did you hear? I love you. Bye."

He hangs up, picks up the briefcase again, and again walks toward the door.

Boris next.

R AFAEL FIRST MET HIM DURING HIS COLLEGE DAYS. BORIS would show up at the school quite often; he represented various publishers of technical books, so he would say, but in fact he was a salesman. And what a salesman he was, that slightly-built Jew with bright eyes and a rather ironic smile. He was good at persuading the instructors to recommend his textbooks to their students, he offered gifts to anyone who bought over a certain minimum amount of books, he sponsored dinner parties to welcome first-year students. And Rafael himself was unable to resist his sales pitch: He bought several books on economics and mathematics. They were good books actually, Rafael had no complaints. The two of them had hit it off right away; after class they would go somewhere for a beer and talk late into the night. The stock market was already Boris's hobbyhorse. He would say modestly that he knew nothing about the subject—he was a high-school dropout—and he would ask Rafael to explain to him the theory behind the stock market. In fact, Boris's knowledge, empirical though it was, was far superior to his; Rafael was amazed at the vivacity, at the sharpness of Boris's mind. "You'd make it in the stock market," Rafael would say. But Boris would dismiss the idea with a gesture:

"I don't think so, Rafael. Such things are not for me. They're for people with a long tradition in this line of work, not for the son of a communist tailor."

After quitting college, Rafael lost touch with him; when they ran into each other again years later, Boris already owned a small brokerage firm; from there to opening his own finance company, it was one single leap, a quick trajectory that Rafael followed, already in his capacity as director of the company. And as friend. At least once a week Boris would have lunch at Rafael's place. He felt at home there; you're my family, he would say, and it was true—he couldn't stand his relatives, who, he claimed, were only after his money. He was very fond of Suzana, would bring her gifts, take her to the circus, or to a movie in the afternoon. But he never married. And nowadays, a hardened bachelor, he leads the life of a mogul, of a tycoon, living in a big house in Vila Assunção, a veritable manor with swimming pools, tennis courts, huge garages for his imported cars, kennels for his Dalmatians. He entertains frequently and is constantly surrounded by gorgeous and famous women. With his arms around them, he lets himself be photographed for the gossip columns, something that Rafael disapproves of, not because of moralism, but because this kind of behavior could mar the image of the finance company. Paradoxically, this hasn't been the case: on the contrary, the more Boris's name appears in the newspapers and magazines, the more he gets new clients; it seems that people want to partake of the secret of this successful social-climber by investing their money in his company.

On the other hand, Boris himself seems to attach little importance to all this luxury surrounding him. He says that he remains a simple man, the difference between his present lifestyle and his lifestyle at the time when he was a book salesman being merely a matter of degree. The Mercedes Benz is just a bigger, more comfortable Volkswagen; as for women—whether it's one, two, or three—what difference does it make? One single woman can offer as many varied and exciting experiences as three or four of these actresses everyone so admires. A swimming pool? Just an outsized bathtub in the open air. Imported wines? Some of them can't hold a candle to our own white rum. Caviar? In the stomach, digested, it's just like any other food. People starving to death? Sure, it happens; it's not his fault, though. There's no use feeling guilty. What's important is to keep money in circulation, to create jobs for these wretchedly poor people. The greatest satisfaction that one can derive from an enterprise such as the Pecúnia, he argues, is to be able to accomplish—and what's more, accomplish in an atmosphere of constant excitement—a job that has no pre-set routine, a job that brings in daily surprises, as if it were a game. He pays a price for this: he is distrusted, envied, even hated; besides, there are few people whom he can trust. "I have no friends," he says, "just contacts."

In the Mercedes, Rafael is taken to Boris's house. The chauffeur, a likeable mulatto, chatters away, he talks about the weather, he discusses soccer, and before he starts commenting on the situation of the finance company, Rafael asks him to turn on the radio—he wants to listen to the noon newscast. Franco remains in a coma, a minister (not the Minister of Finance) arrives in Rio Grande do Sul to sign agreements, there was an accident on Highway BR-101. The newscast ends with the signature tune. Nothing—luckily—about the Pecúnia. Soon after the ARE YOU READY FOR THE GREAT ADVENTURE OF YOUR LIFE? the chauffeur, at Rafael's request, turns off the radio.

They arrive at Boris's mansion, the gatekeeper opens the wide gate to let them in. The butler conducts Rafael to Boris. Wearing dark glasses and a spiffy wine-colored robe, he lies stretched out on a deck chair by the swimming pool. By himself, Rafael can see, relieved. Well, that's something. No gossip columnists or women in scanty bikinis. By himself, sipping whiskey. Boris signals to him to sit down. Rafael sits down uncomfortably on the edge of a deck chair; dressed in a suit and tie, he feels rather ridiculous sitting on a deck chair by a swimming pool. Boris doesn't notice. He seems rather withdrawn today.

"I'm glad you asked me to come over," begins Rafael, "because I really must talk to you. In private."

"All right, Rafael, and I must talk to you too." Boris's *r's* have a pronounced trill—the kind of articulation Rafael used to think of as being typically Jewish, until he met Julio, who also rolled his *r's* heavily. Not being Jewish, Julio looked upon this peculiarity of his as a lucky sign: "Maybe I'll get to be as rich as the boss," he would say, alluding to Boris in a slightly mocking tone. Poor Julio. Not even his *r's* saved him.

The butler approaches.

"What are you having?" asks Boris.

Rafael hesitates: Another whiskey at this time of a working day seems unadvised. However, he asks for one. The butler serves him with measured, but in a way, elegant gestures. Rafael waits until he moves away, then he begins:

"Well now, Boris, it's this matter with—"

He is cut short by a clamor that comes from the house, where some heated argument is going on. Soon afterward a woman bursts through the back door:

"Ah, there he is! I knew he was home! What a pack of liars, finks, all of them!"

Rafael recognizes her; she's Lina Andrade, a television

actress with whom Boris was involved for a long time; she was in Rio recently, playing a minor role in a soap opera. Fuming, she advances toward them:

"You told them to tell me you weren't home, Boris! You wanted to deceive me! Me, of all people! Me, who has never played dirty tricks on you!"

Embarrassed, Rafael rises to his feet; Boris, however, doesn't even budge; impassive, he watches the woman shouting, her finger raised:

"I want my money, Boris! I want my money and the apartment that you promised me! A shelter in Leblon, remember? I want them now, Boris! Everybody's saying you're on the brink of bankruptcy. Whether you're broke or not, I don't give a damn, but if you try to double-cross me, I'll go to the newspapers, Boris, you bet I will. I'll tell all about your little parties, do you hear?"

Boris is unfazed. The young woman, furious: "You scoundrel!" Grabbing a glass, she hurls it at him. Boris ducks; then, leaping from the deck chair, he slaps her on the face so violently that she staggers, loses her balance, and falls into the swimming pool. She sinks—her wig is afloat—but soon she rises to the surface, flouncing about and shouting that she'll come down with pneumonia, the water is ice-cold.

"A lie," says Boris. "It's a heated swimming pool."

He asks the servants to get her out of the water and to drive her to her hotel. Then he turns to Rafael, who stands dumbfounded.

"But go on with what you were saying, Rafael."

"Later," says Rafael. "Not now, not under these circumstances. . . . You can see for yourself, Boris. It's impossible under the circumstances."

Boris sits straight up on the deck chair, takes off his glasses:

"Listen, Rafael. We've got to talk. About a very serious matter."

"At the Pecúnia, then."

"No, not there." Boris hesitates. "Are you staying for lunch?"

"No." Rafael can barely disguise his irritation. "I can't, Boris. I'm up to my neck in work."

That's a clear accusation, which Boris chooses to ignore:

"All right," he says. "But listen, we really have to talk. I'll phone you later, Rafael."

Rafael rises to his feet: "I'm leaving now," he announces. They gaze at each other for a moment, and what is in their gaze? Trust, and at the same time, distrust. Affection, and at the same time, anger. And—perplexity. In Rafael's gaze, perhaps more distrust; in Boris's gaze, perhaps more affection, an affection generated by a long friendship. But in Boris's gaze there's also a minute component of mockery; and mockery, irony, are alien to the makeup of Rafael's character. Perplexity, yes, it has to do with him, especially under the present circumstances. But the perplexity doesn't neutralize the irony, and if their gazes were, say, laser rays, and if the outcome of the fight between the two men were to depend on the intensity of such rays. . . .

No. They do not fight against each other. Occasionally Boris challenges Rafael to a game of tennis, which is played according to a veritable ritual, with Boris in an impeccable outfit, holding his excellent racquet by the handle, and Rafael, rather awkward in his bermuda shorts and old tennis shoes, marching abreast toward the tennis court, and then taking their positions, like real gentlemen; true, once the game starts, it's the usual frenzied scramble, with Rafael, a poor player, running like crazy for the ball, hitting it frantically, trying to get rid of it at all costs. Today, though, there won't be a tennis match, just an exchange of glances full of minute components. Saying goodbye, Rafael departs.

R AFAEL GOES INTO HIS OFFICE, SITS DOWN, STARES DEJECTEDLY at the stack of papers before him. I'm not up to it, he concludes. He decides he'll get out of the office, take a walk about the premises, sound off the morale of the staff. He walks down the halls past several departments. Through the open doors of the offices he sees the employees absorbed in their work. Are they aware of the situation? Quite likely. However, they are probably not very worried. After all, to them the Pecúnia represents merely a job; a good job—Boris pays them very well—but nothing more than a job. At the end of their working day they turn off the calculators, cover the typewriters with dust covers, and leave in a hurry. They go home to play with their children, to watch television. If the Pecúnia goes under, chances are they'll find another job with another finance company; or with a store or a bank. From the office previously occupied by Julio, his replacement, an accountant, greets Rafael deferentially.

Poor Julio. In his early thirties at the time of his death. A thin young man with intense eyes. On second thought—a bit crazy, but always properly dressed. His neckties perhaps a touch too bold, but not bold enough to attract attention or to rouse suspicion.

An only son, his father had wanted him to study medicine or engineering; Julio, however, had other plans. This country is booming, he would say, and anyone with a keen nose will make a fortune. Julio believed in his personal magnetism; he had taken a course in the psychology of salesmanship, he had memorized good jokes, which often fell flat because of a certain anxiety in his voice. Ever since joining the finance company in 1968, Julio had been waiting for the big chance. When prices in the stock market began to rise, he believed that the right moment had come. He sold his house, persuaded his father to lend him his savings, and even went as far as—this came to light later—to embezzle money from the finance company. He drew on the dollars—quite a large sum it was—that Boris had given him for safekeeping. But Julio had every intention of making restitution of everything.

Prices in the stock market were skyrocketing. Sell, his friends would say. Sell, certain shadowy forms kept saying in his dreams. Sell, his wife said timidly and he slapped her in the face for meddling in his affairs. A while longer, he would say, just a little while longer, and I'll be a millionaire, and then yes, then I'll sell my shares and start my own investment company.

And then prices began to fall.

At first Julio wasn't fully aware of what was really happening. His contacts in Rio and São Paulo informed him that it was nothing serious, that the stock markets were having the jitters, that they would soon recover.

The markets didn't recover. Prices kept plummeting. There was still a moment when Julio could have sold without suffering a loss; but he was unwilling to lose even one cent of his profits. To exclude himself from the winner's team? No way.

Later, it was no longer a matter of profits, but a matter of saving something, anything, a matter of handing over the rings in order to keep one's fingers; and in the end, not even the fingers could be saved. Julio was growing thinner and thinner; his eyes now looked hallucinated; at times he would show up for work unshaven, without a necktie. He confided in Rafael what was happening; even knowing that things were pretty bad, he still wouldn't sell his shares. There must be some manipulation going on behind the scenes, he would say; investors are waiting for prices to hit bottom before they buy everything back. Then, lowering his voice: *I know from a reliable source that the multinationals are about to invest zillions in the stock market.*

ONE FRIDAY JULIO ANNOUNCED TO HIS WIFE THAT HE intended to spend the weekend at the seaside. "In this rainy weather?" she asked. "I have to do some thinking," he said. She offered to go with him, but he rejected her suggestion.

He didn't return home on the following Sunday, nor on the following Monday and Tuesday. On Wednesday his car was found abandoned on a deserted beach; but there was no sign of Julio. The possibility of suicide was raised; it was expected that the Atlantic would eventually return the body, although changed beyond all recognition. The newspapers reported briefly on the incident and soon dropped the subject, much to the relief of Julio's widow, who didn't want any scandal. The only relative to show up at the finance company was his brother-in-law, who came to collect Julio's personal belongings; before leaving the premises, he told Rafael that he held Boris responsible for what had happened.

Rafael was outraged: "Why didn't you tell him, Boris, that Julio had stolen thirty thousand dollars from you?"

"What for?" said Boris with a shrug. "Julio is dead. We'll respect his memory. I liked him, Rafael, I really did. A nice fellow. Serious, dedicated, he could have had a brilliant career as a financier—but he was irresolute, he vacillated. And in this business, as you know, moral fiber is needed. Besides, we mustn't lose our cool over thirty thousand dollars."

He hesitated for a while, then he added:

"Besides, it was counterfeit money."

"Counterfeit?" Rafael was flabbergasted.

Boris lit a cigarette.

"It can happen. Even to me, it can happen. Somebody passed me bogus dollar bills. Somebody I trusted. On the day when Julio disappeared I got a phone call from Miami saying that I had been taken in. I still tried to find the whereabouts of this person, but with no success. . . . Fate, Rafael."

Respect his memory. Rafael wondered, had the dollars been genuine, would Boris still have felt the same way? He came to the conclusion, reached first with sorrow, then with anger, that he didn't know. And he didn't want to know.

He never brought up this subject again.

Rafael goes back to his office, takes the notebook out of the drawer, opens it at random. *Malato está el fijo del rey.* What does it mean? Yes, something like *the king's son is ill*; but which king? Why did his father write down this poem? He opens the briefcase to put the notebook inside— and there it is, Professor Samar-Kand's leaflet.

I've got to see this man, Rafael thinks. I've got to see him to get to the bottom of this matter. What do you know about my father, sir? Why did he go to Spain? How did he die? Where is he buried? Questions, questions: he needs the answers. Today. This very day. At least these questions will have answers. That is: maybe.

The phone rings. It's his secretary.

"There's a newspaper reporter here."

Rafael dials Boris's secretary:

"What's going on? What's this reporter doing here?"

"He's been coming every day. He wants information about the Pecúnia. I've spoken to Boris, he wants you to see the man."

"But where is Boris?"

"At home. He said he would be in later."

Shit, mutters Rafael, hanging up. That's all he needs now: a newsman. And Boris doesn't want to talk to him. Boris, who knows how to deal with newsmen, who often boasts about being favorably portrayed in the press—the intrepid financier who started from scratch and worked his way up—Boris now doesn't want to talk to the press. Rafael sighs, then tells his secretary on the interphone to send the newsman in.

A young man in shabby clothes, but wearing a necktie, walks in. Pencil and paper at the ready, he wants to know— what else?—about the situation of the Pecúnia. Any truth behind these rumors afloat throughout the city?

Before replying, Rafael considers him for a moment. What is this young man trying to do? What kind of a reporter is he? A left-winger searching for a scandal that will expose the evils of capitalism? An opportunist using his position to gain access to the financial circles? Or an impartial drone who bureaucratically carries out the task he has been assigned? Impossible to tell. He won't know until the story appears in the newspaper—if it does. Because Boris might already be pulling strings.

For half an hour Rafael discourses on the situation of the financial market; he chooses his words carefully, and successfully parries the more embarrassing questions. The reporter scribbles. At the end of the interview, he says goodbye with a smile and leaves.

Wiping his forehead, Rafael sits back in the chair. Boris will have to do something, he will have to use his connections. It's not the first time that the finance company is going through a tumultuous phase; Boris has always managed to find a way out, either with the help of some politicians or of certain friends in Zurich, in South Africa—gold in the first instance, diamonds in the second. But now Rafael doesn't even want to think about this. He's had a bellyful. With an abrupt gesture, he closes the briefcase and gets to his feet.

"I'm going out," he announces to his secretary on the interphone. "I don't know if I'll be back in the afternoon."

But he doesn't head straight for the address in the leaflet. He decides to stop at his mother's house, which is on the way out there. He doesn't quite know yet what he'll do at his mother's: Should he tell her that he has received a box containing his father's belongings? Show her the notebook?

What for? To upset her? Why should he make her rake over old ashes?

He arrives at her house—the same old house of his childhood days. His mother lives there with an old servant, despite Rafael's and Helena's efforts to persuade her to move closer to them. Once they even rented a small-but-decent apartment for her in a building with a caretaker and electronically monitored main entrance. In vain. Alzira Mendes, who is over sixty, remains as stubborn as ever: She says she doesn't want to live near her son and her daughter-in-law, that there's no reason why she should, and that she's not afraid of burglars—a fact reaffirmed now as Rafael finds her front door wide open. And there she is, seated before the television set, a small woman, thin and prim, wearing an old (but clean and befitting) dress. Standing next to her—for Alzira has never allowed her servant to sit down in her presence—is the black old woman who was only a young girl when she first came to work for Alzira; now she's almost blind, which is why she keeps asking: "And now, Mother, what's happening now on the television, Mother?" She calls Alzira mother, which Rafael used to find amusing; now, however, it strikes him as merely sad.

"Good afternoon, folks."

The face of the old servant lights up. "Look who's here, Mother!" Groping about, she draws closer to Rafael, then embraces him effusively.

"Our boy, Mother! Our little Rafael!"

She touches his face with the tips of her tremulous fingers.

"Getting more and more handsome, this boy! Don't you think so, Mother? Don't you think so? You can see better than me."

Alzira doesn't reply. It's part of the game: For a few minutes she'll ignore the presence of her son, her eyes fixed on the television screen; then she'll finally turn to him, asking abruptly: "So, what brings you here, glad or sad tidings?"

But Rafael doesn't feel like following the usual ritual. He removes the notebook and the photograph from the briefcase.

"What's that?" she asks, suspicious.

"Something I received early this morning, Mom. I think they were Dad's."

She is startled, but she controls herself and feigns indifference.

"Your father's? I doubt it. Who would have your father's things in his possession?"

"A man. A genealogist—"

"A what?"

"A genealogist. A person who studies family history."

"I see," she says, cagey. "And what has he got to do with your father?"

"That's what I intend to find out. Listen, Mom, I've got to know: Did these things belong to Dad?"

"I don't know." She averts her eyes.

"How can you say you don't know when you haven't even looked at them? There's this notebook with annotations. . . ."

Again, she flinches; and again, she controls herself.

"Looking at them wouldn't make any difference. Not without my glasses."

"What happened to your glasses?"

"I broke them."

It's now Rafael's turn to become angry:

"Is that so? You broke your glasses. And why didn't you let me know?"

She hesitates, shifts in her chair. And when she finally replies, it is with sullenness, like a child who's been scolded by her father; but at the same time, she's obviously pleased to have attracted the attention of her son—of her only son, her little Rafael.

"I couldn't. The phone is out of order."

"Out of order? But I talked to you on the phone several times last week!" Rafael, too, is now pleased. A dialogue with mutual reproaches? He'd rather have it so, at least there is a dialogue now and not just silence.

"There's . . ." she hesitates again, she's obviously telling a fib, like a child, "there's something wrong with the rotary dial. It won't dial."

He walks over to her, lays a hand on her shoulder.

"Come on, now, Mom. Couldn't you have gone to the grocery store and phoned me from there? I would have come right away, you know I would."

She bursts into tears.

"No! You wouldn't! You never worry about me, neither you nor your wife, nobody cares."

He heaves a sigh, decides to steer the conversation back to the original subject matter.

"This man says he has some of Dad's writings. Do you have any idea what they could be?"

"No, I have no idea. Whatever I know, you know it too,

I've already told you a thousand times your father all of a sudden made up his mind to go to Spain and fight in the war there. I did everything I possibly could to make him change his mind, but with no success, he went and got himself killed, he's buried in a common grave near Madrid. . . .'' She turns to him, her eyes brimming with tears.''But why bring up this subject again, Rafael, why talk about such painful things? Isn't it enough what I had to go through, what both of us had to go through? Isn't it enough all the sacrifices I made to raise you single-handedly, a woman all alone?'' Taking a handkerchief tucked inside her sleeve, she wipes her eyes with a trembling hand. Rafael kneels down by her side and hugs her:

''All right, Mother. We won't talk about it anymore.''

Annoyed, she struggles free.

''Leave now, Rafael. Go away.''

He makes for the door.

''Rafael.''

He turns around.

''What is it?''

Now she stares at him, pathetic:

''Rafael,'' she says in a quivering voice, ''look after Suzana. Look after your daughter.''

''Why, Mom?'' he asks, suddenly alarmed. ''Why do you say so? Has something happened? Tell me, Mother! Is there something you know?''

''No . . . I know nothing, Rafael, you know that she's just like you, she hardly ever comes here. But one night last week she came. She was out of her wits, Rafael.''

''And what did she tell you?'' says Rafael, anguished. ''Tell me, for heavens' sake!''

''Nothing, she told me nothing, Rafael. All she did was cry. She cried for a long time. And then she left. There's something the matter with this girl, Rafael. Something really serious. That's why I'm telling you: Look after her. We must look after our own, Rafael.''

He opens the door and leaves.

R̲AFAEL WANDERS ABOUT THE STREETS OF THE LOWER CITY, walks up to Praça da Matriz, sits down on a bench, and there he remains watching the children at play. A certain peace descends upon him; at this hour, two o'clock in the afternoon, birds twitter in the treetops and the public square is peaceful, surrounded by austere and imposing façades: the Government Palace, the Legislative Assembly Building, the Cathedral, Courthouse, São Pedro Theater, Public Library. Yielding to a sudden impulse, Rafael rises to his feet and goes to the Cathedral.

Not too many people there. The usual women dressed in black, naturally (Azorian widows?); three schoolgirls who whisper, giggling; an old man wearing sunglasses. Rafael kneels down, something he hasn't done in a long time; a Catholic, or rather a lapsed Catholic, he rarely thinks of eternal life. Now, however, he feels like praying: *Our Father*, he murmurs, *who art in heaven*. They comfort him, these words that generations upon generations have murmured in the demi-dusk of chapels, catacombs, cathedrals. It's good to have faith, to be part of something greater than yourself, something transcendent; it's good not to depend exclusively on a strange Jew, on a rebellious daughter.

He finishes his prayer, crosses himself, leaves. He is bedazzled by the afternoon light, but only for a moment; soon he starts climbing down the steps, then walks along Rua Duque, heading for Alto da Bronze. He is going to the house of one Professor Samar-Kand.

An old house, squeezed between two tall apartment buildings. The faded paint, and the broken panes in the windows with tattered lace curtains, give the impression that the house is abandoned. Who knows, maybe it is. Maybe it's now the dwelling of vagrants or petty criminals—who can say? Rafael hesitates. Finally he pushes the iron gate, which creaks open; he follows a narrow path paved with slimy flagstones and trimmed with a row of neglected plants in ancient pots. He searches for the doorbell but can't find it, so he knocks on the door, on which are tiny windows with bars. Nothing. After a while he knocks again, then stands waiting with his head lowered, eyes fixed on the shriveled wisps of grass growing amid the stones. With a start, he raises his head; from behind one of the tiny windows two eyes peer at him curiously. A moment of tension—and then the door is opened. Standing before Rafael is a short, pudgy man in a shabby wine-colored dressing-gown that is so long that it trails on the floor. He's quite old, this diminutive man: The hair, although foppishly long, is completely white, but the blue eyes behind the metal-rimmed eyeglasses have an expression that is curiously child-like; and the voice, wispish and nasal, is also childlike.

"Is there something you want, friend?"

All of a sudden, Rafael finds this situation so comical, so unreal, that he can barely refrain himself from bursting into laughter. However, he manages to control himself:

"Are you professor—"

"Samar-Kand. That's me."

"I received your note . . . My name is Rafael Mendes."

The words produce an immediate response: The face of the old man lights up, a smile replaces the air of suspicion.

"Oh, yes. So you're Rafael Mendes, sir. Why didn't you say so right away? Come in, please, do come in."

Rafael follows him down a long corridor. On either side are shelves crammed with books—and articles of clothing, and jars of preserves ("I'm partial to preserves," explains the old man as they walk past, "I practically live off preserves and cookies.") and bottles of medicine, stuffed animals, bibelots. The farther they advance into the house, the stronger the smells—dust, mustiness, old paper, food gone bad.

The corridor ends in a large room, poorly-lit by the low-wattage light bulbs of a chandelier decorated with glass beads. It's a big, spacious room; there are shelves, similar to the ones in the corridor, and like them, cluttered with books and all kinds of strange objects—among them, the skeleton of a snake and the heads of three dolls. The walls are lined with pictures: maps of the sky, Zodiac symbols, the Tree of Life, everything rather vulgar. However, the big round table of dark wood occupying the middle of the room and the set of old chairs padded with red velvet are magnificent. "Please, sit down," says the old man.

Both of them sit down. There's a crystal ball on the table.

The old man looks at it, first casually; then he takes it in his hands, examines it attentively, a frown creasing his forehead; with a sigh, he puts it back where it stood before—on a pedestal made of dark granite:

"Chipped. Practically a brand-new crystal ball—and already chipped. And it cost me quite a bundle, let me tell you. Believe me, they don't make crystal balls as they used to do in the old days. Actually, it's good that they don't—then we are forced to innovate."

He has a plan for developing an electronic crystal ball to be operated by the client himself. It looks like an ordinary crystal ball, but it contains electronic sensors capable of detecting and registering various characteristics of a person's hand. Starting with the lines of the palm: the line of life, the line of fortune, the line of the head, the line of the heart, the line of the liver. Then, the presence or absence of callosity or other signs that might indicate the person's occupation. The presence of gold rings. The size of the fingers. The pressure exerted by the fingers—thus revealing what some would call claws. The temperature of the hands, the amount of perspiration: important psychological clues. The data thus collected would then be fed into mini-computers and transformed into visions of the future, which would appear inside the crystal image itself in the form of images of liquid quartz, like the ones in the Japanese watches.

"Yes, I could develop this plan and many others as well—I am well-versed in many branches of human knowledge. I understand the way systems work, I know the theory of play. I can mount a flow chart in seconds, no matter how complex the situation. I'm a psychologist, a parapsychologist, and a physiopsychologist. Have you ever heard of physiopsychology? It's a relatively new science, it studies the psyche through the body functions. I can tell everything about a person by noting the volume of a tear, the degree of viscosity of the saliva, the arching of the jet of urine into a urinal; the amount of tension a wisp of hair can withstand and for this purpose I use a small device I myself have developed, I call it a psychocapillarymeter. I can interpret a person's character by examining his—pardon me the word—feces. Pencil-thin feces indicate a situation of anxiety, of self-consciousness, generally a result of dependency on calculations done with a pencil. Small, hardened feces, like a goat's, point to a temperament which is—can you guess?—that's right, similar to the goat's:

reserved, self-centered, suspicious. Well-formed feces are indicative—which is only logical—of a well-formed soul. As for diarrhea, it's nothing more than the result of a storm—such as the storm that forced the frightened seamen to cast the prophet Jonah into the sea—except that this storm is internal.''

He becomes vehement all of a sudden, shaking the crystal ball:

"I know all of this might seem in bad taste. But I can assure you, sir, it's superior to the old way of predicting the future, examining the viscera of birds as the Romans used to do, a method which some people would like to see reinstated. I'm not going to mention any names, I don't want to give the impression of being unethical, sir, but you have probably been approached by people who use such methods. Some people even use chicken for this purpose, imagine! That's a method with no scientific basis whatsoever. Yes, I know that Father Vieira used to say in his sermons that the ancients were right to have chosen the viscera and not the head to read fate: *He who is able to love is a better prophet than he who is able to reason.* Well, it was the seventeenth century then, and Father Vieira was a fanatic, a Quixote, a romantic ahead of his time. Whereas I, my dear sir, I work only with science. I'm always studying and researching, as you can see by the amount of books I have here; a lot of it is old stuff, but there are also many recent publications to keep myself abreast of what is going on. I'm old, but not old-fashioned, my friend. I'm all for progress, it's wonderful, I've been thinking of introducing Porto Alegre to the computerized horoscope and the computerized family tree, using the Cobal and the Fortran languages. Would you be interested in financing one of these projects, sir?''

Rafael, dumbfounded, doesn't know what to say. The little man puts the crystal ball back on its pedestal, and sighs.

"No, you wouldn't. You don't believe in such things, sir. Never mind. Anyhow, I'm not a fortune-teller by profession, I tell fortunes just to bring in a little money on the side. My specialty is genealogy—now that's something serious. An old science. Consider, for instance, the Bible: What is it if not a monumental family tree, illustrated with stories of a religious nature? And from biblical times down to today, genealogy has never stopped growing. Ah, never. In Europe it's wonderful, every city and town, no matter how small, has its own genealogist—every one of them highly competent. True, they have all kinds of resources over there, such as historical archives. Whereas here I have to overcome the greatest difficulties in order to do my research. The worst of it is that very few people appreciate this kind of work. Rio Grande do Sul, my friend, doesn't have a history. Nobody here knows a thing about their ancestors, and they don't want to know. There are exceptions, of course; Celina Cordeiro, have you heard of Celina Cordeiro, sir?—you must have, everybody in Porto Alegre has heard of her—she was one of my clients. I reconstructed her family tree. We became good friends, she still visits me. But she's an exception. There isn't much chance of genealogy ever succeeding here. That's why I've branched out into other areas."

He hesitates before adding:

"Successfully, if I may say so. I have several irons in the fire, I can assure you."

Rafael stares at him, stunned; stunned and dejected. Where in the world did I end up? he thinks to himself. The little man, coming to his senses, realizes that his impassioned harangue might have created a bad impression:

"Pardon me, sir. I allowed myself to be carried away with my enthusiasm. That's how I am, don't mind me. Let's go back to the main point: So you received your father's belongings, did you? And my note as well?"

"That's the reason why I'm here, sir," says Rafael, cautious. "As you know, my father deserted us many years ago; I was only a little boy then, and I can hardly remember him. Ever since—"

He stops short. The little man looks at him with sympathy, with interest, even with affection. How long has it been since someone has looked at him in this way? There's a lump in his throat, he tries to go on but can't, and then he breaks down and weeps convulsively: He cries not just because of his father or the memory of his father, it's because of everything: his daughter, the predicament of the finance company, all the tension he's been under—the torrent has burst through the barriers and he cries unrestrainedly before the astonished little man. Finally, Rafael manages to pull himself together; he takes a handkerchief out of his pocket and wipes his eyes.

"I'm sorry. I'm not in the habit of breaking down like this. I'm a restrained man, believe me. I don't get upset easily. But lately I've been through some difficulties. And just now as I remembered my father. . . ."

"I understand," says the old man. His sympathy seems genuine; whether madman or con artist, he feels compassion. And who wouldn't at the sight of a man's tears?

They remain silent for a few moments. Then the old man clears his throat:

"Let me explain about that note. I met your father many years ago. He was interested in genealogy, that's why he came to me. I did some research—and I was astonished."

Then, waxing enthusiastic again, he says:

"What a family tree it was, Senhor Rafael! One of the most magnificent I have ever come across. An oak tree, a sequoia, a veritable genealogical forest! The Mendeses have roots all over, in several countries, in several continents. We spent months researching your ancestors. We would work until the small hours; sometimes he would stay overnight; those clothes I sent you, he left them behind when he went to Spain. . . . Did you know, sir, that he went to Spain at the time of the civil war there?"

"Yes, I knew. But I don't know why—"

The old man cuts him short with a gesture:

"I'd rather not go into any explanations. Look: Your father left two other notebooks with me, in addition to the one with the annotations already in your possession. The first contains stories of your ancestors, or rather, stories that he wrote about your ancestors. Your father was endowed with imagination, Senhor Rafael. He was a man who would marvel at the things that happened in life and in the world, and for this reason, he had to write. The first notebook, then, contains Genealogical Stories—the title is his own. The other notebook is about himself; he tells about something that happened to him, something that changed his life, and this notebook even provides an answer to your previous question about his journey to Spain. Valuable material, I'd say. Valuable in general, and valuable in particular to a son."

"Interesting," mumbles Rafael. He feels odd in this place, a bit nauseous; it must be the smell, he concludes. He decides to end this conversation:

"Yes. And how can I have access to these notebooks?"

The old man shows him a parcel wrapped in brown paper:

"Here they are. And they can be yours. . . ."

He pauses.

"For ten thousand dollars."

"What?" says Rafael, incredulous: It is so bizarre to hear

the old man mention dollars, ten thousand dollars, in this archaic, phantasmagorical setting that Rafael thinks he didn't hear it right:

"Ten thousand dollars, did you say, sir?"

Ten thousand dollars? Does the old man know what he's talking about? Does he know how much the exchange rate on the dollar is right now? Ten thousand dollars: It's the sum Rafael has in the safe hidden behind a painting in his study. Money that he keeps for emergencies. Ten thousand dollars? He feels like sending the old man to the devil. Barely controlling his indignation, he forces a smile:

"You know, strictly speaking, this material doesn't belong to you. You yourself said, sir, that it was my father who—"

"Your father left these notebooks in my possession, Senhor Rafael. They are, therefore, my property." Then, conciliatory: " But I don't intend to make a mountain out of a molehill. After all, the contents of the notebooks concern you. They are, let's say, a message. A message from the hereafter." Then, pleased with this figure of speech: "And I'm willing to hand this message over to you. Except that I'm charging for the storage and the delivery of the material. Isn't that what the post office does?"

"But ten thousand dollars, that's absurd!"

The old man smiles.

"That's what you say. However, these are the writings of your father, about whom you claim to know so little. If people want information, they'll have to pay—in cruzeiros, dollars, or any other currency. I prefer dollars."

He shifts in his chair.

"There's something else too, which I haven't mentioned yet. I never got paid for my services, for your father died before he could have done so. He was a friend of mine, of course, and I didn't bear a grudge against him, but the fact is that he owed me an honorarium for the fruits of my labor."

A pause.

"Besides, genealogical work is not easy. In the case of your family, I had to consult dozens of books I have in my library, which is really huge, the only library of its kind here in our country—it's worth a fortune. Climbing up and down stairs and handling dusty books can really kill a person. Not to mention the mental effort. Genealogy is pretty much like a detective's work, Senhor Rafael. Sometimes we have to start from negligible details: a coat of arms engraved on flatware, an old painting, or mythological allusions—to the Gold Tree, for instance. Also, in the case of your family—well, it wasn't a minor job. It wasn't a mere 'family shrub' I had to deal with, Senhor Rafael, I can assure you.''

"But—'' Rafael isn't convinced. "Why dollars?''

The old man shrugs.

"Strong currency, that's why, naturally. You're in the money business, sir; you know that we cannot put our trust in the cruzeiro. Pay me in Swiss francs or German marks, if you want, it doesn't matter as long as it's a strong currency. Ten thousand dollars, let's agree, is not all that much for someone in the financial market. Ten thousand dollars for the evocation of a father? Please, do me a favor, Senhor Rafael. Don't repeat Judas's mistake. Don't betray a loved one for thirty coins.''

The slur angers Rafael, but he's now set on continuing with this dialogue to the very end—he wants the notebooks, and he also wants to find out what's behind this whole story.

"How do you know, sir, that I can pay?''

The old man shifts again in his chair.

"Because of the crystal ball.'' He breaks into histrionic laughter, then becomes serious: "I know a lot about your life, Senhor Rafael. My son used to talk about you.''

"Your son?''

"Julio.'' The little man smiles sadly; all of a sudden, he looks much older than his years, an old gnome of a man, shriveled, melancholic. "Julio, Senhor Rafael. He worked with you.''

So he's Julio's father, this old man. Rafael's suspicions are now confirmed: There was something fishy there, something more than just the notebooks and the dollars. Julio, of course. How else could the old man have met Celina Cordeiro? Julio. This clears up the mystery. Rafael now recalls the stockbroker occasionally talking about his father. A weird old man, he would say, I don't get along very well with him, he has never forgiven me for working for a finance company.

Julio's father! But this complicates matters. There could be something else behind this sensational deal that has just been proposed to him—revenge. Revenge taken on the Pecúnia, which the old man must surely hold responsible for his son's misfortune. Revenge taken on Boris and on Rafael.

As if guessing at Rafael's thoughts, the old man says:

"But that's all in the past, Senhor Rafael. My son is dead,

may God keep his soul, and I bear no grudges against anyone
or anything. Besides . . .''

He hesitates for a moment; then shaking his head as if to
free himself from a disturbing thought, he goes on:

"But let's get back to the main point: I'm making you the
following offer: Take the notebooks with you, examine them
as much as you like. And then, if you want to keep them,
you'll pay me ten thousand dollars. Agreed?''

Rafael, still wary, can't help smiling:

"Aren't you afraid, sir, to trust me with the notebooks?''

"No,'' replies the old man. "I know you're a decent man.
That's what my son used to say: This Rafael Mendes, he's a
decent guy. I trust you, sir, and I'd be happy to have your
friendship too, as I had your father's.''

He pauses for a moment, then goes on:

"Besides, there's something else I'd like to offer you as a
token of my regard for you. There's a third notebook.''

"What? A third notebook?'' says Rafael, creasing his forehead. What kind of trick is he trying to pull off now?

"Yes. Or rather, there isn't one yet. Not yet, but there
might be: I can start writing it at any moment.''

"You?!''

"That's right. Me. And furthermore: It will be a notebook
entirely devoted to you.''

"To me?''

"To you. Are you skeptical? Don't be.'' Then leaning
forward, he says: "There's a lot I could write about you,
Senhor Rafael: About things that happened, things that are
happening, things that *will* happen.''

He straightens up in his chair and stares at Rafael, triumphant. *I bet*, thinks Rafael, he's now going to bring up the
electronic crystal ball.

"Don't worry,'' the little man hastens to say, "for this
notebook I won't charge you a cent. It's included in the ten
thousand dollars. Let's say it's a genealogical gift thrown
in.''

Rafael looks at him, not knowing what to say.

"This third notebook will be of great importance to you,''
the old man goes on. "As important as the other two. After
all, I do know a lot about you. I've been following, although
indirectly, it's true, a good part of your life; therefore, I
believe I know you thoroughly, more than you think I do.
Even your gestures are predictable to me, Senhor Rafael.

This morning I could imagine your astonishment when you came upon the box I sent you—"

"By the way," Rafael cuts in, "you could have phoned me first, sir. You would have spared me a shock."

"Mystery and uncertainty add to the value of things," retorts the old man. "You, who operate in the money markets, must know this better than I do. But to answer your previous question: You'll come back, Senhor Rafael, I'm sure you will. You'll come back because you're honest; and you'll come back because you want to know more. More than what you know now; and I'm in a position to tell you what you want to know, sir."

"Well," says Rafael, "if you, a fortune-teller, are so certain that I'll be back, then surely I'll be back. And if you mentioned ten thousand dollars. . . ."

He falters, but it's too late to backtrack, he's now at the point of no return, he'll have to go on all the way to the end:

"If you mentioned ten thousand dollars, it's because you know that I'll pay you ten thousand dollars. And I will indeed. If I find at least some of the answers I've been searching for, I'll pay you, sir."

Rafael shakes the hand—small and delicate like a child's— that the old man holds out; for a moment they gaze at each other, smiling, until they come to their senses, both of them embarrassed. Picking up the parcel, the old man says:

"Let's get down to business."

Quickly he unwraps two old notebooks:

"Here they are. The notebooks of Dr. Rafael Mendes, your father."

He adjusts his eyeglasses, then leafs through one of the notebooks:

"This one here is particularly interesting, genealogically speaking. It begins with the most distant of your ancestors—a biblical prophet."

"A prophet?" asks Rafael, with disbelief.

"A prophet, yes. And many other distinguished figures. For instance, a famous Hebrew philosopher and physician who lived in Moorish Spain . . ."

"Wait a minute," protests Rafael. "Where did you get this idea that I'm a Jew?"

"I didn't say that you are a Jew," corrects the old man. "What I said was that you come from a Hebrew lineage. A noble lineage, by the way, as you'll see."

"But I was baptized a Christian."

"New!" exclaims the genealogist. "A New Christian, a *cristãonovo*, you, and your ancestors: They converted to Christianity, they were the New Christians, a term applied to Christianized Jews. Haven't you ever heard of it? Very common here in Brazil. Many of us are of Jewish descent because the first Portuguese settlers who came here were mostly Jews. Didn't you know, sir, that soon after the Portuguese discovered Brazil, the entire Brazilian territory was conveyed by charter to a group of New Christians headed by Fernão de Noranha?"

"I didn't know that," says Rafael.

There is a silence. A tense silence.

"I bet I know who you're thinking of now," says the old man. "Boris. You're saying to yourself that the two of you after all have something in common. Even though this Jew—"

"I ask you," Rafael cuts him short, "to drop this subject. I don't know what kind of grudge you might have against Boris, but he happens to be a friend of mine."

"Well," says the old man, sour. "There's no disputing about tastes, or friendships for that matter. My opinion about Senhor Boris—"

"I'm not interested," Rafael says. He rises to his feet: "Excuse me, I'm late. Can I have the notebooks?"

"Of course, of course." The old man wraps them up, hands them over to Rafael.

With the parcel in his hand, Rafael hesitates:

"And . . . how do I get in touch with you, sir?"

"I'll phone you," says the old man. "Tonight, or if not, tomorrow."

"For an historian, you sure are in a big hurry," remarks Rafael, bitter.

"With financiers one has to be in a hurry," retorts the old man not less bluntly. "After all, I'm giving you credit, my friend. Full credit—in your trustworthiness."

He suddenly seems so very old and frail. Ashamed, Rafael feels the blood rise to his face. Without a word, he puts the notebooks in the briefcase and leaves.

Getting out of this house feels like emerging from an unreal subterranean world: Suddenly bedazzled by the brightness outside, Rafael Mendes, his head swimming, hesitates, not knowing what to do next. He looks at his watch: three-fifty.

He decides to go home to read the notebooks he's carrying in the briefcase.

To go home, however, is not all that simple. He goes into a bar, orders a cognac, drinks it down in one gulp. He orders another one. The bar owner, a fat bald man with a mustache, watches him in silence.

"Rough going, is it?"

"Yeah. Very," Rafael agrees.

"I know how it feels," the man says. "There are times when I need my shots of cognac too."

He smiles sympathetically. Rafael smiles back, pays. He walks back to the parking lot where he left the car and drives home.

He enters the apartment. Helena is sitting in the living room, watching television.

As soon as she sees him come in, she leaps to her feet, her eyes wide open:

"What happened, Rafael? Did something happen to Suzana?"

"Relax," he says. "Nothing happened, it's just that I've come home early, there are some documents I have to look over and I decided I'd work here."

She lets herself fall into the armchair:

"What a scare you gave me, Rafael! That was quite a turn you gave me."

He strokes her hair, does his best to soothe her. Then he heads for his study. Before going in, he turns around: "Helena, I don't want to be disturbed, tell the maids not to knock on my door."

"All right," she murmurs feebly.

Sighing, Rafael goes into the study and locks the door behind him. He sits down in his armchair, opens the briefcase, takes out the parcel containing the notebooks, unwraps them.

Two old composition books, exactly like the one that came in the box. On the covers are the titles *The First Notebook of the New Christian* and *The Second Notebook of the New Christian*. Strange titles. As strange as Rafael Mendes, his father, must have been.

He leafs through the notebooks. Pages and pages covered with a small, regular handwriting. Is it his father's script? Again, he isn't sure. But the notebooks are certainly quite old: The sheets of paper are yellowed, moth-eaten, and the lilac ink has faded, rendering the words almost illegible in some passages.

Rafael Mendes opens the first notebook. He plunges into it just like the prophet Jonah must have plunged into a billowy sea. He travels swiftly inside the belly of time, like the prophet inside the fish, heading for a destination still unknown.

THE FIRST
NOTEBOOK
OF THE
NEW
CHRISTIAN

Perplexed, Jonah received from the Lord the gift of prophecy and the mission of denouncing the corrupt city of Nineveh.

My NAME IS RAPHAEL MENDES. I AM A PHYSICIAN AND A genealogy enthusiast. By searching the roots of my family—a search that involved the study of documents, of old books, of coats of arms engraved on flatware, and even of lullabies—I was able to track down someone named Jonah as the most distant of my known ancestors.

My conclusion is based on various clues: in the twelfth century, the coat of arms of the Mendes family displayed the effigy of a whale, but the typical spout of water had been replaced by a stylized tree—the Gold Tree, undoubtedly. This association of the whale with the legend of the tree which had been with the family for generations, is certainly very significant. And as with Jonah, perplexity is a distinguishing trait of the Mendeses, too: What is happening? What happened? What will happen? Like other people, they, too, searched for the Gold Tree, but without great conviction; in fact, they would have much preferred peace of mind and tranquility—which they never succeeded in attaining—to riches. Throughout the ages, they fled from place to place, from country to country; they crossed oceans, they scaled mountains, living strange adventures, sensing a disturbing summons.

NEWS SPREAD QUICKLY THAT JONAH HAD RECEIVED THE gift of prophecy from the Lord. People found it strange: Jonah? Why Jonah? An ordinary man, unendowed with any sort of clairvoyant abilities, incapable of even predicting the weather for the following day—so, why him? In public, however, they tried to rejoice at the news. After all, it was a distinction for the village to have a prophet among its inhabitants. But that's not how Jonah's wife felt; dejected, she foresaw a bleak horizon for her husband. She was partly right: True, prophets were respected in those days—but they were hated, too. They would *say* to the rich and the powerful things that ordinary people hardly dared to *think*. If some potentate had a banquet, the prophets had to hasten to his place, burst into the premises, assail with fiery words all persons present and curse their food, which would punctually spoil—such a waste, because then not even would the poor, who were usually the recipients of any food left over from the love feasts, be able to eat. Hence prophets, while feared by the powerful, were also abhorred by the humble: "Prophets? They're useless. They are only interested in foretelling the future, and what do we care about the future? In the future we'll all be dead."

This, however, didn't prevent numerous people from seeking out Jonah to ask him to intercede with the Lord on their behalf. Desperate women wanted him to help them get pregnant; discredited priests yearned to share the divine word with him. Grain speculators offered him money in exchange for harvest predictions; soldiers consulted him about the advisability of certain military operations. And when Jonah's father began to urge him to find out from the Lord the location of the Gold Tree—you owe it to your family, to your community, Jonah, we've had enough of this life of poverty—Jonah decided to renounce his mission and run away: After all, Jonah thought, I have nothing to do with Nineveh. Are the Ninevehites fornicating? Let them fornicate, I couldn't care less. Nineveh there, I here: Why should I hitch my fate to a city I've never even been to? I'm going to run away.

He ran away. At Yafo he boarded a boat bound for Tarshish. The sea was tranquil, at first; then came the storm. The sailors believed that someone on board was attracting the divine wrath. They drew lots; Jonah was pointed out as the culprit. He was thrown into the sea. A fish swallowed him.

A fish swallowed him. Jonah found himself inside a huge stomach, full of undigested remains. A terrible smell, total darkness. Groping about, Jonah found sand, two silex stones, and some old rags. He managed to produce sparks, which ignited the rags. On a surface of sand and stones he made a fire, and felt better: pleasantly warm, even sheltered.

He could—should—stay there and wait for the fate that Jeovah had in store for him; instead, he began to explore the insides of the fish. He improvised a torch and began his expedition. The stomach extended to the narrow tunnel of the intestines; a short way down the intestines, however, there was something resembling a chamber, where, to his surprise, he came upon a group of people, eleven men and one woman seated around a small fire. Jonah's arrival didn't surprise them. One of them, an old man with a long beard, addressed the prophet in Aramaic; he welcomed Jonah and invited him to sit down.

These people were there for different reasons. Like Jonah, some had been punished for having run away from missions that Jeovah or other deities from the Fertile Crescent had entrusted to them; others were well-known sinners, thieves, murderers. To many of them the belly of the fish was a prison where they were serving sentences whose duration—and this added to the harshness of the punishment—was unknown to them. The old man had been there—he guessed—for over twenty years. He could only guess because he had no way of measuring time:

"When I was first swallowed, this fish was so small that I could barely fit in its stomach. Now, this hollow can house a legion. That's the way dishonesty, hypocrisy, and above all, indecision and perplexity, keep growing in this world."

Jonah was no longer listening. His eyes were fixed on the woman.

Still young and very beautiful, she had a dark complexion, long black hair, dark eyes. A woman of haughty bearing. A priestess of Astarte, as he was to find out later.

The old man invited Jonah to have lunch with them. How did he know it was lunch and not dinner? How could he tell daytime from nighttime in that place? Maybe he was a prophet. "We have fish," said the old man, "fish swallowed by our fish." The way he stressed the *our* showed irony, yes, but also pride—as if the fish were his master, his god.

"The smaller fish are swallowed by the bigger fish, which, in turn, are swallowed"—said the old man with pride—"by the biggest of them all (again: pride). It's a war waged by all against all. But why should we concern ourselves with this war when it's thanks to it that we survive?"

Jonah declined the invitation. He felt uneasy among these people; he was especially disturbed by the presence of the beautiful priestess, who kept looking at him with a smile. Excusing himself, he went back to where he had come from.

A surprise awaited him: The fire had died. Lying amid the ashes he saw a blade of some transparent substance, glittering in the light of the torch. Jonah had discovered glass.

(It was quite simple: the stones upon which Jonah had built the fire were—although he knew nothing about this—soda, which had been the cargo of a boat swallowed by the fish. Through the action of the fire, the soda and the sand changed into glass.)

Jonah examined this material, but because he wasn't actually an inventive or creative man, he never imagined even one of its thousand practical uses. It never occurred to him, for instance, to cut an opening through the flank of the fish and fix the blade of glass there, thus creating some kind of a scuttle, which would become hermetically sealed by the healing process triggered along the edges of the wound. Through it he would have been able to sight the sunken ships lying on the bottom of the sea, ships that might contain treasures. He could have become rich! But this possibility never occurred to him. Neither did he think to use the glass to make lenses, or mirrors. Mirrors—what wouldn't the women have given to see themselves! The mirrors then in use were made of silver; they were expensive and the image they reflected wasn't very accurate, which afforded the opportunity for deceptive practices. Thus, to their rich customers, merchants would sell mirrors that flattered their physical appearance, either by eliminating wrinkles or by slimming down waistlines. Whereas the women who were poor had to satisfy themselves with any scrap of metal more or less polished. These paupers, however, would sometimes look at the rich women and, much to the women's consternation, burst into laughter. Was the laughter of the destitute women yet another sign of the age of debauchery in which they lived, or was it triggered by some grotesque defect that the imperfect mirrors failed to reveal? Who could the rich women trust to help them clarify such agonizing self-doubts? Not their husbands, who made only flattering remarks; not the servants. Only good, faithful mirrors. Jonah could have manufactured and sold such mirrors, thereby not only revealing the truth—which is expected from a prophet—but also earning lots of money. But precisely because he wasn't a prophet yet, he couldn't foresee this possibility. A prophet? Not when it came to glass and mirrors.

"Prophet Jonah!"

Startled, he turned around. It was one of the men he had just met, a thin bald fellow with a big scar on his face: a sinister type, more like a bandit than a prophet. Really strange, the way Jeovah and other gods selected their envoys.

"Could we talk?"

Jonah invited him to sit down. The man went straight to the matter:

"Would you like to get rich, Jonah? Really rich?"

For a moment Jonah thought that the man wanted to talk to him about the Gold Tree. But that wasn't the case; he wanted to disclose a plan of his, a plan to bilk wealthy Ninevehites out of their money:

"Everything points to the fact that you'll be in Nineveh soon. The city has reached the sum of its corruption; Jeovah must be eager to punish it."

He leaned forward—terrible, his breath, worse than the emanations from the stomach of the fish—then he spoke in a low voice:

"Now listen carefully: As soon as you arrive in Nineveh, you prophesy that because of its sins, the city will be destroyed, and its inhabitants will die amid excruciating pains; in short, you'll make a really good prophecy, and in this way you'll fulfill your mission. Soon afterwards, however, you offer to placate the divine wrath by acting as a go-between. Naturally, you'll charge for this service, and you'll ask them to pay in advance; and the more frightened they are, the more you can charge."

Appalled, Jonah listened to him.

"With this money," the man went on, "you'll hire boats

and good fishermen. They'll catch this fish here and set us free. Now, you may ask: Why should I save a man I barely know? Can't you guess why?" Smiling, he added: "Some prophet you are!"

He paused, then went on:

"Because I happen to know where the Gold Tree is," he whispered, his eyes glittering. "And I'm willing to lead you to it in exchange for my freedom. So? Is it a deal?"

Ah: So at last, he came out with it—the Gold Tree. But under the guise of an offer, which was surprising and merely raised Jonah's suspicions. As if anticipating them, the man was ready with an enticing offer, which he announced with a leer:

"The priestess of Astarte. She'll be very grateful to you, Jonah—and mind you, she really knows how to please a man she's grateful to. . . . So? Is it a deal?"

Jonah remained silent, which disconcerted the other man:

"Of course, you don't have to give me an answer right away. Think about it. But I ask you not to wait too long to make up your mind."

Suddenly he was entreating, clinging to the prophet:

"Don't let us down, Jonah! Please, don't let us down! I—"

Then pulling himself together, he wiped his eyes, got to his feet, and left. Jonah sat there, deeply disturbed by what he had heard.

J ONAH WANTS TO MULL OVER THIS MATTER, TO SORT OUT HIS thoughts. All of a sudden, soft arms encircle his neck. It's the priestess of Astarte: already naked, lustful. Jonah heard that these priestesses worship sex, but he had no idea they would go this far. He wants to repel her, it's not the right place nor the right time—he is on a divine mission—besides, he is afraid the others will show up. Lust, however, wins out; he returns the woman's caresses and ends up by taking her right there in the moist, slimy entrails of an enormous fish traveling at an incredible speed across the depths of the ocean.

Later on, lying side by side, they talk. The young woman tells him that she's there as a punishment: Destined for the High Priest, she had, however, fornicated with a wealthy Babylonian merchant. She was then cast into the sea and swallowed by the fish.

"I have nothing to do with Jeovah," she says. "But I know that your God is powerful . . . that he can summon up plagues, that he can part the waters of the sea. Therefore, he'll be able to rescue us from this place too. *You* will be able to. Take me out of this place, and I'll be yours. So, what do you say to my proposal?"

What can he possibly say now, having held the woman in his arms, having shared with her the fruit of sin? Only that he'll think about it:

"I'll think about it."

"I depend on you," she murmurs. She rises to her feet, puts on her tunic, and departs, leaving Jonah once more to his guilt and to his doubts. They want him to give in, these people in the belly of the fish; they want him to humble himself before Jeovah, they want him to obey His command—which amounts to sowing death and destruction throughout an entire city. Yes, the Ninevehites have sinned, but then who hasn't? They are human beings, worthy of compassion. On the other hand, the people inside the fish—who have defied the Lord—they, too, are human beings, they, too, are worthy of mercy. What a dilemma. But, damn it, why did Jeovah have to choose him for this mission? Why doesn't He change his plans—being God, he could—and send him, instead, to some unknown country? A country with beautiful landscapes (a bay, that's what he envisions, a beautiful bay, with waves lapping on the pure white sand of the beach; coconut trees, brightly colored birds wheeling in flight, a gloriously blue sky), a country inhabited by friendly people (bronze-skinned men, women and children, their faces painted in gaudy colors, their long black hair adorned with feathers), in such a country he would at the most have to admonish a few naughty pranksters for their small offenses. In such a country it would be easy to be a prophet. But Jeovah is cruel. Cruel to sinners, cruel to His chosen people.

Inside the belly of the fish there is no concept of time. Holding the blade of glass in his hand, Jonah meditates, he tries to. But the man with the scar on his face is back, he wants to know if Jonah has come to a decision about his

earlier proposal. "I'm thinking about it," replies the prophet,
already annoyed. "All right," says the man, "but don't
forget that we're waiting for an answer."

"We?" asks Jonah, intrigued. "We, who?"

Then it dawns on him: The two of them are in collusion,
the beautiful priestess and the man with the scar are in
cahoots, they're trying to pull a fast one on him. Incensed,
Jonah asks the man to go away: "Go away, you scum! Go
and enjoy your courtesan!"

Muttering insults, the man leaves. Jonah, overcome by a
sudden rage, drives the blade of glass into the stomach of the
fish. Blood spouts out, extinguishing the torch; he is tossed
about in the darkness: The fish, driven insane by pain, thrashes
about in the sea frantically. Finally, the fish spews up Jonah,
who, as if catapulted, flies up into the air, then flops down
into the water. Free! At long last, daylight and fresh air! After
swimming a few hundred meters, Jonah comes ashore. Exhausted, short of breath, he remains lying on the beach.

Then rising to his feet, he sets out on his way. He walks
and walks. And finally he arrives in a big city surrounded by
walls. White-washed houses, temples, palaces glitter in the
sun; through the main gate, caravans of camels flow in and
out of the city.

Nineveh.

I N NINEVEH JONAH DENOUNCED LUST AND PROPHESIED, AS THE
Lord had commanded, that in forty days at the most, the city
would be plunged into chaos and destruction. The people
believed him, and began to fast and to pray; nobody was
fornicating anymore. Such things were not enough for Jonah:
"It won't do you any good," he thundered in the main
squares, "you've sinned and now you're doomed." Much to
Jonah's chagrin, however, Jeovah didn't make the threats
come true: The days went by and nothing happened to Nineveh.
Jonah was deeply disappointed. Addressing the Lord, he
voiced his complaint:

"I knew I was doing the right thing when I ran away to Tarshish. There's no way the two of us can ever work together: I, perplexed, and you, enigmatic, it just won't work. I've had enough."

He went outside the ciy walls and there he remained, seated on the ground, waiting to see what Jeovah would finally do to Nineveh—or to him, His prophet. The rays of the sun, hitting him squarely on the skull, made him ill with calenture. He felt his brain boiling, and had terrfying visions: The gentle, bronze-colored men, whom he had imagined he could see in the country of the beautiful landscapes, were now being attacked and massacred by warriors in steel armors. Blood stained the white sand. . . .

God then took pity on Jonah.

On the parched soil before him, a tiny plant sprouted, and it soon began to grow into a small, but leafy, tree. Disturbed as he was, Jonah didn't see in this occurrence a sign of Divine mercy; he didn't lie down in the shade of this tree so that he could rest and get well again. Instead, he began to rave like a madman:

"It's the Gold Tree! I've found the Gold Tree!"

And he began to tear out its branches, searching for the pods with their precious seeds. Jeovah, angered, then sent a grub of the desert, and in the twinkling of an eye, it devoured the entire tree, and then it transformed itself into a butterfly, which flew away and disappeared.

At first Jonah couldn't believe it. When he finally realized what had happened, he burst out laughing. He laughed and laughed; he was rolling about on the ground, laughing; he laughed so much that his belly ached; he would stop laughing for a moment, wipe his eyes, and then succumb to another fit of laughter.

Finally he stopped laughing, rose to his feet, and heaving a sigh, set out on his way; he was going back home, to Judea. On the way he walked past a craggy mountain, situated south of Jericho, near the Dead Sea. In that bleak landscape, perhaps because of the intense heat, he had a premonition: One day, he murmured, a descendant of mine will climb this mountain in search of his destiny. Centuries later, the prophecy was fulfilled.

HE IS YOUNG, THIS MAN NOW CLIMBING THE MOUNTAIN, THIS Habacuc ben Tov, my ancestor.

He wears a coarse tunic, and rustic sandals. Tied to his waist, a goatskin pouch. Empty: the last of the water drunk hours ago. Covered with dust, his mouth dry, he labors up the steep cliffs. And he is thinking not of Jonah's prophecy but of an incident that happened to his father. One summer day, this man, a humble farm worker, decided to take a break from his tedious work and go for a dip in the cool waters of the Sea of Galilee. He was enjoying his swim, when all of a sudden the area was hit by a violent storm. Frightened, and interpreting the phenomenon as a sign of divine disapproval of his self-indulgence, the man dived into the water: There he stayed submerged, fearful of being struck by lightning. He endured the situation for as long as he could; finally, unable to hold his breath much longer, he lifted up his eyes in a mute request for mercy—and what did he see through the clear waters? Feet walking upon the surface of the lake. *A man was walking upon the waters*. He didn't suppose at that moment that it could be Jesus Christ walking toward a transcendent destiny; as a matter of a fact, he didn't suppose anything at all. Instead, his attention was focused on the examination of those feet. Beautiful, well-shaped feet; the skin on their soles was smooth, with no callosities. From this fact he concluded—erroneously, as it turned out—that those feet belonged to a contemplative, to a person capable of floating above reality. When he finally emerged from the water, there was no one in sight; however, the image of the feet upon the water was to haunt him, and on his deathbed, he said to Habacuc: "Search for men who are above." "Above what, Father?" "Above everything." Respectful but disappointed, Habacuc listened to him in silence; he would have preferred that the old man had relayed to him, say, the secret of the Gold Tree. Being a poor man, with a family to support, Habacuc ben Tov was

84

forced to think of prosaic matters, such as earning his daily bread. However, hidden in the enigmatic words of his father was a message, whose validity circumstances would soon demonstrate.

I N ROMAN-OCUPPIED PALESTINE, INTRIGUE, CORRUPTION, wretched poverty, discontent, are rampant. The small farmers are bankrupt; their wheat cannot compete against the Egyptian wheat, which is much cheaper. The small farms are being taken over by the owners of latifundia, who prefer to use slave labor, much to the shame of the people of Israel. The impoverished masses flock to the cities, and there they live in constant struggle. In Jerusalem, where Habacuc lives, there is a succession of political and religious crimes, the result of confrontations among various factions. Sadducees, Pharisees, and others. Hired assassins, high on hashish, mingle with the crowds. Suddenly, a scream, and a man, covered with blood, collapses: A merchant, suspected of collaborating with the invaders. Or a priest who has adopted Greek practices. Sickened by all this madness, by all this fury, Habacuc decides to leave, deserting his wife (who has been betraying him with a Roman legionnaire) and three children. He goes away in search of purity, of redemption. In search of the legendary Essenes, the sect that holds the key to the harmony of the soul and to eternal life.

F INALLY, HE SIGHTS THE HOLY CITY—ASSEMBLAGE OF AUSTERE stone houses, strategically built on the top of the mountain. A man comes to meet him; he supports him, gives him a drink of water. He is Eliezer, the friend who had joined the Essenes

many years before, and with whom Habacuc exchanged secret messages.

Before being accepted into the community, Habacuc has to
go through a period of initiation: fastings, prayers, medita-
tion. His mentor is Eliezer, who offers him support when he
loses his courage. With the help of his friend, Habacuc
surmounts one by one all the stages of his painful initiation.
Finally, the great day arrives. Before the entire community
gathered in the main square, Habacuc takes an oath. He
promises to obey the law of Moses exactly as it was revealed
to the sons of Sadoc—the Essenian priests. And during the
final battle against the Children of Darkness, he will stand
side by side with the Children of Light. He will follow the
Angel of Truth against Satan. It will be a terrible battle, when
even the dead will rise from their graves to fight: their
decomposed bodies brandishing swords of light. Finally, Good
will triumph, and the Messiah will reign sovereign. "Blessed
be the Lord!" shout the priests when Habacuc is through with
the ceremony. The believers break into applause: Habacuc
has been accepted as one of their own. Since he is still a
novice, he is not yet a full-fledged member of the community
of the definitively pure; but God willing, one day he will be.

T HAT NIGHT—AND WHAT PROMPTED HIM TO DO SO? A TEST
of confidence? A daring gesture? A residue of his former
Jerusalemite arrogance?—Eliezer invites Habacuc to go with
him to a cave located on the outskirts of the city. With great
difficulty, the two of them push aside a huge stone—and
Habacuc can hardly contain an exclamation of surprise: In the
light of the torch that Eliezer carries, he sees bangles, necklaces, bracelets, statuettes; gold, silver, diamonds, rubies. So
it is true! The legendary treasure of the Essenes does exist!
But Eliezer has something even more surprising to show his
friend: a phial containing small, glittering metal grains.

"Do you know what they are? Seeds from the Gold Tree."
Then Eliezer adds, "The fact that we don't sow these seeds

and that we keep our jewels in this cave is proof of our selflessness.'' He seems convinced of the truth of what he is saying and yet, Habacuc detects in his voice a faint, yet definite, tone of falsehood: No, Eliezer doesn't really believe in what he's saying. But why, wonders Habacuc, perplexed. After so many years amid the Essenes, after so much fasting and so many hardships, shouldn't Eliezer have attained that degree of moral superiority that reflects itself in a tranquil disregard for material possessions? It doesn't seem that this is the case. . . . Hm, there's something wrong here. . . . Unaware of Habacuc's suspicions, Eliezer continues to talk about the treasure. ''All this wealth,'' he says, ''is reserved for the Messiah. His arrival will be celebrated with a huge, fabulous banquet. The partakers of this love feast will make their entrance into a spacious hall, lit up by scores of gold candelabra, in the following order: the High Priest; the priests in general; the Messiah in person; the heads of family. The High Priest will then bless the bread and the wine; the Messiah will also bless the bread; and then delectable choice dishes will be served.''

W HO IS THE MESSIAH?'' HABACUC WANTS TO KNOW. ''THE Messiah is the Master of Justice,'' explains Eliezer. ''A long time ago, he lived amid the people, preaching the divine word; but they didn't listen to him; aggrieved, he then went away. But riding a beautiful white horse, he'll be back one day, in search of the righteous—that's us.'' ''But,'' persists Habacuc, ''how will we know that he is indeed the Messiah and not an impostor?''

''Because,'' says Eliezer, beginning to feel annoyed at all these doubts, ''he has the divine commands engraved on his tongue.''

''On his tongue?'' Habacuc is stunned.

''On his tongue.''

''On his tongue, well, who would have guessed,'' murmurs Habacuc, quite impressed. He remains silent for a moment, but is soon asking another question:

"Is the Messiah this Jesus, the one who was crucified?"

"Jesus?" Eliezer laughs. "No. Jesus was a kindly man, but he wasn't the Messiah. Do you think the Messiah would have let himself be crucified? No way. With a single glance he would have exterminated thousands of those Romans before they even had a chance to touch him." Impassioned, he adds: "Ah, all the traitors will be exterminated! Woe to anyone who has drawn away from the divine word, from the Well of the Spring Tide!"

His vehemence surprises and disturbs Habacuc. From a holy man he would expect meekness and gentleness, not this outburst of ferocity. However, he says nothing. He helps Eliezer replace the stone. Then, in silence, they walk back to the small stone house that they share with another five or six people. Habacuc undresses and lies down on his hard cot. His first night amid the Pure is haunted by terrifying nightmares.

I T'S A GRUELING EXISTENCE. THE ESSENES GET UP VERY EARLY; the sky is still dark when they leave for work. On small terraces they cultivate vegetables, making the best of the scanty amount of water that has been carefully collected in reservoirs—it hardly ever rains in this region. The sun rises, the heat becomes unbearable. Down below lies the Dead Sea, dense, saturated with minerals, whose crystals, encrusted on the logs that lie about the shore, glitter in the shimmering light.

Habacuc and Eliezer have been assigned an arduous task: the building of cisterns. They have to cut stones, transport and put them in place, then seal the cracks with bitumen and pitch. In the distance, they can see the women baking bread in round-shaped ovens.

Habacuc would like to ask questions about the women. He doesn't dare; he knows, however, that many of the men are single and chaste. Eliezer is one such man; he is forty years old, and has never known a woman. One day he confided to Habacuc that he would like to take the daughter of one of the priests as his wife. But the girl is only fifteen years old, and according to what the Law prescribes, she can't marry until she's twenty—even though she already has the body of a woman, with breasts bulging under her tunic. Eliezer's sleep is restless, he moans. Habacuc knows why. He, too, secretly desires this same girl, this Naomi.

ONE NIGHT HABACUC GETS OUT OF BED AND GOES FOR A walk. A huge yellow light shines upon the hills of Judea. The air is saturated with dust and odors. From the distance the wind carries strange sounds—laughter, moaning. In the Holy City, the Essenes lie asleep. They rest their exhausted bodies after a day of hard work, a day that has brought them closer to the Great Happiness. Only Habacuc, driven by anguish, has to walk on and on, the sweat running down his face, his chest.

Suddenly, the feeling that he is being watched. He turns around. Did a window close quickly? Perhaps. Habacuc keeps on walking now at a slower pace. His ears, pricked, detect footsteps. Habacuc stops: Somebody is following him, he wants to know why. Is he doing something wrong? Does walking at night make him one of the Children of Darkness?

A figure approaches. A small, delicate hand takes him by the arm. To his astonishment, Habacuc is being led to a cave near the one with the treasure. The cave has a narrow entrance, but soon reveals itself to be spacious, like a hall with a domed ceiling, faintly lit by the moonlight that barely penetrates this place.

They stand, the two of them, face to face. An abrupt gesture, and the cloak drops to the floor, revealing a girl to Habacuc's surprised eyes. Naked! It's the priest's daughter, and she is naked! Naked and quivering! "We haven't got much time," she whispers, and throws herself upon Habacuc. They roll on the ground, she tears away his tunic, kisses him ravenously on the mouth, the neck, the chest, and then on her knees, she takes his member in both her hands, gazes at it

with near fervor—and then proceeds to perform fellatio on
him, the sinful practice introduced by the Romans. "No,"
protests Habacuc, "don't," but his terror is already giving
way to pleasure and he lets himself go. What a tongue, oh,
God in heaven. What a lecherous demon she is with this
tongue of hers!

Habacuc possessed her one, two, three times. Both of them
insatiable: He, full of lust that has been accumulating in deep,
invisible cisterns ever since he left Jerusalem; and she, she
seems demoniac. She must be an incarnation of Lilith, the
she-devil—Adam's first wife, the one who chose to live
among demons; or an incarnation of Potiphar's wife.

Suddenly, she rises to her feet. She wraps her tunic about
her. Habacuc tries to hold her back, but she extricates herself
and leaves, not before murmuring: "Here, tomorrow."

T HEY MEET EVERY NIGHT. SHE ALWAYS LUSTFUL, ARDENT
"You're a real man," she says, "the only man amid all these
sanctimonious fools." She makes it quite clear that she doesn't
believe in anything, neither in the Messiah nor in the last
battle; she was even considering running away from the Holy
City. "And then you came, my love. You, my savior, my
Messiah! My inexhaustible well of love!"

Although flattered, Habacuc can't help feeling apprehensive. What if they find out, he wonders. And even if they
don't—how is all of this going to end? What makes him feel
even guiltier, however, is his betrayal of his friend Eliezer,
who continues to talk to him about Naomi in the most glowing terms. Doesn't he suspect anything at all? Habacuc can
hardly believe that anyone could be so naive; maybe Eliezer
is plotting something, maybe he is leading Habacuc on, just
to see how far he'll go. So, when one night Eliezer invites
him to go for a walk—we have a lot to talk about—Habacuc
is in a near panic: It's now, he thinks, it's now that he's going
to get even with me. He can't, however, decline the invitation. Tense, he accompanies his friend. Under his tunic,

Habacuc firmly holds his dagger by the handle, the dagger he never got rid of, not even after opting for an ascetic lifestyle. But Eliezer doesn't have a clue about what is going on between Habacuc and Naomi. What he wants is to confide an astonishing plan to Habacuc: He can't stand this existence among the Essenes anymore, the fastings, the penances, the waiting for a Master of Justice who will never come.

"This banquet!" he shouts, enraged. Then controlling himself, he lowers his voice: "For years now I've heard them talk about this banquet with the Messiah, Haba. For years I've been preparing myself for the arrival of the Master. I'm fed up with all of it."

A pause, then he goes on:

"I can't bear being without a woman anymore. I just can't, Haba. Every night I have these dreams, I ejaculate in bed. I'm wasting my semen, I'm getting weak. And old. I want the priest's daughter, Haba. And I'm sure that she wants me just as badly. The way she looks at me . . . She's crazy about me, Haba. Crazy. And I'm just as crazy about her. I want her now. And I'm willing to go to any lengths to get her."

He discloses his plan. He will go down the mountain, search out the Roman troops, which are camped nearby. He will reveal the location of the treasure. In exchange for the information, he will ask their commander for a share of the riches—and for Naomi.

Habacuc listens, horrified: "But it'll be a bloodbath," he exclaims. "Nobody here knows how to wield a weapon, all you hear is this talk about swords of light." Eliezer shrugs. "I couldn't care less," he says in a dull tone of voice. "I've made up my mind, I want this woman, I'll have her no matter how." He holds Habacuc by the arm: "Can I count on you, Haba? You'll get your share of the treasure, too. I'll be generous, I promise you."

Habacuc stares at him, at a loss for words.

"Even without your help, I'm going ahead with my plan," threatens Eliezer. "In two days' time I'll approach the Romans. Until then, you have time to think it over."

T HAT NIGHT HABACUC AND NAOMI LEAVE THE HOLY CITY. Behind them are the quiet houses. On a cot, his eyes wide open, lies Eliezer—dead, with Habacuc's dagger buried in his chest.

Walking during the night and hiding by day, they finally reach the coast. They run into a group of refugees, who like them, want to flee the country. They will have to charter a ship; there's a Greek captain who is willing to oblige, but for a high sum of money. But neither of them has any money. As Habacuc argues with the Greek, Naomi begins to pull him by the arm. "What is it?" he asks, annoyed, "can't you see I'm busy trying to solve this problem?" "Come over here," she says, smiling, "there's something I want to show you." After they step aside, she removes the pouch that hangs from her neck, and opens it: rings, necklaces, tiaras; gold, diamonds, rubies. "How beautiful," marvels Habacuc, "where did you get them?" Then it dawns on him—and he blurts out:

"And what about the seeds of the Gold Tree? Did you bring the seeds of the Gold Tree? With the Gold Tree—"

He stops short: By the expression on her face, he realizes that he has made a mistake. He tries to apologize, but it's too late. From now on things won't be the same between them. They will no longer be able to surrender themselves to each other with their former passion. Greed has poisoned their lives. Like Adam and Eve after eating the fruit of the Tree of the Knowledge of Good and Evil, they, too, won't have any peace.

T HE SMALL SHIP SAILED FROM AN ANCHORAGE AT YAFO ON A dark moonless night. The campfires of a nearby Roman encampment glowed in the blackness; the fugitives could even hear the laughter of the legionnaires as they celebrated their latest victories over the fanatically insurgent Jews. Carried by favorable winds, the ship glided rapidly away; by dawn they had left the coast far behind.

Two days later, as they coasted some islands, a sudden lull took the wind from the ship's sails. Seated on the deck, the crew and the passengers traded worried looks. What did it bode, this unexpected change in the weather? Nobody knew, not even the experienced Greek captain.

Night fell. The ship swayed gently in the dark. The silence was broken only by the squealing sound of the vessel's timbers. Snuggled against Habacuc, Naomi slept. The others, apprehensive, sat waiting.

Suddenly a voice, from afar: *Habacuc! Habacuc!* Twice. Roused from their sleep, the voyagers, terrified, whispered: "Answer, Habacuc, answer." But he kept shaking his head stubbornly. Only when the voice called him for the seventh time did he rise to his feet:

"I am Habacuc! Who calls me? Why do you call me?"

"Your crime didn't go unnoticed," replied the voice. "Because of the sins you and others have committed, a god has died, Habacuc. As punishment, your descendants will wander the earth until they finally hark to the word of the Children of Light. Have I made myself understood?"

"Yes," murmured Habacuc, livid, his forehead damp with perspiration. "This is my message," said the voice. There was a silence; and then the wind rose. Reassured that this matter didn't concern them, the sailors then hoisted sail.

Six days later the boat arrived in Sefarad (later called Spain). There Habacuc and Naomi joined a small Hebrew settlement. They prospered, thanks to the jewels Naomi had brought with her. To the end of his life Habacuc suffered

pangs of remorse for having deserted the Essenes, for having
drawn away from the Well of the Spring Tide, and for having
robbed a father of his only daughter even though it had been
with her consent. For having forsaken the land of Israel. For
having killed a man. For having caused the death of a god.
Despite his guilt, however, Habacuc drank and ate well and
was in good health; he lived to a "ripe old age." His children, grandchildren, and great-grandchildren lived in Spain,
in cities like Toledo, whose name comes from *Toledoth*,
meaning the city of the generations, first under the rule of the
Romans, then of the Visigoths, and later of the Moors.
Among the Moors lived a famous ancestor of the Mendeses:
Moses ben Maimon, better known by the Greek form of his
name: Maimonides.

B ORN IN 1135, WHEN THE IBERIAN PENINSULA WAS UNDER
Arabic rule, Maimonides was educated by his learned father
and by Muslim masters. From an early age he dedicated
himself to philosophy. He wrote treatises in which he wondered about the meaning of life, which filled him with anxiety—
but by and large, he was happy.

In 1148 the Omayyads, who had until then ruled over
Arabic Spain, were overthrown by the fanatical Almohads.
This was followed by the expulsion of both Christians and
Jews. Maimonides's family moved to Northern Africa, and later
settled in Cairo. After their father died, Maimonides and
his brother David set up a jewelry business. David, who loved
jewels, would spend hours lovingly stroking necklaces, bracelets, rings. It was painful for him to part with these precious
objects. "If I could," he would say with a sigh, "I'd spend
the entire day admiring these. The more I look at a precious
stone, the greater the wonders I find therein. Some stones
have the warmth of the sun, others have the mysterious glow
of the moon. Signs, my brother—signs of fate. And the Gold
Tree! Ah, if only I could find the Gold Tree!"

Maimonides, however, was completely indifferent to jewels. He would take them to their customers, who were noblemen in the court of the sultan Saladin. Reclining on silk cushions, they would examine the goods while Maimonides stood lost in thought. What is the meaning of the human condition? What is the relationship between God and the universe? The customers would ask him about the price of the jewels; the question had to be repeated three or four times before he came to his senses, and then, in a flurry, he would blurt out something: either a preposterously high or a ridiculously low price, which made the noblemen burst loudly into laughter. Some, irritated, would send him away, saying they didn't want to do business with such an idiot. As a result, his brother David's workload increased. It even fell to him to charter ships and to travel to Cyprus, to Byzantium, in search of new customers. It was in the course of one such voyage that David died in a shipwreck. His body was never recovered.

His brother's death was a severe blow to Maimonides, who for several days sat on the beach, staring out at the sea, grievously striking at his chest with his fists. He had to be taken home against his will. Then, shutting himself up in his room, he began to write his masterpiece, *The Guide for the Perplexed*, which was an attempt to guide himself, and others, through the major issues of life and death.

There were, however, far more pressing worries. Now that his brother was dead, the support of the family became his responsibility. What should he do? He disliked the jewelry business, and with David gone, he wouldn't have the slightest chance of succeeding in this line of work. So he decided to take up medicine, a respected and lucrative profession. Besides, medicine was close to philosophy: Maimonides secretly expected that in the humors secreted by the diseased bodies, in the whispered words of the dying, in the hallucinations of the lunatics, he would find the answers to the questions that kept disturbing him.

At that time Arabic medicine was flourishing under great physicians, such as: Avicena! (or Ibn Sina.) Avenzoar! (or Ibn Zurh.) Averroes! (or Ibn Rushid.) Maimonides—or Musa Ibn Maimun, as he was known—became Averroes's favorite disciple.

Maimonides learned how to prepare infusions of medicinal herbs. With a sharp knife he was able to remove a cataract in a matter of minutes; he would then examine the tiny lens, milky and opaque like the pearls his brother used to admire so

much, and with a sigh, he would discard it, unless the patient
requested to have it as a souvenir; in this case, he would put it
in a phial with alcohol.

In accordance with the best Hippocratic tradition, he learned
how to interpret the signs of disease. By examining urine, he
was able to tell from its appearance, smell, taste, and the
deposits it left, whether the patient was going to die or get
better. If the fever went down fast, he would sigh with relief;
but if a low-grade fever lingered for days or weeks, or if at
twilight the cheeks of the patient flushed, Maimonides would
be alarmed, for he was well familiar with the disguises of
tuberculosis. Like Joseph in the Bible, he, too, was interested
in dreams; he could tell which particular remorse was tormenting a person by analyzing the shapes of the figures that
appeared in his dreams. And he also had a special interest in
the pathology of the unusual or exotic.

He became respected and well-known. He settled in Fostat,
near Cairo; soon afterward, he could write to his relatives:
"Due to my reputation as a physician, the powerful hold me
in high regard. My antechambers are always crowded with
patients. I arrive in the morning, dismount my horse, wash
my hands, and proceed to attend to the sick, who keep
streaming in until sunset. I'm so tired at night that I can
barely talk—tired but happy."

He was making a lot of money. His former doubts about
the meaning of life still obsessed him, but to a lesser extent.
The lives he saved absolved him from his faults. He was . . .
happy. Happy. He was married to a beautiful, gentle, understanding woman. It's true that at times, after they made love,
Maimonides had difficulty falling asleep; restless, he would
toss about in bed. When he finally drifted off to sleep, it was
to find himself submerged in a deep sea, confronting what he
was afraid of finding: the body of his brother. Fish swam
through the empty eye sockets, crustaceans sidled out of the
mouth. Tied to his dead brother's neck, a pouch with precious
stones: pearls, emeralds, rubies. *Take the jewels*, whispered a
distant voice. A series of muffled bangs began to reverberate
in the depths of that sea, growing louder and more distinct
until they finally woke him up; it was someone battering
away at the door. Someone calling him to attend to a sick
person.

Throughout the Jewish community in Egypt, the *Rambam*
(an acronym standing for Rabbi Moses ben Maimon) was

truly venerated. People came to him not only because of his medical skill but also because of his great wisdom. "Me? a sage?" he would say. "But I'm the most ignorant of the ignorant." But they thought otherwise. They all came for comfort and advice, gathering at his door.

One day a stranger came to see him.

He walked in disguised in a long mantle, which he didn't take off; he declined the wine that a servant had offered him, and when Maimonides asked what had brought him there, he ignored the question and started to fire questions of his own at the physician: Wasn't Musa Ibn Maimun overworking himself? Wasn't he getting tired of looking after so many patients? Intrigued but not angry, Maimonides replied to each one of his questions. He knew human nature too well to be offended by such impertinence. Besides, he knew that the sick tend to be suspicious, demanding explanations before submitting themselves to the care of a physician.

When the stranger was through with his questioning, he proffered a remarkable opinion: He believed that the physician was overworking himself, he had too many patients. "Wouldn't it be better to have fewer patients?" he asked. "Say, ten, or five—or, even better, just one patient willing to pay him royally for his services?" "I don't think so," replied Maimonides, wary. "A physician should attend to anyone who needs him. Now, if you'll excuse me, I have to get back to my work."

He rose to his feet. The man rose too, and flinging aside his mantle, he revealed his opulent attire. He identified himself as one of Saladin's ministers: He was offering Musa Ibn Maimun the position of personal physician to the sultan.

Maimonides quivered. The proposal amounted to an official recognition, the greatest recognition to which he could aspire; however, despite being the physician of many a dignitary, he now hesitated about accepting responsibility for the health of a ruler of empires. The minister noticed his uncertainty. "Allow me to remind you that the sultan's invitation amounts to an order," he said.

The man's authoritarian tone of voice and arrogance angered Maimonides; his first impulse was to reply haughtily *then take me with you, but you will have to kill me first;* however, he knew it would be impossible for him to say this. He was responsible not only to his family but also to the Jewish community in Egypt, of which, in the eyes of the

Arabs, he was the official representative. He couldn't take a stand that might put other people in jeopardy. "All right, I accept the offer," he said. The minister, pleased, outlined the details of the proposal: Maimonides would move to the sultan's palace, where he and his family would live in private lodgings. He would have as many servants and assistants as he needed, as well as books, medical instruments, medicines. He mentioned the payment—a sum so high that even Maimonides was impressed: "Am I worth all this much?" The minister smiled: "The sultan pays handsomely for what he wants."

Finally the minister mentioned the main stipulation: Musa Ibn Maimun was to be at the sultan's beck and call. He was not to attend to anyone else—one of the reasons being the risk of his hands transmitting another person's disease to his employer. Then, rising to his feet, he said:

"Is everything clear?"

Sighing, Maimonides said it was. "Let's go then," said the minister, "I have camels waiting outside."

"But I need some time," said Maimonides, "to look after a few matters; there are also the patients waiting to see me—"

"They will be informed," said the minister with impatience. "Call your family and let's go without any further delay."

And SO MAIMONIDES IS TAKEN TO THE PALACE: ON A CAMEL, shielded from the stares of the populace by a richly ornamented baldachin. As soon as they arrive, the minister takes him to the sultan.

A corpulent man, this Saladin; vitality exudes from the piercing eyes, from the vigorous gestures. He looks Maimonides up and down: "So, this is the physician then? Welcome, physician, welcome." Respectfully, and choosing his words carefully, the minister suggests that the sultan submit himself to a physical examination right away, for he is scheduled to start out on a journey very soon. Good-humored, Saladin acquiesces. Everybody leaves the hall, and he remains alone with the physician. Maimonides questions him about his dietary habits, his bowel movements, his sexual drive, the shape of his feces and the force with which the stream of urine comes out. Saladin, willingly but rather impatiently, replies to every question: "I've never been ill, physician, why all these questions?" Intimidated, Maimonides proceeds to the clinical exam: "Would you, Your Excellency. . . ."

"Take off my clothes?" Laughing, the sultan undresses, lies down on the cushions.

Maimonides recognizes at once the sultan's excellent physical condition, but being in a fluster, he makes mistakes typical of a greenhorn; however, he has no trouble noticing that the sultan's forehead is cool, that his mucous membranes are pink and moist, that there is no furring on his tongue, that his pulse is regular, a touch too full, perhaps, a touch too strong, but taking into account his age, still within normal range. No signs of disease, Maimonides concludes, nothing to prescribe, and so he informs the sovereign. "Aren't you afraid you'll lose your job now?" asks Saladin, laughing. Both physician and patient laugh together. The sultan's laughter is deep, he laughs slapping his hands on his thighs, he laughs until he gasps for breath. Finally, he asks Maimonides if everything is all right with him, if Musa Ibn Maimun is happy.

Maimonides is suddenly serious. He doesn't reply right away. He thinks for a while, his eyes fixed on the rug. Finally—surprised at his own frankness—he says that everything is not all right. He feels honored by his position as royal physician, but he would rather attend to many patients, not just one.

"I'm not 'just one,' " Saladin says dryly. "I'm many. I'm everybody. And now leave. You're dismissed."

Maimonides leaves.

Days, months go by. Maimonides sees Saladin but occasionally. Claiming he doesn't have the time, the sultan refuses to see the physician. Maimonides has to turn to Saladin's closest associates for information: Does he sleep well? How is his appetite? Does he pass wind? Does he belch? He neatly writes down the answers in a special logbook, then spends hours mulling over his notes, trying to guess at the condition of the humors, of the pneuma, of the pituitary from the observations that he wrote down. On his desk, thick volumes written in Latin, in Arabic, in Greek, in Hebrew, keep piling up; these books, brought by Saladin's envoys, who travel all over the world to get them, epitomize the medical knowledge of those days. They contain descriptions of exotic diseases, of new forms of treatment. Maimonides doesn't read them. What for? He lacks the opportunity to put this knowledge into practice. Motionless, he sits staring at the books. At times his fingers twitch—the fingers are eager to touch a wrist, to palpate the contours of a tumor. There are no wrists, there are no tumors. There is nothing.

In the evening Maimonides locks his office and goes to his private lodgings. His wife waits for him. Ever since her husband became the sultan's physician, she has experienced contradictory feelings. On the one hand, she's proud of the envy that her status causes in the friends that come to visit her and to whom, with affected insouciance, she relates the latest gossip of the court. On the other hand, she is worried, for she realizes that her husband is unhappy. But she chooses not to say anything to him, hoping that it's just one of those ephemeral depressions that from time to time afflict Maimonides, a melancholic man by nature.

Affecting unconcern, she asks her husband about his day. "So, so," he says. "And how's the sultan?" "Fine," he says, then correcting himself: "I think he's fine. It seems that his headache is better."

Trying to cheer him up, she tells him about the flattering remarks that the Jewish community keeps making about the Rambam, their greatest representative. Maimonides listens in silence. He rises to his feet, goes to his room. He sits there, leafing through his own books, especially *The Guide for the Perplexed*. In this work he advocates applying Aristotelian logic to the Jewish religion itself—which perplexes the more Orthodox Jews, who are, as a matter of fact, invariably suspicious of any Greek trend: Logic, in religion? How? And now Maimonides himself wonders: Under the present circumstances, what good does logic do to me? Could there be something deeper, something not on a conscious level, that would explain what happens? Perhaps supra-individual forces, or historical laws? Such ruminations are cut short by the arrival of his wife, who comes in with a glass of milk: "Go to bed," she says, "it's late, you'll have to be in your office tomorrow."

On the following day everything starts all over again.

Maimonides devotes himself to treating imaginary patients. At first there's only one, a young man afflicted by mysterious fevers; then, Maimonides adds a woman with jaundice, a man with tuberculosis, and an old man with an abdominal tumor. They moan, they call for him. He imagines that he is examining them, that he is looking at their tongues, for example; and so vividly does he imagine the scene that he can actually see the furring on their tongues, the blotches with contours that suggest maps of mysterious countries. Then leaning over, he places his ear on imaginary chests, listening to the beating of hearts that have never existed—and he is amazed at their strange rhythms, rhythms that no Ibn Sina has ever described. To him, it is music, music of the spheres. From this reverie he is roused by the voice of his wife:

"Moses! Dinner!"

At the sound of her voice, he sighs. Does a person who doesn't work, who doesn't help others, have the right to eat bread? However, in his case it's not bread, but delectable dishes—so, he rises to his feet to eat dinner.

ONE DAY THE SULTAN AGREES TO SEE HIM, BUT ONLY RELUCtantly, making it quite clear that he has acceded to the requests of his ministers, but he doesn't believe in medicine or in physicians.

"I only want to make sure that you are in good health," says Maimonides somewhat apologetically.

An idea occurs to Saladin; his eyes glitter; he smiles lewdly:

"So, you really want to see if I'm in good health, is that right, Musa Ibn Maimun? Well, let me show you."

Grabbing the physician by the arm, he drags him through the corridors of the palace as far as a pavilion with an iron door, at which stand two armed guards. Maimonides is puzzled: that's the harem. What is Saladin up to? The sultan pushes him indoors: "Go in, physician, there's no need to be afraid, there aren't any lepers in here."

Around a fountain in the hall, there are some twenty or thirty women wearing transparent silk; reclined on cushions, they talk, they sing. Upon seeing Saladin, they fall silent, puzzled: A man here? And brought in by Saladin?

"You'll see how healthy I am," says the sultan, taking off his clothes.

He looks around, then calls one of the women: "You! Lie down here!" The young woman complies, and Saladin throws himself upon her, and takes her. Then he gets up and calls another woman. Again, he has sex with her, and then with a third woman—afterward, he rises to his feet. Then he asks the shocked, embarrassed Maimonides: "So, what do you think? Am I in good health or not?"

Maimonides doesn't reply. Saladin puts on his clothes. "There's no need for my ministers to worry anymore," he says grinning. "Wouldn't you agree, physician?"

Maimonides agrees. Excusing himself, he then leaves. He locks himself up in his room: to cry. More than perplexed, he feels lost. Hopelessly lost. Not even God can help him.

HE CANNOT LEAVE THE PALACE. IT'S FORBIDDEN. BUT FROM a small window he watches the city, the crowds that fill up the streets, the market. Small dark creatures enveloped in rags. What does he know about them, about the populace? Nothing. To distract himself, he makes diagnoses from a distance: That man over there has scabies . . . that woman there is chlorotic . . . that other man there seems to be suffering from dropsy. It's A.D. 1192. On April 6 Maimonides notes a certain restlessness in the city, a certain disturbance that keeps growing during the following days; observing the panic displayed by the people, he deduces that something very grave must be happening. Masses of people begin to leave the city, taking their possessions with them. Cloaked figures appear on the streets, carrying stretchers on which lie corpses, which are then thrown into the fires that burn every-where. "There's some terrible disease going around, Musa

Ibn Maimun,'' his valet tells him confidentially. And he disappears: he, too, has fled the city.

It's cholera, concludes Maimonides, what the Hebrews called *chole ra*, the cruel disease, the ancient plague of the Orient. It's cholera, and nothing can be done, except what Saladin himself—without deigning to consult him—has already ordered: Burn the corpses. As a matter of fact, consulting Maimonides would have been useless. Maimonides doesn't know. Nobody knows. The cause of the disease is unknown, and so is the manner by which it is spread. With a sigh, Maimonides closes the window and returns to *The Guide for the Perplexed*.

In the third week of this epidemic, he wakes in the middle of the night with a sudden and extraordinary intuition: *The disease stems from the water*. From the water in the great communal well near the market, a well used by most of the townspeople. In the darkness of the room he can clearly see the depths of this well, the subterranean rivulets that feed it; into this crystalline water flows a muddy liquid: excrements, the copious fecal discharges from the cholera victims. A deadly vicious circle is thus established.

The day is barely dawning when he hastens to see the minister to request an audience with the sultan. The minister wants to know why. Maimonides says he wants to see him about the cholera; he outlines his ideas about the disease, claims that he can save the townspeople from this plague—at least he can try. The minister listens to him with a frown, and says nothing. "So?" says Maimonides. "Forget it," says the minister, "you're the sultan's physician, the diseases of the rabble are none of your business." Maimonides still tries to reason with the minister, but he puts an end to the interview, saying he's much too busy. He's making preparations for a military expedition: Saladin is going to confront the Christians in Palestine.

Devastated, Maimonides returns to his lodgings. However, he manages to pull himself together; he won't let himself feel depressed. He spends that night writing nonstop; what he writes amounts to a treatise on cholera: causes, manner of transmission, treatment. But in the morning, in a frenzy of despair, he throws the manuscript into the fire. From then on, his state of mind deteriorates quickly. He shuns his wife, he doesn't want to talk to his children. He has frequent fits of crying. He prays and prays, but even religion cannot give him solace. He considers putting an end to his life. . . .

One night there is a loud banging on the door. Alarmed, Maimonides gets up, opens the door. It's a guard: Maimonides is being summoned to the palace. The physician dresses in a hurry and follows the man. They walk across the inner court-yards of the palace, which are bathed in moonlight. Maimonides shivers in the cold wind. What's in store for him at the palace?

He is taken to the Council Room. All the ministers and court dignitaries are gathered there. Also present is a messen-ger who has just arrived from Saladin's encampment in Da-mascus. He is the bearer of bad tidings: The sultan is ill.

Maimonides interrogates the man quickly; from what he hears, he is convinced that the sultan's illness is serious. Orders are given to make preparations for a journey; Maimo-nides is to leave for Damascus immediately. He returns to his lodgings to pack a few articles of clothing, his medical instru-ments, a few books; then saying goodbye to his wife, he joins the escort already waiting for him. They'll travel by sea as far as Palestine; from there they'll proceed on horseback to the encampment.

Three days later Maimonides arrives at his destination. He is met by Saladin's generals; their worried faces convey to the physician that his arrival represents their last hope. Little information is given out. Saladin had just ended his campaign against the Christians, who were led by Richard of England. Even though he had been defeated twice at Yafo, he was negotiating a highly advantageous peace treaty. Upon return-ing to Damascus, he was suddenly taken ill.

Maimonides is taken to a large tent, where there is only a couch. The man he sees lying on it, the seriously ill man who at times tosses about deliriously, this man is Saladin.

Maimonides removes the mantle that covers him, exposing the ailing body: a strange, unknown country. He is gripped by terror, the same terror of the nightmares in which he sees his dead brother. Clumsily, his hands palpate Saladin's abdomen; the sick man moans, the hands hastily withdraw. The hands hesitate, not knowing whether they should take the pulse or percuss the thorax. Relax, Maimonides murmurs to himself, stop acting like a madman; think, damn it, think.

He tries to coordinate his thoughts, to reach a diagnosis. There's lethargy, he notes, there are tremors; the muscle tone is weakened, the eyes are sunken, the abdomen, depressed and sensitive. What could it be? He doesn't know.

He glowers at his patient: It's his own fault, Maimonides says to himself. He took me away from my practice, he shut me up in a palace, away from my patients. I've lost my skills, my insights. But he's now paying for it: He has condemned himself to death, this Muslim dog.

Maimonides leaves the tent. Alone, he wanders among the soldiers' tents, comes to the well, stands staring at the moon reflected in its dark waters.

Somebody grabs him by the arm. It's the minister.

"The man is very sick, Musa Ibn Maimun."

A statement or a question? Maimonides chooses not to reply. The minister looks at him; it's a look that disturbs the physician. What next?

"I'm not going to beat about the bush, Musa Ibn Maimun," says the minister in a low, ominous voice. "I don't know whether you can cure Saladin or not; the point is, he must not survive. He must not, understand?"

He stops talking: A group of soldiers walks by. The minister waits until they are out of earshot before he goes on: "This treaty with the Christian king . . . this treaty is going to be fatal to us. And it will affect you too, as a Jew. The blood of your people will flow, Musa Ibn Maimun. In Palestine, and everywhere else. Therefore, it's imperative that Saladin die."

Maimonides says nothing. He wants to leave, but the minister seizes him by the arm: "Remember what I've told you," he says. And then he threatens: "It's either Saladin's life—or yours."

Maimonides returns to the sultan's tent. The ministers and the generals are gone; only Saladin's old nursemaid is there, pressing compresses on the sick man's forehead. Dismissing her with a gesture, he sits down by the couch, and there he remains, immersed in deep, sorrowful contemplation.

Suddenly he is aware of Saladin's wide-open eyes fixed on him. There's mockery in the dying man's eyes; the physician is transfixed by this look. "You don't know what's wrong with me," he murmurs. "Of course I do," says Maimonides in a trembling voice. "It's a pretty common illness—congestion, biliousness." "It's none of it," says Saladin, "you're lying." His voice shows no rancor; on the contrary, there is even a certain tenderness in it. "You don't know what's wrong with me," he repeats, "and I'm going to die. Today." "Shut up," says Maimonides, anguished, "I haven't even started . . ." "There's nothing that can be done," Saladin cuts him short, his voice now weak and sorrowful. "And even if you could cure me, they would kill me. My ministers, my generals. I know all about the conspiracy, Musa Ibn Maimun. I know everything."

Exhausted, he stops talking. They remain silent for a few moments. Then reaching out his hand, Saladin lays it on Maimonides's arm. "But you, physician," he says with a smile, "you can benefit from my death. All you have to do is to convince them that you caused it."

"Never!" Maimonides rises to his feet, upset. "I would never do such a thing!"

He bursts into tears. He cries helplessly for a long time. Saladin looks on in silence. Finally, Maimonides wipes his eyes, and sighs. Then something crosses his mind, and he bursts into laughter: "Remember that epidemic, Saladin? That mysterious disease? Well, I traced its cause to the water from the well. The water, imagine!"

"Who would have guessed," murmurs Saladin, sighing. He looks at the physician with entreating eyes: "Could it be cholera that I have, Musa Ibn Maimun? There's a well here too. Could it be cholera?"

"Who knows," replies Maimonides.

They fall silent again. They hear the distant barking of dogs, the mournful singing of a soldier.

"The water," says Saladin, "who would have guessed."

He bursts into laughter. Into uncontrollable laughter, which shakes his body. Astonished, Maimonides stares at him. Then he, too, begins to laugh. The two of them laugh and laugh, delightedly, unrestrainedly; Maimonides laughs so hard that he rolls about on the couch; and there he remains, panting, lying alongside Saladin; finally, tired out, he falls asleep.

When Maimonides wakes up, Saladin is dead. He then flings the doors wide open, and asks Saladin's aides to come in and take the body away. And he leaves, walking past noblemen and soldiers, slaves and professional mourners.

Y EARS LATER, MOSES BEN MAIMON—MAIMONIDES—DIED; his descendants returned to Cordoba; they lived in peace, begetting children, rocking them to sleep with lullabies sung in Ladino, the Judeo-Spanish dialect:

> Duerme, duerme, mi angelico
> Hijico chico de tu nación . . .
> Creatura de Sión,
> No conoces la dolor.

Later they went to Portugal. The name of the family kept changing: Maimonides, Maimendes, Memendes, Mendes.

The Mendeses settled in the mountainous region of Trancoso, in northern Portugal. A wealthy, God-fearing family, they hadn't forgotten Sion, where they hoped to return one day.

At one time they had in their employ a poet-shoemaker called Bandarra, whose visions were expressed in lyric verses that moved and impressed everybody. But it was of his shoemaking skills that Bandarra was particularly proud. An exacting craftsman, he insisted on personally selecting the leather for the sandals and boots that he made; as time went by, however, he was no longer satisfied with this—he had to inspect the cows from which the leather would come while they were still alive. He would carefully palpate them and listen to their mooing. To the chosen ones, he would then deliver a brief panegyric: Your leather will protect the feet of men of goodwill from the asperity of the paths of life; distinguished toes will be grateful to you for having spared them calluses. You will be evoked with tenderness: A good animal, people will say of you, a creature of God that gave us its own skin. After his speech, Bandarra would then kill the animal with blows delivered by a maul made from the solid wood of trees that grew in the Holy Land.

At the age of fifty, suspecting that death would not be long in arriving, Bandarra decided he would produce the masterpiece of his life—the best pair of boots in the world. For a long time he had been getting ready for it: He had raised a calf of excellent pedigree, had grazed it on the best available grassland, had massaged it daily with premium beer. The animal was now at the right stage; a little while longer, and age would affect the pliability of the leather. Therefore, Bandarra couldn't—shouldn't—wait any longer. Before killing the calf, however, he retreated to the mountains, where he spent three days praying and feeding on nothing but milk and herbs. Weakened in body but strengthened in faith, he returned to the village. He took the calf to the main square and, in front of the assembled villagers, delivered his usual panegyric. Then he spat into his hands, grabbed the maul and delivered a powerful blow. He missed; perhaps it was the fasting that made him miss. Instead of killing the calf, he broke the stake to which it was tied. The animal ran away.

Bandarra chased after it, cursing. The calf climbed up mountain trails—with Bandarra, huffing and puffing, in pursuit. Finally the calf came to the edge of a cliff; it was cornered.

Slowly, Bandarra advanced. As he raised the maul, the calf gazed at him in such a way that he shuddered: it was the look of a human being, the look of someone sentenced to death. Bandarra wavered, but only for a second; then he struck a blow, a terrible blow. The animal staggered, but was still on its feet; it kept stepping farther back until it tumbled down the abyss. Bandarra couldn't help uttering an imprecation. What would remain of the animal after a drop from this height? Nothing, certainly. With great difficulty he clambered down to the bottom of the precipice, clinging precariously to rocks and bushes. As he had feared, the animal was all mangled, the skin bloodied and torn by the rocks and the sharp pointed ends of broken bones; he wouldn't even get a pair of slippers out of it. One of its eyes, however, was still intact, and was gazing at him ironically, with the same expression that had disturbed him earlier. Pulling out his knife, Bandarra cut that eye out of its socket. He examined it intently; there was something strange there . . . Impelled by an unconquerable urge, he peered into the dilated pupil. He then had visions that deeply affected him. Unknown lands; a beautiful landscape. A bay, a blue sea, waves breaking upon the white, very white sand of a beach. Coconut trees. Exotic, brightly colored birds in wheeling flight against the magnificent blue of an uncharted sky. On this beach strange creatures suddenly appear—men, women, and children with bronze-colored skin, their faces painted in gaudy colors, their long hair ornamented with feathers; they kneel down—before whom? The Messiah? A king yet to be born? One of the Mendeses? Bandarra couldn't tell. Slowly the vision faded, and the eye became again what it had been before, the eyeball of a dead calf.

Disturbed, Bandarra went back to the village. He didn't know what to tell his masters, the Mendeses. How to explain what had happened to the calf? And the visions he'd had? Strictly speaking, the visions belonged to the Mendeses, for the animal was theirs, and consequently, the magic eye into which he had peered was theirs, too; but would they believe his story? Probably not. However, there was something he knew: he knew there were distant lands, seemingly fertile, bountiful lands—the place, if not of the Gold Tree, at least of a future kingdom. And it wouldn't be fair to keep this secret to himself. So he began to exhort the young Mendeses to become navigators. "Study the art of sailing," he would advise them. "Learn how to read nautical charts; one day these skills will come in handy."

Whether as a result of this advice or not—it's hard to tell—the fact is that the Mendes family produced a cartographer.

His name was Rafael. He had been given this name (from the Hebrew *rapha,* physician, and *el,* God; physician of God) as a tribute to his illustrious ancestor, the great Moses ben Maimon, who could well have been the physician of God. As a matter of fact, this name would be transmitted from generation to generation. Why, when Jews do not name their sons after their fathers? Quite simple: As a shrewd disguise, as a way of deceiving the Inquisition.

At that point in time the stage for the performance of the Iberian Holy Office had been set. In Spain, Torquemada kept demanding from Ferdinand and Isabella the expulsion of the Jews; in Portugal, where one fifth of the population was of Jewish origin, there were similar and no less insistent demands. The Jews aroused jealousy and fear, for they were the physicians and the poets, the astronomers and the philosophers; but above all, they were the merchants and the financiers.

Throughout the Middle Ages, the Jews were the only commercial link between the West and the East. They spoke all the important languages: Persian, Latin, Arabic, French, Spanish, the Slavic languages. From Spain and France they would take furs, swords, and eunuchs to India and China; they would return with musk, aloes, camphor; clove and cinnamon; Oriental fabrics. In order to buy such valuable goods, however—as well as mount their frequent military expeditions—the feudal lords needed money. Since the lending of money at interest was forbidden to Christians, such activity was reserved to Jews—a situation that suited the feudal lords wonderfully well: If unable to pay back their loans, all they had to do was to trigger a massacre.

In England this process was simplified by the existence of the *saccarium judaeorum,* a place for the registration of Jewish vouchers, on which a ten-percent tax, collected for the royal treasury, was levied. In case of breach of contract, all the aristocracy had to do was to solemnly burn the vouchers deposited therein.

At the time of the voyages of discovery, money became necessary to finance the oceanic expeditions. This situation placed the Jewish financiers in a dilemma: On the one hand, the rise of the bourgeoisie heralded freedom of speech and of religion, as well as the destruction of the barriers that separated peoples and regions; on the other hand, this greater freedom also permitted new bankers, such as the Fuggers and the Medicis, to enter the money business. Money lending at interest was no longer a sin; on the contrary, accumulation of capital was soon to become a Christian virtue. A critical time: The old era was dying, the new one not yet born; and standing at this historical crossroads were the Jews. Standing there too were their enemies, determined to seize the Jews' wealth or to prevent them from using it to destroy the feudal world. Heresy must be checked, Torquemada maintained. The world is not round, there are no new sea routes, maps are messages from the devil.

RAFAEL MENDES, CARTOGRAPHER, HAD FREQUENT ARGUMENTS with his father, a calligrapher by profession. The old man wanted to persuade his son to take up calligraphy, an art highly valued in the fifteenth century. "Letters," the old man would say, "are well-defined, codified symbols, they have the exactness of logic. Moreover, they allow for flights of the imagination: In a curlicue, for instance, you can see everything, from the dance of the flames to the image of a serpent; or, if you prefer, the sinuous roads of fate. Fate is often contained in one single letter. When drawing an A, for example, you go up, then you go down; with one single stroke, you cut across it; and there you have, in three movements, a summary account of life. How could we ever appreciate the written word if it weren't for calligraphy? Calligraphy makes the writer responsible for every single letter he traces; the effort, the concentration, the dedication necessary to accomplish this task compel him to be wise, prudent, and restrained in his writing. Calligraphy effectively holds whatever is vulgar in check; it reserves books and their beautiful illuminations for the few who are able to appreciate them. As for maps," he would go on, "what are maps? Nothing but winding lines traced at random; even when accurately traced, these lines merely reproduce geographical accidents, which don't follow any human design. But I," he would say, irritated, "I don't put my trust in maps at all. When someone

shows me an irregular figure, telling me it's Terceira Island—
I don't believe him. Who can assure me that it is indeed
Terceira Island? Now, a *B* is a *B*, an *R* is an *R*.''

Rafael Mendes, cartographer, would not argue with his
father. Out of respect? No. It was because he wasn't even
listening. He was floating in space, so to speak; and what he
saw from those heights were far-off landscapes, mysterious
and fascinating. It was the vision of a bay; waves breaking
upon the white, very white sands of a beach. Coconut trees.
Exotic, brightly colored birds. The magnificent blue of an
uncharted sky.

How to reach such places without maps? It wasn't that the
young cartographer undervalued calligraphy; he, too, would
draw letters fancifully—but he would draw them on maps, or
on the globes which his client, Christopher Columbus, imagined the world to resemble.

A strange man, this Columbus. Little was known about
him; it was said that he was a Jew, but he didn't identify
himself as one. Anyhow, he had a reputation as a skillful
navigator. Rafael had met him through the master cartographer Abraão Zacuto, whom the Genovese had commissioned
to chart an expedition that he was preparing; unable to do the
job on his own, Zacuto had asked the young Mendes to help
him out. Officially, Columbus would be searching for a new
sea route to India; however, it was rumored that the voyage
had some other purpose. Perhaps the discovery of new lands
. . . Anyway, there was an aura of mystery in the whole
story. Despite the high price charged, Columbus always paid
promptly, in cold cash, for cartographic work. Where did he
get the money? Who was financing his expensive and hazard-
ous expedition?

"The people from the nation," the elder Rafael would say,
gloomily. "The people from our own Hebrew nation." He
disliked this Columbus, but recognized that he was an insinu-
ating person, capable of fascinating the rich Jewish financiers
with his schemes of finding territories inhabited by the descendants of Israel's lost tribes: Jews of a strange physical
appearance, tall and strong, with copper-colored skin, who
lived—and this would fire the imagination and arouse the
cupidity of his listeners—in cities paved with precious stones:
Eldorado! The country of the Gold Tree!

With this fantastic country could be established a profitable
commercial intercourse: manufactures from the mother coun-

try would be exchanged for precious metals and spices. In addition, this country would be a safe haven for Jews in case of persecutions. The elder Mendes didn't want to hear about such folly. "A haven? What for? If all Jews minded their own business, the way I mind my art," he would say, "nobody would bother us." His son would then remind him of the massacres at the time of the Crusades led by Richard the Lion-Hearted, among others. "Crusades, my foot!" the old man would shout. "That's all in the past. And don't you talk to me about Columbus. Columbus, Columbus! It's all I hear, Columbus. I'm sick and tired of this Columbus! Who asked him to come to Portugal to upset us? Why didn't he stay in his own country? Damn Columbus! I hope he dies in a shipwreck! Yes, I hope he does. And that the fish will devour his eyes, and that the crustaceans will crawl in through his nostrils. I hope a sea serpent will devour him! And that Neptune will tear him to shreds with his trident! And that he'll go to hell! I hope he'll suffer throughout eternity, this man who has turned my son's head."

Dona Ana would calm her husband and ask him not to hurt the feelings of Rafael, who was a sensible young man of good character—his only flaw being this passion of his for cartography. At the word cartography, not wanting to miss the opportunity, the old man would lash out at maps:

"Maps will destroy your youth, my son. Consider for a moment: Peninsulas keep you awake, archipelagos disturb your good sense, bays turn your head. As for this unknown land . . . It's like a beautiful woman, my son, who lures you by flinging away her transparent tunic. As soon as you get closer, however, like a siren, she'll vanish into the sea. Give it all up, take up calligraphy, which won't bring you any sorrows and will last for centuries. Nothwithstanding," he said with almost imperceptible disquiet, "these experiments now being undertaken in Mainz, where people are printing texts with movable types made from wood. Something only visionaries would dream up; friends of this Columbus, no doubt. Like those other people who want to measure time with mechanical gadgets—what do they have against the sandglass, the clepsydra? Can't they see that the passing of the hours can only be estimated by the slow trickling of sand or water, by a candle that the flames consume, by the shadow that the sun casts? No, they must resort to weights that fall down, or to coiled metal springs, which, forcibly restrained, angrily unwind; and if they could, they would make crystal vibrate in order to measure minute fractions of time in its nervous, tortured quivering. But they won't succeed, my son, I assure you. No machine will ever replace a man's hand—least of all a calligrapher's hand. Try to find peace within yourself, not on maps or in exotic countries."

All this haranguing ended up undermining the young man's convictions. "Why don't you travel across the Mediterranean like all the prudent navigators?" he once asked Columbus, who had come to pick up his maps. The Genovese didn't reply; he smiled and paid cold cash as usual. He was about to leave when an idea occurred to him. He took from his pouch an ivory box. "This is a game I've invented," he said. "I propose that we play a game. If I win, you give me back the money I've just given you; if you win, I'll pay you three times as much; is it a deal?"

"I don't know," replied Rafael, timidly. "I'm not in the habit of betting."

"Well, then you're not in the habit of living," said Columbus; "in life, dear Rafael, as in business and in navigation, we have to take risks."

"Well, then, I'll give it a try," said Rafael.

It was some kind of a chess game; instead of rooks, however, there were miniature caravels, which, after the king and the queen, were the most important pieces. Rafael was quick to learn the rules. They played, he lost. Columbus pocketed the money and predicting better luck for the cartographer, he took his leave.

That very night Columbus left the city of Oporto to see their majesties Ferdinand and Isabella. Some weeks later, an emissary brought a letter to Rafael Mendes: Columbus's expedition had the approval of the sovereigns. He invited Rafael Mendes to accompany him as the official cartographer.

"Madness," said the calligrapher Mendes when his son talked about going. "You're crazy, young man, completely crazy. But I'll take care of you."

The old man didn't take him to a physician because he had no confidence in them. "After our ancestor Maimonides there hasn't been a decent physician in our nation." He took Rafael to a rabbi. "My son is possessed," he declared. "A wandering soul has entered his body and won't leave him alone. He wants to roam the world. Is it a curse, rabbi? If it is a curse, I ask you to free him from it."

The rabbi asked to be left alone with the young man. And to this quiet man, with gentle eyes and a long white beard, Rafael poured out his soul. He talked of his love for maps; and he talked of journeys, venturesome journeys. He mentioned Eldad Ha-Dani, the mysterious Jew who appeared in Spain in the ninth century, saying that he was a surviving member of the Dan tribe, one of Israel's lost tribes. And he related the travels of Rabbi Benjamin de Tudela, who, having left Navarra in 1159, went to Babylon, to the cities of Tema and Teumira, inhabited by Rehavita Jews; to Basra and to Shushan; to Shiraz and to Samarkand. Like these dauntless people, Rafael Mendes wanted to discover new places; but mostly, he wanted to reproduce on maps the contours of unknown continents—Atlantida, among others. In short, he wanted to accompany Christopher Columbus.

T HE RABBI HAS HEARD ABOUT THE GENOVESE. HE KNOWS that funds are being secretly raised to finance his expedition; that a company is even being established in order to explore the riches to be found. And as in Isaiah's prophecy: "The islands will be waiting for me; and the ships of Tarshish will transport your children; and also gold and silver to honor the Everlasting." (Tarshish, the rabbi knows, is Tartessus, in Spain.)

It is undoubtedly a new era that is being heralded. What can one say of the alchemists' amazing discoveries? And of the new mechanisms, such as the clock, so much abhorred by the calligrapher Mendes? To the rabbi, it seems at once marvellous and terrible that a mechanical device can register the inexorable flow of time. It won't be long before the small, closed guilds and associations are replaced by establishments with hundreds or thousands of workers. This will require substantial funds, so the financiers are counting on the gold and silver from the unknown lands. The rabbi also knows that the feudal lords watch such movements with mistrust; the

Inquisition is well-informed, and the Jews live in fear of mass arrests, of executions.

Such are the thoughts that go through his mind as he observes the young man's lit up face and wild eyes. Yes, the calligrapher is right: He is possessed.

Rafael stops talking, the two men remain silent. Finally, the rabbi begins to speak. Cautiously choosing his words, he offers his advice to Rafael Mendes: No, he should not accompany Christopher Columbus. It would be better for him to stay with his family in Oporto. He can draw as many maps as he wants, the rabbi will have a word with his father concerning this matter, and ask him to be more tolerant; but as for this voyage, no. It's fraught with dangers. The storms, the sea serpents, the savages in the unknown countries . . . It would be better for Rafael to stay home.

The young man says nothing. He remains silent, his head lowered, as the rabbi invites the elder Mendes, the calligrapher, to come in, saying that everything is all right.

"He's not possessed. A bit restive, that's all. But it will pass, it's a phase that youth goes through. I've given him some advice."

He's Gog, the young man says to himself as he stares at his father with hatred. He's Gog, the tyrant, wanting to oppress him. Only Columbus can free him. Columbus is his Messiah.

IN JANUARY 1492, THE YOUNG RAFAEL MENDES RUNS AWAY from home. Traveling during the night, hiding by day, he finally arrives in Castela and goes straight to the La Rábida monastery to see Columbus. An emotional moment: Rafael, in tears, pleads with the Genóvese to let him join the expedition. Columbus hesitates. He has already hired all the men he needs, including a cartographer, whom he engaged when he didn't hear from Rafael Mendes again. Besides, he knows how the young man's father feels about this voyage, and he doesn't want any complicatons. Finally, he proposes that Rafael and he decide the issue on the chessboard.

After a few moves, the young man is trapped. Enraged, he flings the miniature caravels away. Soon afterward, however, he smiles: He took a risk, he lost, now he must willingly accept the designs of fate. So, saying goodbye to Christopher Columbus, he returns home.

On August 2, 1492, Ferdinand and Isabella issue a decree: Becoming effective at midnight that day, no Jew is allowed to remain on Spanish soil. At eleven o'clock that night, the last of the crewmen went on board Christopher Columbus's three caravels, at anchor in the Port of Palos. Among them were Jews who hoped to find freedom and wealth in a New World. . . .

In 1497, King Manuel of Portugal issues a decree: All Jews must convert to Christianity.

In 1536, the Tribunal of the Holy Office of the Inquisition is established, with the purpose of spying on the New Christians so as to ensure that they are practicing the Christian faith. People are carefully investigated in order to weed out those of Jewish ancestry; only "noblemen of pure blood" can hold positions in the civil service. The denunciation of Judaistic practices, which can be made anonymously, is encouraged. Confession is obtained by torturing the accused. For this purpose the rack is used—it resembles a bed, to which the prisoner is tied with ropes, which are then gradually tightened until they cut into the flesh—and other such instruments of torture. The trial is conducted according to the precepts of secret rules known only to the Grand Inquisitor and a few functionaries of the Holy Office; the solemn pronouncement of judgment takes place in a public square—this ceremony is the auto-da-fé, the first of which was held in Lisbon in 1540.

Sometimes the defendants are acquitted; sometimes they are sentenced to wearing the sanbenito, a sackcloth garment to be worn by the penitents; as for the impenitents, the flames see to their purification.

TWO NEW CHRISTIANS, RAFAEL MENDES, THE SON OF THE cartographer of the same name, and his friend Afonso Sanches, are arrested by the Inquisition, and accused of Judaistic practices. Due to lack of space in the dungeon, they are thrown into the same cell. Daily, they are submitted to interrogations: Rafael first and then Afonso; or Afonso first and then Rafael; the order in which they are called is unpredictable, as unpredictable as the designs of the Holy Office.

Through dismal corridors, Rafael is taken to a hall with a domed ceiling, where the interrogations take place. Seated behind a huge table, under a colossal crucifix, three inquisitors wait for his arrival. He must stand in the center of a red circle ("the mouth of hell") painted on the floor. His eyes move apprehensively from the faces of the inquisitors to a side door, and from there to the crucifix.

This heavy side door of solid wood has a peephole through which his denouncers can peer. They don't have to say anything. When they want to confirm an accusation, they manipulate a pulley so that the head of the crucified Christ nods. At the sight of the head with a crown of thorns nodding with a rigid, mechanical movement, Rafael's terror is doubled. It's as if Christ himself were accusing him. But even so he refuses to answer their questions. Afonso and he have sworn that they won't reveal anything. And they won't. At least not while their strength holds out.

They do their utmost to keep up their morale. They have devised an intensive program of activities. After waking up early in the morning, they pray fervently. Then they hold a debate on such topics as: Did Jonah commit a sin by refusing to fulfill the mission the Lord had entrusted to him? Was Maimonides really a perplexed man? The discussion, although heated, is always marked by courtesy and held in a low voice to prevent the guards from overhearing them. As for the verdict, it is reached by mutual agreement: The loser should frankly acknowledge defeat.

After the debate, another praying session; as they stand on their feet, facing east, the direction of the distant and beloved Jerusalem, they sway their bodies imperceptibly as they murmur the holy words: *Baruch ata Adonai . . .* Blessed art thou, oh Lord. . . .

This is followed by other, more joyful activities—games. They play chess, a game they both enjoy very much. There isn't, of course, a chessboard, nor chess pieces, which, however, doesn't prevent them from having chess tournaments: They use their imagination. "Queen on the bishop's fifth square," says Afonso, grimacing with displeasure at the word *bishop;* Rafael, engrossed in the game looks at him carefully: What is his opponent plotting? "Castle on the king's fourth square," he announces. "But did you still have a castle?" asks Afonso, suspicious. "And would I lie to you if I didn't?" retorts Rafael. "Remember, my friend: between us, nothing but the truth." Accepting Rafael's well-reasoned argument, Afonso admits defeat.

On the other hand, aware that muscle atrophy precedes moral decay, they are careful not to neglect the physical activities. With rags, they have improvised a ball; in the confinement of their dungeon cell—two meters by two meters— they compete against each other in a game: One of them is supposed to kick the ball against the wall, while the other is supposed to prevent him from doing so. Rafael has named this game *ludopédio,* meaning foot game. For thirty to sixty minutes they kick the ball furiously while the guards, amused, look on: "Strange creatures, these Jews," they say. When the game is over, they sit down, exhausted.

Then it's time for some melancholy moments: They reminisce about their families, their friends; they weep together; and then, the interrogation starts again.

The inquisitors are particularly interested in Rafael. They know about his father's connection with Columbus; they want to get to the bottom of this matter. They want the names of the Jews who financed the Genovese's expedition. They want to know about the gold and the jewels. And they also want the names of the alchemists, of the cabalists, of the inventors who have designed diabolical mechanical contraptions that can spin and weave thread, print books. They want to know about those vehicles that can move under the sea like fish of steel. The crafty Grand Inquisitor, trying to persuade Rafael

to disclose willingly everything he knows, promises him full
acquittal and even a commission on the holdings and proper-
ties that are confiscated. Since Rafael persists in his stubborn
silence, the interrogation session ends, logically, in torture.

F OR THIS, THERE IS A SPECIAL ROOM EQUIPPED WITH CONTRI-
vances designed by one of the inquisitors, a very inventive
man (he looks Jewish, remark the others, full of suspicion).
The prisoner is made to lie naked on the rack. The torturer
then begins to tighten the ropes. The poor devil screams out
with pain. The screams startle a canary kept in a cage (A),
making it flutter about wildly. A cat placed on a point (B)
below the cage, leaps up, trying to catch the canary. Then a
dog tries to chase the cat, but it can't because it is held on a
leash; the action of its paws make a conveyor belt (C) move,
and this motion is transmitted by a system of pulleys to a small
wooden mallet (D), which then begins to hit the prisoner on the
head. In fact, as the Grand Inquisitor remarks to visitors, it
is the prisoner himself who inflicts punishment on himself:
the guiltier he is, the more he screams, the more the canary
flutters about, the more the cat jumps, the more the dog runs,
the more the conveyor belt moves, the more the small mallet
delivers blows. Were the accused man fortified by his alleged
innocence, the punishment inflicted would be less severe.

The inquisitor makes an analogy between this instrument of
torture and the Jewish conspiracy. In both instances, he explains, we have a system that operates by chain reaction, their
goals being Goodness in the first instance, Evil in the second.
By setting off one system against the other, we can turn the
sorcery against the sorcerer; the cabala against the cabalist;
the philosopher's stone against the alchemist. It's the victory,
magnificent albeit sanguinary, of Goodness over Evil, of
Godliness over diabolism.

R AFAEL MENDES AND AFONSO SANCHES COME OUT OF THE
torture room in a wretched condition. They cannot even stand
on their feet; the guards have to carry them to their cell,
where they spend the night moaning. Only at daybreak do
they sometimes get some sleep.

One day Rafael Mendes is brutally awakened from one of
those meager scraps of sleep he manages to get. It's Afonso
shaking him awake. Rafael sits up: His friend is staring at
him in a stange way. "What is it?" he asks, startled.

"You were laughing," says Afonso, gloomily.

"Laughing?" asks Rafael, surprised. "Me, laughing,
Afonso?"

"Yes. You."

"But I can't even laugh, Afonso, not with my face hurting
so badly, you know. Not with my lips split open like this."

"But you were laughing," Afonso persists. "You were
roaring with laughter. You were laughing your head off.
You were splitting your sides with laughter. You even woke
me up with your laughter."

"Strange," murmurs Rafael. "What could I be laughing
at? Is there anything to laugh at? Not under these circumstances. Laugh at what?"

"That's what I'd like to know," says Afonso, and his tone
of voice is now openly suspicious. "What were you laughing
at? Because I can see no reason to laugh."

Rafael puts forth a conjecture: Maybe it was a dream that
made him laugh. Upon hearing this, Afonso rises to his feet,
incensed.

"A dream? I've never heard of anyone laughing in their
sleep, Rafael Mendes. I know there are people who talk, even
walk, in their sleep—but laugh? No. And what kind of mirth-
ful dreams can you possibly have in this place? Do tell me.
Because I, Rafael, have nothing but nightmares: Even in my
dreams the inquisitors keep torturing me. But even so I value
this sleep, it restores my energies, so that I can resist my

121

torturers. Whereas you, you waste in laughter precious moments of rest. And what's worse, you prevent me from getting any."

"I'm awfully sorry," says Rafael with contrition. And he promises: "It won't happen again, Afonso, I assure you."

The other man, however, continues to glare at him, full of mistrust:

"You still haven't told me what made you laugh."

"I don't remember," says Rafael. "Honestly, Afonso, I don't."

The arrival of the guards interrupts this conversation. And for the rest of the day neither of them brings up this subject again.

That night Afonso once more rouses Rafael from his sleep.

"You were laughing again, Rafael!" he shouts. "You did it again! You were laughing happily, like a pleased child."

Rafael sits up. And now he's the one who is angry:

"Stop it, Afonso, stop it! You've gone too far, do you hear?"

"Me, gone too far?" says Afonso, upset. "You're the one who has gone too far. Who do you think you are, anyway?"

Puzzled, Rafael stares at him. An idea crosses his mind: He must be insane, poor Afonso. All this suffering, and the blows from the mallet, no wonder he has a screw loose. Rafael is overcome by a great feeling of compassion. Drawing closer to Afonso, he puts a hand on his shoulder: "All right, I did laugh, but it won't happen again, I promise."

Afonso rebuffs him:

"Take your filthy hand off me, you traitor! Go away, you Christian asslicker, you pig!"

He's crazy all right, concludes Rafael, horrified. It's not the first case: Many have lost their minds in the dungeons of the Inquisition. That was what happened to the prisoner who previously occupied their cell. Sentenced to death, he was taken to the stake to burn. It was a cold day, and upon seeing the flames crackling, he turned to the judges:

"Kindly Christians, I thank you for having lit this fire to warm me up. That's what I really needed. I have arthritis, the cold is bad for me. . . ."

He drew closer to the fire and whistling softly, he warmed his hands. Then, pleased, he greeted the judges and walked toward the exit. He was seized and thrown into the flames.

Crouched down in a corner of the fetid cell, Rafael watches Afonso, who paces back and forth, muttering:

"He has joined the enemy, this dog. They are in cahoots to break my spirit, to make me kneel down before their deity. But if they think that I'll surrender, they are wrong. I'll fight to the very end. They don't know who they're dealing with."

"Enough of that!" Rafael leaps to his feet. "That's enough, Afonso!" He's distraught over the seriousness of the situation: They mustn't fight against each other, not now, not when the inquisitors are watching out for the slightest signs of weakness in them. It's important to bring Afonso to his senses: "You're crazy, my friend. Raving mad! What you're saying is insane. I'm Rafael Mendes, I'm from your nation, too, we're brothers!"

On an impulse he produces his penis, shows him that it's circumcised.

"See? I, too, bear on my flesh the sign of the Divine Covenant, Afonso. Like you."

Impassive, Afonso looks at him steadily.

"Please," Rafael pleads, "believe me, Afonso! I admit I laughed but I have no idea why. Perhaps it's weakness or . . . madness."

He moves a step forward:

"That's it, Afonso. I must be losing my mind. And if I am, I need your help. We can't afford to antagonize each other, Afonso. More than ever we must join forces. We owe it to our elders, Afonso. To our nation, to our God, the God of Abraham, of Isaac, of Jacob."

In silence, Afonso turns this matter over in his mind. The words in the Book of Daniel occur to Rafael: You've been weighed in the balances. . . . Afonso is weighing him, for sure. And what will he find in his deranged gauge?

"All right," Afonso finally says. "Here's what I'll do: If you laugh again, I'll call the guards. I'll tell them that you've been laughing at the Inquisition, that you've been jeering at the wounds of Christ, that you have secrets you haven't told them. And then we'll see: If you are in cahoots with them, they won't harm you, but then I'll kill you. And if you are not on their side, they'll burn you at the stake. So, you'd better control yourself and not laugh."

The day is breaking. And throughout that day Rafael is tortured by anxiety: He fears that Afonso might suddenly do something crazy, that he might call the guards. At nightfall, he makes a decision: He won't sleep. He will resist sleep as much as he resists his interrogators. After dinner—watery soup, a few rotten potatoes—Afonso lies down on his pallet, and is soon snoring, but Rafael knows that he is not asleep: He pretends he is. Although knowing he is being watched by the other man, Rafael finds sleep invincible, and has to fight hard to keep it at bay. He resorts to tricks: He opens his eyes wide, pinches himself, thinks up problems such as, three shepherds are tending one thousand and three hundred sheep. The oldest shepherd is tending twice as many sheep as the second shepherd—in vain, for he drifts off into sleep.

From which he is abruptly aroused: Somebody is shaking him. He rubs his eyes: He is surrounded by guards. Terror-stricken, he scrambles to his feet. Afonso looks at him with a sinister expression on his face.

"Afonso!" he shouts, desperate. "Afonso, my friend, my brother—what have you done? You've called the guards, Afonso!"

"I warned you," says Afonso.

B Y ORDER OF THE GRAND INQUISITOR, RAFAEL IS TAKEN TO the torture room. He won't leave it for two weeks: he's tortured night and day: The canary is tired of fluttering wildly about, the cat can barely leap up, the dog, exhausted, lies collapsed on the conveyor belt. The Grand Inquisitor himself undertakes the task of hitting the prisoner on the head with the small mallet, which now displays a cleft.

"What were you laughing at? Answer me!"

But Rafael says nothing. The Grand Inquisitor is finally convinced: It's a hopeless case. This Jew is posessed by Satan, he'll resist to the very end. He sentences him to burn at the stake, as a warning to others.

T HAT SAME NIGHT, HOWEVER, SOMEBODY OPENS THE CELL door. It's one of the guards. He signals to Afonso to keep quiet: "The people of the nation have sent me," he whispers. And he opens his hand to reveal a Star of David, in gold, which Afonso immediately recognizes as his brother's amulet.

Picking up the unconscious Rafael, they carry him down the corridors to a secret passage that opens onto the river, where a boat is waiting. On board, Rafael regains consciousness; Afonso then explains to him what is happening. Rafael opens his burst lips into a painful smile. Afonso smiles back, then Rafael begins to laugh, Afonso laughs too, and the two of them laugh and laugh; every once in a while Rafael stops laughing and moans with pain; but soon they are taken with another fit of laughing, and the boatman begs them to be quiet, for God's sake. Finally, Afonso manages to control himself; wiping his eyes, he says, still gasping for breath, that there is something he must tell Rafael:

"During the days I was alone in the cell, I made a very important discovery, Rafael: You had told me the truth. You weren't laughing."

He hesitates, then goes on:

"It was me, dreaming that you were laughing. This happened several times: I would fall asleep and then wake up with your laughter. But it was a dream, Rafael. A dream."

"Everything is a dream, brother," murmurs Rafael. "Everything is a dream. Possibly this place we're heading for, this distant country, is nothing but a dream."

Of the caravel that carried him to Brazil, Rafael Mendes was to remember the creaking of its timbers, the wind whining in the ship's rigging, the shouts of the sailors, the darkness and the stench in the hold of the ship, where, as fugitives, they were confined. And the rats. Huge rats that kept attacking them and that they kept driving back with kicks. This ordeal lasted for weeks. It was not until they were near the coast of Brazil that the captain allowed them to go up on deck. Gaunt, bearded, in tatters, their pathetic grins exposing gums swollen by scurvy, the two men emerged into the light.

The sailors were suspicious of the two strangers, the officers sneered at them. *Sta fermo, Moise!* shouted the first mate, a Genovese who claimed to be related to Christopher Columbus; he was alluding perhaps to the biblical Moses, or perhaps to that other Moses, Ben Mainon. Neither Afonso nor Rafael would say anything in reply; leaning on the gunwale, they would stare out at the greenish sea. Thus they spent their days.

All of a sudden, the weather changed. The wind, until then favorable, died away, and an eerie wind-lull immobilized the vessel. Black birds kept fluttering over the caravel and a huge fish swam around it, at times revealing its dark back, which resembled a rock. "Divine punishment has befallen us," muttered the sailors, "for we are harboring two heretics, two descendants of Christ's killers." Tension kept mounting, and one night Rafael and Afonso woke up with shouts and the clangor of swords. It was a mutiny! Officers and sailors were fighting like demons against one another; an officer lay on deck, with blood spouting out of his slit throat. "Save yourselves," the captain shouted at them, "jump into the sea." Without hesitation, Rafael and Afonso jumped over the gunwale and plunged into the ocean. They swam all night, occasionally letting themselves float in order to rest. "Hanging on, are you?" Rafael would shout in the darkness. "Yes," Afonso would reply, "and what about you?" "Me too," Rafael would say. "Then, keep swimming," Afonso would encourage him, "don't give up." Afraid of drowning, afraid of dying, afraid of having his eyes devoured by fish and his nostrils invaded by crustaceans, Rafael kept swimming. He swam and swam.

The day was dawning, a beautiful day it was; they sighted birds—which lifted their spirits: Land must be near. And indeed, soon afterwad, with the help of the current, they came ashore to a white, sandy beach dotted with coconut trees. They stretched out on the sand and fell asleep. Theirs was a sound, dreamless sleep. Upon waking up, they found themselves surrounded by Indians.

ABOUT THIRTY OF THEM. NAKED, THEIR BODIES PAINTED with annato, they stood staring impassively at the two men. Frightened, Rafael and Afonso scrambled to their feet. Rafael was trembling so much that his teeth chattered; it was Afonso who showed presence of mind. He took out of his pocket a mirror which he, being rather vain, always carried on him. Their curiosity aroused, the Indians drew closer. Upon seeing their painted faces with wide-open eyes reflected on the polished surface, they began to laugh. They laughed delightedly, like children. Any murderous rage that they might have been harboring dissolved at that moment. "Friends!" Afonso kept saying and the Indians would repeat: "Friends, friends!"

Friends, and yet they couldn't make themselves understood. Not even through mime. The Indians eventually got bored and headed for their settlement. Rafael and Afonso followed them.

The tribespeople were eating. With gestures, Rafael and Afonso tried to tell them that they were hungry; but it wasn't until Afonso offered them his belt buckle that they were given food: fish, corn, manioc, fruit. A copious meal, hinting at the ease with which food could be obtained there. "I think that anything you plant in this land will bear fruit," said Afonso.

(Later Rafael was to recall the glitter in Afonso's eyes as he spoke those words. At that moment, however, he was more interested in the food itself.)

In the evening they were taken to the *oca*, the communal dwelling of the Indians. Men, women and children slept there in hammocks or on the dirt floor. Rafael and Afonso stretched themselves out on the floor and were soon fast asleep.

Soon afterward—but was this going to be the norm in Rafael's trouble-ridden life?—they were wakened. Four Indians were shaking them; they signaled to Rafael and Afonso to follow them.

They left the communal dwelling and got into the bushes. After walking for a long time along a rough-hewn trail cut through the jungle, they arrived at a clearing. At the door of a shack, they saw a very old Indian squatting before a fire. When the Portuguese drew closer, he got to his feet and inspected them with his small blinking eyes. Then, at a sign from him, the Indians who had escorted them withdrew. The old man opened his arms:

"*Bruchim habaim,*" he said, smiling.

"Did you hear that?" said Rafael, astonished. "He spoke in Hebrew!"

"In Hebrew?" asked Afonso, who was not well-versed in the language of the nation. "And what did he say?"

"That we're welcome. But how does he know our language?" Rafael couldn't get over his astonishment.

"Ask him," said Afonso.

Rafael addressed the old man in Hebrew. And he heard an interesting story.

"Many, many moons ago," the old man said, "one of King Solomon's sons had a misunderstanding with his father. He wanted to have access to the harem. The king didn't consent to his son's request, claiming that one of the women there, he didn't know which one, was the young man's mother; if he had sexual relations with her, he would be committing incest, a very serious sin. Feeling resentful, the young man then began to conspire against his father and he succeeded in stirring up revolt in some of the palace guards. Just as he was about to be killed, Solomon was changed into a multicolored bird, which flew away. Later on he came back in his human form, accompanied by many soldiers. The rebels were overcome and the king himself passed sentence on them. Solomon ordered that they be put, together with their wives and children, in a rudderless ship so that they would drift aimlessly: a befitting punishment for people who had gone astray.

"After a long time, their ship came to these shores. We are the descendants of those Hebrews. Because we gazed into the sun, our eyes narrowed like this, and our skin turned bronze-colored. Many of us no longer speak Hebrew; but in each generation, there is always one person in charge of taking care of the Torah, which our ancestors brought with them from Jerusalem."

He signaled to them to enter his shack. And there, by the weak light of an oil lamp, they saw the scrolls of the Law.

With devotion, Rafael stroked the parchment, which was

rather damaged by the effects of time, of humidity; the letters were almost completely faded, but even so he was able to read a few sentences of the holy text.

They talked for a long time because the old man was curious to know how the descendants of the Hebrews fared in Europe. At daybreak, he put out the light and said: "Let's go outside and take a leak."

As they urinated, Rafael watched the old man stealthily. He was indeed circumcised, but his member was deformed. "Here we have to use a conch to perform the *brit mila*," he explained self-consciously. "We lost the ritualistic blade. Besides, we lack the ancient skills. . . ."

Squatting by the almost-extinguished fire, he closed his eyes, and softly began to intone a tuneless chant, no longer in Hebrew but in the language of the Indians: He was again just an old aborigine, ugly and toothless. Rafael and Afonso returned to the Indian settlement.

AFONSO ENDED UP MARRYING THE CACIQUE'S DAUGHTER, A great beauty, whom he affectionately called Little Dove because, as he explained to Rafael, of her small breasts, which were round and firm. As for Rafael, he remained faithful to the wife he had left behind in Portugal. He cultivated the land and prayed together with the old Indian patriarch.

Afonso learned the language of the Indians. Although he liked them, their laziness irritated him: "We have to put these people to work," he would say to Rafael. He had a plan: to grow sugarcane. "In Europe sugar is worth its weight in gold." "Yes," Rafael would argue, "but who's going to buy the crops?" Afonso didn't have an answer to this question. He would fall silent, but it was obvious that he wasn't going to give up his plan.

As good luck would have it, a Portuguese ship sailed into the bay. Rafael, afraid of the Inquisition, wanted them to go into hiding; Afonso, however, went to the ship in a pirogue. He came back bursting with excitement: He had struck a

bargain with the captain. He and Rafael would plant sugarcane; in the next voyage, the ship would bring them a sugar
mill, dismantled; they would start producing sugar right there.
They would strike it rich!

It wasn't an unreasonable expectation.

As a matter of fact, according to historian Cá da Mosto,
ever since the fifteenth century, sugar had been "a luxury
item used in the kitchens of the wealthy." Pounding or
pressing the sugarcane released a dense, foamy juice, which
after going through a boiling process for three or four
times, turned into crystallized sugar. Such sweetness! And
what a pot of money it was! However, sugarmaking was an
industry that required substantial capital, an industry that
would be of interest to the Genovese and the Florentines,
people like Cesaro, Spinola, Lomeltini, and Paolo di Nigra, a
friend of Columbus's (the same Columbus who had taken
cuttings of sugarcane to Hispaniola, where it thrived, as he
informed the Castilian monarchs in a letter sent in 1494, its
quality leaving nothing to be desired when compared to the
sugarcane grown in the Old World); and of interest, too, to
the New Christians, who, through their connections, would
be able to raise the necessary capital. Through the captain,
Afonso sent a letter to Fernão de Noronha, the father-in-law
of Admiral Pedro Álvares Cabral, requesting that, "in the
interests of the nation," he arrange for the shipment of all
parts needed to assemble a sugar mill, and that he also
arrange for the financing of the project because "the sugar to
be produced here will soon become even more valuable than
the highly renowned brazilwood."

"Why go in search of the Gold Tree, which nobody knows
where it is?" he would cry out. "We'll make a fortune with
sugarcane!"

T HE INDIANS, HOWEVER, WERE LOATH TO DO ANY PLANTING— except for their own consumption. In vain Afonso tried to explain to them that their efforts would be rewarded with many mirrors, glass beads, and belt buckles. The Indians would laugh at him. Enraged, Afonso resorted to cruelty, becoming the scourge of the tribe. Armed with a whip, he would chase after the savages, trying to force them to work. Terror was rampant in the village, especially because Afonso had become—after the cacique died, of a broken heart, undoubtedly—the sovereign ruler. One day the old man of the Torah sent for him. Afonso went, hoping that the elder would support him in his endeavors to get the Indians to work. He came back foaming at the mouth with rage. Not only had the old man refused to back him but he had also warned him not to mistreat the Indians: "Mistreatment is not sanctioned by our faith," he had said. "Our faith!" vociferated Afonso. "As if I and this old savage belonged to the same faith!"

He took to beating his wife. One night, as Rafael lay asleep in his straw-thatched hut, he felt a warm body next to his. It was Little Dove; the poor thing, in tears, snuggled up against him. Rafael tried to persuade her to leave, but with no success. The young woman spent the whole night there, with Rafael fighting off desire—he didn't want to betray his friend.

At dawn, he woke up with the yells of Afonso:

"Come out here! Come out here, you cur!"

Rafael crawled out of the hut. Afonso stood naked in the yard, with a cudgel in his hand; like an Indian, he had painted himself with annato.

"Come here, I want to kill you, traitor!"

The Indians, motionless, looked on. A child was crying. "For God's sake," said Rafael, "don't do anything foolish, Afonso. I—"

"Come and fight, you bastard!"

A shudder passed over Rafael; Afonso's words made his blood boil. He went into the hut and came out with a cudgel.

"Are you ready?" bellowed Afonso.

Rafael was ready. The cudgels clashed in the air. The fight didn't last long: Livid with rage, Afonso kept missing his target and stumbling over his own feet. He ended up by falling on the ground. Rafael then bashed his head in.

The Indians ate the body of the Jew Afonso Sanches, a fugitive from the Inquisition. On the following morning, as a caravel appeared on the horizon and the Indians were getting ready to set out on a warpath, Rafael left the village after saying farewell to Little Dove and to the old man of the Torah, who presented him with a fragment of the holy book. Taking with him enough food for a journey of many days, he headed south.

H E FINALLY ARRIVED AT A VILLAGE INHABITED BY HIS COUN-trymen, the Portuguese, who received him with suspicion. He told them about the shipwreck and the long period of captivity among the Indians. He was allowed to stay. He devoted himself to commerce and he even prospered. Later on he sent for his wife in Portugal; the couple then settled in Olinda. In that town, Rafael made friends with Bento Teixeira. Bento, a New Christian, believed that the knowledge of Latin and arithmetic, disciplines that he taught, was indispensable to the Hebrew nation:

"It was through Latin, friend Rafael," he would explain, "that the Christians controlled the world. They transformed the language of their former torturers into a weapon of victory. Besides, Latin is the language of the Holy Office of the Inquisition, so it's a code into which we must initiate ourselves for our own good. As for arithmetic, it's fundamental: The four operations are as important as the four elements—air, water, fire, and earth. Arithmetic is the idiom of finances, an idiom as universal as Latin, my brother. We need both to defend our nation—until the day when we can resurrect our former grandeur, the grandeur of Solomon. As a matter of fact, I'm making a prophecy, a prophecy of peace: Like the phoenix, we, too, shall rise from our own ashes.''

The phoenix? Rafael Mendes didn't care for such comparisons. The phoenix was an invention of the Greeks, the same Greeks who had kept the Jewish people subjugated until the advent of the Maccabees. Good-humoredly, Bento Teixeira would explain that it was merely a simile, poetic license.

Bento Teixeira was the first poet of Brazil. His masterpiece, in his own opinion, was a long poem called *Prosopopoeia*, dedicated to Captain Jorge de Albuquerque Coelho, the governor of the captaincy of Pernambuco. By singing the glories of the Albuquerque family, he intended not only to pay homage to Brazil, "beautiful, warmhearting country, a daughter of Sion," but also to enlist the sympathies of the governor, which could undoubtedly prove extremely useful to the people of the nation. His purpose was to sensitize Jorge de Albuquerque Coelho to the sufferings of the chosen people. He gave a copy of the poem to Rafael Mendes, who didn't think that poetry writing was a very good idea; in his opinion, the people of the nation should remain quiet; they should move about silently, like the fish in the depths of the ocean. However, he promised that he would read the poem and give his opinion.

On the night of September 20, 1593, when he was already in bed, he called his wife, to read aloud to her a few lines from *Prosopopoeia*:

> *Oh, cruel, fickle Fate,*
> *Always usurping the rights of the good.*
> *Always favoring what is most abominable*
> *Always berating and loathing what is perfect.*
> *Always favoring the least deserving*
> *While spurning the most deserving.*
> *Oh fragile, fickle, brittle Fate,*
> *Forever robbing us of possession's and justice!*

Then he said:

"Tell me, does this rigmarole make any sense to you? Do you have any idea what these lines mean?''

She didn't reply.

"A certain poet," Rafael Mendes went on, "claims that these lines describe the sufferings of the nation. Do you think so?''

His wife remained silent.

"That's it," said Rafael Mendes, sighing. "We are condemned to perplexity, wife. Good night."

He fell asleep and never woke up. He died that very night, silently, without disturbing anyone.

On the following day, Heitor Furtado de Mendonça, an emissary of the Holy Office, arrived in Pernambuco. And thus began an investigation aimed at rooting out suspected heretics. In 1595 Bento Teixeiia was arrested and sent to Lisbon. After being tried, he was then forced to repudiate his heresy publicly in an auto-da-fé. He died of consumption in 1600.

In 1601, the editor Antonio Álvares publishes Bento Teixeiia's *Prosopopoeia* in Lisbon, with the imprimatur of the Holy Inquisition (undoubtedly obtained by the Albuquerques). On the front page, the coat of arms of the Albuquerque family; at the end of the poem, a quotation in Latin, but taken from Solomon's *Song of Songs, Fortis est ut mors dilectio,* love is as strong as death; and an emblem: the phoenix rising from its own ashes. It was at that time, too, that the phoenix appeared as an emblem elsewhere: in the Judeo-Portuguese synagogue of Amsterdam, the *Neveh Shalom (The Prophets of Peace),* built by the marranos who had escaped from the Inquisition.

F EARFUL OF THE INQUISITION, RAFAEL MENDES' MOTHER WHO, had been born in 1591, had her son baptized a Christian. But Rafael Mendes knew that he was from the nation. And he knew that he had to keep his identity secret. What had happened to that imprudent New Christian, Branca Dias? In church, at the moment of the consecration of the Host, Branca Dias would murmur: *There are dogs kept in chains.* She was arrested, tried, and sentenced by the Holy Office. Rafael Mendes wasn't going to let words betray him. He hardly spoke, and then only when necessary, which earned him the nickname "Tight-Lips." He would attend church, kneel down, pray, receive communion. Not that he believed in any of it. But he didn't want to be harassed.

On the other hand, his quick-tempered wife, Ana, also a New Christian but in her heart a fervent Jew, made him secretly practice the Hebrew faith. On Fridays she made him bathe and put on a clean shirt; and on Yom Kippur she made him fast. As soon as the servants brought the meal, Ana would dismiss them, then pour the contents of the serving dishes into leather haversacks, which were later burned. So as not to arouse suspicions, she would leave scraps of food on the dishes and flatware; on that day they wouldn't touch food, much to the displeasure of Rafael Mendes, who was very partial to roasted meat. However, he would follow his wife's wishes without arguing, he didn't want any hassles of any kind. He minded his store, played chess with his friend Vicente Nunes, went fishing once in a while: He caught small fish only. And didn't want much more from life.

Vicente Nunes, also a New Christian, had a different way of thinking. He was an ambitious man; a sugar mill and plantation complex wasn't enough for him. Big business, that's what he had in mind; he wanted to make it to the top. He had good contacts; among them, Diogo Dias Querido, of Amsterdam; a Jewish merchant born in the city of Oporto, Querido had lived in Brazil until the arrival of the Holy Office of the Inquisition, when he fled to Holland. There, Querido established an import-export business. He was one of the staunchest supporters of the idea of sending the West Indies Company of Holland on an expedition to Brazil.

In December 1629 Vicente Nunes let Rafael Mendes in on an extraordinary plan: He knew from reliable sources that the Dutchmen would soon be disembarking in Pernambuco. They wouldn't have to fear the Inquisition anymore; the Batavians, known for their tolerance, would allow freedom of religion. Besides, Vicente was sure that the Dutch were going to invest heavily in Brazil, especially in the sugar industry. Allied to the Dutch, it would be possible for them to take over the European markets. Recife would become the New Amsterdam: A prosperous city, with beautiful streets along which the well-dressed and well-nourished burghers would stroll with their families.

Some measures would have to be taken, and for this purpose, Vicente Nunes needed the cooperation of "Tight-Lips." First of all, Rafael Mendes was to send two of his most trusted employees to meet the Dutchmen and show them around. In addition, he was to hire the services of one Calabar, a shrewd man, very familiar with the region, who sometimes came to Rafael's store.

"But," said Rafael Mendes, perplexed, "you're asking me to collaborate with the invaders!"

"Why not," retorted Vicente Nunes, "we'll eventually reap benefits from this collaboration."

Rafael Mendes turned this idea over in his mind for a few minutes.

"All right," he said finally, "let's decide this issue in a game of chess."

He called a man servant, asked him to bring them wine, told him they were not to be disturbed, then closed the door. He got the chessboard.

"I see," said Vicente Nunes, "if I win, you'll side with me."

Rafael Mendes smiled:

"Every game," he said, "has one unknown factor. This one has two: its outcome and my decision. The perplexed are entitled to an enigma."

Vicente Nunes lost the game. Rafael Mendes rose to his feet: "I'm with you, come what may."

D ESPITE PUTTING UP A FIERCE RESISTANCE, RECIFE FELL TO the Dutch. Vicente Nunes was bursting with pride. He had himself circumcised in public; during the operation he howled like a madman; soon afterward, still enveloped in bloodied bandages, he showed the brethren of the nation his prepuce, which he later buried in the soil of New Amsterdam. Exhorting them to return to the faith of their ancestors, he then announced that he and his wife Philipina were changing their names: From then on they would be Abraão and Sara—the patriarch and the mother of the people.

Rafael watched the scene. Calabar was also present, with his enigmatic smile.

At Ana's insistence, Rafael Mendes had his son, already a

grown boy, circumcised. However, as a precaution, he decided not to change the boy's name, which remained Rafael Mendes. "But this is a paradox," protested Ana. "The perplexed are entitled to paradoxes," retorted her husband. And "Tight-Lips" made no other pronouncements. Years later he died, as quietly as he had lived.

TWO FRIENDS, RAFAEL MENDES (THE SON OF THE MERCHANT of the same name) and Joseph de Castro lived in the city of Recife, the New Amsterdam—or, as Rafael would say, the Jerusalem of the New World, a city where the splendors of the Mosaic faith could be celebrated in a magnificent synagogue entirely decorated with jacaranda and gold.

They were partners in business. Lens grinders by trade, they had learned their craft from a Dutch master and they were among the first such craftsmen in Brazil. Of the two, Joseph was the more dedicated to his work: He would arrive at their workshop before sunrise, and wouldn't leave until very late at night, often working by the light of candles. Rafael kept remonstrating with his friend about his imprudence: "You're damaging your eyes," he would say, "the most precious gift that God has endowed us with." Joseph, however, didn't take heed of what Rafael said. He was a stubborn, quick-tempered man.

Joseph had few friends. And he couldn't find a woman willing to put up with him, despite all the efforts of Rafael's wife, an active matchmaker. He never went out, he didn't go to parties; and even during joyful celebrations—such as Purim, the feast in honor of Queen Esther—he would not join in the general merriment as people recalled the punishment the king had inflicted on his cruel minister Haman, the persecutor of the Jews living in Persia, and in a way, the forerunner of the inquisitors.

Joseph read extensively. He admired the works of the nation's philosophers; he knew the entire corpus of Michel Eyquem de Montaigne, whom he often quoted: "I hold on to freedom to such an extent that were I denied access to even one of the remotest corners of the West Indies, this would be enough to make me rather discontented with life," and he particularly respected the defiant Uriel da Costa, who preached a Judaism freely interpreted. He corresponded in Dutch with Baruch Spinoza, who was then living in Amsterdam. While studying at the school *The Tree of Life* and at the *Academy of the Crown of the Law*, Spinoza had become familiar with the works of Maimonides and so, he was quite delighted to learn that Joseph's partner was a descendant of the author of *The Guide for the Perplexed*. In their letters they discussed everything, from the original sin to the grinding of lenses, which was also Spinoza's occupation; the philosopher was proud of the eyeglasses he made, but, he would say, it's absurd to talk about the imperfection of the blind, because in essence every human being can see. It was from Spinoza that Joseph acquired a passion for freedom and an abhorrence of superstition. They continued to correspond even after the philosopher, a free thinker, was excommunicated by the Jewish community of Amsterdam, following a lengthy and scabrous trial; in passing sentence, his judges said in part: "By decision of the angels and the judgment of the saints, we excommunicate, expel, execrate, and curse Baruch Spinoza . . . May he be cursed by day and cursed by night; cursed when he lies down and cursed when he gets up; cursed when he leaves home and cursed when he returns home. No one is to have any spoken or written communication with him; no one is to do him a favor, or remain under the same roof with him, or be within four yards of him; no one is to read anything written or transcribed by him." In a letter to Joseph, Spinoza transcribed the text of his excommunication; commenting upon the letter, Joseph said with a sneer: "Here I am, Rafael, reading something written and transcribed by Spinoza; I'm committing a serious sin, but if it weren't for his letter, how would I know I was committing a sin?"

Such paradoxes, such tricks of reason, delighted Joseph. His father being a descendant of the famous Isaac, the Blind, Joseph was familiar with the works of the ancient cabalists of Languedoc. As for other esoteric subjects, Joseph had read not only Jean Bodin's *The Demonomania of the Sorcerers*, a treatise on the efficacy of numbers and the power of the stars but also the prophecies of Michel de Nostredame, known as Nostradamus; both these writers were from the nation. In addition, Joseph had contacts with the Gnostics, the Rosicrucians, and the Freemasons.

He knew about the existence of the Gold Tree. He claimed he would be able to find it at any time he wanted. However, he didn't think that it was right for anyone to obtain gold by means that he considered predatory. Now, alchemy was different. He thought it would be more appropriate for a person to obtain this precious metal by dealing with the hidden nature of quicksilver, by laboriously manipulating kilns and retorts. Although he had never tried, he thought he would succeed in such an experiment; he also thought that he could make a homunculus or a giant from mud, and that a righteous man could breathe life into it. By assembling lenses, he had manufactured an apparatus which enabled him to see tiny creatures of various shapes living in the least expected places: in stagnant water, in feces, in the entrails of fish; even in his own semen, which he collected in a phial with the help of fantasies—a sin for which Onan had been severely punished, and to which he had added the sin of heresy: "To the best of my knowledge," he would say with a snigger, "these tiny creatures were never counted in the Garden of Eden, or in Noah's Ark."

Like Galileo Galilei, he, too, would arrange lenses together in order to make telescopes. On starry nights he would climb to the roof terrace of his house, and from there he would scan the Brazilian skies with his complex tubular contraption. He would search for the planet to which the prophet Elijah had fled in a chariot of fire. He knew that from time to time Elijah returned to earth in search of righteous men and women. Out there in space, a community, similar to Francis Bacon's New Atlantis, had been established. In that place, lost somewhere in the firmament, people had rosy skin and eyes moist with emotion. Nobody ever starved or froze. And no baby, he would add sarcastically, was ever circumcised there: Any kind of pain was forbidden. People could address God directly; all they had to do was to close their eyes, and presto, they were in direct communication with the Lord. They communicated among themselves without speaking—through telepathy, a principle that Joseph planned to use later in his efforts at finding a better system to replace the unreliable postal system of the time.

The inhabitants of that enchanted kingdom used glittering metal vehicles to move in space, and steel fish to travel in the depths of the water. They didn't have to work. Machines did everything; they even cultivated the land, which yielded watermelons over a meter in diameter, and ears of wheat with grains as big as the eyes of a calf. "And the slaves, what do they do?" Rafael would ask. "Slaves?" Joseph would say, irritated. "There aren't any. Nobody enslaves anybody, nobody mistreats anybody. Love reigns on Elijah's planet."

How strange that Joseph, such a lonely, sour man, should speak of love, Rafael would say to himself. One day, as if guessing at Rafael's thought, Joseph confided to him that he was sure that the woman of his dreams lived in that remote planet. He hadn't seen her yet through his telescope, although he suspected that a hazy face glimpsed amid a group of young people singing in a choir . . . From such a distance, it was impossible to tell.

Nobody could figure out why Joseph, who wasn't an astronomer, would spend so many hours gazing at the sky through a telescope. "Why do you have to find beauty in other worlds?" the Dutch painter Frans Post, one of Joseph's few friends, would ask. The painter was forever marvelling at the Brazilian landscape, so serene and at the same time so exuberant. "Even if I were blind, I'd still be able to paint here," he would say, carried away by the success his paintings were enjoying. "Why can't you be content with Brazil?" "You don't understand me," the embittered Joseph would say. "There's but one place in the universe where I could be happy . . . And this place is out of my reach. There's nothing I can do but wait for the prophet Elijah to take me there in his chariot of fire."

Then, impassioned, he would wonder: "But, will the prophet ever come here? Intrigue and corruption reign in Recife. And the people of the nation have sold out to sugar!"

Although Rafael smiled at such remarks, he worried about the rebellious tone in Joseph's voice, and particularly about the implications of such statements, clearly heretic. He tried to persuade his friend to give up his extravagant ideas. Why couldn't Joseph be content with being a lens grinder, with doing his work to the best of his abilities? "There are so many people out there in need of our expertise," Rafael would say, "so many short-sighted and cross-eyed people, so many old people who are almost blind. And they pay well, too." But Joseph ignored his words. He despised material possessions, he wanted neither palaces with purling fountains nor concubines wrapped in silk. He wanted no rings, no bracelets, no necklaces, no gold, no diamonds. "The only thing he wants," Rafael's wife would remark sarcastically, "is to sow hatred; he wants to bring us nothing but pain and misfortune, as if we didn't suffer enough at the hands of the Inquisition."

She kept nagging at her husband to break with his business partner. But Rafael wouldn't. First of all, he considered Joseph a competent optician. Besides, Rafael liked him, and didn't want to desert him—which would probably amount to hurling this man, already weird, headlong into the depths of a well of insanity, there to sink into its putrid waters. And finally, he recognized some truth in Joseph's words, although it was an annoying truth. When it came to truth, Rafael would much rather have the biblical truth, the truth that the rabbi of Recife proclaimed in a stentorian voice in the sermons he delivered every Friday. Yes, that was a good truth, at times bitter, at times sweet, but always nourishing, always comforting. Around this kind of truth the Jewish community could gather, without having to break off relations with the Dutch, who respected the ethics of the Old Testament and who were, like the Jews, a nation of merchants. It was from this truth that Rafael Mendes derived the strength he needed to face the sneering laughter of the malevolent Joseph.

Joseph was also eyed with suspicion by the Dutch administration because of a disagreement between him and the Batavian commander, who had heard marvellous things about his telescope. It was said that with such an instrument, even a rather careless observer would be able to spot a Portuguese sailing ship still at anchor in the harbor of the city of Oporto. When invited to clarify this matter, Joseph refused to either confirm or deny the alleged qualities of his invention; neither was he willing to give a demonstration to the military authorities. The commander was furious. He knew that there were New Christians who continued to maintain contact with the Portuguese, which puzzled him: Why would the Jews want to have anything to do with their former persecutors? Why were they in league with the Portuguese? What kind of interests were at stake? Lands? Concessions to export sugar? "What perfidious creatures, willing to sell themselves for thirty coins," the Dutchman concluded; if it weren't for their traditional skills—in business, in finances, in the art of cutting diamonds and grinding lenses—it would be better to crucify them, just as they had done to Christ. From then on, Joseph de Castro became the number one suspect on the Batavian government list of suspected people.

THE LATENT CONFLICT BETWEEN THE JEWISH COMMUNITY AND Joseph came to a head when he published a booklet titled *The Tiny Creatures of the Sugar Business*, whose opening paragraph read:

"The price of sugar is high in Europe, where it is a luxury item: eighteen grams of gold for one *arroba,* or fifteen kilograms, of sugar. Since their lives are so insipid, sugar is necessary to sweeten their mouths, to make them merry, and to help them grow fat. Fat is beautiful. The Dutch, for instance, love chubby, rosy faces, prosperous bellies, ample buttocks; that's how they are portrayed by Rembrandt and Hals. On the Batavian tables, which cave in with the weight of various delectable delicacies, there is a succession of assorted meats and fish topped with rich sauces, followed by syrups, baked meringues, pastries and cakes, candied fruit. Sugar gives them the energy they need to conquer lands where more sugarcane will be planted so that they will have more sugar, which will increase their strength so that they . . . A spiral leading to the domination of the world. But you, dreamer, you are not concerned with such matters. You despise material possessions. That is why I ask you to gaze at a crystal of sugar. Observe how it glitters! Like a diamond. Keep gazing. Observe how the crystal grows before your eyes, how it expands and becomes round until it is transformed into a ball, into a big crystal globe. Inside this globe you will see enrapturing scenes." In the globe the reader would then be able to see strange tiny creatures; with the help of a magnifying glass he would be able to recognize them as "miniature human beings who feed exclusively on sugar. They are Jews; Jeovah has punished them for their pride, reducing them to insignificant proportions."

In another passage Joseph told of a nobleman who had an entire city built of sugar: sugar houses, a sugar castle with sugar turrets; the windowpanes were thin, translucent blades of sugar. If a guest in this castle wanted to have a better view of the scenery, all he had to do was to lick a windowpane until it dissolved; he would then see rolling sugar hills, on which grazed tiny sugar cows. The city even had a lake of sweetened milk; a breed of carp, especially adapted, was developed for this lake. Very tame, these fish let themselves be caught by even the most inexperienced of fishermen, because they could be lured by an ancient Spanish song *Si la mar era de leche*, if the sea were of milk; upon dressing the fish, its flesh showed itself whitish, and pale and sweet was its blood.

What the nobleman feared the most was a heavy rainfall (like the one in the Deluge: Jeovah's punishment for his whimsy) which would dissolve this enchantment, washing away tons of sugar, which would end in muddy rivers and stormy green seas. To ward off this danger, a gigantic white umbrella was kept permanently open over the city.

This lampoon caused indignation throughout Recife's Jewish community. Several hundred copies of the booklet were burned in a public square; an enraged group of people threw stones at Joseph's house, forcing him to seek refuge in the home of a priest whose eyeglasses he had once fixed. From then on he was insulted on the streets, and spat at by children as he walked by. Rafael's wife threatened to leave him if he didn't break with this lunatic. Rafael decided it was time for him to take action.

He sought out the prominent members of the Jewish community and pleaded with them to forgive Joseph. "He doesn't know what he's saying," Rafael would reason with them, "but deep down he's a good man, he needs compassion and help." The prominent people then met with the rabbi to talk this matter over. After meeting behind closed doors for several hours, they called Rafael to announce their decision: They were willing to absolve Joseph from his wickedness provided that he submit himself to public humiliation. He was to come to the synagogue wearing sackcloth and holding a black candle in his hand. Before the community assembled there, he was to declare that he had truly repented. Upon which he was to receive thirty-nine lashes from a whip; then he was to remain lying at the door of the temple so that people could step on him as they went out.

Appalled, Rafael listened to them. He couldn't refrain himself from falling on his knees before those men to beg them to be less severe. In vain: the sentence had already been drawn up.

In a daze, Rafael left the synagogue. He didn't know what to do. He would have to talk to Joseph, but he wasn't up to it. I'll have to pull myself together, he kept murmuring to himself. I'll have to talk to him calmly, as if nothing had happened.

As the day drew to its close, Rafael went to their workshop. Joseph, whistling softly, was busy grinding a lens. Distressed, Rafael stammered an account of what had happened; he told Joseph about the proposal of the religious leaders:

"Do accept it, Joseph! Please, accept it! Do it for your friend!" The other man said nothing. He continued to grind the lens, and when he was finished, he put it into a small box lined with velvet. Only then did he look at Rafael. He smiled. Without a word, he got up and left.

On the following day he didn't show up for work. Alarmed, Rafael went to his house. The door was open. He went in: nobody. In his room, as usual, books and sheets of paper scattered all over. But no sign of Joseph.

He went back to the workshop. He worried all day, unable to concentrate on his work. He didn't know what to make of Joseph's disappearance. Deep in his heart, he hoped that Joseph had run away; that, fearing the community, he had fled to Bahia or to Rio de Janeiro. Which would solve Joseph's problems; Joseph's as well as Rafael's.

At night he went back to Joseph's house. Empty. He climbed up to the roof terrace. No, Joseph wasn't there. The telescope, however, was in place, the metallic structure pointing to the sky. An absurd idea crossed Rafael's mind: Could it be that the prophet Elijah . . . ? He looked through the telescope. He saw nothing. Not even the moon, which enormous, was shining in the sky.

Two days later Joseph's body was washed up on a beach, his eyes had been eaten up by the fish, crustaceans were sidling off his nostrils. He was buried in the Jewish cemetery of Recife, but next to the wall, as a suicide.

Rafael became the only optician in town. He charged high prices, and if a customer remonstrated, he would retort with scoffs: "Don't make me cry, I'm made of sugar and I dissolve easily."

For a long time his wife kept bugging him to sell Joseph's telescope to the Dutch commander. The sale would bring in quite a bit of money and it would give them distinction. Rafael would say nothing. One day in a fit of rage he threw the apparatus out of the window, threatening his wife with the same fate. She stopped nagging him and from then on he was relatively happy. His son, Rafael Mendes, wasn't as lucky: After the Dutch were defeated, the persecution of the Jews was resumed, and he was indicted in a judicial inquiry for allegedly having in his possession books on witchcraft that had belonged to Joseph de Castro. Hard times were those. In less than a decade, the price of sugar had dropped by thirty-three percent; on top of religious skepticism there was also financial uncertainty. Rafael Mendes decided to run away.

T WO NEW CHRISTIANS, FELIPE ROYZ AND RAFAEL MENDES, are on the lam, heading for Maranhão. Now that the Dutch have been expelled from Pernambuco, they are afraid of the reprisals with which the people of the nation are threatened. In addition, Felipe Royz has a goal: He wants to kill André Vidal de Negreiros, who was appointed governor of Maranhão as a reward for his bravery in the fight against the Batavians. Vidal de Negreiros insulted him: In front of everybody he accused Royz of having collaborated with the Dutch; he called Royz a treacherous dog and a filthy marrano. His plan of revenge, however, is forgotten as soon as they arrive at their destination. That's because, once in Maranhão, Felipe Royz, with the help of the people from the nation, becomes a settler. As he grows tobacco and sugarcane, he no longer thirsts for revenge, especially because Vidal de Negreiros's sojourn in Maranhão is brief; having arrived in 1654, in the following year he was already leaving for Minas Gerais in search of gold.

The learned Rafael Mendes takes up teaching; as a teacher,

he makes friends with Father Antonio Vieira. He suspects that this Jesuit priest is from the nation, too, not only because of the worried and rather wild expression in his eyes, but mostly because he is a passionate defender of the Jews, whose enterprising spirit he keeps extolling. As early as 1649 this priest had backed the formation of a Trade Company, with bankers of the nation as shareholders. He's at sixes and sevens with the Holy Office; and he is looked upon with suspicion because he defends the Indians: "In the State of Maranhão there is no gold nor silver more valuable than the blood and the sweat of the Indians. Their blood is sold to their enslavers and their sweat is transformed into tobacco, into sugar." Royz keeps criticizing Rafael for his friendship with the Jesuit; in the priest's references to tobacco and sugar Royz sees an allusion to his own cultivated lands, where he uses Indian labor:

"And why not? What else are Indians good for, if not for work? Or would you rather see them wandering about, with their bodies all painted with annatto, killing people and eating human flesh?"

Rafael Mendes doesn't reply. He doesn't want to get into a polemic; he agrees with Father Vieira, the enslavement of Indians is not part of the ethics of the nation, but he knows what Royz will say in reply—that in their Indian settlements the Jesuits also make use of Indian labor; and if Mendes then reasons with him, saying that the priests act in accordance with their religious purposes, the embittered Royz will sneer at him: "The salvation of souls? It's rather the salvation of their purses." No, Mendes doesn't want to argue about such controversial matters. On the other hand, Father Vieira has enemies far more powerful than the harmless Royz. The long arm of the Inquisition reaches him; in 1661, due to the intervention of the Holy Office, the priest is forced to return to Europe. Two years later, Father João Felipe Bettendorf, a commissary of the Holy Office, arrives in Maranhão; his mission is to root out bigamists and sodomists, witches and crypto-Jews. The holdings of the Jesuits are extended; the number of Indians under the priests' custody increases, and the clashes with the settlers escalate. One settler is particularly angry: He is Manoel Beckman, nicknamed Bequimão, the owner of a sugar mill and plantation complex, and an alderman. A New Christian? Possibly. His uncle João Nunes de Santarém, a wealthy Lisbon merchant, who had acted as mediator between the Portuguese and the Dutch, was known as being a New Christian; and it was quite possible that his father-in-law, João Pereira de Cáceres, was from the nation. A New Christian for sure. Whenever a steer was slaughtered on his farm, Bequimão would tie the animal to a cross; and he referred to the corral as the *sacrarium*.

It was stories like these that helped create an image of Bequimão surrounded by an aura of mystery, an image that fascinated many people, among them Maria de Freitas, the *Maria-of-the-Blazing-Ass*.

This woman (whose nickname was due to her real or alleged preference for anal copulation) was known as a witch, and was even given to boasting about it. "I'm a sorcerer, a witch, and everything else that they say I am," she would state with pride. Fake pride it was, though: In fact, she was a frustrated witch. To start with, there was the problem of her name: It had fourteen letters. Why fourteen? Had it thirteen letters, people would utter the name Maria de Freitas with awe and fear. But no. At birth she had been given a name with fourteen letters and she was stuck with those fourteen letters until the day she died. Once she went as far as to ask the governor permission to change her name to Maria d' Freitas. Vidal de Negreiros had laughed: "How can you eliminate the *e* and then put an apostrophe before a name that begins with a consonant?" Besides, the change would be less than satisfactory, for the apostrophe could always be construed as a letter; skeptics would no doubt take advantage of the situation: "A witch? But only if it's with an apostrophe!"

AN IGNORANT WOMAN, MARIA DE FREITAS HAD NEVER really been initiated into the arts of magic, whether black or white. Everything she knew was from hearsay. She resolutely applied herself to her work; however, she never succeeded in achieving anything practical or useful. She would make a wax effigy of a hated neighbor and stick into it a hundred long pins, some of gold; instead of pining away to nothing, the neighbor would even put on weight. Likewise, the evil eye she cast upon the plantations of the wealthy merely made the sugarcane and the tobacco plants grow more luxuriantly. Levitation? A flop. Flying across the skies on a broom? Another flop. She would gallop on a broom, and confidently propelling herself skyward, she would leap up in the air—here I go!—only to come crashing down wretchedly. She would try to foretell the future by examining the viscera of animals; where others saw the weather forecast, victorious armies advancing, the price of sugar on the London or Amsterdam markets, she merely saw the giblets of a rooster; a black rooster it was, a good game bird, killed in accordance with the ritualistic precepts; but still, giblets, pure and simple. What else could she do except eat the giblets? Which she did, cooked.

She was never invited to the Sabbaths of the witches; her attempts to communicate with the dead always ended in failure, nothwithstanding her frequent visits to the cemeteries on Friday nights. She would have gladly submitted herself to incubi and other demons; as a matter of fact, she lusted after their grotesque penises, which she pictured as big and reddish. Rolling about in bed, she would murmur, passionately: "Come, demons, come and take me. I have a delicious ass." They wouldn't come: least of all the Devil, whose asshole she longed to kiss, the *osculum obscenum* being the great dream of her life. She would invoke him, but with no success: "Eko, eko, Azarak! Eko, eko, Zamelak! Eko, eko, eko." Nothing would happen; what she most desired—to have the mark of the devil branded on her flesh—she never got. Sometimes she would notice something, a blotch, a swelling; but no, it was just a boil, or a sore. The mark of the devil? No.

She blamed Maranhão for her failures; this place here is a backwater, how can anyone do a good job when conditions are so unfavorable, nobody takes anything seriously; and she would quote Father Antonio Vieira, to whom Maranhão meant: *muttering, mockery, malevolence, misinformation, meddling, mendacity.*

On the other hand, her own slave Grácia Tapanhuna, a scatterbrained young Negro girl, succeeded—and without any effort—in everything that she, Maria, aspired to achieve. Grácia would predict rain; the sky being blue, people would make fun of her; soon after, however, dark clouds would gather, and not long afterward, there would be a rain shower.

She brought luck to gamblers, she made barren women pregnant merely by laying her hand on their bellies, and she could wither the leg of a fat man by merely looking at it sidelong. She could levitate at will, rising a span or more in the air, and she had sexual intercourse with demons at least twice a week, on Saturdays and Sundays, and also on all holy days of obligation. "Ah, Dona Maria, you can't imagine how good it is, ma'am," she would say about her experiences, rolling her eyes.

Such resounding success deeply mortified *Maria-of-the-Blazing-Ass*. She would have liked to ask Grácia Tapanhuna for advice, but it wouldn't do to diminish herself; after all, Grácia was a slave. If she had to associate with anyone, it would be with Manoel Beckman, Bequimão. She believed that the New Christian had secret powers; otherwise, how to account for his ascendancy over the people of Maranhão? He must know the cabala, for sure; the secret of the Essenes; the works of Michel de Nostradame and of Jean Bodin. If Beckman wanted to, he could turn her into a first-class witch, into a really malevolent sorcerer. Maria de Freitas would be the reincarnation of Lilith, Adam's first wife, an insatiable female, a magician of extraordinary powers.

But Bequimão simply ignored her existence. Deep in thought, he would walk past her on the street, barely greeting her, notwithstanding the ardent glances she kept casting at him. Maria de Freitas wanted the Jew not only as a mentor but also as a lover; she wanted to surrender herself to him, not only to derive magical powers from the carnal union but also to reach peaks of orgasm time after time. However, how could she hope to have him when the love potions that she prepared were nothing but malodorous concoctions containing the blood and parts of repulsive animals? It just didn't work.

One night, driven by lust, she became bold enough to knock on the door of Bequimão's house. "I must talk to you," she whispered when he came to the door; "in private." Beckman, embarrassed, said that it wasn't the right time, but she insisted. They went then to the corral, where letting her robe fall to the ground, she embraced him, quivering:

"I'm yours, magus. Take me!"

At once thunderstruck and outraged, Bequimão stood staring at her; then he coldly ordered her to put on her clothes and never to come to him again.

Humiliated, Maria swore she would take revenge on him.

For this purpose, she used the naive Grácia Tapanhuna; at Maria's request, the slave girl denounced Bequimão to the Holy Office of the Inquisition. What she told them was already common knowledge: That Manoel referred to the corral as the *sacrarium*, that before slaughtering a steer he always tied it to a cross, but to this she added that she had seen him perform on his slaves the ceremonial washing of the feet.

"Did he wash the feet of his Negroes?" João Felipe Bettendorf, who was taking testimony from Grácia, asked in disbelief.

"Of his Negroes, yes, sir," she confirmed.

The commissary of the Holy Office closed his face: To wash the feet of Negroes, in imitation of Christ, who had washed the feet of the apostles! A serious breach, an affront to religion, something only a heretic or a Jew would be capable of doing. Beckman was indicted.

The investigation of Beckman by the Holy Office went on for two years, from 1678 to 1680. In charge of the investigation was Father Antonio de Affonseca, who, incidentally, at one time had owned the slave Grácia Tapanhuna.

The accusations were serious and involved the entire Beckman family. Then the process was suspended by order of the king of Portugal, who considered Manoel an honorable man. However, from then on, Manoel began to openly contest the government policies of governor Sá e Menezes and of the Portuguese Crown. He would say that the settlers were suffering hardships, that there was a shortage of hand labor; that freightage was costly, that foodstuffs were in short supply, that taxes were high. Meanwhile, the Jesuits were exempt from export taxes; and the Trade Company of Maranhão and of Grão-Pará had a monopoly on imports and on the slave trade, as well as special privileges and exemption from taxes. "They're sucking our blood," Bequimão would vociferate at anyone who cared to listen to him. "These foreigners are sucking our blood." Rafael Mendes listened, perplexed: foreigners? But Beckman himself wasn't a Brazilian, he had been born in Portugal. And what did he hope to accomplish with all this clamor? Wasn't being a New Christian troublesome enough? Wasn't it bad enough to have the Inquisition at his heels?

Rafael tried to calm him down by reasoning that things could be settled amicably. "You're just a coward," Bequimão would say, "you're good at giving advice, but I don't need any advisors, I need supporters." And he did get them: He could count on the support of at least sixty of the most influential individuals in Maranhão. His brother Thomaz, a poet and minstrel like the shoemaker Bandarra, was an enthusiastic propagator of his ideas.

On February 24, 1684, there broke out an insurgency led by Manoel and Thomaz Beckman. The governor was ordered not to put up any resistance; a junta, called "The Junta of the Three Estates"—the nobility, the clergy, and the people— was established. The laws restricting trade were abolished; the Society of Jesus was ordered to leave Maranhão.

Beckman himself read the decision aloud to Bettendorf, the rector of the College of the Society of Jesus: "I, Manoel Beckman, as the elected procurator of the people, justly angered by the vexations they have suffered due to the fact that Your Excellencies hold temporal power over the Indians in our villages."

Father Bettendorf listened to him in silence. Deep in his heart he liked Beckman; there was between the two men mutual admiration. After assuring the priest that the holdings of the Society of Jesus would be safe, Beckman then ordered that the Jesuits leave for Pernambuco immediately. The priest didn't argue. "We'll see how things turn out," he said with a faint smile.

The revolutionary government lasted fifteen months; and from the very beginning, it became clear that it wouldn't get the support of the neighboring provinces. The Senate of Pará, whose concurrence would be vital, decided to remain loyal to the Crown, and so did the captaincy of Santo Antonio de Alcântara.

Put under a blockade, Maranhão was isolated. The Junta exhorted the people to prepare themselves for a long siege and for the hardships they would have to suffer: The final victory will be ours! Full power to the Junta!

BECKMAN IS A BELIEVER; HE FIRMLY BELIEVES IN THE REVOlution, in a glorious future. As he paces the floor back and forth in a state of agitation, he outlines his ideas to Rafael. He foresees a better world, a world of justice and brotherliness.

A world where nobody will starve or freeze. The cultivated lands, the sugar mills, the ships will belong to everybody; from each according to his abilities, to each according to his needs. Science will make progress; the ideas of Copernicus, of Galileo will be developed. Machines will do all the work; people will move in space in flying vehicles. "And what about the nation, what will happen to it?" Rafael ventures to ask.

"But it's about the nation that I'm talking!" bellows Bequimão, impatient. "I'm also talking about the nation! These ideas come from the nation, from its prophets, from Isaiah, and others. The nation? Everybody will belong to the nation!"

Making no reply, Rafael Mendes goes home. His wife and children complain: "We're suffering many privations. With the blockade, even food is hard to come by."

One day Maria de Freitas comes to see Rafael on the sly; she wants to talk to him about a very important matter. They go to the corral, where Maria de Freitas discloses that someone has put a jinx on Bequimão. He is under the spell of Úrsula Albernaz, a badtempered hussy whom Maria knows well: They were together in exile before they came to Maranhão.

"A witch. A witch of many powers. She has turned his head, I'm sure."

She can well guess at what lies behind this scheme. Úrsula wants a job with the Administrative Council. Her intention is to get official sanction for her witchcraft practices; if possible, she will even create a Ministry of Witchcraft to be headed by some magician of her choice.

"But," adds Maria de Freitas, "I can undo the hex. All I need is to sleep one night with him."

Rafael stares at her, in disbelief.

"Bequimão won't be able to resist my charms," the woman insists; and to prove it, she sheds her clothes.

Rafael looks her over. She's no longer young; a wrinkled face, sagging breasts, flabby buttocks. The signs of any former beauty are dissolved. What is left is a bag of loose, pendulous skin. If Beckman's return to sanity depends on this . . . He heaves a sigh. He, too, is old; he has a twenty-year-old son, a nineteen-year-old daughter. And Beckman is pushing seventy. Rafael promises Maria de Freitas that he will talk to his friend and arrange for a clandestine rendezvous.

"Let me know, then, will you?" says Maria de Freitas,

taking her leave. "But don't breathe a word of this to Grácia Tapanhuna. I don't trust her. And watch out for Úrsula Albernaz."

She walks away but then turns back. An idea has occurred to her:

"If I win Beckman's love," she says with a foxy smile, "and if I become the Grand Witch of the captaincy of Maranhão, you'll be rewarded, Rafael Mendes. At the very least I'll get you an aldermanship, you can count on it."

The constrained Rafael, trying to keep his promise, tells Beckman that Maria de Freitas wants to sleep with him. Beckman casts such a reprimanding look at him that Rafael is almost frightened: He realizes that he is now dealing with a man driven by fixed ideas, a fanatic.

As Beckman's power increases, so does his wrath, his holy wrath, as he puts it. He wants to completely eliminate all vestiges of corruption, and do away with luxury, with ostentation; he wants the people of Maranhão to live like the Indians used to, a simple, pure, innocent life. And so he proposes to the Junta that all superfluous expenses be cut, that women in general be forbidden to wear ribbons, and that the *mamelucos*—the women of European and Indian descent—be forbidden to wear silk mantles. The *mamelucos* are outraged: "What? Why can't we wear silk anymore? What are we supposed to wear? Bird feathers, like the squaws?" Beckman is booed on the streets: "Let's burn this infamous Jewish dog," people shout at him. Widespread discord has now replaced the initial enthusiasm of the supporters of the movement. The only member of the Junta Beckman can trust is the Negro Francisco Dias Deiró, the people's representative. The situation is serious: The blockade has created difficulties for the merchants, and for the owners of the sugar plantations and mills. Besides, Bequimão's outlandish ideas raise eyebrows; it is rumored that the Jew is crazy, stark crazy. As if all of this weren't enough, a grave incident is about to stir up feelings even more.

A ship of the Trade Company has just arrived from Guinea with two hundred Negroes, and this event precipitates a riot. Due to the shortage of hand labor caused by the blockade, people start fighting over the slaves; in the middle of the street, two merchants cross swords with each other over a young Negro, and end up by killing the poor devil. To prevent such excesses, the Junta decides to raffle off the slaves. On the raffle tickets, some people write down witty remarks, risqué statements, insults—which triggers new arguments, new fights.

Then the new governor, Gomes Freire de Andrade, arrives in the province. Taking office, he promises to restore law and order. The Jesuits return; the trade monopoly is reestablished. Manoel Beckman is in hiding; his godson Lázaro de Melo discloses his whereabouts to the authorities. Beckman is arrested, together with several other leaders. And so is Rafael Mendes, for being a sympathizer. He is taken to the same dungeon where Bequimão is imprisoned.

And there they are, the two friends, Rafael Mendes and Manoel Beckman, waiting in a dark dungeon cell to be interrogated. Rafael Mendes hesitates; for a long time he has wanted to clarify a suspicion regarding Beckman, but he isn't sure if now is the right moment. Finally, he decides he'll ask, anyway:

"Are you really from the nation, Beckman?"

Taken aback, the other man stares at him, wary. He, too, hesitates before replying:

"From the nation? No way. I'm a Christian by the grace of God."

"But," says Rafael, "when the emissaries of the Holy Office accused you of being a Jew, you didn't deny it."

"True," says Beckman, "I didn't deny being a Jew."

"And why not?" insists Rafael. "Why didn't you, if I may know?"

Beckman remains silent; finally, he says that he can't give a reply right away; he needs time to think it over.

"How much time?" asks Rafael Mendes.

"Some time."

"A lot of time?"

"No. Not a lot of time."

"But, as you know, we might not have much time left," warns Rafael.

"Yes. We might not have much time left," says Bequimão with a sigh. "But don't rush me. I need time."

Rafael looks around. They are in a dark, damp cell; water drips from the ceiling. Rafael points upward:

"See that leak? The water keeps dripping with a regular rhythm. So—"

"How do you know it's a regular rhythm?" Bequimão cuts him short.

"By correlating it with the beats of my heart. It's one drop for every two heartbeats."

"And who says that your heartbeats are regular?"

"I'm the one who's asking the questions," retorts Rafael.

"Are you from the Inquisition?" asks Bequimão, irritated.

"No. But I'm a Jew. And you?"

"Give me time," says Bequimão.

"How much time?"

"Some time."

"After twenty-four thousand drops," says Rafael, rising to his feet, "I'll return to this question."

And he begins to count: *one, two, three, four* . . . His voice trails off; at ten thousand he merely murmurs; and at fifteen thousand, he can no longer speak, he counts in silence. As he comes to drop number 18,412, Beckman says:

"Now. I'm ready now."

"So?" says Rafael, exhausted. "Why didn't you deny it when they accused you of being a Jew?"

"Because to them I am a Jew," replies Beckman; "in their eyes I want to be a Jew."

Laughing, Rafael Mendes lets himself fall upon the pallet. "So you're a Jew," he cries out, joyfully. "Of course you are a Jew."

"Am I a Jew?" asks Beckman, perplexed.

"You are a Jew."

"It's true!" shouts Beckman. "It's true! I'm perplexed: I'm a Jew! I'm a Jew, Rafael Mendes. I'm a Jew by the grace of God. A Jew like Jacob, who struggled with the angel, a Jew like Jonah."

But Rafael is no longer listening; tired out, he has fallen asleep.

The day of the execution arrives. The entire population of the city heads for the main square to watch the hanging; among them is Rafael Mendes, who has been set free so that he, too, can watch. Standing by his side is Maria de Freitas, who ceaselessly invokes all the demons to save the man she loves. But to no avail, no chariot of fire descends from the sky to whisk away Beckman; the earth doesn't split open, night doesn't suddenly fall, winds don't rise, whales don't get out of the sea. In despair, she appeals to Úrsula Albernaz, to Grácia Tapanhuna: "Do something, save him!" Úrsula Albernaz smiles; she has lost interest in Bequimão, she'll be investing heavily on Gomes Freire. Grácia Tapanhuna doesn't want to jeopardize herself, either; she doesn't like Beckman, he has never washed her feet.

As for Rafael Mendes, he watches the events, perplexed. Why didn't Bequimão flee? The populace would have helped him, even Father Bettendorf had openly repudiated the denunciation. Does he want to die, then, this man? Like Christ? But if he is from the nation, why die like Christ? If he wants to change the world, why surrender himself to the executioners?

The drums roll. The ceremony is about to begin. The hangman proceeds to hang a black dummy dressed in tatters; it symbolizes Francisco Dias Deiró, who being a fugitive, has escaped hanging. The crowd laughs as the grotesque figure sways from the rope. It is now Beckman's turn. He refuses to be blindfolded; he also requests that his hands be left free. He removes the dummy from the hangman's noose, kisses it, then carefully lays it on the floor of the gallows. He places the noose around his own neck; turning to the crowd, he announces that he is happy to die for Maranhão. For Maranhão? wonders Rafael Mendes, perplexed. Why not die for the nation? Or for humanity? Beckman is no longer able to supply answers to these questions: The trap door is opened, he drops abruptly; dexterously, the hangman then steps on Beckman's shoulders so as to speed up asphyxiation. At this moment, Maria de Freitas lets out a scream; casting aside her clothes, she throws herself upon the ground, and there she remains, screaming and rolling. When Rafael Mendes comes to her aid, he notices on one of her buttocks a reddish blotch in the shape of a flower: *Maria-of-the-Blazing-Ass* has finally succeeded in getting the devil's mark.

A few days later she died, but not before letting Rafael Mendes in on a secret: The Gold Tree existed, and it was to be found in Brazil.

"It's in the south, Rafael. Go south."

Rafael didn't go in search of the Gold Tree, but for many years the idea haunted him like an obsession. An old man, the arduous journey was not for him. So, he called his son and told him about what had happened.

"I have no riches to bequeath you," he said. "I'm passing this secret on to you, use it in whatever way you see fit."

The younger Rafael was rather skeptical about what his father told him; but the story roused the ambition of his friend Álvaro de Mesquita.

"Let's go south, friend Rafael," he said, his eyes glittering with cupidity. "Let's go in search of fortune."

T HEY PENETRATED DEEP INTO THE JUNGLES OF BAHIA. THEY
trudged across dense vegetation, a pistol in one hand, a
machete in the other, their hearts pounding: they feared the
wildcats, they feared the snakes, they feared the Indians, the
demons, the ghosts, the agents of the Holy Office. While one
of them slept, the other kept vigil: On the 34th day of their
journey, however, exhaustion won out and they both fell
asleep at the same time in a clearing carpeted with leaves of
cacao trees.

Upon waking up, they found themselves surrounded by
Negroes. About thirty of them, wearing loincloths, and armed
with spears and cudgels. Still dazed, Rafael and Álvaro scrambled to their feet—and soon realized that any attempts at
resistance would be futile: They had fallen into the hands of
run-away slaves.

"You're our prisoners," said the one who seemed to be the
leader, in excellent Portuguese.

Their captors were not going to stand for any foolishness:
They tied their hands with bast, then prodding them with their
spears, they made the prisoners walk. After a forced march
lasting several hours along a narrow, rough-hewn trail cut
through the jungle, they came to a large clearing as the day
was drawing in. There, surrounded by a high stockade made
of wattle, was the *quilombo*, the village of the run-away
Negroes. Rafael and Álvaro were taken straight to the presence of Zambi.

Zambi of Palmares. A hefty Negro, with gloomy eyes.
Seated on a crude chair made from trunks of trees and decorated with the teeth of animals and the feathers of exotic birds,
he awaited their arrival. A man of kingly bearing; and haughty
like a king he addressed them. He wanted to know what they
were doing in the jungle. Rafael and Álvaro hesitated, they
exchanged glances. Finally, Rafael decided he would tell the
truth: They were Jews, they were escaping from the Inquisition.

Wary, Zambi considers them. Clearly, he is making conjectures, assessing the situation. Two white men? They could well be traitors. On the other hand, if they are running away from the Inquisition, from the Portuguese, then they could become two allies, two soldiers. Two workers. At the very least, two hostages to be used, should the need arise. A shrewd man, he doesn't disclose his thoughts. "Burn them alive," he orders his men in Portuguese. And he adds, "If the Inquisition can burn white people, so can we, and for stronger reasons." On hearing the verdict, Rafael and Álvaro throw themselves upon the ground, weeping. Álvaro invokes his mother, Rafael remonstrates with his God, saying it's not fair—they've escaped from the Inquisition, they've faced the wild beasts of the jungle, and now they're about to die an inglorious death—and for what crime? For no crime, for no wrongdoing. It's not fair, it's not fair!

Zambi watches them with ill-concealed satisfaction: he's not loath to humiliate the white men.

"Get up!" he orders sternly.

They try to stand up but can't, despair weighs them down. Grabbing them by the arm, the warriors force them to rise to their feet. And on their feet they stand, wailing, leaning against each other.

Zambi keeps staring at them. Strange creatures, Jews. He had met a few before, including—this happened back in Africa—a black Jew, a wayfarer, who, having been condemned by some obscure curse to wander the earth, had left the east coast of Africa and walked across the entire continent. His haughty bearing had made quite an impression on the young Zambi; and so had the story the man told him:

"I'm a descendant of Menelik, the son of King Solomon and Queen Shebah. My illustrious ancestor, an African born Negro, lived in King Solomon's court from the age of thirteen—when he was *bar-mitzvahed* and initiated into the Jewish faith—until the age of twenty-five, when his father sent him back to Africa. As a parting gift, Solomon gave his son a copy of the Tables of the Law; however, by means of an artful ruse, Menelik succeeded in exchanging them for the real Tables of the Law, which he then took with him to Africa. Thus, we Negroes became the true keepers of the divine word."

He said in conclusion:

"We have rights, my brother. And we must assert our rights—if not by force, then by shrewdness."

It was a lesson that made a deep impression on the young Zambi and filled him with admiration for the Jews. Paradoxical admiration, though, for among them are slave traders, whom Zambi, naturally, abhors; but he is deeply impressed by the strength, the perseverance, the finely tuned instinct of survival of these people, traits that propel them to permeate every nook and cranny of society, however small, so that once inside the social structure, they can fill up the gaps, thus making themselves indispensable and progressively irksome, until they are finally expelled and the cycle starts all over again somewhere else.

No, Zambi won't kill his prisoners. Partly because he sees them as brothers in misfortune; partly because he is loath to shed the blood of defenseless men—whether or not they are white, whether or not they are Jews. While he decides on a course of action, the prisoners will be kept under strict surveillance. And in order to deserve the food that they will receive, they will work in the building of fortifications—from sunrise to sunset, like the rest of the inhabitants of the *quilombo*, the village of the run-away slaves.

B ACKBREAKING WORK IT IS. TO FELL TREES IN THE JUNGLE, to lop off branches, to haul logs along muddy trails; to set up the stockade, to shore up the logs; to dig trenches, to build stone walls—three days of this, and Álvaro and Rafael are exhausted, their hands covered with blisters. At night, Rafael collapses on his hard pallet and falls sound asleep, much to the amusement of his guard: "No need to worry about this one, he's too pooped out to run away."

But not Álvaro. Even though he feels tired, he doesn't go to sleep. Accompanied by his guard, he strolls about the *quilombo*, greets the occasional person, strikes up a conversation with them. Suspicious at first, the Negroes eventually get used to him. And thus he makes friends with M'bonga, one of Zambi's chief advisers. Into the mind of this kindly but unsophisticated man, Álvaro begins to instill certain ideas. . . .

Quilombos, he says, shouldn't be conceived as mere hideouts for fugitives but as true republics in embryo, potentially strong and well-organized. Of course, something along these lines is already at work here in the *quilombo* of Palmares; there is division of labor, some people being in charge of planting, others of manufacturing wooden and clay utensils. However, it is possible to move further; it is possible to *Progress.* For instance, it will be possible to build *machines.* Machines capable of replacing the human arm in the heavy work of felling and hauling trees, of digging holes in the ground. Machines that will manufacture cloth, domestic utensils, and also—and this is very important—weapons. Machines that will move in the air or in the depths of the ocean, like big steel fish. Machines that will build buildings; and machines inside these buildings that will transport people from the lower to the higher floors, and vice-versa. The machines will do everything; the people of the *quilombos* will spend their time singing and dancing to the sound of drums and of percussion instruments. Pleasure will be the word of command. "Really?" interjects M'bonga, his eyes glittering. "Really," Álvaro assures him. But, he cautions, it won't be easy to make this dream come true. Fortifications and good warriors are not enough. What is needed is a government capable of maintaining interchange—especially commercial interchange—with the other republics. A republic must integrate itself into the worldwide financial system. And for this to happen, it will need coin.

"Coin?" M'bonga creases his forehead. Surely, he knows what it is; however, he hasn't thought of it as being important; at least not important in Palmares, where money is unknown, for everything belongs to everybody, and nothing is bought.

Coin, yes. Carried away by excitement, Álvaro begins to describe the coin unit he envisions for Palmares, a beautiful gold piece having its value on one side, and the effigies of the heroes of Palmares on the other: Zambi and his Finance Minister.

"Me, Finance Minister?" M'bonga is getting more and more astonished, he has never dreamed of such glories, he doesn't even know what a Finance Minister is supposed to do. "Ah, yes," says Álvaro, "no self-respecting country can do without a Ministry of Finance. And who would be better suited to fill the post than M'bonga, the creator of the coin of Palmares?"

(M'bonga: a name adopted by the runaway slave João de Deus upon joining the *quilombo* of Palmares; a name of African origin; a name its bearer utters with religious fervor. M'bonga!)

A coin that will pass into History. A coin that will be exhibited in museums, together with the cruzado, the doubloon, the escudo. "And what do we have to do in order to have it?" asks M'bonga, waxing enthusiastic. "Quite a lot," cautions Álvaro. A financial system: a government mint, banks. But men with a great deal of experience in finances, such as Álvaro himself, would look after such matters. However, all of this will be useless if there is no gold reserve; that's what gives coin validity and substance. Gold.

"Gold?"

"Gold. Without gold, nothing done. No coin, no banks . . . No Minister."

"Hm . . ." says M'bonga. "Gold." He falls silent, turning this matter over in his mind. Cautiously and skillfully, Álvaro begins to question him. "Was there, by any chance, gold in the surrounding areas? A few nuggets, maybe, in some purling creek? Or on a tree?" M'bonga roars with laughter. "Gold? Where would us poor Negroes get gold? And what's this about gold on trees? Lunacy."

No, there is no gold. But this idea of Álvaro's, this coin system, has bewitched him. He'll see what can be done. He'll speak to Zambi, the chief trusts him, M'bonga has saved his life more than once.

He accompanies Álvaro back to the small straw-thatched hut that has been assigned to the prisoners and says good night. Álvaro goes in. "We are on the brink of some sensational events, friend!" he announces glowing with joy, but Rafael doesn't want to hear about it: He wants to sleep.

O N THE FOLLOWING DAY, M'BONGA, RADIANT WITH JOY, wakes them up. He has already spoken to Zambi. Although reluctantly, the chief has approved of the idea. M'bonga is now the Finance Minister (his appointment, though, is to remain secret for the time being—Zambi fears infighting for the control of power). Álvaro is given permission to go ahead with his project of devising a financial system.

"As for gold," says M'bonga after hesitating for a moment, "Zambi hasn't said anything about it. But we'll take steps to get it. We'll do so in good time."

After he leaves, Rafael turns to his friend:

"What's this all about?" he asks, intrigued. "What's going on?"

Álvaro quickly briefs him on the matter.

"But this is madness," protests Rafael.

"Shut up," snarls Álvaro, "it's our chance of saving our skins. And of getting rich!" His eyes are glittering. "Rich, Rafael!"

Álvaro is convinced that M'bonga is not telling him the truth, that he is playing dumb; that there must be gold somewhere in this area, perhaps a mine, perhaps the Gold Tree. Otherwise, why did the Negroes run away from their masters, leaving behind their homes (even if they were only plantation slave quarters) and guaranteed meals (even if they consisted of plain portions of food) and go into the jungle? There must be something behind all of this. Like gold.

Before Rafael can say anything, M'bonga is back. He comes in with stationery, booty taken from the Portuguese troops.

"There you are!" he says, triumphant. "You can start working."

Rafael has no other alternative, for however crackbrained Álvaro is, he can't now abandon him to his own fate.

They embark upon their assignment. At first, they apply themselves to the task of drafting fiscal laws and regulations;

162

soon, however, they realize that there are far more pressing matters that have to be dealt with first. It's pointless to have legislation if there is no government, no structuring of the powers. As Rafael Mendes gets more deeply involved in his work, he undergoes a disturbing transformation. It dawns on him that the *quilombo* is not a mere agglomerate of runaway slaves but possibly an incipient nation, and by some mysterious design, he has been given the honor of witnessing the birth of a nation. Will he measure up to this historical role? Álvaro sneers at his anxieties: The idea is to hoodwink the Negroes, bilk them out of their gold, and then get the hell out of there.

"But what gold?" asks Rafael, perplexed.

"The gold they're going to get."

"How?"

"By selling primary products, that's how."

" But what kind of primary products?" Rafael is more and more puzzled. "The inhabitants of the *quilombo* live hand to mouth, what they plant and hunt is barely enough to feed them."

Álvaro laughs: That's not the kind of primary products he has in mind.

"*They* are the primary product."

"They who?"

"They. The Negroes. The slaves."

He explains: There's no shortage of Negroes in this village of runaway slaves, and there won't be any—he has already noticed the high fertility rate among the women; maybe because feeling free, the Negroes copulate more often. So, it's only a matter of making connections with the slave traders (he happens to know one from the Antilles, a New Christian like them, and like them, a fugitive from the Inquisition), of delivering a certain number of Negroes, preferably young, and of receiving payment in gold, some of which will go to the ministers, as their commission, and some will be set aside as gold reserve to give stability to the coin system to be created.

Rafael's astonishment turns into indignation: "You mean you want to send these poor people back to slavery? You want them to sell their own children for gold, is that so? But when they don't even need gold! They're happy the way they live!" "Don't yell at me," says Álvaro, coldly. "Yes, they need gold. If M'bonga, their leader, says that they need gold, and that they need coin, it's because they need gold, and they need coin. And if that's the case, they must sacrifice one generation so that the other can reap the benefits of a sound financial structure.''

And he concludes by saying: "It's a question of options."

Distressed, Rafael looks at him. They've known each other since they were children; they played together; they had their *bar mitzvah* together; Rafael always thought of him as being kind; somewhat roisterous, perhaps, but basically honest and hard-working. And now he has cooked up a plan for selling the Negroes who have harbored them. That's villainy, to say the least. An idea crosses his mind: Could it be that Álvaro is insane? That he has lost his mind, due to the hardships they've been through? No. He doesn't act crazy. He is self-possessed, he expresses himself clearly, he knows what he is talking about. No, he's not crazy. Unfortunately not. Maybe his true nature is finally showing through, maybe he's giving vent to his feelings by casting aside the chaste mantle of virtue to reveal the furry beast of prey that he really is.

"I can't accept something like this," says Rafael, rising to his feet. He begins to pace back and forth. Álvaro watches him. It's obvious that his mind is already made up. That's what he says:

"I've made up my mind, friend Rafael. I'm going to present this suggestion to Zambi, with or without your approval. We can mention our differences of opinion to him. It will then be up to him to decide which of us he will choose as his advisor."

Then rising to his feet, he leaves the hut. Rafael hesitates; finally, he follows him, cursing. Álvaro stops to wait for him; then taking his friend by the arm, he says:

"Hold on! I've just had a bright idea. An idea that reconciles my plans with your qualms."

He explains: They won't actually sell the Negroes, but just go through the motions of a real sale. They'll get the money from the slave trader, but when he comes to collect the slaves, he'll be in for a surprise; he'll be met by well-armed warriors, ready to put up resistance. And he'll have no choice but to beat a retreat and go back to the Antilles.

"So? What do you think?"

Rafael thinks that it is a viable alternative. They'll be cheating one of their own—but after all, he is a slave trader, a sinner; it will be stealing from a thief.

They present their proposal to M'bonga. At first, he has some reservations about it; he considers it dangerous to deceive a white man. However, he acknowledges that the strength of the lion is worthless without the cunning of the fox; if deception is necessary to give his people a future, then he will deceive. And he'll persuade Zambi to do likewise.

That night there is a festive celebration in honor of a black deity. They eat roasted kid goat, corn, summer squash, and they drink the powerful firewater that is distilled in the *quilombo*. Soon everybody is singing and dancing merrily. Álvaro chases after the young Negro women, pinches their bottoms. M'bonga averts his eyes, pretending not to have noticed.

Suddenly, there is a blast of cannons. They are being attacked! Under an intense fusillade, the Negroes scatter every which way. Zambi yells out orders, vainly trying to set up a defense. Rafael grabs Álvaro by the arm, he wants them to take cover. Shaking his friend off, Álvaro runs toward the gates of the *quilombo*, and opens them wide:

"Stop it!" he yells. "Stop it, you white shit asses! Don't damage my goods!"

A bullet hits him on the chest, he throws his arms open and sinks to the ground, dead.

There's nothing Rafael can do, except flee, and he flees.

H E ARRIVES IN CACHOEIRA, A TOWN LOCATED IN THE VAST and fertile coastal region of the state of Bahia known as the *Recôncavo*. There, in 1705, he meets Bartolomeu Lourenço de Gusmão, who is finishing his studies at the Seminary of the Jesuits, in Belém. They become friends; the young seminarist often comes to see him to talk. Which doesn't surprise Rafael: the young man is a future Jesuit, yes, but didn't that other Jesuit, Father Vieira, also befriend the Jews? All priests are not alike; besides, Rafael had heard that Bartolomeu is from the nation, too. Which, again, doesn't come as a surprise. The same used to be said about Father Vieira.

Bartolomeu is an enthusiastic young man with the gift of gab. He is keen on learning; he has read—secretly—the works of Bacon, Copernicus, Galileo, and Thomas More's *Utopia;* he is well-versed in the art of magic; he has some knowledge of alchemy; he can fix clocks; he has built a manual printing press; he has plans to improve the sugar mills. But his greatest dream, the great ambition of his life, is to fly. To fly like the Brazilian birds: the brightly colored macaw, the garrulous parakeet, the freakish black vulture. But—how will he be able to fly? By means of a balloon, naturally, a balloon big enough to carry people and cargo. He has made sketches and even a prototype of this balloon, which he has named Big Bird. And he ends up disclosing his reason for having sought out Rafael Mendes: He wants to donate his Big Bird to the nation, to the New Christians. He envisions a safe sanctuary for the persecuted: it's the *New Zion*, to be located on a gigantic wooden platform, five leagues long by five leagues wide. On this platform, houses, schools, workshops, a synagogue will be built; there will be reservoirs to collect rain water. In big containers filled with soil, potherbs and trees will be planted. There will be space to raise animals and even a small lake for fish culture. One hundred and twenty Big Birds will raise this monumental structure about a league and a half high up in the air; then, at the whim of the air currents, they will crisscross Brazil, from north to south, from east to west. At that height, the Jews will be closer to God; they will be able to pray, with nothing intervening between them and heaven. And, as they lean over the rail, they will be able to admire far below the magnificent Brazilian landscape, with its verdant forests, mighty rivers, vast meadows; they will hover over cities, towns, and villages, well above hatred and intrigue, deceit and corruption. And, should they so desire, one day they will land on the central plateau and there, in that immense wilderness, they will found a city, which they will govern as they see fit. And it is even possible that the winds will carry them across the seas; it's possible that they will arrive in Palestine, and descend upon the mountain of the Essenes, or upon Jerusalem, the Golden, the millennial dream finally come true, thus making the *New Zion* no longer necessary.

"So?" he asks eagerly. "What do you think?"

Rafael gazes at him, perplexed.

"Are you from the nation?" he finally asks.

Gusmão hesitates.

"Yes. Let's say I'm from the nation. Yes, I'm from the nation."

He grabs Rafael by the arm.

"I need your help. Convince your friends of this possibility. Tell them it's a unique opportunity."

But Rafael is rather reluctant; deep down, the whole story strikes him as absurd—and couldn't it be a trap set up by the Holy Office to catch crypto-Jews? Could it be that Bartolomeu Lourenço de Gusmão is a useful innocent, or even a spy? He promises to think about it. Then a few days later Pedro Telles pays him a visit.

It is common knowledge that this Pedro is a real scoundrel: ex-slave trader, ex-hawker, ex-jewelry dealer, ex-mercenary soldier. He is always mixed up in some swindle or other, and although he is from the nation, the New Christians shun him as much as possible, but even so, they feel compelled to invite him to their secretly held religious ceremonies, during which he displays unusual fervor (pretense, according to some; a guilt-ridden conscience, according to others).

Pedro Telles has heard about the Big Bird, and he is interested. He has plans of his own for this invention: He wants to use it to capture Indians and Negroes:

"Have you ever thought of it? It's bound to be a success, Rafael!"

He would fly on the Big Bird over a village, capture—with a lasso, if need be—the most able-bodied of the Indians and then flee, as quick as the wind (exactly: as quick as the wind). With the Big Bird he would be able to smuggle slaves, transport riches, relay information (say, on the price of sugar) from Portugal to the colonies.

"And speaking of gold, we might even succeed in finding the Gold Tree. All we have to do is to keep flying over the forests until we spot the metal glittering on the top of a tree."

Stunned, Rafael Mendes stares at him. Such possibilities have never occurred to him; the truth of the matter is that Pedro Telles's ideas are indeed bright. Of course, Rafael is loath to enter into partnership with a person with such a bad reputation; on the other hand, wouldn't it be an opportunity for him to make lots of money? Rafael Mendes is a poor man, with a wife and children to support. He promises Pedro that he will speak to the inventor. The talk has to be postponed because Gusmão is being ordained a priest; however, a few days later, Rafael has the opportunity to meet with the Jesuit alone and he then discloses Telles's ideas to him.

Gusmão is incensed: "To use my invention to capture Indians? Never!" It grieves him to see Rafael as the bearer of such an indecorous proposal.

"You're right," says Rafael, embarrassed. "It's indeed indecorous."

And he tells Pedro Telles that Gusmão refuses point-blank to accept his proposal.

Telles, however, is not a man to give up easily. If not through Rafael Mendes, then he'll find other means to achieve his goal. . . .

Weeks later a beautiful young woman arrives in town. She seeks out Father Bartolomeu Lourenço de Gusmão, and introduces herself as Bárbara Santos. She would like to talk to him in private—about certain sins, which are so terrible that it's impossible for her to even mention them in the holy sanctuary of the church. Would he receive her in his own private quarters? Naively, Bartolomeu assents, without suspecting that this Bárbara is a courtesan from Recife, whom Pedro Telles had sent for. The priest is even proud: He'll be hearing confession for the very first time. The harlot doesn't have the slightest difficulty in seducing him; afterward, while Gusmão sleeps off his drunkenness, she absconds with the sketches of the Big Bird, which she promptly hands over to Pedro Telles. The New Christian then hires a foreman—and workers—and the construction of the balloon begins.

Shameless as he is, Pedro Telles is not in the least anxious about keeping the project under wraps; on the contrary, he even promotes the balloon in leaflets, claiming that it is suitable for warring expeditions, the transportation of goods, recreational trips, and naturally, the capture of Indians or fugitive Negroes.

Upon reading one of the leaflets, Bartolomeu Lourenço de Gusmão lets out a yell and collapses on the floor as if struck by lightning. For three days he lies unconscious, without eating or drinking.

Rafael Mendes, being a devoted friend, nurses him, never leaving the room, not even for a minute.

Little by little, Gusmão recovers. However, he is now a much changed man; he has become quiet, taciturn. Only once does he speak to Rafael Mendes; he wants to know when the

inaugural flight of the balloon being built by Telles is scheduled to take place.

"Later this week," says Rafael, worried. What could the
priest be plotting? He soon finds out: On that very day
Bartolomeu Lourenço de Gusmão goes to the emissary of the
Holy Office of the Inquisition and denounces Pedro Telles as
being a crypto-Jew and a warlock. Telles is arrested and sent
to Lisbon, where after a brief trial he is put to death by the
Inquisition.

Bartolomeu Lourenço de Gusmão recovers his sketches and
then he gets ready to travel to Lisbon. Before going aboard
the ship, he shows Rafael a letter that he will personally
deliver to the king of Portugal. In it he extols the commercial
and military advantages of the Big Bird, which could also be
used in the supervision of the colonies: "By preventing the
maladministration of the Conquests, Your Majesty could then
reap the riches they produce."

J EWS CONTINUED TO BE HUNTED DOWN. RAFAEL MENDES HAD
no other alternative but leave Bahia for Rio de Janeiro.

There he established himself in business. Two routes: the
Old Road, via Paraty, and the New Road, which was shorter,
linked Rio de Janeiro to Minas Gerais, the region of the
general mines, thus turning the city into a commercial and
import center that traded in all kinds of goods imported from
Lisbon: salt, olive oil, wine, silk, damask, plush, weapons,
gunpowder, mirrors, glassware. All of this was resold in
Minas Gerais at a fabulous profit. One *arroba*, or fifteen
kilograms of fresh meat, which cost 200 *réis* in Rio, would
fetch 6,000 *réis* in Minas; a horse priced at 10,000 *réis* could
be resold there for 120,000 *réis*.

It wasn't long before Rafael became a rich man. "The
Gold Tree?" he wrote in his journal. "What for? What I have
here is better than any Gold Tree." He and the people from
the nation continued to practice their religion in secret, of
course, but nobody bothered them. His only disappointment

was his son, Rafael Mendes, who didn't have the slightest aptitude for business. He contemplated a career in the theater. As if this weren't unfortunate enough, there was also the young man's friendship with one Diogo Henriques, a rebellious, fanatical individual, feared by the Jewish community of Rio de Janeiro because of his reckless statements. Diogo Henriques believed that only through the theater would the Jews be able to act their role of the conscience of the nations, and he would say things that although seemingly silly, were in fact profound and powerful veracities. "But for this to happen," he would say, "the theater will have to go to the people, rather than the people go to the theater." He had a plan: The city would have to be entirely rebuilt around a central public square, where the theater would stand, a small theater, incidentally, consisting only of an enclosed stage on which the actors would perform. A system of tubes would spread out from the stage, connecting it to every single house in the city, and by means of a complex play of mirrors in this tubular contraption, images would be carried to each residence. Thus, without leaving home, people would be able to watch the performance through this kind of periscope.

When Rafael Mendes ventured to reason that such an undertaking would cost a lot of money, Diogo, irritated, would retort: "I want none of this Jewish way of thinking." Diogo, however, ended up settling for the building of a conventional theater. For this project, Rafael Mendes had to ask his father for money; the entire fortune of the elder Mendes was spent on this undertaking.

I N 1738 THE THEATER IS READY TO BE INAUGERATED. THE OPENing play will be *Hijinks in the General Mines,* a comedy satirizing the gold rush in Minas Gerais, written by Diogo himself. The coming performance hasn't roused much interest— nobody takes Dioguinho Screwball seriously. Rafael Mendes and Diogo's wife, Isabel, will play the leading roles.

Beautiful, this woman. Beautiful, sensual, provocative.

Right from the start Rafael feels uneasy with her; and when, according to the script, he has to embrace her, he feels that she responds with an unexpected intensity. What could it mean? Rafael soon finds out. One night the two of them are rehearsing. Diogo watches them; more irritable and critical than usual, he gets angry at everything they do, saying that what they're doing is not theater, it's syrupy idiocy; finally, he gets up and leaves. Isabel shrugs, laughing. "Let him go," she says, "we're better off without him—aren't we, Rafael?"

She goes to her dressing room. She returns naked, her body glowing in the candlelit stage. Rafael takes her right then and there. And from then on, a series of clandestine trysts take place; they even make love on the beach as they lie on the damp sand.

The entire city knows about this affair; Diogo, however, remains silent. One day he calls Rafael and Isabel to announce that there will be a change in the program. He will present a play based on texts written by Antonio José da Silva, the Jew. A playwright born in Rio de Janeiro, he was taken to Lisbon as a child, together with his father, a prisoner of the Holy Office. At hearing the news, Rafael winces; it's that Antonio José da Silva himself is being tried in Lisbon by the Inquisition and chances are he will be convicted. Rafael tries to reason with Diogo, who remains, however, adamant; he has made a decision and he will stick to it. Isabel asks what role she will be playing. Diogo smiles:

"None. It's a monologue. I'll be the only actor."

Something in his tone of voice makes Rafael Mendes uneasy. What is Diogo up to?

The news about the change in the theater program excites vivid interest, which is undoubtedly heightened by the rumors about the backstage goings-on. As a result, all the tickets are sold out; the monologue is a success in advance.

The opening night has arrived. It's a full house; on every face, an air of expectancy; matrons and young ladies whisper behind their fans.

Rafael Mendes is visibly worried; nervous, he keeps fidgeting on his seat. Diogo wanted Isabel and Rafael to sit in the orchestra: "Then you'll be able not only to watch the performance but also feel the audience's reactions." Isabel looks relaxed; she hums softly, and greets the occasional person.

The curtains rise. Half-naked, Diogo lies tied to a rack, the bed on which the Holy Office tortures its victims.

"Friends!" he shouts. "Do you know what ropes are these that bind me? The ropes of treachery! The same ropes that at this very moment are cutting into the flesh of Antonio José da Silva, the great Brazilian playwright, a prisoner of the Holy Office! Do you think it is fair, my fellow Brazilians? Do you consider perfidy fair? Rebel, my fellow Brazilians. Down with the Inquisition! Down with the Portuguese tyranny! Down with immorality! Down with adulterers!"

There is widespread commotion: booing and catcalls from one side; applause from another. In the ensuing uproar the theater is left in shambles, and many people are hurt.

Diogo Henriques is arrested. Rafael Mendes has to leave Rio. He feels very guilty about deserting his father, now old, sick and bankrupt. And like many others who *got a sniff of the mines, and had to go there in the hope of making it big,* as Dom Luis da Cunha wrote, Rafael, too, heads for Minas Gerais. It's not that he really believes in the existence of the Gold Tree; he doesn't. However, he is indebted to his father and wants to pay him back—in gold, if possible. Which he will never succeed in doing.

Iₙ 1773, Joséi de Carvalho e Melo—the Count of Oeiros and the Marquis of Pombal—finally succeeded in having the king of Portugal issue a decree that was to abolish the distinction between New Christians and Christians of long standing. Rafael Mendes, however, distrusted laws generally. Fearing that the Holy Office of the Inquisition would be back with a vengeance, he decided to keep his true identity secret.

In Minas Gerais he dealt in gold, and he prospered. He settled down and started a family; he had many children and grandchildren. Toward the end of the eighteenth century one of them, named—naturally—Rafael Mendes, settled in Vila Rica. It was there that he met the Second Lieutenant Joaquim José da Silva Xavier, nicknamed Tiradentes, the tooth-puller.

Rafael met the second lieutenant in his capacity as dentist. Having some tooth cavities and abscesses, Rafael went to see him.

The lieutenant made him sit on a hard armchair, and then tied him to it. "What are you doing?" Rafael Mendes asked, startled, but Tiradentes reassured him: "Don't be afraid, friend. It's for your own good."

He examined Rafael's mouth:

"Hm . . . Bad breath . . . Gums in pretty bad shape. Cavities. There's at least one tooth that will have to come out. One of the molars. Completely rotten. Down to the roots."

Opening a box lined with red velvet, he took out the forceps.

"Are you ready?"

Rafael was ready. Or so he thought: The extraction proved extremely difficult, the tooth seemed to be cemented to the jaw bone. Tiradentes kept pulling as hard as he could, his face apoplectic with the effort, his black beard bespattered with blood:

"Out with you! Come out, you dog!"

One final vigorous yank, and a moment later Tiradentes was showing Rafael the extracted molar caught in the tip of the forceps:

"Crooked roots," he explained, "that's why it was so hard to pull the tooth out."

He fixed his eyes on poor Rafael Mendes who, pale and shaky, was wiping the sweat off his forehead.

"Anything with crooked roots should be pulled out. Wouldn't you agree?"

"Yes," said Rafael, spitting out saliva red with blood. He had no idea what the man was talking about, but he was in no condition to argue. Whistling softly, Tiradentes was washing his hands. After drying them carefully, he went up to Rafael, who was still tied to the armchair. Again, he fixed his piercing eyes on Rafael:

"Are you from the nation?" he asked in a low voice.

Rafael's heart jumped. "I don't know what you're talking about," he stammered. Tiradentes smiled:

"Oh yes, you're from the nation all right. But fear not: I'm a friend. And I have something to tell you—something very important."

Then raising his voice:

"I have a beautiful collection of molar teeth at home, friend Rafael. Teeth that I've pulled out. Would you like to see my collection?"

That night, disguised in a cloak, Rafael Mendes, still feeling dizzy, went to Tiradentes's house. He plodded through the narrow alleys, and kept sliding on the cobblestones made slippery by a cold drizzle. He knocked on the door, as agreed upon: four raps in quick succession. Tiradentes himself opened the door. He had been waiting for Rafael, whom he then took to a room at the back of the house. The molar teeth were in little boxes lined with velvet and in soapstone containers, which were kept in a cabinet.

"This one here is yours," said Tiradentes, showing a tooth to Rafael. "The molar. One of the most interesting teeth, Rafael Mendes. The *molar,* a millstone, the tooth that grinds. It lacks the sharp cutting edges of the incisor, and it is unlike the canine, the tooth of the dog. The molar is a self-respecting tooth that does its job properly and unhurriedly, working in the deepest recesses of the mouth. Do you follow me, Rafael Mendes?"

There was a knock on the door. Tiradentes opened it: It was his servant, an old woman with a sinister aspect. She brought in a bottle of wine and two glasses, which she placed on the table. The lieutenant remained silent while she was in the room. As soon as she left, he grabbed Rafael and whispered in his ear:

"She's a spy. I have no doubt about it."

Then, raising his voice:

"As for the canines, you have to watch out. They're apt to betray you when you least expect."

He tiptoed to the door, then threw it open: nobody.

"Ah."

He asked Rafael to sit down, then he sat down opposite.

"There's something I'd like to disclose," he said, his eyes glittering. "I'm with the nation."

He poured out the wine, then raising his glass:

"Cheers!"

Then, hit by a sudden suspicion:

"This wine tastes funny, don't you think?"

Then, resuming what he had been saying before: "Yes, indeed, I'm with the nation. And some members of our family even say that we are New Christians. That we're Jews whom the Inquisition forced to convert."

Musing, he takes another sip of wine. "I've often wondered . . . if there's any truth in it. Well, it doesn't matter. Even if I'm not from the nation, it's as if I were. It's as if I indeed were, Rafael Mendes!" Then suddenly impassionate: "Because of all the humiliations, of all the mockery we've suffered! They treat us like dogs, those people from the mother country! They take away our gold, our silver, our precious stones."

Quivering with indignation, he rises to his feet.

"Enough is enough, Rafael Mendes! It's time we put an end to this situation!"

Agitated, he paces the floor back and forth as he discloses his plan. He wants a free country, a republic in which everyone has rights, and he goes even further: He envisions a better world, a world of equality, liberty and fraternity. A world in which nobody will starve or freeze.

Science will make progress. The ideas of Copernicus, of Galileo will be developed; the existence of other worlds will be proved. Man will no longer be the center of the universe, nor will he be the king of creation; after all, man is nothing more than a good savage, a mammal, an ape that acquired speech, true, but at a price: a set of weak jaws and terrible teeth:

"You have no idea how widespread is tooth decay, friend Rafael!"

(Even tooth decay, however, will be treated by ingenious apparatuses.)

There will be no slaves. Machines will do all the work. People will move in space in metallic birds and they will travel across the depths of the ocean in the wombs of steel fish—an invention for which the future generations will be indebted to the prophet Jonah. It will no longer be necessary to prospect creeks or the entrails of the earth for gold; botanists will create in their laboratories that legendary—or is it merely rare?—tree, whose roots have the ability to seek out the precious metal, which once found, is then solubilized, absorbed and carried in the sap, and finally deposited in the tree's fruits or pods. The same can be done to obtain silver, tin, mercury, lead.

"I'm a dentist, Rafael Mendes. I work in a limited space. The mouth often seems to me a dark, damp cave very much like the caves so common in our region. The teeth correspond to the stalactites and stalagmites; as for the tongue, it is the blind, viscous, slow-moving monster that many people claim to have seen in the underground gangways. All day long I toil inside mouths: the exhalations, far from pleasant, I can assure you. At night, however, when I lift up my eyes to the skies, the stars speak to me of a radiant future. . . . So, what do you think of all this?''

"Interesting," mumbles Rafael Mendes, irritated: His jaw hurts badly, and the sight of all those molars has upset him.

"It's not a mere utopian dream," goes on Tiradentes. "We've been actively working to make it come true. . . . We, my friends and I. We're a united, disciplined group, yet capable of daring flights of the imagination. We're patriots, and should it become necessary, we're willing to shed our blood in order to free this land from Portuguese bondage. We call ourselves the *Inconfidentes*, the 'disloyal ones.' ''

He interrupts himself in order to assess the effect of his words. Rafael dabs at his mouth with a handkerchief, which he then inspects: It's blood-stained.

"I'm sorry—this bleeding—''

"Mallow," says Tiradentes, with a certain impatience. "Rinse your mouth with a tisane of mallow. But you still haven't told me what you think of my plan."

Without waiting for Rafael's reply, he goes on talking about the conspiracy. Some important people are involved: the poets Thomás Antonio Gonzaga and Cláudio Manuel da Costa, and also Colonel Joaquim Silvério dos Reis. They've even devised a password: *On such and such a day I'll be baptized.*

"Baptism," he explains, " can include circumcision. The victory of our movement will mean total freedom of worship. Times have changed. Look at what is happening in France, look at what has already happened in North America. Read the works of Locke, Rousseau, Voltaire. It's the end of oppression! Every person should have the right to do as he pleases. If you decide to be circumcised—in public, if you want—it's nobody's business."

A pause, then he goes on:

"Rights, they include the right to own property. Our gold belongs to us. We need it—to maintain ourselves independently, to improve ourselves. But let me tell you: We can't succeed unless we have the support of many people. We must be united. Look at what happened to Bequimão, so shamelessly betrayed. Look at what happened during the War of the

Emboabas, when those outside adventurers, the *emboabas,* flocked to Minas Gerais in search of gold: people of the nation fighting against people of the nation, killing one another for the vile metal. Do you think it's right? No, it's not right, and it's not right either to smuggle slaves into this region, using the Paraty Road for this purpose. Justice must be above profits, Mendes. So, I ask: Can I count on you?''

Rafael Mendes has hardly listened, so great is the pain afflicting him. He mutters something by way of reply—he'll think about it, he'll let Tiradentes know in three or four days—then, excusing himself, he takes his leave.

For the next several days Rafael Mendes is in intense pain. The inflammation caused by the tooth extraction has spread to his entire face; he runs a high fever. The family doctor, who has been sent for, examines him and is puzzled: He doesn't know what's wrong with the patient. There's lethargy, tremors; there's weakening of the muscles, the eyes are sunken. The fever suggests blood poisoning, but the patient doesn't show any signs of improvement after the application of cupping glasses.

In his delirium Rafael Mendes sees Tiradentes arrested and brought to trial. The Tribunal is in a huge hall with a domed ceiling. Behind a heavy door with a peephole stands the informer—who is he? Every time he wants to confirm an accusation, he manipulates a system of ropes and pulleys so that the head of the crucified Christ nods. Suddenly, this head falls down, then rolls on the floor until it stops at Rafael's feet. He picks it up; it's no longer a wooden head, it's no longer the head of Christ, it's the gory head of Tiradentes. Horrified, Rafael drops it. In his delirium, he flounders about in bed: He wants to warn the lieutenant that someone is betraying him, he wants to get up, but he is restrained from jumping out of bed. *"Save Tiradentes!"* he screams in despair. But nobody knows what he's talking about.

F OR ALMOST TWO WEEKS RAFAEL MENDES HOVERED BETWEEN life and death. Then the fever broke and was replaced by salutary sweating; he began to get better. The day came when, although still feeling weak, he went for a walk. On the main square he stopped short, aghast at the sight: Stuck on a pole was the decapitated head of José Joaquim da Silva Xavier. Rafael moaned with grief. So, it hadn't been a delirious hallucination. So, it hadn't been a dream.

Distressed by what happened to Tiradentes, Rafael Mendes leaves Minas: He doesn't want anything more to do with gold, with caves, with trials. He heads southward, to São Paulo.

It wasn't a random choice. In São Paulo the people of the nation had always enjoyed great prestige, ever since the days of bailiff João Ramalho, whose duty it was to supervise all commercial activities with the Spanish colonies. The people of the nation owned sugarcane plantations, sugar mills, and ships; they regulated the Customhouse and had a monopoly on the collection of taxes. And they were the physicians and the astronomers, the apothecaries and the merchants; and they operated a commercial network that spread throughout the continent. The New Christians also financed, among other ventures, expeditions that were sent out to capture Indians for manual labor, of which there was a shortage, or to prospect for gold and precious stones. However, by the time of Rafael Mendes's arrival in São Paulo, such undertakings are already in decline. He can't even find anyone from the nation.

One night in a dismal tavern, Rafael meets a garrulous old man called Bento Seixas, who offers him a drink. They drink together and get drunk. Rafael Mendes talks about his life and ends up disclosing the fact that he is from the nation. Upon hearing this, the old man breaks into a grin:

"My brother!"

He, too, has Hebrew blood; he, too, is a descendant of prophets: of Jeremiah, to be specific. And being of noble ancestry, he has a dream: He wants to restore the temple of Jerusalem and make it even more splendorous than it was during the glorious reign of King Solomon. For this purpose, Bento Seixas, who is also a descendant of the *bandeirantes*, those flag-bearing pioneers who joined the armed expeditions to the interior in search of Indian slaves, gold, and emeralds, intends to organize an exploratory expedition similar to the ones of his ancestors.

"To capture Indians?" Rafael is puzzled and rightly so; nobody enslaves Indians anymore, nowadays everybody wants Negroes as slaves.

"To capture Indians?" repeats Bento Seixas, impatient. "Of course not!"

He has moral reservations about this infamous trade: How can the Chosen People be involved in slavery?

No, it's not to capture Indians; nor is it to search for the elusive emeralds that lured his ancestors; what he is after—and Rafael quivers when he hears the words—is the legendary Gold Tree. The secret of how to find it was revealed to him by his uncle on his deathbed. Despite the fact that this uncle was a weird man, a loner who shunned everybody, including his own family—or perhaps for this very reason—Bento Seixas is convinced that the secret itinerary, which he has engraved on his mind, will lead him to the magic tree for sure. There's one problem, though: his blindness. In that poorly lit environment, Rafael didn't notice the expressionless eyes; however, as soon as the old man mentions this fact, Rafael realizes that he is indeed blind.

He is blind and until he met Rafael, there was no one he could trust. With enthusiasm, the blind man now makes a proposal to Rafael: "Let's find the Gold Tree, brother. Let's give the grandeur of the past back to our people!"

Despite being drunk, Rafael Mendes is reluctant to accept the proposal, which strikes him as being rather crazy. But he ends up by agreeing: To stay in São Paulo, or to penetrate into the jungle, what difference does it make? Yes, he'll be Bento Seixas's guide.

With mules and provisions, they set out in secret, just the two of them. At first, they travel in a cheerful frame of mind, they sing songs from the nation: *Si la mar era de leche*. . . . After a few days on the road, the first problems arise; there is a sullen animosity, mostly Rafael's, against Seixas (this old coot, he thinks he knows everything, he doesn't know a thing, how could I have been so stupid), an animosity revealed in the rude replies:

"Is there a hill to our left, Rafael Mendes?"

"No. There's no hill to our left. Why should there be a hill to our left? What a stupid thing, a hill to our left."

"But aren't there any hills in sight?"

"It depends on what you mean by hill, Your Grace. In front of us there is an elevation of land, some might call it a knoll, others might call it a hill, it all depends on the eyesight of the observer. But since you're sightless, Your Grace . . ."

"It's a hill! It's the hill!" Strangely enough, the old man didn't seem to notice the sarcasm; and how could he expect sarcasm from a partner, a brother from the nation? He didn't know about Rafael's misgivings about this undertaking; neither did he know about Rafael's secret spites, some of them the result of recent disillusionment (the trial, execution, and quartering of Tiradentes); others, the result of ancient traumas (premature weaning by his mother; then an impatient wet nurse; and ever since, a permanent feeling that he will never come upon any hidden treasure). "Now tell me, dear Rafael, is it a relatively high hill with a rock on the top suggesting a prophet with raised arms?"

"It's a relatively high hill," says Rafael dryly. "Since Your Excellency used the word *relatively*, I can concur with you. And there is a rock on the top. I don't know if it suggests a prophet with raised arms. Let's suppose it does. Which prophet do you have in mind, Your Excellency? Is it the admirable Jonah, or is it that despicable whiner, Jeremiah? As a matter of fact, however—do you really want to know, Your Excellency?—it suggests nothing at all to me."

"Nothing, Rafael Mendes?"

"Nothing."

"Nothing at all?"

"Nothing at all."

"Not even a tiny little bit?"

"No. Nothing. Zilch."

Strange, murmurs the old man. It suggests nothing. Gradually it dawns on him that something is amiss; Rafael Mendes is not being cooperative, that's it, he's not being cooperative at all.

"Is there any scrub growth to our right?"

"I have no idea," he replies with a shrug, and now old

Seixas realizes—by his partner's tone of voice—that Rafael Mendes is shrugging.

"Wait a moment, Rafael! You're shrugging!"

"Since when can a blind man tell someone is shrugging?" retorts Rafael.

"I can feel, you wretched person! I can feel that you're shrugging. You're mocking me, you frivolous rascal! Watch out, I'll get you!"

Drawing his sword, he begins to brandish it every which way. From a safe distance, Rafael looks on:

"A bit farther to the right! Still farther! Oh, you're nowhere near! Move forward! A bit more!"

A few minutes later, the old man, exhausted, lets himself fall on the ground. Then Rafael—whether impelled by a flash of lucidity, or by remorse, or by a mere desire to prolong the old man's suffering for a few more days, whatever the reason—walks up to him:

"Let's go, brother. Don't get all steamed up over this. Let's proceed with our journey. Think of Solomon's temple."

Despondent, Bento Seixas lets himself be led away. Soon, however, the bickering starts all over again:

"Is there a creek in front of us?"

"There's a small river."

"A small river! What's the difference between a creek and a small river?"

"In Minas Gerais we'd call this a small river. But you *paulistas*, you folks from São Paulo—"

"In Minas Gerais! What do you people from Minas Gerais know? That lieutenant, that poor fool . . ."

"Don't disparage him, Bento Seixas!" It's Rafael who is angry now. "Don't disparage that man, do you hear me?"

"I'll disparage him if I want to, him or anyone else."

In retaliation, Rafael Mendes hides himself behind a tree. The old man keeps searching for him:

"Rafael Mendes! Don't do this to me! Don't play games with me, brother! It's cruel! Come on, Rafael Mendes, it's getting dark, I can feel the coldness of the night in my flesh, if I get lost, you won't be able to find me, Rafael. Help! Oh, Lord, have mercy on me!"

Rafael Mendes walks up to the old man, who embraces him, in tears: "Forgive me, brother, if I hurt your feelings by disparaging Tiradentes. I'll never do it again. I'll respect your feelings!"

They become reconciled. On the following day, however, they are at it again:

"Is there a coconut tree with a somewhat crooked trunk standing in front of us?"

" There is a coconut tree all right, but it's not just *somewhat* crooked. It's *quite* crooked."

"You idiot!"

"I've never seen such a crooked coconut tree in my entire life!"

"You pervert!"

"Jeovah himself, even if He wanted to, wouldn't be able to come up with a coconut tree this crooked."

"You heretic!"

"Extremely crooked."

It begins to rain. And as in the biblical times, it rains for forty days and forty nights. Mud, mosquitoes, and swollen rivers to cross. The mules, struck by a mysterious disease, die one after the other. Bento Seixas is so weak that Rafael Mendes has to carry him. However, as they advance, their friendship is rekindled; and when they are 400 leagues away from São Paulo, they enter into a solemn pact, promising each other to remain brothers forever. Rafael no longer has any doubts about their mission: He firmly believes that they will find the Gold Tree. And that they will rebuild the temple. Then one day:

"Is there a small waterfall to our left?"

"Yes, there's a small waterfall to our left."

"And is there a rocky hill to our right?"

"Yes, there's a rocky hill to our right."

"Are there six black birds fluttering over our heads?"

"Yes, six black birds are fluttering over our heads."

"And have we left a long road behind us? And all bitterness?"

"Yes." Tears roll down Rafael Mendes's face. They have indeed left a long road behind them. But all bitterness?

"Brother!" cries out Bento Seixas, his face radiating joy. "Brother, we have arrived! The Gold Tree must be in front of us. Isn't there a tree in front of us?"

"Well . . ." Rafael Mendes doesn't know how to put it. "There is a tree. But not just one. There are many trees, Bento Seixas. Scores of thousands of trees, in rows, as if they were warriors standing in formation. And they aren't exactly trees, they look more like shrubs, and they are covered with berries."

Now it's Bento Seixas who is perplexed:

"No. According to the itinerary, there should be a clearing here, and at the center, the small gold tree. Thousands of shrubs, did you say?"

Then it occurs to him:

"Coffee!"

"What?" says Rafael Mendes, surprised.

"Coffee!" It is heart-rending to see Bento Seixas's despair. "That's what they plant nowadays, this tropical poison! What else could it be?"

He hurls himself upon the ground, rips his clothes to shreds, tears at his hair.

"Ah, my God, such an injustice! Ah, Lord, why do you treat your children like this? Why have you forsaken us?"

All of a sudden, he leaps to his feet.

"It's probably all right!" he shouts, suddenly excited. "It's quite possible, Rafael, that the Gold Tree is somewhere here in the middle of this coffee plantation!"

Rafael takes him by the arm.

"Let's go back, Bento Seixas," he says softly. " Let's go back, brother."

The old man extricates himself.

"No! I won't go back without the gold! I'd rather die here, Rafael."

Groping about, he advances until he comes to the coffee shrubs, then he begins to touch them with his trembling hands:

"It's not this one . . . And it's not this one either . . ."

Rafael Mendes sets out on his return journey. He looks back just once and there is the old man, in the middle of the huge coffee plantation:

"It's not this one . . . And it's not this one either . . ."

R AFAEL MENDES CONTINUES TO JOURNEY SOUTHWARD. WHAT he wants now is virgin land, a place with no gold or coffee shrubs, but also a place free from intrigue and betrayal. Thus, after journeying for months, he arrives at the territory that was later to become the State of Rio Grande do Sul. In the vastness of the pampas, across which the pampero, this purifying wind, blows freely, an idea begins to take shape in his mind. He will head for the Missões, the region of the former mission settlements of the Jesuits; he will look for the people who stayed in the settlements, and he will reunite them so that together they can establish a new Guarani Republic, and thus redress a flagrant historical injustice. He is not afraid that this undertaking will end in failure; he can count on the support of the nation. Yes, because—and this is an important detail—he will convert the Indians to Judaism; and he will name the city to be founded there, New Jerusalem. In the middle of a forest, strong men with bronze-colored skin will rebuild Solomon's temple; and workshops, laboratories and universities will be created in order to foster, in addition to religious belief, a love for the sciences and the arts. That's what goes on in Rafael's mind as he walks along the roads that cross the pampas, shivering with cold in the pampero wind that penetrates his very bones. It doesn't matter: The coldness of freedom is preferable to the bonfires of the Inquisition. It's a good coldness, this one. And the wind seems to purify him; finally, he can still count on the warmth of the ideals that inspire him.

He ends up in the lands that belong to Colonel Picucha, who is notorious for beheading his enemies and using their heads as balls to play *ludopédio,* a foot game.

Eyes watch him from amid the trees; suspected of being a cattle thief, he is captured by the Colonel's men and taken to his presence. The caudillo, however, takes a liking to Rafael; perhaps it is Rafael's air of impoverished nobility, or his circumspect arrogance; perhaps the Colonel, remotely related to the nation, can hear the voice of the blood whispering in his ears. Whatever the reason, he sets Rafael free and engages him as tutor for his daughter. When the girl grows into an elegant young woman, Rafael falls in love with her. His love is returned. The young woman becomes pregnant. Fearing the Colonel's wrath, they elope. They roam the pampas in a big wagon, similar to the ones used by the gypsies: a veritable house on wheels, with doors, lace curtains on the windows, and smoke always curling out of the chimney. Children are born to them, times goes by. The family eventually settles down in Viamão, near the Mato Grosso Road, which links their village to Porto Alegre. There they buy land. . . .

B Y THE TIME THE WAR OF THE *FARRAPOS*, OR THE RAGA-muffins, as the insurrectionists were called, breaks out, Rafael Mendes is already a teenager. His father leaves home, saying he will join the war. It is not known if he really will, or if he is lying; the fact is, he never returns home.

Little is known about this father. He seems to have been a kindly man, quiet but friendly. He had worries he never talked about, he didn't sleep well, he often dreamed about warriors and prophets. He used to tell stories: about the Gold Tree, among others. The image that Rafael will keep of his father shows him as a strange yet affectionate man who would take him in his arms, and lull him to sleep with a lullaby sung in Ladino, the language of their remote ancestors:

> Duerme, duerme mi angelico.
> Hijico chico de tu nación . . .
> Criatura de Sión,
> no conoces la dolor.

Yes, Rafael Mendes knows that he is from the nation; however, he hardly knows anything about Judaism: a few prayers, the rudiments of Hebrew, and that's about all.

He longs for his father, whom he can barely remember. He

longs for the sea, which he has never seen. He wants to see his father again, he wants to listen to the stories he used to tell; and he wants to be a sailor, and sail to faraway, mysterious places, Angola, Egypt, Palestine: He wants to see white sandy beaches, coconut trees, exotic birds. To this strange man, to his father, he wants to say, come back home, mother is waiting for you.

In this two-fold objective he is helped by chance. David Canabarro, the leader of the *Farrapos,* is preparing an expedition to the town of Laguna; he is enlisting volunteers for the fleet of the Rio Grandense Republic. Rafael Mendes asks his mother for permission to join the warriors; she is unwilling to let him go, she has already lost her husband and fears she will lose her son, too, in a shipwreck or in the battlefield. But Rafael insists, threatens to enlist anyway; sighing, the poor woman ends up by giving her son permission to carry out what she considers a crazy plan.

A haversack slung over the shoulder, a knife at the waist, Rafael Mendes sets out southward. He heads for a region near the Capivarí River, where, he has been told, the *Farrapos* are camped.

On a densely foggy morning he comes to a meadow, turned soggy because of the recent rains. Spotting a few trees in the distance, Rafael Mendes walks toward them. It's a weird-looking thicket: Some of the trees are very short, others very tall. As he approaches, he is surprised to see that the tall ones aren't trees at all. Although covered with foliage, they aren't trees: They are the masts of the ships lying at anchor in the Capivarí River.

"Stop!"

From amid the trees emerge heavily bearded men dressed in tatters, wielding weapons. Frightened, Rafael Mendes raises his arms; he's shaking so badly that his teeth rattle. "I'm a friend!" he says. "A friend!" His captors, however, are not taking any chances; they tie his hands and take him to Garibaldi.

There stands the legendary rebel everybody talks about, the hero who came from Italy to help out the *Farrapos,* the Ragamuffins, against the imperial government. A bearded man looks at Rafael with his pale blue eyes, in which mistrust and amusement are mingled. Then he orders that the prisoner be set free. Moved by gratitude, Rafael tries to kiss his hands; Garibaldi rebuffs him rudely:

"Fermo! Sta fermo!"

Startled, Rafael freezes.

"Who are you, anyway?" asks Garibaldi. Rafael tells him his story, to which the rebel leader listens, his eyes fixed on the boy.

"He's a fool," he says at last. "Send him away."

But Rafael doesn't want to go: "Please, general, allow me to stay with you, sir. I have good reasons, I must find my father. He left us, me and my mother, to join the *Farrapos*. I want to fight side by side with him, I want to take him home after the war is over."

After hesitating for a moment, he adds: "Besides, I want to be a sailor."

"A sailor?' Garibaldi laughs. We don't even know if we'll ever be able to sail, son. The loyalists are the top dogs."

The boy doesn't give up: "I'm strong I can make myself quite useful; give me a chance, general."

Garibaldi is reluctant, and even more so when he learns that the youth doesn't have any sea experience. Then an idea occurs to him: "Do you play chess?" he asks. "Yes, sir," replies Rafael, surprised.

"Well, let's then play a game of chess," says Garibaldi. "If you win, you can join us; if you lose, you'll be given thirty-nine lashes and sent away."

Garibaldi may well be a skillful strategist, but when it comes to chess, he is not so at all. Despite being a mediocre player, Rafael has no difficulty defeating him. And so he gets what he wants: Rising to his feet, Garibaldi declares in a solemn tone of voice that from now on Rafael Mendes is a sailor in the fleet of the Rio Grandense Republic. The men fraternize with him, offer him white rum and unsweetened maté.

However, disappointment follows this cheerfulness: Rafael Mendes's father is not among the men under Garibaldi's command. And no one there has ever heard of him. A man given to singing *duerme, duerme mi angelico*? Nobody knows of any such man. But, they would add, it's possible that his father is with some other detachment. Perhaps Rafael will run into him in the course of the long march ahead of them. Because they won't be sailing in the near future. In order to outsmart the vigilant loyalists, Garibaldi has devised a fantastic plan: They will transport the fleet's two ships—the Seival and the Farroupilha—overland as far as the town of Tramandaí, located many miles to the north; from there, they will go by sea to the town of Laguna, in the state of Santa Catarina, where they will attack the imperial forces, caught off-guard.

It is an undertaking of extraordinary complexity. The Seival is a ten-ton boat, the Farroupilha even bigger. Therefore, first of all, they take the cannons, the ammunition, and anything heavy out of the two ships; meanwhile, the head-carpenter Joaquim de Abreu and his assistants make twelve gigantic wheels of solid wood rimmed with iron bands that turn on axles made of huge logs. The wheels are then taken down a slope to the Capivarí River. Waiting in the water are Garibaldi's men, including Rafael Mendes. Six men take hold of each wheel and at a signal, they all dive together into the water, trying to place the axles underneath the hull of the boats. Finally, the operation is successfully completed and the large barges are ready to leave the water. Sixteen yokes of oxen are hitched to each of the two boats; the air is filled with the shouts of the cowboys: Come on, Pet! Forward, Piebaldy! Let's go now, Half-Boot! Come on, Slobberer! The oxen pull steadily, their hooves sinking into the mud of the river bank; slowly, the boat Farroupilha, its wooden framework squeaking and creaking, its mast tilting dangerously, begins to come out of the water and onto the bank. The men fling their hats up into the air, Garibaldi dances a tarantella with Rafael Mendes, who by now has been adopted as the mascot of the troops.

They are on their way. Pulled by the long-suffering oxen, the boats make a slow advance across the pampas of Rio Grande do Sul. The men walk ahead of them, watching out for bogs; Rafael Mendes is the only person given the privilege of traveling aboard the boats, his mission being to ensure that everything is all right, that there are no breakages or cracks. Standing at the helm, he sings cheerfully. Mornings, when everything is shrouded in a dense fog, he has the feeling that he is sailing across a tranquil sea, the backs of the oxen being gentle furry waves. As soon as the sun rises, he clambers up a mast to unfurl the flag of the Republic of Piratiní. He has but one worry: When will he find his father? The *Farrapos* try to cheer him up: "Maybe when we get farther up north, boy."

Nights, when the boats are at rest and the *Farrapos*, tired out, lie asleep by the campfires, their ponchos wrapped about them, Rafael climbs to the crow's nest, where he remains gazing at the stars; he misses his mother, he sings the songs that she and his father used to sing together:

Si la mar era de leche
yo seria un pescador
pescaria mis dolores
con palabritas de amor.

The days go by. The barges keep advancing. Here and there in the underbrush, there are now patches of white sand. And straw-thatched huts, with the natives of the region standing at the door, small, thin men with rotten teeth, women with sagging breasts, sallow-skinned children with distended bellies. Upon seeing fishnets hanging from poles, Rafael, excited, concludes that the sea cannot be far away. In fact, one night he hears the roar of the waves. In the morning, from the crow's nest, he sights the sands of Tramandaí.

"Sea in sight!" he cries out, his hair ruffled by the wind. The *Farrapos,* who are making coffee, laugh. Rafael slides down the mast, dashes to a nearby brook, washes up, and is back, huffing and puffing, shaking off water. Someone gives him a piece of jerked beef and a mug of hot coffee; and now, it's time to work, shouts Garibaldi, but Rafael pays no heed to his command; he is busy talking to the fishermen who have gathered curiously around the boats, asking them if they've seen such and such a man, a quiet but friendly man given to singing a song about a sea of milk. "No," say the fishermen. And they laugh: "A sea of milk, that's funny. If the sea were made of milk, our children wouldn't have to starve," they say.

When Rafael returns to his post, he is severely reprimanded. "Who ever heard of a warrior that fails to obey orders?" roars the general. "I was trying to locate my father," murmurs Rafael, close to tears.

"Your father!" shouts Garibaldi, irritated. "The future of the world is at stake and you are looking for your father!"

Indignant, he falls silent. Then, cooling down, he touches the sheepish-looking Rafael on the shoulder.

"All right, son. We're going to find your father. It's a promise."

That night, when everybody is seated around the campfires, Garibaldi and Rafael have a long talk. The revolutionary speaks of a better world; a world in which people will have ruddy complexions and eyes misty with emotion. Machines will do everything, there won't be any slaves, people will spend their time singing and dancing: Pleasure will be the word of command. The realm of poverty will give way to the realm of freedom.

Rafael Mendes listens, but in fact he is thinking of something else. Taking advantage of a pause in Garibaldi's speech, he shoots the question which he has had in readiness for a long time:

"Are you from the nation, general?"

"What?" says Garibaldi, astonished.

"I asked you," says Rafael, now haltingly, "if you are from the nation. If you are a Hebrew."

"A Hebrew?" Garibaldi bursts out laughing. "No. Me, a Hebrew, son? Of course not. What makes you think I'm a Hebrew?"

What made Rafael think that Garibaldi was from the nation? He has no idea. The fact is that he has thought of this possibility; and on his list, he has also included David Canabarro, because of the biblical name. And Bento Gonçalves—the name Bento could well be the Portuguese version of the Hebrew name Ben Tov, meaning a good son, a term of endearment used by Rafael's father; or a version of *baruch*, blessed.

But no, none of them are Hebrews. Perhaps the Azorians who live in Porto dos Casais are Hebrews, but none of the leaders of the *Farrapos* are.

L AGUNA WAS CAPTURED WITHOUT OFFERING ANY RESISTANCE, which rather disappointed Rafael Mendes for he had anticipated a bloody battle. Windows and doors were flung open and people took to the streets to fraternize with the revolutionaries.

The Juliana Republic is proclaimed.

Garibaldi takes up administrative functions. During the day he works at the Town Hall, rendering decisions on official matters; in the evening, as a measure of precaution, he goes aboard the Seival, which is berthed in the harbor. At dawn, before going on land, he carefully scrutinizes the town through a telescope.

This telescope is a powerful instrument, built in accordance with the ideas of Galileo Galilei. It consists of a complex tubular structure through which Garibaldi can gaze at the stars in the nighttime and spy on his enemies in the daytime.

I T IS THROUGH THIS TELESCOPE THAT HE FIRST SEES ANITA. A beautiful, haughty woman. She is in her living quarters, getting ready for her bath; she takes off her silk gown. On seeing her naked, Garibaldi heaves a sigh. Rafael Mendes, who is always hanging around, overhears him murmur: *Tu deve essere mia!*

Ever since that day Garibaldi has changed completely. Later, having enticed Anita away from her husband, he strolls with her in the streets of Laguna, unconcerned about the reproachful eyes of its inhabitants.

Rafael Mendes grieves. He wants to ask Garibaldi when they will start searching for his father, but the general won't even see him, enthralled as he is by his Anita. Rafael considers going home; however, he is a disciplined warrior, he won't desert his post.

One night, while wandering sleeplessly about the outskirts of Laguna, he seems to hear the words of a very familiar lullaby brought by the wind: *Duerme, duerme, mi angelico. . . .*

He runs in the direction of the words. It's not his father that he finds there, but a group of loyalist soldiers on patrol.

After being arrested, Rafael Mendes undergoes interrogations, which are followed by various forms of torture. Unable to endure the ordeal, he discloses everything that the loyalists want to know. With this information in hand, they prepare a successful attack: The town is recaptured, the *Farrapos* beat a retreat. Garibaldi and Anita go to Italy. There, in the country of Galileo Galilei they will continue to fight.

Set free by the loyalists, Rafael Mendes returns home. He will never sail again. He will never find his father.

Rafael Mendes set up shop as a leather exporter, and he was somewhat successful. He married and fathered a son on whom he lavished affection; however, even though he used to lull his child to sleep with the song *duerme, duerme mi angelico*, Rafael never told him that he was from the nation, partly because he had a spite against his own father, and partly because he believed that this secret belonged to the past and in the past it should remain; he hoped that his son would enjoy life, with no guilt and no need for dissimulation. He provided his son with all the comforts of home and a sound education. Rafael Mendes, one of the very first engineers to have graduated in Rio Grande do Sul, went in for railroad construction. For a while he worked for the Rothschilds of France, who were then investing in railroads. It wasn't a pleasant experience; Rafael Mendes, a distrustful man whose sleep was haunted by nightmares, hated those financiers, even though he had never met them because he conducted business exclusively with the Brazilian agents of his employers. Somehow, this experience left him with a deep resentment against Jews. And yet, when his own son was born, how did he lull him to sleep? Well, by singing *duerme mi angelico*; he couldn't resist the pull: Because that's how ancient things are: powerful and mysterious.

RAFAEL MENDES: AN INTER- MISSION

J UST BEFORE MIDNIGHT RAFAEL MENDES FINISHES READING THE first notebook. Setting it aside, he sits motionless for a moment. Then he rises to his feet, opens the door of his study.

The apartment is quiet. Helena is asleep; Suzana, as usual, isn't yet home. He goes to the living room, opens the balcony door, stands gazing at the city, at the lights twinkling in the distance. They twinkle because of the alternating current. Rafael knows this: The electric current changes direction at regular intervals. It's one of the few certainties he has. As for the stories he has just read, he doesn't know what to make of them, and even less so of the man who wrote them. What's the significance of all this succession of historical characters, Jonah and Habacuc ben Tov and Maimonides and all the Mendeses?

What good is it to him to know that one of his ancestors—if he really existed—talked to Tiradentes—if he indeed talked to him? Rafael doesn't know. Neither does he know whether what he has read is true, or false, or a mixture of half-truths and lies. He remains just as perplexed as before; he has merely found out—and cold comfort it is—that this perplexity of his is of long standing. Centuries-old.

The telephone rings. Startled, he makes a dash for the phone.

"Well, Senhor Rafael, have you read them yet?" The genealogist, naturally.

Rafael can barely contain a sigh of irritation.

"I've read the first notebook."

"And what do you think?"

Rafael hesitates:

"Fiction, isn't it? Fiction. Plenty of made-up stuff."

"It's like I said." The man sounds somewhat disappointed; but what did he expect, that Rafael would burst into tears over the telephone? "Your father had a fertile imagination . . . but you'll get to know him better in the second note-

195

book. It's through a series of forward moves that we come to the genealogical truth, Senhor Rafael.''

Philosophy at this hour of the night? Rafael is losing his patience, but the little man doesn't beat about the bush:

"I'm phoning to know if I could get the money.''

"At this hour?''

"It's that . . .'' the other man wavers, "I didn't want this day to end without . . . But it doesn't matter, I can wait until the morning. It's even possible that the dollar will go up during these hours, isn't it?''

"Yeah,'' replies Rafael dryly.

"So, I'll be there first thing in the morning. Good night.''

"Good night,'' mutters Rafael and he hangs up.

"Still up, Senhor Rafael?'' It's one of the maids, the little mulatto with the pert face. Heading for the fridge, no doubt, always eating, these creatures. For a moment Rafael stands staring at the girl as she walks away. A nice piece of tail. If she weren't his servant, and if it weren't for all the hassle . . . Rafael heaves a sigh. He goes back to his study, locks the door, picks up the second notebook and sinks into the armchair.

THE SECOND NOTEBOOK OF THE NEW CHRISTIAN

T HE MENDESES PUT DOWN ROOTS IN RIO GRANDE DO SUL; as time went by, they became a traditional family, although they didn't belong to the so-called rural aristocracy. Among my ancestors who settled down in Rio Grande do Sul one was a farmer, another was a merchant, my father was an engineer; but the name Mendes was held in high respect, at least in my circle of friends. As for the distant roots, nobody had ever talked to me about the New Christians, or the Inquisition, or the Essenes, or the prophets—or the Gold Tree.

And yet there was *something*. A certain attraction for the exotic, the mysterious, the secret; a certain fascination for paradoxes; a certain perturbation whenever walking past a synagogue; a feeling of dissimulation and perplexity. Not the wide-eyed, open-mouthed, speechless kind of bewilderment; a lesser confusion, embryonic but nonetheless disturbing. So disturbing that it necessitated the help of a guide for the perplexed, if available. But it wasn't.

Like Maimonides I too turned to medicine. Like any other physician, my foremost desire was to heal myself. I was a sickly boy; the measles, rubella, fevers, chicken pox, the croup, you name it, I had them all in due course. Maybe I attributed my anxieties to my sickly body, I don't know. All I know is that I wanted to become a physician. As soon as I finished high school, I began to prepare myself for medical school.

The year was 1929. In New York, there was the stock-market crash; desperate financiers were jumping off high-rises, but, they didn't fall into my arms, which were as a matter of fact far from strong. The economic depression was something very remote from me; my really pressing problem was admission to medical school. I used to study together with a childhood friend, Cuvier de Souza, named after the French naturalist Cuvier. The son of a physician, he had handled his father's microscope ever since he was a child, and was passionately interested in fungi, protozoans, bacteria.

Later he was to become an outstanding bacteriologist; even in those days he was already known as Microbe—partly because of his small size and restlessness.

It was from Microbe that I first heard about Débora. A few days before the university entrance exams he came running into my house in a state of agitation: "There's a girl sitting for the entrance exams," he said. "She's Jewish, imagine! And they say she's a brain."

A woman, and Jewish to boot, in the Faculty of Medicine? Amazing. Medicine was for men, as everybody knew. "I'll bet she's a dyke." Microbe was indignant. "A witch, at the very least."

No, she wasn't a witch. She was rather beautiful, as I had the opportunity to ascertain a few days later, as we sat side by side to write the first exam, which happened to be on the Natural Sciences. A Hebrew type of beauty, of course, the nose somewhat hooked, and the legs somewhat thick. But she had beautiful greenish eyes and nice brown hair and a well-shaped mouth. She looked at me; I can't say I wasn't disturbed; yes, I was disturbed by the sight of this Hebrew girl—what did I know about Jews, whether male or female? Very little. I didn't associate with them, I hardly ever went to Bom Fim. But the expression of her eyes stirred me. . .

The examination topics were announced; she leaned over the desk and began to scribble away at an incredible speed, covering pages and pages. Microbe was right, she seemed to know everything. Later, however, when the list of the successful candidates was published, we saw that she came out 24th in the exams, a rather modest placement; she wasn't, as we would soon find out, the genius we had supposed her to be. Intelligent, yes, but not brilliant. Anyway, she did better than I did—I came out second to last, and better than Microbe, who came out 25th.

She was the only girl in the class, but not the first woman ever to attend the Faculty of Medicine; there had been others before her. Anyhow, her presence created perplexity. And irritation. Irritation that translated itself into disguised hostility or wisecracks—the disguised hostility easily turning into open aggression, the wisecracks into coarse jokes. Trying to forestall problems, the Dean of the Faculty of Medicine invited her to a meeting of the Faculty Association. He started by asking her to let them know about any discourtesy on the part of the students, "As you know, the presence of young

ladies in this Establishment is unusual," and then he asked
her how she would like to be treated. "Like everybody else,"
she said. A proud reply. She was haughty—a haughty Jewish
girl. From her father, a shoemaker, already deceased, she had
inherited a sense of dignity—which was somewhat strange,
but touching. This man had always dreamed of his daughter
becoming a physician; and he had also advised her to hold her
head high, no matter what. That's what she was doing now:
holding her head high.

The faculty members listened to her in polite silence. At
the end of the meeting, a professor of Clinical Practice of
Medicine went up to her; his name was Brito, and he came
from a traditional family and had a reputation for being
arrogant. "Welcome, young lady," he said, "but let me
warn you: This isn't a profession for women, nor is it a
profession for upstarts. As you'll soon find out for yourself."

Débora made no reply; she turned her back to him and
walked away. On the following day she was invited to meet
with the executive of the Students' Association; they wanted
to know if she would submit herself to hazing. "I will, like
all my fellow students," she said, with a touch of contempt:
She considered hazing a silly, infantile activity, unworthy of
university students. But even so, she went to Praça da
Alfândega, stepped into the public fountain there, and put up
with the railleries of the idle onlookers. She came out of the
fountain shivering with cold, it was an exceptionally cool day
in March. I offered her my coat; after a brief hesitation, she
accepted it, and thus we struck up a friendship. The three of
us—she, Microbe, and I—would study anatomy together,
dissecting the same cadaver.

The morgue was a cold, gloomy, poorly lit place; the air,
saturated with vapors of formalin, stung our eyes. Such things
didn't bother Débora; scalpel in hand, she would dissect the
thorax and interpret the anatomical findings.

I couldn't keep my eyes off her. "Here's the upper chest
cavity," she would say, but my eyes weren't on the cavity,
they were fixed on her—did I love her? I didn't know. And
yet I kept staring at her. Which, incidentally, she seemed not
to notice; she took things seriously, was conscientious to a
fault, and worked hard, ignoring all banter. There were some
who wouldn't forgive her for being so bold as to be there
among men, wielding a scalpel—which, like knives and dag-

gers, is a male's prerogative. Thus the sniggering, the wise-cracks, the practical jokes—which once went way too far.

It was a rainy winter morning. Débora arrived, wearing a smart checkered coat; it was a new coat, and some of our fellow students made flattering remarks about it, although in my opinion, the coat looked more grotesque than elegant, but that's beside the point. She took off her coat, hung it on a hanger, put on her lab smock and set to work. Just before noon we completed that morning's assignment, which was the dissection of a foot; she went to the hanger, put her coat on. Suddenly, she noticed something; putting her hand into the pocket, she took out something that had been placed there.

A penis.

A huge penis from a cadaver, a good-sized rod, a stupendous prick; a tremendous chink stopper, a fine pecker, a magnificent pestle, a gigantic cock.

A silence fell upon the morgue, a tense silence. Her head bowed, she stood staring at the penis in her hand. Without a word, she laid it on the table; and then she looked at each one of us in turn. There was no anger in her gaze; sadness, yes; hurt feelings, maybe; but anger, no.

(I was angry; I was fuming. I should have leaped to her side: You cowards, aren't you ashamed, how can you do such a thing to a girl, whoever did this, step outside if you're man enough. But I didn't; why not? Perhaps because of an unwillingness to get involved in a quarrel that didn't—didn't it really?—concern me; perhaps because of fear; perhaps because of a sense of solidarity with the males in the class. Medicine, as everybody knew, wasn't for girls; why did she have to butt in where she was unwanted? Why didn't she stay in Bom Fim and marry a Jewish merchant? Why didn't she devote herself to raising children, like all other women? Anyhow, what those jerks did was vicious, wicked, loathsome.) When I came to my senses again, I realized that she was gone—and there I stood, perplexed, not knowing what to do next. Should I go after her? I didn't know. The fact is that I didn't go after her; I dithered, I took my time taking off my lab coat. Meanwhile I joined in the laughter, but unlike the others, I wasn't roaring with laughter, I wasn't laughing my head off, I wasn't splitting my sides with laughter; still, I was laughing at least a little, enough not to draw attention to myself, enough not to be excluded; and as soon as the others went back to their cadavers, I dashed out into the street, hoping against hope that I'd catch up with her. But she was nowhere to be seen, she was gone. I went back to the morgue and we—Microbe and I—began to dissect the lower chest cavity of a cadaver. "It serves her right," Microbe kept muttering, "a meddler, that's what she is." "Shut up," I said, and that was all: On that day, at least, that was the only thing I did to side with her.

D URING THE FOLLOWING WEEK PREPARATIONS FOR THE FRESH-men's Ball were under way. Débora wasn't going: "She doesn't have a date," said Microbe with a little laugh of derision—he *really* disliked her. On an impulse I decided I would be Débora's escort; I would proffer her my arm; together we would enter the brightly lit ballrooms of the Commerce Club. . . .

I spoke to her about it. "A ball?" She opened her eyes wide. And she blushed; for the first time I realized that deep down, this Jewish girl was shy, and I felt a rush of tenderness. But she soon reacted, said she wouldn't go—a ball, well, no, that was something for the smart set only. Noticing my annoyance, she amended herself, she didn't mean it, it hadn't been her intention to offend me; finally, resting her hand on my arm (a gesture that made me quiver; did I love her?), she said that yes, she would be delighted to go with me.

I prepared myself carefully for that ball. Like a general preparing himself for a major battle, like a politician preparing himself for a major pronouncement, but also like a lover preparing himself for a major conquest. I rented a tuxedo; I made arrangements for a taxi, a black Oldsmobile with glittering chrome work, an impressive automobile it was; I reserved a table at a restaurant, where we would dine after the ball. I had orchids delivered to her house. And so, on a balmy evening in April I went to pick her up. She lived on Avenida Cauduro, a side street with rows of dinky little houses, each one with a door and a window at the front. I had to wait for her under the suspicious gaze of her mother, a fat old Jewish woman, and her brothers, of whom there were quite a few, all of them snivelling. Finally, she appeared.

She didn't look dazzling, not by a long shot. She was wearing an unattractive dress, the orchids weren't pinned quite right, she hadn't had her hair done. And yet, she looked beautiful; she was smiling, and I couldn't help feeling moved (did I love her?). "I'm afraid we're late," I said rather awkwardly; we were indeed late, but the car took us in no time to the Commerce Club and a moment later we made our entrance into the ballroom, already packed with people.

In the eyes fixed on us I could detect: curiosity, sympathy, scorn, and perplexity, sometimes in combination: curiosity and sympathy, sympathy and perplexity. I couldn't care less whether or not they stared; let them stare and whisper. At least, that's what I kept repeating to myself as we slowly made our way across the hall: I couldn't care less. But did I really feel that I didn't give a damn? Probably not: I wasn't feeling absolutely self-confident, my mouth was dry, and the smile that I was determined to keep on my face at any cost had become a grimace. Anyhow, the orchestra started to play and we were soon dancing amid scores of other couples, and so we no longer drew attention to ourselves. Débora wasn't a good dancer: She kept treading on my toes and apologizing: "I'm not used to dancing." To make her less self-conscious, I steered the conversation into a different subject, medical school. And right away she began talking enthusiastically. "Medicine means everything to me," she declared, and proceeded to explain what she expected from a career in medicine—not wealth, as many of our fellow students did, nor higher social status; what she really wanted was to tread the road of science; she wanted the joy of a new medical breakthrough, and she wanted fame, too, but well-deserved fame. I was listening to her, but just barely, because her body pressed against mine had given me a hard-on; fellow student or not, Jewish or not, she was a woman, a beautiful woman, and I was falling in love, I was on the verge of falling in love, I was only a few centimeters, a few millimeters away from passion; I tried to hold her closer to me . . . Abruptly, she withdrew. "I don't like this sort of thing, Rafael," she said dryly, on her face an aggrieved expression. Self-consciously, I mumbled a vague apology and we continued to dance—apart—but I was then feeling irritated. Very well, so she doesn't like this sort of thing. And what is it that she likes then? Hm? What does this Jewess like? Not a good prick, one could see that. She must be a dyke all right, as Microbe had so aptly diagnosed. Or frigid. At the very least, frigid.

On the way back to her home neither of us spoke; on the following day, a Sunday, we didn't see each other; on Monday, however, when we ran into each other at the door of the morgue, she said she had to talk to me, so we went to a snack bar on Avenida Osvaldo Aranha for a cup of coffee. She started off by apologizing; it hadn't been her intention to hurt my feelings at the ball; however, she really had no intentions of having a boyfriend, at least not while she was attending medical school. She wanted to devote herself exclusively to her studies, to research work, and she hoped I would understand. I said that I understood, that everything was all right. That's what I said that morning while I stared, with my head lowered, at the tiny iridescent bubbles of coffee. I didn't want to raise my head; I didn't want to look at her; I was afraid to look at her; afraid I would find out that I *loved her*;* afraid I would plead with her; afraid I would cry. To cry right there, in front of her, in front of the bar owner, a fat Portuguese man wearing a torn T-shirt? Never. From my father, who had worked hard all his life, and who had died of tuberculosis, I had learned to be tough; stoic, at least. No, I wouldn't dissolve in tears.

She went on talking, seemingly unaware of my perturbation; as for myself, I was no longer listening. Finally, she said: "So, Rafael, will we remain friends?" And I got my wits about me and said that sure, we would remain friends.

And friends we remained. Ours was a cordial relationship, we would study together, take in a movie once in a while. On such occasions my arm sometimes brushed against hers; whether accidentally or not, it did, and the effect was electrifying—a thrill I both feared and desired; however, to her it was nothing, seemingly nothing. She would merely move her arm away. She wouldn't cringe or stiffen up, just move her arm away, without taking her eyes off the movie: "What a great actress, this Greta Garbo, isn't she, Rafael?" She would leave the movie theater sighing: "I hope I'll find fulfillment in medicine just as this woman has found self-fulfillment in the cinema." Débora had no other ambition, no other interest;

*Did I love her? (R.M.)

she barely took notice of what went on around her. One day we were downtown, when all of a sudden there was some unusual commotion, people began scurrying about, and groups of citizens were arguing at the top of their voices; and a moment later, the whole thing coalesced into a political rally: "Down with the oligarchies!" an inflamed orator was shouting. The Revolution of 1930 had just broken out. That's what I told Débora on the following day: "We have witnessed the outbreak of a revolution," I said. She shrugged: "I'm not interested, I've no use for revolutions; all I want is to become a great physician."

However, as time went by, it became harder and harder for her to make this burning desire materialize. Débora was not at all a brilliant student. Others were already beginning to stand out—Microbe, for instance, had already been invited by his professor of bacteriology to work with him after his graduation—whereas Débora wasn't even doing well in her coursework. Once she entered a competition to win a prize that a pharmaceutical laboratory was offering to medical students; her paper, a monography entitled *Calcium and Phosphorus: Some Considerations on their Role in the Metabolism of Human Beings*, was placed second to last. On the front page of the monograph, the chairman of the evaluation committee had remarked in his own handwriting: *The A.'s considerations are inadequate, inopportune, impertinent, inconsequential, irrelevant, and to a certain degree, immoral.* Débora didn't let such opinions, such failures, weigh her down; she attributed them to her being both female and Jewish. And she would soon come up with another idea, another project. During her first years in medical school, she had considered going into laboratory research; however, when we began our courses in clinical practice of medicine, a whole new horizon opened up for her, a horizon represented by patients—hundreds of them—scattered in the wards of a gloomy hospital. Such a wealth of pathological cases! Such an abundance of research material! What exotic diseases could explain the unrestrained moans, the emaciated faces, the edematous limbs? She would rush from one ward to the next, from one bed to the next, in search of the complex, of the transcendent; of the extraordinary, of the astonishing. Forever in search of rare cases, of peculiar syndromes, of freakish anomalies. Like Hellwig and Didonaeus, she, too, was in search of women who menstruated through their eyes; or through their ears (Spindler, Paullini,

Alibert); or through their mouths (Meimobius, Rhodius); or through their scars (McGraw). Cases of false pregnancies, like the ones documented by Weir Mitchell, fascinated her: A woman wanting very much to become pregnant sees her womb grow . . . and grow . . . and grow until "that great student of semiology—Time—rectifies the illusion, (Weir Mitchell). There is no baby! There is no pregnancy! The womb became distended for nothing, for nonsense! Queen Mary of England had been one such case.

Ah, if only she would come across an enormous ovarian cyst, like the one mentioned by Morand, from which 425 pounds of liquid were extracted over a period of ten months. And what about bodies that burst into flames? Taylor talked about spontaneous combustion in human beings: People catching fire while asleep, and then burning, without ever waking up, until finally they are reduced to cinders. Lord Bacon himself, a great humanist, had also made references to such facts.

Great, too, was her interest in teratology: Ah, if only she would come across a bifid or supernumerary tongue; teeth growing on a lower eyelid, like those mentioned by Carver; eyes with multiple pupils. In the absence of such things, she would be satisfied with interesting signs, such as the pulse of the water hammer, the dance of the arteries, Medusa's head, a sardonic smile, a leonine face, the hand of an obstetrician, some fingers holding a drumstick about to beat a drum, an equine foot, the flick of a fillip, the puff of breath in the peep of a seagull, the rhythm of galloping; a joint in a cogwheel, a geographical tongue, the bridge of a nose. Nothing.

D ID I LOVE HER? ONE DAY—WE WERE IN OUR FOURTH year—as I watched her auscultate a patient, I came to the painful conclusion that I loved her. Because of a strand of hair falling over her face, because of her lips, which were parted and slightly more moist than circumstances warranted, because of the graceful curve of her neck . . . Whatever the reason.

The fact is that I was still fond of her, indeed I was, notwithstanding the succession of girlfriends and lovers I had had. I remember heaving a deep sigh in that autumn afternoon; I remember an almost comatose patient opening his eyes wide, surprised at this sigh; I remember my embarrassment. But I also remember how much I loved her at that moment, and how much it hurt to love a woman who was not interested in me or in anyone else, a woman whose only desire was to devote herself to medicine and through it seek a fame that would certainly remain beyond her reach.

"Why do you have to ask such stupid questions, doctor?"

Brito, professor of Clinical Practice of Medicine, disliked Débora and he made no bones about letting her know.

"If you were to put greater effort into learning how to percuss instead of being interested in whatever is out of the ordinary, you'd do much better."

She would be furious; and when furious, even more beautiful. At least I thought so. Microbe thought she was ugly: A dyke. What other woman but a dyke would want to puncture, to cut, to sew up people; always trying to come up with some fancy diagnosis. *Professor Brito, we have here a case of Basedow-Graves's disease. Not at all, lady doctor, it's not a case of Basedow-Graves's disease, it's a case of simple colloid goiter; you know nothing, young lady, your place is at home, looking after domestic affairs.* She would storm out of the room in tears, slamming the door behind her. Some would laugh, others would glower, annoyed at the professor's rudeness (some of our fellow students were finally beginning to like her; besides, everybody in the class hated Brito). As for myself, I neither laughed nor glowered; I didn't know what to do; I loved her; I thought I did; but since my love was not returned, why should I stick my neck out to defend her? Maybe one day I would leap from my chair, yelling: *Take back your insulting remarks, you scoundrel*; maybe I would. But I always wavered for one second, or half a second, and then she was no longer in the room. One day it occurred to me that this minute fraction of time in fact stood for an insurmountable barrier, an abysmal moat between my loving her and my not loving her. I didn't love her, I concluded, or wanted to conclude. I didn't love her because I vacillated, because I wanted to reconcile love with convenience. I knew what convenience was, but love? What was love? In the fourth year I had made up my mind: I'd go into surgery. Thus

I opted for objectivity, for asepsis, for incisions made with a steady hand, and for dispassionate assessment. In the fifth year I changed my mind slightly: Orthopedics. Bones: hard and white, I liked the idea. Besides, wars and accidents had given a tremendous impetus to this specialization. Microbe, naturally, would devote himself to bacteriology, Frog wanted to become a neurologist, Afrânio would certainly work with his father, a famous general practitioner, Medonho would inherit his father's professorial chair, Veloso planned to practice surgery in Rio de Janeiro, Ambrósio had already been offered an administrative position with a hospital—in short, in the fifth year everybody already knew what he was going to do, that is, everybody except Débora, who still didn't know because of that terrible need of hers for self-assertion, a need that made her scramble frantically from ward to ward: A case of Fallot's disease! A case of a kidney shaped like a horseshoe! A case of this, a case of that; research this, research that; and everybody laughing at her. The intensity of her obsession would even frighten her: "Am I crazy, Rafael? Tell me, do you think I'm crazy?" I didn't know what to say, but Microbe had no doubts about it: "She's daffy, Rafael, nutty as a fruitcake."

We graduated and she still didn't know what she would be doing. She didn't want to set herself up as a practitioner; she couldn't go to another country because of her mother; neither the interior nor the suburbs appealed to her. And she wouldn't give up her aspirations to engage in research, to have her work published. Then, without pay, she started to work in a hospital ward, whose director had ambitions similar to hers. Right away, they decided to experiment with a new drug, imported from Argentina, to treat high blood pressure. Thirty-five patients were selected for the experiment, and the initial results showed that the medication was effective; however, this drug—a hormone by-product—had a disturbing side effect: feminization. Old cowboys began to develop large breasts and voluptuous curves. After the attempted suicide of one of the patients, the experiment had to be interrupted, which didn't really disappoint Débora: A preliminary report that she had presented at a meeting of the ward's medical staff had been well received. Her other experiments, however, weren't successful. At one time she worked with a doctor who tried to extract diuretic substances from aquatic plants—without success. Then she worked together with another colleague, who envisioned lighting up the human body with searchlights of the kind used in the war and making a diagnosis by examining the shadows projected by the organs. This experiment ended in failure. As did all the others: Using intra-abdominal balloons, whose insufflation could be regulated, to lift sagging organs: a flop. A chamber of rarified air for the treatment of tuberculosis: a flop. Severely burned patients kept afloat by means of balloons filled with hydrogen: a flop. Injections of extract of the cartilage of small rodents to treat arthritic conditions: a flop. Nothing worked, nothing succeeded; nothing, nothing. Each failure plunged her into deeper depression. It was then that she met Kurt Schnitzel.

German by birth, Kurt had emigrated to Brazil in the early thirties. He set up a repair shop in Porto Alegre for medical equipment: sphygmomanometers, spirometers, electrocardiographs. A big hunk of a man, almost two meters tall, with a booming, stentorian voice and a Pantagruelian appetite, Kurt had an unusual talent for working with electric and mechanical gadgets. Not only could he fix, adapt, or improve any machine, he could also invent gadgets for the most disparate purposes. He had devised and built a mechanical heart, a complex machine to treat cardiac insufficiency. It worked like this: The beats of the diseased heart, collected by the chest piece of a stethoscope (A) applied to the patient's chest, would alter the pressure inside a system of rubber tubes (B), thereby activating an accelerator of high precision (C), which would then inject the right amount of gasoline into the internal combustion engine (D), which in turn would set in motion the pistons of the pump. The blood of the patient, which had been initially diverted to a flask (E), was then reinjected into the patient by means of the pump (F).

Débora watched as the machine was being put to the test. She saw a dog, which had suffered sudden and acute cardiac insufficiency after being injected with an almost lethal amount of quinidine, recover quickly; soon the dog was barking cheerfully. There was no longer any doubt in her mind: It was an invention that would revolutionize medicine. She decided to use the mechanical heart on a twelve-year-old boy who suffered from a serious form of rheumatic cardiopathy; the boy had been given up as incurable by various physicians, including professor Brito, who had sent him home to die. Débora hoped she would at least be able to keep him alive. The experiment, however, ended in disaster, due to an unfortunate circumstance. On the appointed day, Kurt fell ill; the assistant who replaced him got mixed up, he confused the rubber tubes of the gas tank with the tubes of the flask of blood. So, instead of blood, the machine pumped about three liters of gasoline into the boy, who died instantly. In his attempt to stop the apparatus, the young man struck it with a small iron sledgehammer; the sparks caused a fire that razed the entire ward and charred the corpse. Débora managed to clear herself in the inquiry that was held—the young man declared that the patient was already dead when he was hooked to the machine—but she became so depressed that she had to be hospitalized in a psychiatric clinic. "This will put an end to her crazy ideas," Microbe assured me. He was wrong. When Débora was discharged from the hospital, she had a new project, which was the direct result of her being in contact with the mental patients: "The future of medicine lies in psychiatry," she assured me with confidence. Having read extensively on the subject, she now intended to devote herself to psychoanalysis, still a novelty in that year, 1935. She was eager to go to Buenos Aires, where she would look up a Dr. Ernesto Finkelman—a Jew, naturally; everybody was then saying that psychoanalysis had to do with Jews—in order to initiate herself into the secrets of his specialty. Her mother, who had never lost faith in her daughter, sold the few jewels she owned, and so, one day in November 1935, Débora left for Buenos Aires.

I T WAS WITH A CERTAIN ANXIETY THAT I SAW DÉBORA OFF AT the railroad station. In what kind of a muddle would she find herself next? This psychoanalysis thing reminded me of cabala, of magic. And it stirred something inside me. Why? Cabala—what did I have to do with cabala? I didn't know, then. But I was disturbed.

In Buenos Aires, Débora looked up Dr. Finkelman. He received her coldly; when Débora said that she would like to get professional training in psychoanalysis, he told her that there was no such thing, that there were no courses or anything like that that people could take. If Débora wanted to become a psychoanalyst, she would have to undergo analysis herself, a long, difficult process. His words felt like a cold shower, but Débora didn't let herself feel disheartened; right away, she decided:

"Then I would like to be analyzed by you."

Finkelman smiled, with a superior air:

"By me? Impossible. I'm booked solid for the next three years."

She couldn't believe what she heard:

"Have I then come all the way from Porto Alegre for nothing?"

"Buenos Aires is a city with plenty of attractions. I'm sure you'll find ways of amusing yourself."

He wanted to put an end to this interview—they were at the headquarters of the Medical Association, where he was scheduled to give a lecture—but Débora wasn't going to give up. She took him by the arm:

"Will you refer me then to someone else?"

He extricated himself free:

"I know of no one who could help you: There aren't many analysts here in Buenos Aires. Why don't you try New York? Many European analysts have been heading for that city, fleeing from the Nazis."

"New York?" said Débora, desperate. "But I don't know any English, doctor!"

The man shrugged:

"I'm very sorry. I'm afraid there's nothing else I can say."

Anyone else would have given up and returned to Porto Alegre; not Débora, though. On the following day there she was, seated on a bench in a public square, right in front of the building where Finkelman had his office. She wasn't quite sure why she was there, but she hoped that an idea would strike her. Resentfully she sat looking at the ugly, gray façade extravagantly decorated. Caryatids, griffins, sphinxes—but what were they supposed to be, anyway? What did those figures with their clearly threatening expressions represent? She shrank in her overcoat, lit a cigarette. In Porto Alegre she never smoked in public; but in Buenos Aires and under the circumstances, she didn't give a damn.

A black limousine pulled up in front of the building. The

chauffeur leaped out and rushed to open the back door. Finkelman hurried into the building. A moment later lights went on on the fourth floor, where he had his office. All she could see from the public square was a bowl-shaped lighting fixture made of chrome-plated metal. She couldn't see Finkelman, or what he was doing with his patients. It was indeed a mystery, psychoanalysis. Débora sighed.

It was then that she noticed the For Rent sign on the fifth floor. Which gave her an idea. She went to the real estate agency, and after ascertaining that the empty suite was located exactly above Finkelman's office, she rented it. Then she went to a hardware store to buy a flashlight, a hammer, a chisel; at nightfall, she went into the building. There were no lights on in Finkelman's office—he had already left, which suited her just fine.

Shunning the elevator, she climbed up the old stairway; as she stealthily opened the door, her heart was pounding, not just from exertion but also from emotion. Switching on the flashlight, she looked around. Two adjoining rooms, empty: completely bare of furniture. Nothing but old newspapers and cardboard boxes.

Sitting down on the dusty floor, Débora unfolded the floorplan with which the real estate agency had provided her, and it showed not only her floor but Finkelman's as well. With the help of a tape measure, she determined the exact location of the lighing fixture in Finkelman's office. And then she set to work. With the hammer and the chisel she managed to pry off a few parquet blocks, and then she proceeded to bore a hole in the floor. The cement slab wasn't very thick and soon she succeeded. She wasn't worried about the debris, they dropped into the bowl of the ugly lighting fixture. Finkelman's taste in decoration was terrible, but quite providential under these circumstances.

When the hole was ready, she carefully rounded its edges and then obliterated it with a bung painted in white. Unless the psychoanalyst was in the habit of studying the ceiling, he would never notice a thing. Satisfied with her work, she returned to her hotel.

Quite early next morning she was already at her post, peeping through the hole. Finkelman was late; she was chainsmoking, and getting impatient: Why didn't he keep to his schedule, this distinguished gentleman? Could he afford the luxury of sleeping in? At long last the door opened:

Finkelman walked in. Crooning softly to himself, he took off his overcoat, hung it in the closet, sat down in an armchair, and began to read the newspaper. Fifteen minutes later the doorbell rang. He got up and answered the door. It was a patient; obviously a patient; a young man, very agitated. He came in, barely greeted Finkelman, and lay down on the couch. There he remained, with his mouth half open, staring at the ceiling. For a moment Débora was afraid that he would notice the hole—but no, the young man was looking at nothing; glassy-eyed, he stared vacantly. And he was silent. Once in a while he sighed but didn't say a word.

A quarter of an hour went by like this. Débora was growing more and more intrigued: What kind of treatment is this? They don't speak, they don't do anything—where is this great scientific novelty? She was beginning to feel anxious, not just for the patient, who was unable to speak, but also for the doctor (what a waste of time), when the young man finally stirred on the couch:

"I smell," he said in a strangled voice, "something burning."

Finkelman remained silent.

"I smell something burning," the patient repeated.

Finkelman still silent.

"Quite pronounced, this smell," persisted the young man.

Finkelman cleared his throat:

"Last week," he finally said, "it was a rotten taste in your mouth. Now, a smell of something burning. Rotten, burned; burned, rotten. Let's consider the implications, Juan. What is turning rotten? What is burning?"

The young man, restless, was squirming on the couch like an eel. All of a sudden, Finkelman leaped to his feet:

"By golly, there is indeed a smell of something burning!"

Only then did Débora notice: Engrossed in the psychoanalytical session, she had forgotten about the lit cigarette, and it had set the old newspapers on fire! Jumping to her feet, she quickly extinguished the flames with her coat, then tore down the stairs—one second before Finkelman came out of his office, shouting for help.

The incident had its beneficial aspect. Débora (enough of hair-raising experiences! enough of fires!) felt it was high time she developed some common sense; which she did. Upon returning to Porto Alegre she began, like any other physician, to frequent the wards of the Public Charity Hospital, where she would discuss cases, assist in operations, deliver babies. For she had made up her mind: She would move to the interior, together with her mother. The old woman didn't like the idea; she even came to see me, requesting that I have a word with Débora, that I try to talk her out of this idea. But there was nothing I could do. Besides, I didn't want to get involved. My life seemed to be on the right track; I was engaged to Alzira, a good girl from a traditional family: Her father was an influential person in state politics, a personal friend of Getúlio Vargas, the President of the Republic. Well, in a small, provincial town such as Porto Alegre was in those days, my friendship with Débora was looked upon with spiteful suspicion. I always made a point of saying that we were nothing but colleagues. And that's what I said to Débora's mother: "We're just colleagues, ma'am, I cannot interfere in your daughter's life."

Débora came to my wedding. When she appeared at the door of the reception hall, alone, with that forlorn expression of hers, anxiously glancing around her, I felt a lump in my throat: It was now too late for hesitations—or for hopes, which might or might not be fulfilled; our paths had now definitely diverged. I hoped from the bottom of my heart that she would look at me mockingly so that I could hate her; so that I could compare her Semitic features, her wishy-washy appearance, with the aristocratic bearing of my bride Alzira; so that I could say, without any remorse, without any of that sour grapes feeling, go away, you Jewess, make yourself scarce, you dyke, disappear from my life once and for all, you worthless creature. But she didn't; with a disarming expression, she wished us happiness and said goodbye: She was leaving for the interior that same night. Keep in touch, I said, my voice sounding so strangled and strange that Alzira stared at me, wondering. Saying that of course she would keep in touch, Débora left.

Upon returning from my honeymoon there was a letter from her already waiting. She was living in a small town located in the region of the former mission settlements: ". . . Mother and I live in a small house on the top of a hill. A beautiful panorama unfolds before my bedroom window, at which I now sit writing—there's a meadow, where cows graze placidly, and in the background, the ruins of São Tolentino's Church, which belonged to the mission settlements built by the Jesuits. A beautiful view, but I must tell you, a tranquil landscape is not what I was after. What I'd really like to do is to frequent hospitals; to study, do research, publish papers, attend conferences. But here, I don't even have anyone I can talk to. My friends are the pharmacist, the school principal, and the priest, who is an intelligent, learned man. But there's plenty of work to keep me busy. My waiting room is always full of patients, and I handle everything: general practice, surgery, obstetrics. The people here really like me. At first they would look at me askance; to them, a doctor, particularly a doctor practicing in the interior, had to be a man. A woman, and Jewish to boot, was inadmissible! Then they got used to me, and now they won't take a step without first consulting with me. Even the mayor, who doesn't like women, respects me. And Mother is happy. . . ."

AFTER THE WEDDING, MY LIFE SETTLED INTO A PLEASANT routine: In the morning I operated; in the afternoon I saw patients at my office. Two or three times a week I went to my club to play cards with friends, but this was not a matter of discord between me and the sweet Alzira. On Saturdays, a party or a dance.

So everything was fine—and yet, there was this strange feeling: a certain emptiness, a certain anguish. All of a sudden I was struck by the urge to study—history, philosophy—and I would spend hours shut up in my study, leafing through books written by obscure authors. Until then I had never been much of a reader; my friends were amused. "You're turning into a doddering old man before your time," Microbe would say.

But life was peaceful. We celebrated our first wedding anniversary with an intimate dinner attended by relatives and friends. Before taking his leave, my father-in-law took me aside; then, after hesitating for a moment—he was by nature reserved, this typical frontier gaucho—he announced that he was very pleased with me:

"You're making my daughter happy, Rafael. I admit that

there was a time when I had some misgivings about this marriage. What with all that gossip about you and that colleague of yours, that Jewish woman . . . Nonsense, but it did upset me. If you had made Alzira miserable, I would have killed you, Rafael. Upon my word, I would have, Rafael. But now I'm no longer worried. And I have a present for you.''

H E HANDED ME A THICK ENVELOPE. IT CONTAINED AN ADvance copy of the government's Gazette, which would be in circulation on the following day. And listed there was my appointment as Head of the Department of Communicable Diseases of the state of Rio Grande do Sul. Puzzled, I looked at him.

"It was Doutor Getúlio himself who authorized the appointment," he said, pleased. "I've been pulling strings for quite some time . . . But I never said anything to you. I wanted it to be a surprise."

I didn't know what to say. Choosing my words carefully, trying to be as tactful as possible so as not to hurt his feelings, I said that this position wasn't suited to an orthopedist; also, I was already very busy; besides, I didn't need a job, I was making good money with my own practice. With a gesture, he dismissed my reasoning:

"I know how busy you are, but you won't even have to go there, everything has been taken care of: There's someone there who will be looking after things. It's an important position; besides, it will provide security for a rainy day."

"But—"

He closed his face.

"Let's not discuss it anymore, Rafael. Tomorrow you go there and take office, they'll be waiting for you." Alzira came up to them, he smiled at her: "I was telling your husband some good news, my daughter."

He took his leave. I told Alzira the news; she listened without being impressed, for she was quite used to her father's impulsive acts of generosity:

"He's a very kind man. People like him are a rarity nowadays."

The following morning I went to the Department of Communicable Diseases, which was located in an old mansion on Rua Duque de Caxias, near Praça da Matriz, not too far from my own office. All the government functionaries were waiting for my arrival; as I came in, they broke into applause, which rather embarrassed me; however, I was also pleasantly surprised—I had never been applauded before. I greeted them one by one, the old bureaucrats and the smiling secretaries, as well as the two physicians—Artêmio, an elderly man nearing retirement; and Raul Castellar, a well-known bon vivant who spent his days playing snooker and had no other job on the side. After I was shown into my office, they brought me some papers to sign—nothing of any consequence; when I was through with signing, the administrative officer said:

"That's all, doctor. You're free now."

On the following day it was the same thing; and so it was on all the succeeding days. My father-in-law was right: The job was no sweat and it made no demands on my time. And it gave me prestige: During Getúlio Vargas's next visit to our state, I was one of the officials that had been invited to welcome him, and my photograph appeared on the front page of the newspapers. As for the communicable diseases—well, they were taken care of by old Dr. Artêmio, a taciturn, cantankerous man but a highly competent sanitarian, totally devoted to his work in the department. He attended to everything: He investigated all cases of contagious diseases, visited hospitals and health clinics, traveled to the interior whenever necessary, often driving his own jalopy. It was rumored that he was a communist. I didn't care what he was. As long as he found solutions to problems, I saw nothing wrong with him. Besides, I had no intentions of getting embroiled in politics.

Everything was fine. On January 1, 1936 my little Rafael was born. We were at my father-in-law's farm, where we had gone to spend New Year's Day. Soon after midnight, Alzira began to feel pains. Fortunately a physician who practiced in that region, a competent obstetrician, was a guest at the farmhouse; labor progressed with no incidents, and at sunrise there was the boy, howling. What a joy! To celebrate the birth, my father-in-law invited four hundred people to a *churrasco,* an outdoor barbecue party; we even got a telegram of congratulations from Getúlio Vargas.

Everything was fine. Was it? In Spain a civil war was raging, and people were saying it was a prelude to a world war. In Brazil, after the failure of the communist uprising of 1935, Getúlio Vargas began to consolidate his position, but in many states—including his native Rio Grande do Sul—people were conspiring to overthrow his government. None of these things concerned me, of course, and everything could indeed be fine—however, not everything was. There were sensations, forebodings, strange happenings. "What's this song you keep singing to lull little Rafael to sleep?" Alzira asked me one day. I didn't know what to say, I didn't know where it came from: *Duerme, duerme, mi angelico/ hijico chico de tu nación.* I was then reading voraciously; reading and working. Performing operations provided me with a diversion; there was something comforting, soothing, about a white bone emerging from the gory flesh.

One night I came home to find Alzira worried.

"Dad phoned. He wants you to go to his house right away. He has some urgent business to discuss with you."

I was tired and hungry; my first reaction was to send the old man to the devil; but I couldn't, obviously. I took the car and drove to his house.

The silent manservant showed me into my father-in-law's study. There I found him, not seated in his favorite armchair but standing on his feet, talking to his friend Doutor Saturnino, a wealthy rancher from the region of the former mission settlements, a great-grandson of the notorious Picucha, the Cutthroat; upon seeing me, the worried expression on my father-in-law's face cleared up somewhat:

"Ah, there you are. I'm glad you came, Rafael. Sit down, do sit down. It's Saturnino here who's having a problem."

Without a word, the rancher handed me a newspaper clipping. SQUATTERS VOW TO PUT UP A FIGHT, read the headline: A group of Indians—men, women, and children—led by a white man were squatting on Doutor Saturnino's lands and they refused to budge.

"And what is it that they want?" I asked.

"The land," replied my father-in-law. "They claim it's theirs, that it's been theirs ever since the days of the Jesuits. That they've been expelled, and that they're now back to reclaim their land. And that they'll only leave dead."

"This is what they say?"

"What this white man says. He's their spokesman."

"And who is he?"

"Well, that's the point. Nobody knows. Probably a rabble-rouser; a communist, for sure. They haven't yet learned their lesson from the recent communist revolt."

"The problem, Dr. Rafael," Saturnino cut in, "is that it wasn't the Indians themselves who started all this. This is a snake that someone has deliberately planted, my dear doctor. It's not just me that they want to hurt; they are after Doutor Getúlio, who is a personal friend of mine. And they know he is."

"They who?" I asked. I didn't like this at all; it boded no good, it looked like a real imbroglio, and I wanted no part in it, I didn't want to get entangled at all.

"*They*. Those people, here, in Rio, in São Paulo, who are conspiring to overthrow Getúlio." Saturnino, a short-tempered man, could barely control himself.

"But I don't see . . ."

"Where you come in?" It was my father-in-law. "Simple, Rafael: According to the latest reports that we've received, some of these people are ill. And it's apparently something contagious. All you have to do is to order that they be sent to the Isolation Hospital, and then you make the hospital off limits to the press."

Which would require that the Brigade be called in, of course. No, I didn't like this at all. I tried to find a way out:

"But are they really ill? Rumors sometimes—"

"That's the information we've received. Of course, you'll have to go there in order to find out for sure."

"Me?"

That was all I needed: To leave my patients, the hospital. However, it wasn't the right time to argue about such details. "Leave it to me," I said. I already knew how to solve this problem. I would dispatch the discreet and efficient Dr. Artêmio to the scene.

On the following day, I sent for him as soon as I arrived at the Department. The secretary looked up at me, surprised:

"But didn't you know, sir? Dr. Artêmio doesn't come in anymore. He has retired."

"What?"

"That's right: He has retired. You yourself okayed his application for retirement, don't you remember?"

Well, this came as a total surprise. What should I do? I couldn't entrust the irresponsible Raul with this mission. I made a decision. I sent for the chauffeur:

"Do you know where Dr. Artêmio lives?"

"Yes, sir."

"Then let's go there."

It was a modest house near Ponta da Cadeia. Dr. Artêmio, in his pajamas, was sitting in the verandah, reading a newspaper—exactly what one would expect a retired person to do. He didn't give me a chance to address him first:

"I know what brings you here: those squatters."

"Yes, I'd like you . . ."

"I won't go there."

"Listen, Artêmio—"

"*Doctor* Artêmio," he said dryly. "Retirement doesn't invalidate my degree."

Why this sudden aggressiveness in a man usually courteous? I tried to appeal to his noble sentiments:

"But some of those people there are sick. We're in a desperate situation. . . ."

"You are. I'm not. I'm sitting here in my pajamas, relaxing like any other pensioner."

"But . . ."

He folded the newspaper. "Well, I can see I won't be able to read in peace." Taking off his glasses, he fixed his eyes on me:

"Listen, young man. I'm going to tell you something: I've been in this business of public health ever since my graduation in nineteen fifteen. I've crisscrossed this country. I worked with Oswaldo Cruz on his campaign to eliminate yellow fever and bubonic plague. I was one of the very first doctors ever to go to the Amazon Region to fight malaria. I devised a plan to control the disease caused by tropical parasitic flatworms, and another plan to control Chagas's disease. I've received awards for my work in Public Health, I ended up here in Rio Grande do Sul; you know—or should know—that I worked hard until my very last day. Well, during all those thirty years I was never promoted to department head. I was always pushed aside because of political protegés like yourself. But now I no longer have to put up with this sort of thing, understand? I've had it. Therefore, do me a favor, will you, get the hell out of here so that I can read my newspaper in peace."

"Well, there's no need to fly off the handle." I was trying to take it as a joke. "After all, this is not something that—"

He leaped to his feet. He was shaking:

"Get out!" "But, doctor—"

"Get out, do you hear me? Get the hell out of here or I'll set my dog on you!"

I left.

"The little man sure flew into a temper," remarked the chauffeur, who had witnessed the incident. But I barely listened, worried as I was about how to get out of this tangle. At the hospital I got a phone call from my father-in-law:

"I thought you were already on your way, Rafael."

"Take it easy. This thing can't be too—"

"It is, Rafael. A very serious thing! I was downtown a while ago. The squatters are the talk of the town. The matter has now become a political issue, Rafael."

I hung up. I had an operation scheduled for that morning but I cancelled it. There was no other way: I would have to go to Doutor Saturnino's ranch. On my way home, though, a news item I heard on the car radio was to change the course of events. *Drastically*, as I was to find out later. According to the news, the squatters had entrenched themselves in the ruins of the old São Tolentino's Church, which was located on Saturnino's land. I was immediately reminded of Débora's letter, the one in which she said she could see the ruins from her house; and it occurred to me that I could ask her to investigate the situation there. So, I drove to the Governmental Palace, where I found the Director of the State Health Department and several aides of the *interventor*, the temporary state governor appointed by the President of the Republic as his direct agent—they were all worried: Getúlio Vargas himself had phoned from Rio, wanting to know what was going on. I reassured them: I already had the situation under control.

Communications with the region of the mission settlements were difficult, but using the radio transmitter of the Governmental Palace, I succeeded in getting hold of Débora through the garrison of the Brigade. Yes, of course, she had heard about the situation. No, she hadn't been there; nobody had sent for her. If she could go there and examine the sick people? Sure. She would do so right away and then report back on the situation.

"But be careful," I warned. "I understand they're armed."

She laughed: "A woman still commands respect in Rio

Grande do Sul," she said, "and even more so if she happens to be a doctor too."

Then I went to my office; in my state of worry, indeed of anxiety, I didn't attend to my patients properly. At six P.M. the phone rang; it was from the Governmental Palace: There was a message for me from the lady doctor. So I went there, and read the message that a captain had written down: "Among the ruins, she came upon a makeshift tent—inside, on the floor, seventeen corpses of Indians, men, women, and children—some still warm, suggesting sudden death—bluish and yellow blotches on their faces, chests, arms—one person, a white man, is alive—"

Soon afterward the radiotelegraph operator reestablished contact with the garrison at São Tolentino. Débora wanted to speak to me. Her voice sounded very excited over the earphones: She would be driving to Porto Alegre, and she would bring the patient, the white man, with her—she wanted to study this case carefully, it was certainly an exceedingly rare situation, possibly a new disease, something worthy of being published:

"It could well bring us fame, Rafael!"

Fame. Well, now, things were really getting complicated. How stupid of me to have brought Débora into this case. As if I didn't know that something unpredictable or crazy was bound to happen whenever she was involved. Sighing, I removed the earphones. They were all looking at me: my father-in-law, Saturnino, the politicians, the top military men. "The situation is like this," I began, then stopped short. How to tell friends from enemies in that room? I didn't know; all I knew was that I was treading on a minefield, I would have to watch my step. I put the message into my pocket: "Everything is under control," I said. Then they began to leave; finally, only the ones I could really trust remained: my father-in-law, Saturnino, and a couple of other people. To them I relayed Débora's message.

"But isn't she that Jewish doctor?" My father-in-law creased his forehead. "Did you entrust her with this task?"

"Débora practices medicine there," I retorted. "And as for her ability to handle this situation, I have no doubts whatsoever."

Suspicious, he stared at me, but said nothing. We then began to discuss the situation. We all agreed that it was indeed a serious matter and that it should be kept secret. I ordered that an entire ward of the Isolation Hospital be blocked off; the patient—we only knew his nickname, Redhead—would stay there, watched round the clock by soldiers from the Brigade. And then we waited.

It wasn't until the following night that Débora finally arrived. The trip had been ghastly: the car had stalled several times on the flooded roads; the patient, in a state of agitation, had to be tied; even so, he had bitten her in the hand, and the bite, fairly serious, had almost prevented her from driving. Fortunately, a soldier from the Brigade had come with her, which had been a blessing.

She had driven straight to the Isolation Hospital, from where I got a phone call informing me of her arrival. I went to the hospital; I found her exhausted, disheveled, but radiant with joy: "A really beautiful case, Rafael, a great scientific opportunity."

I hugged her. We hugged each other. Colleagues, finally; and friends. But I tried to press her tightly against me; or I think I did; and she resisted slightly; or I think she did; yes, she did; there were people watching us, the soldier from the Brigade. But maybe that wasn't the reason why she extricated herself from my arms; maybe it was something in herself (a dyke? a potential dyke?). Maybe the reason was the patient, who was still on the back seat of the car, tied and apparently unconscious; a stocky young man, who looked German. I ordered that he be taken to the ward right away. Débora had requests of her own:

"I want the best possible care for him. And all the tests that are necessary."

She, in charge of this patient? It struck me as rather inconvenient. But it was not the right moment to argue, so I decided I would talk about something else. I asked her where she would like to stay:

"I could find you a room in a hotel."

She looked at me in disbelief:

"A hotel, Rafael? You must be kidding. I'm staying right here at the hospital. I want to follow this case minute by minute."

I was taken aback. Upset, I tried to reason with her, pointing out the lack of comfort at the hospital, a rundown old building, where only the destitute ever went. But she brushed off my arguments. She would stay there:

"Ask them to place a cot by his bed, will you?"

"But, Débora, a cot by a patient's bed, whoever heard of such a thing? What if his illness is contagious?"

She shrugged, smiling:

"It *is* contagious, Rafael. There's no doubt in my mind. But if I'm destined to catch it, I must already have caught it. Don't forget, he has even bitten me."

She held up her bandaged hand. She was absolutely unconcerned about the danger; she was like a little girl playing with her favorite toy.

"But, Débora—"

She was pushing me away:

"Go, now, Rafael. Go home. Leave it to me, I'll look after the patient."

There was no other way. So I instructed that the man be taken to his sickroom and that the hospital staff comply with the lady doctor's requests. Right away she gave them some instructions and ordered some tests.

The following morning I returned to the hospital rather worried. The first news broadcast of the day had reported on the disappearance of the Indians; there was speculation that they had either left the place or hidden themselves in the nearby woods; no mention was made of either the deaths or Redhead. The matter was, of course, an open secret; but I was hoping that time would be on my side, and that the whole thing would deflate on its own.

The difficulty was holding Débora back. She wanted medical examinations; she wanted the opinion of other physicians; she wanted to discuss the case the way we used to in medical school. Tactfully, I tried to make her see that we weren't faced with an academic situation, that there were certain connotations. . . . Impatiently, she cut me short:

"I'm not interested in connotations, Rafael. You've promised to help me, and you're going to keep your promise."

We went to have a look at the patient. There he was, strapped to the bed, apparently in a deep coma, receiving serum and oxygen.

"I don't know if we have much time left," she said. "In all the other cases death came quickly. I'd like to come up with a diagnosis while he's still alive. And I'd like to cure him, if possible."

I sighed:

"So, what is it that you need?"

She handed me a sheet of paper with a new and long list of

tests. I looked at her, then sighed again: None of them could be carried out at the hospital. Outside technicians and radiologists would have to be called in: more people to learn about the case. No, there was no way I could keep this case under wraps.

"All right. I'll make the necessary arrangements. By the way, Débora, you know, don't you, this hospital has its own medical staff. . . ."

"I'm not interested, Rafael. It's my case, I'll see it through. If you want to help me, fine. If not, I'll continue on my own."

"Listen, Débora . . ."

I explained the situation to her, all the events of the last few hours; I ended up by saying that she would have to shoulder the responsibility for whatever happened. She smiled:

"Trust me, Rafael. I can't make head or tail of these political things, but if they depend on a diagnosis, leave it to me. Poisoning, well, that's a good one. If Renard were here, he would be tickled to death. Poisoning, indeed!"

There was a knock on the door. It was the man from the laboratory with the results of the tests that had been carried out in the hospital. She skimmed through the results:

"Everything normal."

Disappointed? No. The results didn't contradict her assumptions. On the contrary, they reinforced her theory that she was dealing with a new disease:

"If it were something known, these routine tests would have told us. Wouldn't you say so, Rafael?"

I didn't want to express an opinion; as a matter of fact, what I wanted was the presence of some other colleagues, of people who were more experienced, and particularly more levelheaded. Débora, however, wouldn't budge on the stand she had initially taken:

"I'll discuss this case with the professors at the Faculty of Medicine. As soon as I have gathered all the facts. I'll be spending the rest of the morning in the library, looking up things to update the bibliography. And I'll write up the material this afternoon."

I had a scheduled operation, but I decided I would stop home first. Alzira was waiting for me, peeved:

"Where have you been? I was getting worried."

Then I realized: I had forgotten to let her know.

"I'm sorry, Alzira. I worked all night."

"With that lady doctor?" she asked, cross.

That was all I needed: jealousy.

"For heavens' sake, Alzira—"

Just then the phone rang. I answered it: It was Doutor Saturnino. An idea had just occurred to him: Why not have the patient transferred to São Paulo or Rio, on the pretext of providing him with better medical facilities? It was a good suggestion, but Débora would never agree to it. And the reporter from that newspaper *Alerta* would raise a squawk. Saturnino was displeased:

"If it were up to me, I'd take this devil out of here," he said, ill-tempered.

Calmly yet firmly, I stated that it was my prerogative to decide on this matter, which irritated him even further. Well, let him be irritated: I couldn't care less.

Anyhow, it would be better to share this responsibility with someone else. Knowing that Débora would be away from the hospital the following morning, I decided to take advantage of this opportunity to bring in Brito—physician to the big shots—to examine the patient. I phoned him; he agreed right away. We decided on ten o'clock next morning. At ten I was already at the hospital. Brito, however, was late as usual; when he finally showed up, he couldn't examine the patient. Débora, who had just then returned from the Faculty of Medicine, burst into the sickroom in a fury:

"May I ask what you're doing here, sir?"

"Me?" asked Brito, no less irritated. "I'm here at the request of Dr. Rafael Mendes, head of the Department of Communicable Diseases, to which this hospital is related. And you, madam, may I ask you what you're doing here?"

"I'm the physician in charge of this case. Didn't Rafael inform you, professor?"

No, I hadn't, and now there was this muddle. To my surprise, however, Débora controlled herself: She said that she was ready to report on the case at the next session on clinical practice at the Faculty of Medicine, and that she had thought of talking to Professor Brito about this matter; therefore, it would be wonderful if he were willing to examine her patient—she would be delighted. But no, there was no way Brito was going to examine the patient now. Glancing at me reproachfully, he picked up his hat and left, but not before fixing on a day for Débora's presentation: the following morning.

I was getting increasingly worried, but Débora was jubilant—just what she had been waiting for, a meeting with the professors of the Faculty of Medicine, with the cream of the medical practitioners in Rio Grande do Sul:

"I've read everything I could find on the subject, Rafael, and I'm now absolutely convinced: It's a new disease, no doubt about it."

Defiant, she stood smiling, her eyes fixed on me. Such was the degree of my desire for her at that moment that I quivered. But what was it, anyway? Love? Once more I shrank away from this disturbing question.

"All right, Débora. Go ahead. But I don't want to hear any complaints later."

I was about to leave, but she held me by the arm:

"Don't you want to examine the patient?"

As a matter of fact, I didn't. It wasn't my specialty, he wasn't my patient; why should I get even more involved than I already was? Besides, there was that nagging suspicion that it was a contagious disease, and I was in a hurry. But with Débora's hand on my arm . . . It wasn't an affectionate press of the hand: I wished it were, but it wasn't; perhaps there was an affectionate component in the way she pressed my arm, but it was mostly a forceful, commanding gesture: Examine him!

I examined the patient. Quickly and reluctantly. I found nothing.

"I don't know what's wrong with him."

She smiled:

"That was rather quick."

I felt like saying something cruel in reply: That she could spare me her opinions, that I knew how to examine a patient, that I was experienced in examining patients, and in many other things which she knew only from hearsay, like screwing, for instance. But I controlled myself and even managed to smile:

"You're right. But as a matter of fact . . ."

I interrupted myself: My eyes were on her cot, still unmade, where she had slept—fully dressed? in a nightgown? naked?—next to a stranger. I didn't see any generosity in her behavior; what I did see was shamelessness, something one would expect of a hooker or a dyke.

"As a matter of fact, I'm in a hurry," I said dryly. "Is there anything else that you need?"

She asked me to inform her mother that she was fine, and that her patients should see the doctor in the neighboring town: It was an arrangement that had worked well on previous occasions.

I left. At the entrance to the hospital I was accosted by a shabby young man with a little mustache and a cheeky air.

"Dr. Rafael? I'm a reporter. . . ."

Well, it had started then. "I'm in a hurry," I said and got into the car. He hung on to the door, preventing me from closing it.

"If I were you, sir, I wouldn't be in such a big hurry to get away. My newspaper, the *Alerta*, has received some interesting information. . . ."

The *Alerta*. My father-in-law was right: They were on top of the situation. The *Alerta* had been on an insidious drive against Getúlio Vargas. It was a satirical, sensationalistic rag, still tolerated because of its small circulation, which, however, was already on the increase. I hesitated; should I appease him?

"Later, maybe," I said. "Now you must excuse me, my friend, I have an operation to perform."

And I told the chauffeur to drive away. In the rearview mirror I saw him standing on the sidewalk, his eyes following the car: Trouble in the offing, for sure. I went to the hospital but never got anywhere near the operating room. Doutor Saturnino had phoned, asking me to attend a meeting at his hotel. This situation was beginning to get under my skin, but I saw no way out of it. When I arrived at the hotel, several people were aleady assembled there: Saturnino, my father-in-law, two aides from the Governmental Palace, and a hefty, fashionably dressed mulatto, who introduced himself as an agent of the Department of Press and Propaganda. Saturnino apologized for having disrupted my work schedule:

"But it's an important matter, doctor. Early this morning I received a telegram from Getúlio. According to their sources there in Rio, the newspapers are going to milk every drop out of this story about these sick Injuns. They'll want to know what has befallen them. And above all, they'll be demanding news about this fellow that is now at the hospital."

The mulatto listened, smiling enigmatically. I told them there was nothing I could state beforehand; I didn't even know what was wrong with the man.

"What about this lady doctor?" asked my father-in-law. "Can she be trusted?"

I replied that I couldn't vouch for her, but neither could I take the case away from her. And I rose to my feet:

"I have a patient waiting in the operating room. An exposed fracture, a serious case, so if you'll excuse me . . ."

The mulatto from the Department of Press and Propaganda accompanied me as far as the corridor in order to tell me that he would handle the press. I didn't want to enter into an argument: I merely thanked him, got into the car, and went back to the hospital. I couldn't operate well: all that commotion had upset me. At the end of the operation, which lasted five hours, I was exhausted. Even so, I decided I would go to the Isolation Hospital. I found Débora quivering with excitement:

"I spent the morning at the medical school library, Rafael. And I dug up some very interesting things."

She handed me a sheet of paper.

"There you are. A copy of my notes."

I read: "In the *Annales de l'Académie de Medicine* of 1898, Renard mentions five cases of a disease characterized by fever and multicolored skin blotches that occurred in the Belgian Congo, but all his patients were black. In 1902, V. Kranz, in a memo to the Institute of Tropical Diseases at the University of Berlin, refers to a disease characterized by fever and yellowish and bluish blotches—but in his patients there was also the occurrence of alopecia in patches as well as gangrene of the extremities—the sputum was fetid, which suggested a pulmonary abscess—the urine was dark, murky. In 1912, in an editorial in the *Journal of Tropical Diseases*, Allen and Dunswick remark upon the *Riu-riu*, a curious disease that strikes the aborigines of Polynesia, a disease which they attributed to a curse from the sacred serpent. Multicolored blotches . . . fever . . . mystic delirium. In 1925, in the same *Journal of Tropical Diseases*, Tate and his collaborators analyze an epidemic outbreak among the natives who were building an American railroad in Panama. In all those cases, however, the ganglions were swollen to a very large size . . . In 1932, Merrill, an Englishman, gathered data on eight cases in Malaysia . . . Multicolored blotches, but also paralysis of the lower limbs . . . In 1935, Bengstrom described twenty cases of a communicable disease characterized by multicolored blotches that struck the members of a safari . . .''

But what the hell was all this about? Renard and *Riu-riu*? Merrill, safari? Perplexed, I stood staring at Débora.

"But can't you see, Rafael?" she asked, elated. "There are no references to a disease similar to this one here. Which means: We're dealing with a new disease, Rafael! Just as I had suspected, Rafael!"

And she began rattling off a list of what had to be done; there was one thing she considered particularly important:

"An autopsy of the deceased. The bodies are probably still there in the ruins of the church—I hope they aren't badly decomposed. Have them brought here, Rafael. Send for them urgently and request that the Faculty of Medicine perform the autopsy."

I assented, or rather pretended to assent. In fact, I was thinking of how I could extricate myself from this tangle— there seemed no way out at the moment. I looked at my watch; I was already late for the office.

"All right, Débora. I'll see what I can do."

I went to my office. The waiting-room was crowded as usual, and I saw one patient after the other until ten o'clock in the evening. When I thought I had seen the last of my patients, my secretary announced:

"There's one more. A young man who didn't want to give his name. He says he's here on a personal matter."

"Tell him to come back tomorrow."

But he was already standing in the doorway; it was, naturally, the reporter from the *Alerta*.

"Go away, please," I said, gruffly.

He smiled:

"I'd like you to peruse this material, Dr. Mendes. You might find it of interest."

They were proof sheets. I hesitated, but ended up by sitting down to read them. It was a report on the deaths at São Tolentino. Saturnino was mentioned by name; there was some reference made to his friendship with Getúlio. And the possibility of poisoning, possibly due to the water from a nearby well, was raised.

Poisoning? Where had they gotten this idea?

"Where did you people get this idea?"

"If you're willing to deny it, we'll print your statement," the reporter said.

I didn't know what to say. "If I decide to make a statement, I'll phone you," I said. Then he left. Bewildered, I plopped myself on a chair. And now, what should I do?

All of a sudden it occurred to me: the D.P.P., the Department of Press and Propaganda. I loathed the idea, but it could well be the solution. I would have to locate that mulatto without delay, before the newspaper went to press. Rather than wait for the elevator, I tore down the stairs. I ran all the way along Rua da Praia, deserted at that hour, then went up Rua Ladeira, arrived at the Palace—the sentry at the door already knew me—and burst into Moreira's office. Fortunately Moreira, who was the aide assigned to this case, was still there; an industrious man, he often worked far into the night. After briefing him quickly on the situation, I asked if he could locate the D.P.P. agent for me. We phoned his hotel. He wasn't there, obviously—it was not for nothing that he looked like a skirt chaser.

"Let's go to Marlene's."

The place was nearby, on Rua Sete de Setembro. Marlene herself welcomed us:

"To what do I owe the honor?"

Yes, the D.P.P. man was there. Without further delay, we burst into a bedroom, where we found him with a woman. She immediately started to scream, while he made a dash for a revolver lying on the night table. Then recognizing us, he relaxed; we gave him a quick account of the situation, and he felt that under these circumstances the newspaper should indeed be prevented from circulating; however, he would have to ask Rio for authorization:

"Unfortunately, it's not going to be easy."

We returned to the Palace. The phone connections were slow, there were delays; and it was always someone else we would have to speak to, so it wasn't until six o'clock in the morning when we finally had an official decision, which came from Getúlio himself: The newspaper was to remain in circulation. We could reply to the accusations, but the newspaper was not to be prevented from circulating. The D.P.P. man was annoyed:

"That's stupid! Real stupid!"

Anyway, by then the paper had already hit the streets: From the Palace we could hear the newsboys hollering out the headlines. Moreira turned around to say:

"The ball is in your court now, doctor."

Was it? Yes, but everything would now depend on Débora. But—how could I make them understand my predicament? Indeed, the ball was now in my court.

I left for the Isolation Hospital, went into the sickroom. Débora was still asleep on the cot that had been placed next to Redhead's bed. I stood gazing at her. What could have been the significance of the fact that I stood gazing at her in spite of the urgency of the situation? Was it love? Some love? How much love? How to evaluate the dosage of love? By measuring the duration of the stationary fascination? By converting this duration into equivalent units (which units?) of passion?

But a moment later she woke up; she was a light sleeper, like many other physicians, who leap out of bed even before an anguished voice begins to cry "wake up, doctor." On seeing me there, she smiled—a sweet smile, or at least I thought so, and how could I evaluate the fact that it had seemed sweet to me?—but she soon turned her attention to her patient, who was still in a coma. A tragic face, that man's: deep-set eyes, a sharp-pointed nose, high cheekbones, a sparse, red stubble. Débora jumped out of her bed—she had slept in her labcoat, as I could now ascertain—and proceeded to examine him.

"There's no change." She looked disappointed. "No new signs, no blotches whatsoever."

Suddenly she remembered:

"What about the autopsy, Rafael?" she asked, turning around. "Have you arranged for the post-mortem?"

I just couldn't bring myself to tell her that there wasn't going to be any autopsy; that as soon as she had left São Tolentino, the soldiers, terrified, had requested over the radio permission to cremate the bodies, which I granted. It was foolish of me, as I now recognized, but at the time it had seemed the best solution to prevent the disease from spreading; besides, Doutor Saturnino didn't want any graves or crosses on his lands.

"It's been arranged," I lied, "but it will take a few more days, our pathologist is away on leave, but don't worry, the bodies are safely stored in the morgue's refrigerators." And before she could ask me any further questions, I left.

When I got home, I found a note from Alzira saying she had left for the farm, where she would be spending a few days with her mother, and that she had taken little Rafael with her. I was not pleased at all; this would soon set tongues wagging. Anyway, it was one more burden I would have to bear. I had lunch by myself, then went to my office. I couldn't keep my mind on my work, so I went back home, stayed up reading until the small hours, but still couldn't fall asleep. It was with both relief and renewed worry that I saw the day dawning.

I arrived at the Faculty of Medicine at the time appointed for Débora's presentation. The auditorium was packed with people; everyone was aware of the importance of this case. There was an air of anticipation. Brito came up and invited me to join them at the table. Débora was sorting her papers. She looked calm; she smiled at me with self-confidence.

Brito rang a bell and declared the session open. He started by thanking everybody for coming. He said that this meeting would be particularly interesting because the subject matter was the outbreak of a contagious disease that had occurred in Rio Grande do Sul. And then he gave the floor to Débora. She rose to her feet and was now visibly nervous:

"Gentlemen: professors, physicians . . ."

Then she stopped. There was an oppressive silence, interrupted only by the noise of traffic and the shouts of the newsboys outside. Holding my breath, I sat watching her, ready to intervene if necessary. But it wasn't necessary. Taking a deep breath, she went on:

"I'd like to present a report on cases of a disease, as yet unknown, that have occurred in the region of the mission settlements."

She began to shuffle her papers, and was again showing signs of nervousness; when she finally resumed her exposition, it was with a faltering voice; stammering, she described the circumstances under which she had found the bodies, and the condition of the man now hospitalized. I looked around; the expressions I saw on the faces showed perplexity, suspicion, irritation. They shot questions at her, which she fielded to the best of her abilities, apologizing for her inexperience and lack of resources; when asked whether autopsies had been performed, she looked at me as if to ask for help. But I said nothing, there was nothing I could say, and then she announced that she hoped to have the data from the autopsies in the near future.

I was feeling ill at ease, terribly ill at ease, the scene reminded me—naturally—of the Inquisition: a helpless Hebrew woman before her unyielding judges. And what was I doing? Merely nodding my head mechanically. Was my behavior honorable? No, it wasn't. I should be doing something, but what? As I wavered, Brito rose to his feet. For a few moments he stood looking at the audience, saying nothing. Then he began in an ominous tone of voice:

"Present at this meeting are the luminaries of medicine in our state. Your presence here, gentlemen, attests to our interest in the medical science."

A pause. A tense pause.

"Regrettably, however, this meeting has been a waste of time. Dr. Feinstein talked about an outbreak of a new disease. But there has been no outbreak, the existence of a new disease has not been substantiated. And I don't even know if there is a disease."

"But there must be something!" shouted somebody from the back of the auditorium.

It was the old Dr. Artêmio. He stood on his feet, shaking with indignation.

"There *is* something, Professor Brito. Go to the Isolation Hospital, and see for yourself, there's a patient there, lying in a coma. There is something!"

"I didn't say there isn't anything," Brito replied coldly. "What I did say was that I don't know if the coma of this patient, whom incidentally I saw but briefly—because our lady doctor here wouldn't let me examine him—can be attributed to a disease."

"To what can it then be attributed?" Artêmio was now advancing up the aisle. "To poisoning, as the *Alerta* claims?"

Brito hesitated—for a second, half a second—but when he tried to give an answer, it was already too late. Facing the audience, his back turned to Brito, Artêmio had already launched forth into a speech:

"Because if it is poisoning, gentlemen, we'll have to clear up this matter. We're no longer living in an age when crime could go unpunished in our country. Nowadays the world clamors for justice, gentlemen. Right now in Spain there is a bloody fight going on for democracy, a fight in which we too are engaged. It is our duty to find out what is behind this incident!"

"Ah, you bastard," shouted Doutor Saturnino, advancing upon Artêmio. With difficulty, the two men were separated; Artêmio was dragged out of the auditorium, shouting. Two soldiers then took him away.

Brito tried to bring the situation under control, but it was impossible: the melee was now widespread, students had invaded the auditorium with clenched fists raised in the air, shouting *down with the dictatorship*. "Things are getting grim, doctor," somebody whispered in my ear; it was, naturally, the mulatto from the D.P.P. I was trying to reach Débora, who looked frightened, to take her away from this place, but my father-in-law was pulling me away by one arm and Moreira by another, and from the door—was he, too, involved in this brawl?—Kurt Schnitzel, holding a sheet of paper in his hand, was signaling to me. Standing on a chair a young doctor, applauded by some, booed by others, had launched into a diatribe against Getúlio. Brito kept ringing the bell, but nobody paid any attention. The situation was finally brought under control by a slightly built university beadle: One by one, he kept pushing people out of the auditorium until only Brito, my father-in-law, Saturnino, Moreira, Débora and I remained. Irritated, Brito, whose jacket had been torn, put on his hat.

"I suppose we can now declare the session closed, right?" he said. Then, turning to Débora: "Congratulations, doctor. If it was an affray you were after, you surely succeeded, no doubt about it." Doutor Saturnino and Moreira wanted to call an urgent meeting, but I was not up to it; taking Débora by the arm, under my father-in-law's suspicious eyes, I left. At the door of the building, that reporter from the *Alerta* stood waiting. "I have nothing to say—" I said, but he cut me short:

"Okay, doctor, this time I'm the one who has something for you. Your friend Kurt Schnitzel was trying to give you this," and he showed me a handwritten sheet of paper, "but that beadle pushed him out of the auditorium, so I offered to deliver it to you. I took the liberty of reading it—after all I am a newsman, right?—and I found the contents most interesting. And let me tip you off: This material will appear in tomorrow's edition of the newspaper."

Schnitzel's note was long:

"I have every reason to believe that the man known as Redhead, now at the Isolation Hospital, is a militant Trotzkyite whom I met in Berlin in nineteen thirty. Although he was then only a young student, he was already under surveillance by the authorities. He was considering fleeing to Latin America, for he was particularly fascinated by the Indians, whom he intended—to use his own words—'to set free from the bondage of the white man.' He went to Mexico, where he lived in seclusion for a long time. He wrote several books under the pen name B. Traven. He made a lot of money from his writing, and he could have led a comfortable life; but, on the one hand, the Nazis kept harassing him, they wanted to do him in; on the other hand, he was obsessed by the idea of inciting the Aztecs to rise up and usurp power. For this reason he had to flee the country. He went to Peru, with the intention of rebuilding the Inca empire, but on socialistic foundations. He was arrested and after two years in jail, he was set free. Then he crossed the border and came to Brazil. Here he ran into a group of his fellow countrymen, who had been expelled from the lands they owned in the state of Santa Catarina. He talked them into accompanying him to Rio Grande do Sul, where in the ruins of the mission settlements they would found a new republic; for this he believed they could count on the concurrence of the local Indians. But somebody tipped off the police in an anonymous letter, undoubtedly written by members of the Nazi movement in Rio Grande do Sul. He then threatened to reveal everything he knew about Nazism in Latin America, including the names of important individuals in the government and in the business sector. . . .''

THIS, OF COURSE, COMPLICATED THINGS EVEN FURTHER AND I was about to say to the newsman, "Don't you dare make any of this public," but when I lifted my eyes from the letter, he was gone. Débora, her eyes fixed, was still standing there motionless, utterly devastated. I considered taking her to lunch at the Palace of Commerce, but it wasn't a good idea; she wouldn't accept the invitation, and anyhow, it wouldn't be pleasant to have lunch with prying eyes fixed on us. I made her get into the car and we drove to the Isolation Hospital. We went to the director's office, which was empty at that hour; she let herself fall into an armchair, and there she sat, in silence. I was at a loss for words and didn't have the courage to look at her. She burst into tears: She wept convulsively, her entire body shook with her sobbing; it was painful to watch. Suddenly she raised her head and looked at me, haughtily:

"No, Rafael. We're not going to give up so easily." She began to cheer up. "I can prove, Rafael, that it is a new disease, which hasn't been described yet. When the data from the autopsies come in—"

She stopped short, intrigued:

"By the way, Rafael, have they finished the autopsies yet?"

Now is the time, I thought, now is the time to clear the air, right now. I took a deep breath:

"There hasn't been any autopsy, Débora."

And I told her that the bodies had been cremated. She couldn't believe her ears:

"But how could you have allowed something like that, Rafael? How could you have been so foolish?" Desperately she asked, "But why, Rafael? Can't you see that this is our undoing? Now there's no way we can prove anything, Rafael!"

I couldn't even look at her. "I've hurt myself, too," I mumbled, but she was no longer listening. She rose to her feet, walked up to the window, stood there motionless, looking out. Without turning around, she said in a clear, steady voice:

"I'll see it through, Rafael. I don't know how, but I'll see it through. This man has a disease which is yet unknown, and I'm going to prove that it is so."

"Don't do anything rash," I cautioned, but she had stopped listening to me. She left and went to the sickroom.

I looked at my watch. It was time to leave for my office. When I got there, the phone was ringing. "It's for you, sir," said my secretary. "It's Senhor Moreira." I thought I wouldn't take the call, but it would be futile; he would keep trying until he got hold of me.

"Hallo!"

"The situation is bad, Rafael."

"I know."

"The *Alerta* is already printing an extra edition with a report on the melee at the Faculty of Medicine. They're going to say there's a political dispute behind this incident."

"What about this D.P.P. guy?"

"I don't even know where he is, probably in a brothel

somewhere. What are we going to do, Rafael? Tell me something, is this Redhead still in a coma? Because if he were to
regain consciousness and say that he hadn't been poisoned . . ."

"Yeah, sure, but he *is* in a coma. So long, Moreira."

I asked that the first patient be sent in, but a moment later
the phone rang again. It was my father-in-law:

"Saturnino is furious, he says he'll set fire to the editorial
room of that newspaper . . . And the worst is that Getúlio
doesn't even want to speak to him, he sent him a message
saying that he doesn't want to get involved in this tangle, and
that Saturnino must fend for himself. Is there anything we can
do, Rafael?"

"Nothing," I said.

"Nothing." His voice sounded sarcastic. "We're now in
the hands of this little lady friend of yours, this lady doctor.
While the two of you are having a good time, we are here,
eaten up by anxiety. She, I can understand: She comes from a
rootless family, they have no self-respect, no dignity, nothing.
But you, Rafael, you come from a good family. How disgraceful, Rafael."

"Listen—"

"*You* listen to me now!" He was shouting furiously.
"*You* listen to me! You'll rue the day if you involve my
daughter in a scandal, Rafael, do you hear me? You'll rue the
day!"

I hung up. The patient sitting before me, an elderly man,
was staring at me in astonishment.

"You may go," I said.

"But you haven't examined me yet."

"And I'm not going to. Not today, I can't. Come back
some other day. Go now, will you?"

I called my secretary and said I wouldn't see anyone else. I
closed the door, took a bottle of cognac and a glass out of the
cabinet. I intended to get drunk; I wouldn't go back home, I'd
stay right there in my office, and would sleep on the examination table; but all of a sudden I missed Alzira and my little
Rafael, my dear son. Maybe they were home waiting for
me. . . .

But the house was dark when I got there. Swaying, I was
trying to insert the key into the keyhole when somebody
touched me on the shoulder. I jumped in alarm and swiped at
the shadowy form, which staggered and fell to the ground.

"What's the matter, Rafael? That's no way to treat a friend."

It was Microbe, my colleague Microbe. He knew about the case at the Isolation Hospital and he wanted to talk about it. I invited him in. He sat down, and with shining eyes proceeded to say that he could cure the patient with a new drug he had just discovered:

"It will make us famous, Rafael!"

I sighed: here we go again, fame: I sighed. But Microbe, enthusiastic, had already launched into an explanation: For some time now he had been studying how fungi and bacteria reacted to each other; even before Fleming, he had succeeded in isolating a substance found in the moulds of the genus *Penicillium*, a substance which he called—before Fleming, mind you, and such a coincidence, isn't it?—penicillin. He knew that the Americans were already manufacturing it on an experimental basis and that they would soon be dumping it into the Brazilian market; however, he wasn't discouraged by this fact. He was convinced that his own penicillin was better, and he had been waiting for an opportunity to prove—dramatically—that it was so. And now the opportunity came with this patient, Redhead. The situation struck him as ideal: a difficult case, a guarded prognosis, a great deal of curiosity about the evolution of this disease not only in the medical circles but also among the general public. After hesitating for a moment, he went on:

"Besides, if by any chance this doesn't work out all right—well, he's a transient and nobody knows who he is . . ."

Then, with growing animation:

"But it's going to work out all right, Rafael. It has to. You should see the guinea pigs getting over an infection . . . As if by magic. Yes, it will work out all right. Penicillin is the drug of the future. I'll establish an industry, I'll supply the entire country with penicillin. We mustn't let the gringos take over, Rafael."

I hesitated. A new drug . . . Maybe it would work out all right, but quite frankly, I didn't have much faith in Microbe. Also, how could anybody be sure that we were really dealing with an infectious disease? What if it were a case of poisoning? Then I asked him: "How do you know it's not a case of poisoning?" He looked at me astonished. "Poisoning? You're talking nonsense, Rafael. Everybody knows it's an infection. There have been outbreaks in the region of the mission settlements, and in Argentina the disease is rare but not unheard of. There are even historial references to it.''

Opening his briefcase, he took out an old, yellowing, moth-eaten booklet. The title: *Recollections of São Tolentino's Church;* the author, Father João de Buarque, S.J. Astonished, I read its few pages.

In the first part, Father João gave an account of how he had been entrusted with a mission, which he called divine. Born in the city of Oporto, he had been steered into the priesthood at an early age. Being exceptionally gifted, he seemed destined to rise quickly in the ecclesiastical hierarchy. One day, however, worn out by fatigue, he fell asleep in the chapel and had a dream that was to change his life. He dreamed that Saint Tolentino appeared to him, surrounded by Indians; the saint asked him to abandon everything and leave for America, where he was to build a church and devote himself to converting the Indians.

It was a revelation. On that same day he asked his superiors' permission to follow the saint's edicts. All attempts on their part to make him change his mind were in vain. ''God inspired my tongue and I refuted their arguments calmly, firmly, and self-assuredly.''

In the second part of the booklet, Father João gave an account of his voyage to Brazil; of his long journey across the pampas; of his meeting with the Guarani Indians, ''so pure and innocent that when I saw them my heart burst with joy''; of his peregrinations on foot across the rolling hills of the region until ''coming upon a certain pleasant place, I heard Saint Tolentino's voice saying that was the place where he wanted to be venerated.'' So, without delay, the Indians built a settlement there; the construction of the church, however, took many years because ''Saint Tolentino kept appearing to me in dreams to say that he wasn't pleased with the temple, there was always something wrong: the door, too big or not big enough; or the churchyard, too large or not large enough; or the right foot of his statue, placed too high or not high enough''—and so on and so forth until the priest, disheartened, began to think of giving up the idea.

It was then that a young Indian arrived at the settlement. He was known as Sepé Tiarajú; and right from the beginning, it became clear that he was a man of strong character, a Guarani ready to challenge everything. He would enter into discussions with the priest, arguing that what the Indians needed were spears, not crucifixes; fortresses, not churches.

"A church is a fortress," the priest would retort. "A fortress of faith."

"But can it withstand cannons?" the Indian would ask, ironic.

"You know everything," the priest would say, baffled and irritated. "You're like Adam after he ate of the fruit of the Tree of the Knowledge of Good and Evil; but don't forget, the only thing he discovered was his own nakedness."

"And quite a discovery it was," Sepé would reply. "It's good to be aware of our own nakedness, don't you think? Except that, had I been Adam, I would have stayed naked. As a matter of fact, that's how we Indians were before you priests arrived. We were happier then."

"But we brought you the Divine Word," the priest would object. Sepé would laugh. "The Divine Word? We already had the Divine Word, Father. Don't forget—you yourself have said so—that we are one of Israel's lost tribes, that we're the descendants of King Solomon."

The Divine Word? No, that was not what he was after. Nor had he any desire to eat of the fruit of the Tree of Life, which would give him eternal salvation; what he was after was the Gold Tree:

"I know that it exists, and I'm going to find it, Father, you can bet on it."

With the gold he intended to buy cannons. But that was not all, he also wanted to build foundries, to import machinery. "Progress, Father, our salvation lies in progress," he would state, his eyes glittering with defiance.

Conversations like these disturbed Father João, who didn't know how to refute Sepé's statements. *Inspire my tongue, Saint Tolentino*, he would beseech the saint in his prayers. His patron saint didn't accede to his request; on the other hand, he stopped appearing in the priest's dreams, and so the construction of the church was finally completed. The first mass was held there in an atmosphere of jubilation, attended by hundreds of Indians as well as by priests from the other Indian settlements. Sepé Tiarajú looked on, smiling ironically. Father João wasn't upset. He decided he would ignore him. He had ascertained himself that the rest of the Indians didn't share the ideas of this rebel. On the contrary: They worked, attended the religious ceremonies, kept up their morale, practiced good habits. Thus Father João had accomplished his mission and now, being an old man, he was preparing himself to die in peace when tragedy struck: They were attacked by the Spaniards. The Indian settlement was quickly wiped out amid a real carnage: "Streams of blood flowed down the streets." The survivors sought refuge in the church, determined to resist until the very end. Father João related at length how his conscience was assaulted by conflicting ideas: Could he desecrate a temple in order to save human lives—the lives of Indians? (Yes—suddenly he felt disgusted with those savages: disgusted and angry with the whole situation—what keeps me here? Why don't I fling the doors open and join the white people, who are, after all, my own kind? Why don't I go back to Portugal, there to spend the rest of my life in peace?) But then Saint Tolentino appeared to him once more in a dream; the saint showed him the sword he held in his hand, a sword of fire; the priest understood the message. He announced to the Indians that he would fight together with them.

The siege continued. Although the defenders of the temple disposed of only a meager amount of weapons, they had stored there much food, as well as water, which was piped in from an underground cistern located nearby; they were in good spirits; but then a sudden event occurred: "On the 32nd. day of this heroic siege, Sepé Tiarajú, the Indian leader, the dauntless warrior whose courage inspired everyone, woke up sick . . . He complained of pains in his legs and arms . . . He vomited a large amount of black bile . . . His body was very hot . . . And upon examining him more closely, I noticed on his forehead a red blotch, which looked like a beauty spot."

The blotches spread quickly, "acquiring different colors, some looked yellow, some blue." These symptoms then appeared in other Indians. The priest's consternation turned into panic two days later when the first Indian died—his death soon followed by another, then another, and yet another. At first he suspected that the enemy, having discovered the hidden cistern, had poisoned it; but later, when he noticed that the animals—dogs, cats, goats—drank of the same water with no ill effects, he concluded that it must be a plague hitherto unknown. And then "a great fury rose in my soul against Saint Tolentino: *You put the wrong people to the sword,* I cried out, *you struck down your own votaries instead of your enemies, you stupid saint!*" At that moment "the wrath of heaven descended upon me; my eyes became dim, my legs felt weak, and I fell to the ground; I don't know for how long I lay there unconscious; my guess is hours, or days, for when I came to I saw the Indians, all dead, piled on top of each other. Sepé Tiarajú had disappeared." Peering through a window, the priest still caught a glimpse of him riding away at a gallop, brandishing his spear. "Thank God," he said with a sigh, "thank God and Saint Tolentino, one of them managed to escape."

Even though being extremely debilitated, with his body burning with fever, the priest was determined not to surrender; he would die with his Indians, and with them ascend into heaven. But then the Spaniards, tearing down doors and windows, burst into the church. What they saw "horrified them to such an extent that they fell on their knees, and weeping, begged for forgiveness."

The priest's condition worsened and for weeks he was "between life and death, beseeching death to take me . . . God, however, chose not to bestow his mercy on me." The priest recovered and returned to Portugal, where he spent the remaining years of his life writing and rewriting his *Recollections of São Tolentino's Church*. . . .

I finished reading; perplexed, I looked at Microbe. Suddenly it dawned on me: Here was the very proof I needed! It was History's own voice speaking through the priest's narrative, a voice more powerful than the headlines of any filthy sensationalistic rag. Jumping to my feet I ran from the room. "Hey, where are you going?" Microbe, astonished, shouted. "We still haven't fixed on a date for the test." But I wasn't interested, all I wanted now was to show Father João's booklet to Débora, it proved that the disease was real, that it wasn't a figment of her imagination, that it wasn't poisoning; Doutor Saturnino's reputation was safe, and so was Getúlio Vargas's, the government wouldn't fall—everything was all right, at last everything all right!

I arrived at the Isolation Hospital and as I was running into the building, I was stopped by the head nurse, who grabbed me by the arm.

"One moment, doctor. May I have a word with you before you go to the sickroom, sir?"

What's the matter, I was about to say, but she was already handing me a letter which an orderly had written to her. I read it, aghast: "Dona Marta, I'm writing this to let you know about something I saw, something that got me worried, when I was on duty last night, I went to the sickroom and saw Dr. Débora with a syringe, she was taking blood out of the patient, I didn't want to interfere, so I said nothing and just stood there watching, and her back was turned to me, so she didn't see me, but I saw her inject the patient's blood into her own vein, I couldn't understand why, so I decided to ask, what's that for, doctor, what are you doing, and then she said it was nothing, just an experiment and that I was not to mention it to anyone but it's a great responsibility for me to shoulder and for this reason I'm relating this incident to you. Yours truly."

"Well, doctor?" She could barely conceal her glee, the bitch. "What should I do? It's a very serious matter. As the head nurse, I—"

"Shut up!"

"But—"

I grabbed her by the arm, and shook her.

"Not a word about this, do you hear me? Or else you'll be fired."

"Is this a threat, doctor?" she asked, defiant.

"You bet it is. And now leave me, will you?"

Muttering, she walked away. I stood there in the hall, not knowing what to do. Then I realized I was still holding the letter in my hand; quickly, I put it into my pocket. As if it would solve the problem. As if it would.

No, it couldn't be true. Débora couldn't have done such a crazy thing; not even a person like Débora would have gone so far.

I went to the sickroom. She was examining the patient. I waited for her to finish, and then I showed her the letter. After skimming through it, she handed it back to me:

"That's right, Rafael." Just like that: As if its contents were of no consequence.

"But why, Débora?" I was aghast. "Why in the world did you do such a thing?"

"To prove to them . . ." she said softly.

"To prove what?"

"You know what: That it's a new disease, and that it's contagious. That it's a disease that can spread from one person to another."

It was frightening, it was a nightmare; it even made me feel sick, my mind was reeling.

"And what's going to happen?" I asked, anguished.

"I suppose," she began in the same calm, controlled voice, "that the first symptoms will be indefinite: fever, an achy body, indisposition, nausea, vomiting. Then blotches will appear. If I'm unconscious, someone should follow the evolution of these blotches on a daily basis, and if possible, photograph them. If ganglions appear, a biopsy should be carried out."

Shocked, I stood staring at her. But it was about herself that she was talking, as if she were some indigent patient or a guinea pig!

"But Débora, listen, we've got to do something!"

She smiled sadly.

"Like what, Rafael? There's nothing to be done."

"But your life is at stake, Débora!"

"That's right." Her eyes, blank, were staring into space. "Yes, my life is at stake. I know."

Suddenly Microbe and his penicillin crossed my mind. And if we were to try? First, on Redhead and afterward—if the drug worked out well—on Débora. I phoned him at home and asked him to come over right away. Fifteen minutes later he arrived with his penicillin—a white powder stored in vials. He diluted it in sterilized water. Before injecting the solution into the sick man's vein—I hadn't told him anything about Débora—he made a dramatic pause:

"An historical moment!"

Then he injected the patient with the penicillin. "Now we'll have to wait, he should improve within hours or days," Microbe said. And he left, requesting that we keep him informed about any unforeseen difficulties.

I stood staring at Débora. I still couldn't believe what she had done; and her air of tranquil resignation filled me with despair. "Ah, Débora, Débora," I groaned. She laid a hand on my arm.

"Go home, Rafael, go home."

I was reluctant to leave her. She assured me that she was all right—so far—and that I could go. The day was already breaking when I got home and the phone was ringing. It was Alzira, with a tearful voice:

"I've been trying to get hold of you for hours, Rafael, the long distance operator said that your phone kept ringing but nobody answered. My God, Rafael, what's been going on? What kind of mess is this woman dragging you into?''

I tried my best to reassure her; then, worn out, I collapsed on the bed. I woke up with the phone ringing again, but it was now nine o'clock in the morning.

Moreira, the aide from the Palace, wanted to talk to me:

"It's that crazy old Dr. Artêmio. He's been circulating a petition requesting that our patient be removed from the Isolation Hospital. He claims that this fellow is in jeopardy there, that Saturnino's thugs are quite capable of snuffing out the patient right there in the hospital."

"That's ridiculous," I muttered, still muddle-headed with sleep.

"Exactly what I said, too: ridiculous. But it would be good if this patient were to last for at least one more week. Couldn't we perhaps send for some drugs from the United States?"

I informed him that we were already using a new drug and that the patient's condition was bound to improve. Then I phoned the Isolation Hospital and asked to speak to Débora.

"She's taking a shower at the moment," a nurse's aide said, "but she asked me to tell you that everything's fine."

"And the patient in the sickroom?"

"The same, doctor."

"Hasn't he improved?"

"No, doctor."

"Not at all?"

"No."

"Not even a little bit?"

"No, he's just the same."

No improvement: and the penicillin? I got into the car and drove to the hospital. I went straight to the sickroom, where I found Débora. She was well; seemingly well, which was a great relief. Soon afterward Microbe came to give the patient another dose of his penicillin. "He's much better," said Microbe, pleased. Better? I didn't think so, but chose not to say anything. Microbe was peering at the patient. "Just like the cases described by Father João," he remarked.

"By the way, have you shown the booklet to Débora yet?"

The booklet: No, I didn't want to show her anything with sickness or death in it. I promised him I'd let her have it later, after this whole business had settled down. I saw him to the front door of the hospital; and then I asked him if this disease could be transmitted by blood—say, by a blood transfusion.

"Certainly." He stared at me, surprised. "Why? Has there been a blood transfusion?"

I dissembled: "Nothing, just curiosity." Then an orderly came to say there was a phone call for me. It was Moreira again:

"The city is seething with rumors because of this petition. Lots of people are subscribing their names to it, it's already been reported in the *Alerta*, and the medical students are going to have a rally in front of the hospital. Saturnino thinks it's time we called in the Brigade. What do you think?"

"I'm sick and tired of all this baloney. I have plenty of other things to worry about. If they want to have a rally, let them."

I hung up, surprised at the way I had given vent to my feelings, and went back to the sickroom. Débora was lying down. "What's the matter?" I asked, alarmed. "Nothing," she replied, "I feel a bit dizzy." I felt her pulse: fast. Not too fast, yet fast enough to worry me.

She was staring at me. And suddenly we found ourselves holding hands, gazing at each other, overcome by tenderness—and love? But all of a sudden she shuddered and withdrew her hands from mine. The arrogant head nurse had just walked in to check the patient's temperature, or on some other pretext.

"And how is our lady patient?" The tone of mockery made me lose my cool. I grabbed her by the arm: "Get out! Out!" I pushed her away and closed the door.

Débora was crying softly. I helped her back to the bed and wrapped a blanket around her; we remained there together, talking and reminiscing about our days as medical students until she fell asleep. It was a restless sleep, which filled me with anxiety: Could it be a symptom of the disease? I sat watching her for a long time; when I left the sickroom, it was almost two o'clock in the afternoon.

Waiting for me at the entrance to the hospital was, naturally, the reporter from the *Alerta*. "What is it this time?" I said, gruffly. He grinned.

"You're not exactly full of goodwill, are you, doctor? Can't blame you. You're getting hopelessly entangled in this mess, aren't you? But tell me something: What's wrong with this lady doctor in charge of the case? Why has she been hospitalized?"

Stunned, I stared at him: How could he already know? And immediately I realized: the head nurse, of course. The bitch: As soon as I had kicked her out of the sickroom, she must have hurried to the nearest phone. As if guessing at my thought, the reporter said:

"We have our sources, doctor. There are lots of people siding with us. I would advise you to follow the example of your old colleague Artêmio and join us. As for this lady doctor Débora—"

I grabbed him by the collar and shook him:

"Leave the doctor out of this, do you hear me? Leave her out of this or you'll regret it!"

I let go of him. Livid, he composed himself; the glance he cast at me was full of hatred, but he said nothing. Then he got into his car, an old Packard, and drove away.

I went to my office. The waiting room was full, but after seeing the first two patients, I felt I couldn't go on; I told my secretary to inform the patients I wasn't feeling well and that all appointments were cancelled. Then I stood at the window watching the groups of people that had gathered on Rua da Praia. Raised fingers, turgid jugular veins, angry voices—the reporter was right, the case aroused controversy, public opinion was divided on the matter.

My secretary came in to say that my father-in-law was on the phone.

"I want to inform you," he said dryly, "that I'm on my way to the farm. Alzira wants to see me. You must know what about, isn't that right, Rafael?"

I said nothing; he went on, barely containing his anger:

"Have you considered the consequences, Rafael? Of a legal separation? To Alzira, to your son? To my family's reputation? To your own reputation, which I doubt is still worth anything?"

I remained silent.

"Rafael! Are you listening? You'd better listen carefully, you'd better heed my words: I told you once that I would kill you if you ever made my daughter miserable. I'm warning you, Rafael, my promise still stands."

He hung up.

Motionless, I stood there holding the phone.

But why didn't I go with him? Why didn't I drop everything, this damned patient, the Isolation Hospital, the Department of Communicable Diseases, the *Alerta*, Microbe, the sickroom, Kurt, Brito, and all the rest of it? Why didn't I leave Débora and join my family at the farm? Why didn't I?

I didn't know why. But I knew I would stay. Oh shit, I groaned, putting the phone back in the cradle, and it immediately began ringing again. It was an orderly from the Isolation Hospital, sounding extremely upset.

"Doctor, there are some men here, they want to take the patient away . . ."

"What?" I was mystified.

"Some men! They are here to take the patient away! They say they're acting on your orders. They're in the sickroom arguing with Dr. Débora. The poor lady is not well at all, she asked me to phone you."

"Don't let them! I'll be right there!"

I tore down the stairs, and on the way out, I grabbed the superintendent, a huge mulatto who on occasion helped me out, and dragged him behind me. We got into the car and ten minutes later, after a reckless drive, we were at the hospital; I burst into the sickroom, and indeed, there they were, Saturnino's thugs—so he had decided to have the patient removed by hook or by crook—four men, one of them holding Débora by the wrist as the others wrapped Redhead in a blanket.

"Stop it! Let go of the patient, you bastards!"

They hesitated, but obviously their orders were to take Redhead away, no matter what. Pulling out a club hidden under his shirt, the mulatto advanced upon them, while I was trying to free Débora. There was a brief scrimmage: the thugs were strong but they were not in their own territory, and the mulatto, in a fury, succeeded in making them flee. Then we carefully picked up the patient, who had rolled across the floor, and we laid him on the bed. Then I turned to Débora. She was pale and shaking. I laid her on her cot and covered her with a blanket, and all the time, her eyes were staring wildly at me. Suddenly she hung on to me:

"Save me, Rafael, don't let me die! Save me! You're a doctor, save me!"

It was awful to watch. It wasn't easy to control myself and keep calm: "Well, now, Débora, that's nonsense, you're not going to die."

"Yes, I'm going to die, Rafael, I know. Oh God, why did I do it? Tell me, Rafael, why in the world did I do such a thing?"

Hiding her face in the blanket, she began to cry convulsively. Just then Microbe came in. "What's the matter?" he asked, alarmed. Quickly, I gave him an account of what had happened; he dashed to the sick man's bed.

"This man is dying, Rafael! What an atrocity!"

It was then that he noticed Débora, and his eyes opened wide:

"But what's wrong with her?"

"I'm afraid she has caught this disease," I said, my voice cracking; I could barely hold back my tears. I asked that he send for Brito urgently. He went to the phone and was soon back:

"He's now at the Portuguese Beneficent Hospital, looking after a patient who's seriously ill. He'll come as soon as possible."

Microbe gave the sick man another injection of penicillin. "Just for conscience's sake, really, I don't think it will do him any good." Then he asked if there was anything I needed. I said there wasn't, and he left. I pulled up a chair and sat by Débora, holding her hand. She shuddered. "It's me, Rafael," I whispered. "Don't leave me, Rafael," she murmured. "I won't leave you," I promised. She didn't say anything else; with her eyes wide open, she lay motionless; she made no reply to any of my questions.

At dawn Brito arrived. He examined Débora and was hesitant about saying anything; at my request, he examined Redhead too.

"It's not the same disease," he said. "Definitely not. In her case, we shouldn't exclude the possibility of a psychiatric problem. She has a history of . . . I'd like a second opinion. With your permission, I'll bring in someone, a specialist."

"Of course, of course," I hastened to say. He left and I sat by Débora, who remained motionless, her eyes closed.

I dozed off. I woke up with a start, with the impression that Débora was looking at me; but no, she wasn't, her eyes were closed; and yet there was something—the expression she wore on her face was strange, an expression at once serene and droll; happy and resigned. What caused it? Delirium? What kind of delirium? All of a sudden, her eyes still closed, she stretched forth her arms and pulled me toward her. I tried to hold back, I think I did, she was a patient and I couldn't, but she was also a woman and I could, I should, I wanted— and did I love her? I had always thought that perhaps I did—and what I had never imagined possible, not even in dreams or in moments of delusion, was now happening, she was embracing me, pulling me down toward her, her warm arms around my neck, and then with her breasts already against my chest, her mouth began searching for mine, and I was overcome by panic, what if she is sick with heaven knows what kind of disease or plague, it could be something contagious, and I had always been afraid of contagion, whenever I was in the ward for tropical diseases I avoided getting close to the typhoid and smallpox patients; but even greater than my fear was my desire, an overwhelming desire, and I began kissing her furiously, and I had a hard-on and I began pushing the bedclothes aside, oh God, I'm going to screw her right here on a hospital bed, next to a sick man, something unheard of, and she's a virgin, I know she is, I'll have to deflower her and the sheets will be stained and the orderlies will no doubt conjecture, no, not the orderlies, but that loathsome nurse will, hell, let her conjecture, let her gossip, ah, these breasts, Débora, my love. . . .

B UT IS RAFAEL STILL IN THERE?"

It was Microbe's voice outside in the corridor: he had come—of course—to give the patient yet another damn injection. Jumping out of bed, I tidied myself as well as I could, he walked in, went straight to the sick man's bed without noticing my agitation, gave him a shot of penicillin, then turned dejectedly to me:

"There are only two doses left, Rafael. Let's pray that he'll pull through."

Only two more doses? What if Débora were to need the drug? No, she wouldn't need it. I was now sure she would pull through. And yet, she remained motionless, her eyes closed. Why? What did it mean?

I went to the office of the hospital's director, stretched out on the couch, and tired out, fell asleep. In the morning Brito phoned to say that he would be coming with a psychiatrist.

"An Argentinean who's teaching a course here. An authority. He was reluctant at first, but I succeeded in persuading him, I explained that a colleague was involved, that the case had implications, that it would be better for us if we could get an outsider's opinion. We're leaving now. His name is Finkelman.''

Finkelman, of course. Who else? They arrived soon after. He was a short, ugly man, who looked at us with an air of superiority. At Brito's request, I briefed him quickly on the situation. He said he would like to see the woman patient.

"Actually, you've met her before," I ventured to say cautiously.

"I know."

He asked to be left alone with Débora. He went into the sickroom and closed the door. Minutes went by; Brito, impatient, kept looking at his watch. Finally Finkelman appeared:

"You may come in," he said.

Débora was sitting up in bed, looking at us.

"She's all right now," said Finkelman. "Aren't you, Débora?"

She nodded in reply.

"Incredible," said Brito. "How did you . . . ?"

"Well, my friend," replied a smiling Finkelman, "we doctors have our little tricks, don't we?"

He looked at his watch: He had to teach a class, there were people waiting for him; Brito would give him a ride. He took his leave, then before getting into the car, he looked at me intently but without saying a word. I never saw him again.

I went back to the sickroom. I hesitated at the door, but I went in. I had to force myself to look Débora in the eye. Her eyes met mine in a steady gaze, her face empty of emotion. With an effort, I spoke.

"So, what happened, Débora? What happened?"

"Nothing, Rafael."

Nothing? What the hell was that supposed to mean? Was she dissimulating, was she crazy, or what? Nothing? How come, nothing?

"Nothing, Débora?"

"Nothing, Rafael."

"Nothing at all?"

"Nothing at all."

"Do you know what I'm talking about, Débora?"

"I think so. But nothing happened."

Calmly, and with a somewhat curious expression in her

eyes, she stood staring at me. Which should distress me but didn't; I was feeling rather benumbed, maybe because I was so tired.

"Nothing."

"That's right. Nothing."

And didn't we embrace each other? I could have asked. And didn't we kiss and caress each other? Questions I could have asked, but chose not to; once again, I opted for perplexity.

Redhead died that morning. In the afternoon the *Alerta* published an extra edition: Among other things, the newspaper claimed that the patient had been used as a guinea pig to test an imported drug, and it raised again the theory of murder, laying the blame pointblank on Saturnino.

Surprisingly, this *fazendeiro*, this owner of ranches and farmlands, decided to take up the challenge. The patient had been killed, yes, but the killing had been perpetrated by people interested in upholding the theory of poisoning. Saturnino discredited the *Alerta* reporter in the news media, saying he had been carrying on with one of the nurses that worked at the Isolation Hospital, a fact that could be corroborated by several of the hospital workers. And he also pointed out that the *Alerta* had connections with certain groups that were conspiring to overthrow Getúlio.

An autopsy, which could have thrown light upon this issue, was never performed. That very night, the body was stolen from the morgue where the post-mortem was to be carried out on the following day; the guard claimed that he had seen nothing. Saturnino and the *Alerta* reporter continued to hurl accusations at each other but the issue finally died down. Anyway, it was a mere drop in the ocean, for political unrest kept growing at an alarming rate, culminating in the coup d'état of November, which gave rise to the *Estado Novo,* the New State.

A week later Débora left for Spain via Uruguay. In Spain she enlisted in the International Brigades as a medical doctor. Why? When she was neither a communist nor a radical; she hadn't even been interested in politics. So why Spain? Why the Civil War? What did she have to do with them? And what about me, didn't I deserve at least an explanation? She left without even saying goodbye to me. Well, I've had enough, that's what I thought.

I was studying History, I was really into History. I had a growing desire to know the past—in the hope of understanding the present. And from the study of History I moved on to genealogy—who am I? Who were my ancestors? By studying their lives I hoped in fact to find out who I was; I wanted answers to the questions that kept tormenting me; I wanted to know what had happened, what was happening, what would happen. I wanted to trade perplexity for wisdom—not for passion.

In this undertaking I was helped by a good friend, a genealogist whom I had met by chance, and who became not only an advisor but also a real spiritual guide. With the utmost equanimity, this man revealed to me astonishing things. That I am a descendant of the prophet Jonah—I would never have imagined. And yet, from which other prophet but the bewildered Jonah could I be descended? From which other physician but the perplexed Maimonides? I developed a liking for them; about them I wrote pages and pages of real or imaginary facts, I was thrilled by their adventures, distressed by their tribulations. While trying all the time to understand their perplexity. My perplexity:

Did I love her? Débora: Did I love her? Oh God, was I ever haunted by her. Haunted by her defiant eyes, her sad smile; haunted by her mouth, her breasts, her body. Oh God, I wanted her; I *had* to find out if I loved her. I decided to leave for Spain.

A GENEA-
LOGICAL
NOTE

A T THE END OF THIS NARRATIVE, THERE IS A NOTE WRITTEN
by the genealogist:

Dr. Rafael Mendes never got to Spain. He died on
board the freighter in which he was traveling, victim,
according to the ship's doctor, of a mysterious fever
whose prodromes had manifested themselves before he
set off on his voyage. Throughout his illness Dr. Rafael
Mendes was often delirious, when he would talk about
things that made no sense to the bystanders, such as:
the eyes of the prophet, the Inquisition, caravels, the
head of Tiradentes. During a brief moment of lucidity
he announced that he would be dying soon; he asked
that his body be cast into the sea so that *like Jonah* (to
use his own words) he could reach his destination. He
didn't clarify which destination he had in mind. His
wishes were carried out: his body, wrapped in the
Brazilian flag, sank into the sea while two Brazilian
crew members sang the National Anthem—not all of it,
just the parts they knew.

Two people were notified of the death of Dr. Rafael
Mendes: Dona Alzira Mendes, his wife; and myself, his
genealogist. In accordance with Dr. Rafael's wishes,
the ship's captain sent me the two notebooks that he
had in his possession, and these I have kept together
with the other personal effects he had left at my house.

Whenever people asked Dona Alzira about him, she
would reply, quite understandably, that her husband,
impelled by his magnanimity, had gone to Spain to fight
for democracy and that he had died there and that he
was buried in a common grave on the outskirts of Madrid.

As for myself, I remained silent. And unless there
are any new developments, the period at the end of this
sentence marks the end of the story of Dr. Rafael
Mendes and of all the perplexed Mendeses.

T HE NOTEBOOK SLIPS OUT OF RAFAEL'S HANDS; HE FALLS
asleep. The day is dawning.

RAFAEL MENDES: THE RACE

H‍E WAKES UP WITH SOMEONE POUNDING VIOLENTLY ON the door.

"Rafael! Open the door, Rafael!" It's Helena.

He leaps to his feet, looks at the watch: eight o'clock. How in the world—

"Open the door, Rafael! Open the door, for heavens' sake!"

He opens the door, Helena walks in, dishevelled, wild-eyed, upset:

"What's the matter?" he shouts, alarmned. "What's the matter, Helena?"

Weeping, she flings herself into his arms.

"Ah, Rafael, what a misfortune! What a misfortune!"

"Come on, tell me, Helena! What happened?"

"It's Suzana. She's gone, Rafael."

"Where did she go? When?"

"Early this morning, Rafael . . ." Sobbing her heart out, she can barely speak. "She came home early this morning, packed a suitcase with clothes, and left. She said we shouldn't worry, she was going away for a while, she would soon be in touch . . ."

"But why, Helena? Why didn't you stop her?"

"I begged, Rafael . . . I begged her to stay. But she said it would be better this way, better for everybody. She said you'd understand. . . ."

"Me?"

"Yes, you. And that's not all, Rafael. The radio, since early in the morning, has been reporting on the finance company. They say it went bankrupt, that there are crowds of people in front of the building, wanting to withdraw their money."

Oh no, moans Rafael, that's the last straw.

"And Boris?" he asks.

"He phoned a while ago, he wanted to speak to you. I said I'd wake you up but he said he couldn't wait, he had to catch a plane. . . ."

263

"A plane?"

Ah, the bastard: the rat running away, abandoning ship. And all of a sudden it dawns on him: Suzana and Boris . . .

"They're leaving together, Helena! The two of them! Tell the doorman to get the car going, hurry!"

He dashes out of the apartment: The elevator won't come, it's stuck somewhere, he bangs on the door, then giving up, tears down the stairway, two steps at a time, and panting, reaches the ground floor. As he goes out the front door, he almost crashes into a little man who's just coming in—it's the genealogist.

"Wait a minute!" shouts the little man. "Where are you going? We have to settle our accounts!"

"I can't just now," Rafael shouts back. "I must hurry to the airport, it's urgent. We'll talk when I'm back."

"The airport?" The little man sounds astonished. "Are you running away? Wait, there! I want my money, my ten thousand dollars!"

But Rafael is no longer listening—he gets into his car, drives off in great haste, making the tires screech, and races to the airport.

Leaving the car at the entrance, he dashes into the building. The lobby is crowded. He runs to and fro, searching for Boris, he can't find him, is he gone already? Suddenly Rafael spots him in a corner, there he is, in a hat and dark glasses, cloaked in a raincoat. But there's no sign of Suzana. That's something: Suzana is not with Boris, they are not travelling together, what a relief! Controlling himself—he mustn't make a scene—he walks up to Boris, touches him on the arm. Startled, Boris flinches.

"Relax, Boris. It's me."

"You startled me." Boris heaves a sigh. Glancing around him, he explains that he's fleeing to Montevideo: There's a warrant to arrest him.

"And do you know who obtained it?" With a bitter smile, he says: "Celina. Our friend Celina Cordeiro."

Rafael sighs.

"But why did you let things get this far, Boris? With your social position you could have saved the finance company . . ."

"No, Rafael." His smile was sad; sad and at the same time ironic, a smile typical of Boris. "I couldn't. I just couldn't hack it anymore. Incredible as it may sound, I couldn't anymore. I was tired, you understand, don't you, Rafael?

Sick and tired of everything. Sick and tired of the dinners with the fat cats, of the formal interviews with the ministers, of the under the counter transactions, of political collusion. Sick and tired of all the lies, of all the crookedness. And do you know why, Rafael? Because I discovered something that really matters. . . ."

He stops speaking: Rafael is not listening.

His eyes are fixed on Suzana, who appeared out of the blue. She is dressed for a trip; with her arms around Boris, she is telling him something—I phoned Mother, or something like that—and she is kissing Boris on the face; and now she is looking at Rafael and there is no defiance in her eyes, just a firm and calm determination.

So, here's the confirmation. The nights his daughter spent away from home, and Boris's conduct, and now this escape— everything has fallen into place. They are lovers. They are lovers and they are fleeing the country together. Boris continues to talk but to Rafael his voice sounds distant, although what he is saying is important (he is talking about how their love for each other started: suddenly; he is explaining why they are leaving together: Because they want to start a new life far away—Montevideo is just a stopover—in a place with an idyllic landscape, a bay, and the sea breaking against a white, sandy beach full of coconut trees, of multicolored birds fluttering against the sky; and they are through with finances or mansions or anything else; all they want is to love each other); and Rafael isn't listening because he is thinking of the little girl Suzana, whom he used to rock to sleep with a lullaby (*duerme, duerme mi angelico*) and of the young girl Suzana and of the young woman. . . .

Over the public address system, passengers are asked to board the plane for Montevideo. Suzana embraces her father, kisses him on the face: "Goodbye, Dad, take care of mother; and don't worry, we know what we're doing, Boris and I. We're after our happiness." And Boris says:

"So long, Rafael, old chap." The sad smile. Sad and sly? "Goodbye, my friend." Ironic? Ironic and affectionate?

Hand in hand, they walk toward the departure lounge as Rafael looks on. Perplexed; above all, perplexed. And suddenly he shouts out:

"Wait!"

They turn around: Boris, Suzana, the people in the airport. "Wait!"

Alarmed, Boris takes hold of Suzana's hand but before they can reach the departure lounge, Rafael tackles him, then drags him toward the lobby. Boris struggles, desperately trying to pull himself free. The two men end up on the floor and then the whole scene turns topsy-turvy, Helena, oh God, Helena is here, she shouldn't have come, Helena screaming like a madwoman, and the old genealogist comes running into the airport lobby.

THE OLD MAN AT THE AIRPORT

RUNNING LIKE THIS DESPITE MY AGE AND THE PAIN IN MY chest, and yet run I must, for Rafael Mendes intends to abscond, he and Boris together, notwithstanding the steps taken by my friend Celina Cordeiro, who has denounced them to the police; and if they succeed in escaping, that will be kissing my ten thousand dollars goodbye, so I must catch up with Rafael Mendes, make him cough up the money before he boards his plane; however, before I can reach them, the secret agents nab them, and in no time, Boris Goldbaum and Rafael Mendes are handcuffed; too late, there goes my money.

And all of a sudden I'm overcome by an intense desire to laugh, and I begin to laugh my head off, and everybody, astonished, turns to stare at me, even the agents, everybody thinking I must be an investor who has been cheated out of his money and is now avenged, but I'm not an investor, just a foolish old man. Taking advantage of the opportunity, I walk up to Rafael:

"Your debt is cancelled," I say.

But he is not listening. His eyes, naturally, are riveted on his wife and his daughter. The wife is in tears, but the daughter supports her while looking proudly at her father, who is now being taken away.

It's over. All I can do now is return home, go back to bed, and write.

269

THE THIRD AND LAST NOTEBOOK OF THE NEW CHRISTIAN

A JEW AND A CHRISTIAN, OR A JEW AND A NEW CHRISTIAN, or in fact, two Jews—in short, two men, are arrested. The charge is embezzlement.

Antecedents. Three days before this incident, Senhora Celina Cordeiro went to see an old friend of hers, an elderly man who practiced, without success, as a genealogist—and also as an astrologer, a chiromancer, a diviner, and other such—a man whom she had been helping out with a small sum of money for many years. She had reasons to believe, she told him, that Boris intended to flee the country. And there was more: "He's taking that girl Suzana, Rafael Mendes's daughter, with him; he and the girl are lovers. I've been entertaining the idea of denouncing him. What do you think?" The genealogist approved of the idea; he had reasons to dislike Boris, whom he held responsible for the death of his only son, Julio, a broker with Pecúnia S.A., the finance company headed by this same Boris. However, he asked that Celina give him twenty-four hours, the time he needed "to pull off a deal of my own," as he put it. On the night of November 17, 1975, as they had previously agreed, Celina Cordeiro denounced Boris to the police. On the following morning, right in the middle of the airport, Boris Goldbaum and Rafael Mendes were arrested and taken to a special jail—a house in a distant neighborhood of Porto Alegre, especially converted for this purpose. Allegedly for security reasons, this arrangement was in fact the result of some string-pulling on the part of Celina Cordeiro. Although she loathed Boris Goldbaum, she had a soft spot in her heart for Rafael Mendes, and wanted him to be at least in comfortable surroundings.

A RATHER SPACIOUS ROOM WAS SET ASIDE IN THE PRISON-house for Boris Goldbaum and Rafael Mendes; it is furnished with two beds with foam mattresses and chenille bedspreads, two bedside tables with lamps, a wardrobe, a chest of drawers, a rug with an Oriental design, and, on the wall, the reproduction of a painting: a bay, the sea breaking against a beach with pure white sand, and birds—one, two, three, four, five, six—six multicolored birds against a bright blue sky. But the birds seem to be frozen; the painter lacked the skill to create the illusion of flight. Still, they're nice to look at. Anyway, for scenes of greater motion, there is a TV, although it's only a sixteen-inch black-and-white without cable, made in the free zone of Manaus, in the distant Amazon region, a mysterious place where Indians and melodious birds with brightly colored plumage are still to be found. To sum up then, this room even has a bathroom ensuite, and it could well be a bedroom in a two-star or maybe even a three-star hotel (depending on the whim of the inspector from Embratur, the Brazilian Tourism Authority).

But there are bars on the windows. Which Rafael notices as soon as he walks into the room. Not the kind of bars usually seen in prisons; less conspicuous, but still bars, iron bars, of good quality iron. There are also bars on the small window on the door (made of solid wood), and when the door closes behind them, which happens as soon as the two men are pushed into the room (perhaps not pushed; shown in; however, shown in with firmness, with determination, and perhaps even with a touch of brutality, let's say, ninety percent firmness/determination; ten percent brutality) it does so with a loud noise (not too loud, though; a noise maybe about twenty decibels; loud enough, though, for someone accustomed to nothing louder than Musak and the whirring of the air-conditioners). Rafael Mendes—he realizes with an anguished heart—is imprisoned.

He sits down on one of the beds, which by tacit agreement,

as usually happens under such circumstances, will be his from then on. Boris sits down on the other, his face still bloodied by Rafael's blows. Boris smiles; despite everything, he smiles enigmatically. By acting on the same impulse that overcame him only half an hour ago, Rafael could fall upon Boris and punch him on the face until he erased that smirk off his face. However, Rafael is so depressed now that the idea doesn't even occur to him.

The door opens. In comes the chief of police. There's nothing belligerent about his manner; on the contrary, he seems an affable man, with something of a math professor about him, but one of those easygoing professors, the type that refers tenderly to the logarithm tables. He goes over the situation: Yes, Boris and Rafael are under arrest and they will remain imprisoned until their case goes to court, or until some other solution is found (through Celina Cordeiro? But does Celina Cordeiro still have any clout—and supposing that she is willing to use it to protect the prisoners, which is a moot point—or did she use up all the clout she had to get them into this special prison? It remains to be seen). Anyhow, they will be well-treated, as the meal about to be served will prove. The chief leaves, and indeed, a moment later in comes a man bringing them dinner. Roast beef, summer squash, pasta with sauce, sago pudding. There is plenty of food and it is pretty edible. Although Rafael Mendes hasn't eaten much during the last several days, he is not hungry. Unlike Boris, who eats, in that avidly ill-mannered way which has always made a bad impression on Rafael and on the high society people; it's his lack of table manners that most clearly identify him as an arriviste.

They don't speak. At times Rafael stares at Boris, who, however, meets his eyes in a steady gaze. There is no hatred in Boris's expression, not even insolence or defiance. Generally speaking, he seems calm, even resigned. One could say that during the short period of time between his arrest and his imprisonment Boris has matured. Artificial maturation? Yes, but maturation nonetheless.

Dinner over, and certainly having come to the conclusion that any attempts at striking up a conversation with his cellmate would be doomed to a self-conscious failure, Boris turns on the television. They watch a soap opera, soon followed by the news. Franco remains in a coma, naturally, but no mention is made of their arrest. Which is odd and rather disturbing.

Their arrest is important enough to be one of the lead stories not only in the local but also in the national news. So why was it never mentioned? Hell, they're not political prisoners. Or are they? No, they couldn't be: They've been arrested for embezzlement, which is, after all, a common enough crime, as the chief of police himself said. True, his supervisors might think otherwise. But then . . .

They'd rather not think. Although not speaking to each other, one thing is clear: Both of them would rather not think about this matter. Each one knows that the other would rather not think about it; they know because there was a time when communication between them was so perfect that they could guess what was on each other's mind, and it wasn't just in the case of interest rates.

After the news, Boris asks if Rafael would mind if he turns off the television. He asks just for the sake of asking, he knows Rafael won't reply; but in such matters he is always courteous, his courtesy to others on a par with his rotten table manners. After waiting for a few seconds—ten seconds, which might be considered a reasonable length of time—Boris gets up and turns off the television. A bright spot lingers on the screen: a reminder of that day's news; a reminder of that day and of all the other days. It's an historical synthesis of exceptional brightness. As for the bedside lamps: each man switches off his own; they undress in the dark. Out of modesty? Maybe. Enemies probably don't like to be seen naked. Boris, of course, doesn't consider Rafael an enemy, and even if he did, he wouldn't mind undressing in front of his former partner. If he has turned off the light, it's because Rafael did so first. Rather tactful of Boris.

It's Rafael who wouldn't be able to bear to see the other man's nakedness. The sight of the hairy chest, of the long ape-like arms, of the big circumcised penis—especially the penis, the size, the circumcision—would unleash an uncontrollable loathing, a murderous fury (this bastard used to sit my daughter in his lap, I bet he was already fondling her when she was a three-year-old kid, this pervert, this heel). Which is quite understandable—after all, Boris is his daughter's lover. But without this aspect, Rafael's hatred cannot be justified. Yes, Boris was irresponsible in the way he handled the affairs of the Pecúnia; flighty even. But Rafael was aware of this fact, and even so he didn't take any drastic steps. If in the past he could accept Boris as a friend, as a boss—why can't he now accept him as a son-in-law or what amounts to one? Why did Boris keep him in the dark about his relationship with Suzana? Maybe to spare his feelings.

Maybe Boris had been waiting for the right opportunity to disclose it. Even though Boris is considered an enemy, Rafael must give him the benefit of the doubt. Such cogitations, however, do nothing to mitigate Rafael's hatred. For it's not just this matter between Boris and Suzana; it is this, plus Celina's betrayal (even though attenuated by the special privileges), plus this humiliating imprisonment. Besides hatred, there's anguish and anxiety over everything that has happened to him ever since he came upon that box containing his father's belongings—a succession of mind-blowing revelations. He wasn't a Jew, but now he's a Jew, or a half-Jew, or a descendant of Jews, or a Judaizer, or a New Christian, or a member of the nation—it doesn't matter: What is certain is that now there is something Jewish about him, nothing to do with circumcision, something else, which wasn't there before, something which is at the very least unpleasant, depressing even. Like finding a cavity in a tooth. Or a leak in a drainpipe in the apartment. Or an ugly birthmark on the buttocks of a beloved woman. The genealogist had tried to convince him that it was something good—of course he would, with ten thousand dollars at stake—but what is the good of being the descendant of a prophet, of an illustrious physician? Actually, judging from his father's description of them, they were weirdos; perplexed creatures. They didn't pass on to him any values, whether material or moral; nor the secret—well, the legend, yes—of the Gold Tree; nor any ennobling instances that he in turn could pass on to his daughter (and would Suzana be impressed by ennobling instances?) or to his grandchildren (he'd better not even think of this possibility, it's far too painful).

He wasn't a Jew, now he's a Jew. He had a good position or at least it looked good; he had a high-paying job, people looked up to him. Now he is unemployed and in prison. If before he knew nothing about his father, at least he had an idealized and somewhat comforting image of him; now he knows that his father was an eccentric who cheated on his wife, walked out on his family and gave up his medical practice because of a woman doctor just as eccentric as he was—bequeathing to his only son nothing save some old clothes, books and notebooks with stories about the nation.

The nation. What a strange nation it is, a nation that includes rebellious prophets as well as blind *bandeirantes*, flag-bearing pioneers; illustrious physicians as well as senile Indians; great financiers as well as swindlers like Boris Goldbaum. Who, incidentally, doesn't torture himself with such issues: he lies sound asleep, and is even snoring. Scoundrels have no problem falling asleep, Rafael observes with bitterness. He gets up and walks to the window. From between the bars he can see a small tiled patio bathed in moonlight; its boundaries are the house itself and a high, moss-covered wall. What lies beyond this wall? An empty lot? A house? Who lives in that house? And what are they doing right now? Eating dinner? Watching TV? Discussing the latest events? Neighbors, can you tell me what happened? Can you tell me what's going to happen?

Rafael goes back to bed and lies down; he tosses about until, exhausted, he falls asleep on a bed that isn't his, in a house that isn't his: It's as if he were in a capsule adrift in outer space.

H IS DREAMS, HOWEVER, DON'T FORSAKE HIM. WHAT IS THIS room if not a stronghold of nightmares? Before the day dawns, the medieval knight steps out of the mists of a restless sleep. He walks toward Rafael, who waits for him, trembling; the knight then devotes himself to his habitual task of encircling his victim's throat with his iron gauntlets. And his grip, now stronger than ever, leads Rafael to believe that this time the knight is in real earnest, that this time he will indeed put an end to the long—long according to the genealogist, but who is to say if everything is not just lies, nothing but the fabrications of a senile and/or unscrupulous old man?—Mendes lineage.

To his rescue comes—who? God? No: Boris. Boris Goldbaum. There he stands, shaking Rafael awake, looking at him with that faunlike face of his, a worried face, true, but still like a faun.

"You were moaning."

Dazed, Rafael stares at him. Then he realizes: He was dreaming, having his recurrent nightmare; then Boris woke him up. He should feel grateful, and for a moment (to what length of time does this moment correspond? To one single pulsation of a quartz crystal oscillator in a Japanese wristwatch, this electronic marvel developed in the country that created the bonsai? To one tenth of a pulsation? To two tenths?) he feels grateful because he is not wide awake yet; but once he is, and on his guard, hatred is back. And the look he throws at his former partner is so rancorous that Boris, caught by surprise, steps back, his feelings certainly hurt, for it was only reasonable to have expected a shred of gratitude for his role as exterminator of nightmares. But is this hatred strong enough? Had it been as strong as Rafael believed it was, shouldn't it have sent Boris flying against the opposite wall as if he had been hit by an electric discharge or by the rays of a cosmic pistol? Rafael wonders. He wonders, but at least for the time being, he would rather not delve into this matter. Anyway, a man (obviously a plainclothesman) comes in with breakfast on a tray:

"Good morning," he says pleasantly.

Irony in his greeting? Probably not. It seems unlikely that this man—stocky, bronze-colored, with Indian features—should have the degree of sophistication needed for early morning ironies. It looks as if the man is merely carrying out a task; and as he learned in the public relations course (duration: twenty-eight hours) he has just completed, any task should be carried out as joyfully and willingly as possible. Thus: good morning!

Bread, butter, jam, salami, coffee with milk: a copious meal, as on the previous day. And, as on the previous day, Boris eats with relish. In silence Rafael bites on a slice of bread and takes a few sips of black coffee with no sugar.

The chief of police comes in. He wants to know if they rested comfortably. Yes, says Boris, it's not like home, but . . . The chief of police laughs; the news he then imparts to them, though, is not encouraging: They are to remain in this "house" for a while; they are not allowed any visitors, be they relatives or lawyers. Solicitous, he concludes by saying, " Should you need anything, just let us know."

As soon as he leaves—it looks as if they are taking turns, but it's just a coincidence, or who knows, maybe they are indeed taking turns yet making it look like a coincidence—in comes the Indian-looking individual. It becomes increasingly more obvious (an obviousness that will probably grow in geometric progression with each appearance of this man) that he is a plainclothesman, despite the fact that he is here—the real reason or a pretext?—to bring them the newspapers. He puts them on the table:

"The newspapers."

Unnecessary words. Or maybe necessary for this man to act the role of the host rather than the jailer; or if he is indeed a jailer, then he must be a special jailer for special prisoners. Or maybe necessary for the peace of mind of this man who perhaps only reluctantly plays the role of the jailer, his dream being getting a job as a receptionist at a three- or four-star hotel. Or maybe the man is overawed by the presence of prisoners connected with the financial world, to him a mythical, magical world; or maybe he is a sensitive man who doesn't mind stating the obvious if by doing so he can break a silence which, he has already noticed (as sensitive people are apt), has become awkward. The fact that he looks stupid doesn't invalidate the last hypothesis. He may well be stupid on the outside and sensitive on the inside.

He leaves.

He leaves, leaving behind a problem.

There are three newspapers—two tabloids, one full-sized paper. Who will read them first, Boris Goldbaum or Rafael Mendes? Rafael Mendes or Boris Goldbaum? Perhaps this is a pointless question. Rafael Mendes wants to read the newspapers, or at least he *thinks* he does; it's quite possible that he doesn't, but it is certain that if Boris reaches out for the papers, Rafael will want to read them. Therefore, it is wise to assume that Rafael does want to read them. It's *possible* that Boris isn't interested in reading them, but assuming both men want to read the newspapers at the same time—how are they going to divide the three newspapers between them? Especially when the newspapers are of different kinds? The possibilities are endless, practically endless. The two tabloids for Boris and the big newspaper for Rafael—that's one possibility. Or vice-versa. Or they could total the number of pages, then divide them by two—but then there's the problem of the various sections: who will get the sports pages, the crime pages, the business news? Besides, who will establish the criteria and make the final decision? Boris? Why should he? At the Pecúnia he was at the top, he was the boss. But now both of them are in jail. On an equal footing. Actually, no: It's Boris who is now in the doghouse, his reputation sullied. (Is that so? Isn't it possible that Rafael, who knew about the embezzlement, is just as guilty?) But is this relevant to the matter of deciding who will read what? Does the guiltier person have a greater or a lesser right to choose than the less guilty? Generally speaking, the guiltier a person is, the fewer the privileges to which he's entitled; however, if one takes into account the fact that the guiltier person will serve more time for his crime, perhaps it's only fair, or at least humane, to allow him to read more. Then again, will reading do him any good?

Boris picks up one of the newspapers. He does so seemingly at random—seemingly, for it is impossible to know for sure. The atmosphere is not suitable for a discussion; they could come to blows. Rafael picks up one of the remaining newspapers and flips through it. Franco remains in a coma; not a word, however, about their arrest. In the business section, a brief news item informs that Pecúnia S.A. Credit and Investment is operating normally, any other reports notwithstanding. Which strikes Rafael as being very strange. How could it be operating normally with the President-Director and his top advisor in jail? Something is up. Could it be that Boris has pulled off yet another sting? Rafael gives him a sidelong look, a perplexed yet spiteful look; fearing however that his perplexity might undermine his hatred, Rafael gives up this silent questioning and returns to the newspaper. Boris seems oblivious to everything. Maybe he is not even interested in any news about the Pecúnia. Maybe he's reading the social column. The scoundrel.

Lunch is brought in by the jailer; just as copious as the dinner on the previous day. Great, says Boris, sitting down at his table. He looks at the tray with a puzzled expression, as if something were missing. Nothing to drink? he asks. Only water, says the man.

"Water!" Boris breaks into laughter. "Water is poison. Wouldn't you agree, my friend?"

Constrained, the man joins in the laughter.

"I agree, Doutor, but . . ."

Boris puts his hand into his pocket, takes out a green bill, crackles it in his hand. It's a twenty-dollar bill. (How many such bills does he carry on him? Quite a few, for sure, considering that he was—they were—about to board a plane, never to return. That he still has this money on him is yet another mystery.) Even though the cop might be unfamiliar with American money, even though he might not know what the current rate of exchange is, he probably realizes that it is enough to buy a great deal of beer. He hesitates: On the one hand, his position, his honesty, his fear that it might get him into hot water; on the other hand . . . But the dollar bill, after being weighed on these quickly assembled scales, is found to be heavy enough; pocketing it, the man leaves, but not before asking if Rafael would like some beer too. No, he wouldn't. Minutes later the man returns carrying under his arm a rolled-up newspaper, inside which is a bottle of beer. The man also supplies a bottle opener and then he leaves, saying—his solicitousness more and more obvious—that he is at their disposal.

Boris pours himself some beer. Before he starts drinking, he silently proffers the glass to Rafael, who ignores the gesture; he would like a beer, but acceptance would amount to surrender. Besides, another thought is now nagging him: After this beer, then what? What is Boris up to? Maybe nothing. Maybe he is just ensuring the future supply of beer. However, knowing Boris as he does . . .

The door opens. It's the chief of police. "A visitor," he announces. "From Brasilia," he adds, with ill-concealed satisfaction. He's enjoying one of the highlights of his life, the chief of police is.

He shows in a man, still young; his cropped hair and thick eyeglasses give him an earnest appearance, very much like that of a well-behaved schoolboy. He wears a striped suit, which hangs loosely from his body, and a gaudy necktie; and he carries the inevitable attaché case.

"How are you, Toledo?" asks Boris, without getting up.

"What?" The chief of police is surprised. "You know each other?"

"Toledo and I are old friends," says Boris. "Rafael here hasn't met him yet. Rafael, let me introduce you to Doutor Toledo, from the Ministry of Finance."

Rafael cannot ignore the man just because it's Boris who is introducing him. Rising to his feet, he greets him; Rafael is courteous rather than effusive; constrained rather than crestfallen (or almost crestfallen). After all, he is in jail, not in his own office. Anyway, the visitor hasn't come to see him, of course. He is there to see Boris, who asks, as he lights a cigarette:

"So, Toledo? Did you have a nice trip?" The usual small talk.

"Pretty much so, Goldbaum." The man is constrained but cordial. "A bit rough-going as we flew over the state of Santa Catarina; otherwise, it was fine. May I sit down?"

"By all means, make yourself at home. It's your house." Boris laughs. "I'm just a guest here."

Toledo chooses to ignore the insolence. He sits down. The chief of police takes his leave, he has other things to do:

"So, make yourselves at home. Anything you need, just give us a shout."

He leaves, closing the door behind him noiselessly. Boris turns to his visitor:

"Well, then, Toledo? What brings you here?"

"Guess, Goldbaum," replies Toledo with what could be a grimace or a nervous tick; it is probably a grimace, a mixture of irritation and fatigue (brought about by the flight? or by something else?), with the addition of a certain amount of glee verging on sadism. This complex grimace, and other grimaces like it, surely would account for the wrinkles and the tortured expression on Toledo's face. "Can't you guess that it is the situation of your finance company? This time you went too far, Boris. People in Brasilia have had it with you."

Then he realizes that Rafael is in the room:

"I don't know if—"

"You can talk freely," Boris cuts him short. "Rafael works with me, he can be trusted."

"Good. So, let's get down to business, I haven't got much time, I'm flying back to São Paulo tonight. My mission is not exactly official, Goldbaum . . . But it's just as important. If not more."

Opening his attaché case, he removes a stack of papers, which he peruses.

"Let me see . . . Yes. Your situation is really pretty bad, Goldbaum. You're in hot water. We have the names of your agents in the United States, in Europe, in South Africa, we know the numbers of your bank accounts, the total amount of the embezzlement. We know enough to make you rot in jail; not in this one, somewhere worse. But . . ."

A smile. A wan smile. A wan and ominous smile.

"You've got powerful friends in high places, Goldbaum.

Somebody has intervened . . . It's to nobody's advantage to let you sink. Or to strike you down. Any intervention now would cause alarm . . . Particularly at this point in time. We're expecting the arrival of an international delegation, Goldbaum. Major investors. The message I have for you is, find a way out of this mess.''

"Find a way . . ." Boris grins, amused. "What way? Any suggestions?''

"Don't play the fool," says Toledo. Angry; the anger of the timid man. It is clear that he normally contains rather than displays his anger, which accounts for the insomnia, the eczema of nervous origin, the duodenal ulcer. In addition, like his wife and his little daughter, he suffers from asthmatic bronchitis, which is the reason why he accepted this post in Brasilia, with its high altitude, dry climate, unpolluted air. Brasilia is good, Brasilia is safe. Toledo dislikes having to travel to the other states; the hotels, even though they are four- or five-star hotels, the restaurant meals, and mostly the missions entrusted to him, are detrimental to his health; his consumption of antacids and tranquilizers rises sharply when he is on the road. And when, on top of everything else, an already difficult and delicate situation involves dealing with Boris Goldbaum, then . . .

"You know far more about such things than I do, Goldbaum. Far more than anybody else. It's your problem. Talk to your friends abroad, or to your own people. They wouldn't let you down.''

"My own people, Toledo?" says Boris with mockery. "My own people have disowned me." The mocking tone in Boris's voice increases in proportion to the other man's visible signs of insecurity. On a graph, Line 1 (corresponding to Boris's levels of mockery), and Line 2 (corresponding to Toledo's levels of insecurity) are almost parallel and sharply ascending. "Do you know that I am reputed to be anti-Semitic?''

Toledo now frowns, and it looks as if he has closed this subject for good:

"You've got to be joking, Goldbaum. But you're playing with fire. I'm laying my cards on the table: You've got some friends in the Ministry, but you've also got enemies who would like to see you dead. Mostly because you are a Jew, and to some people the idea of having a Jew as a scapegoat is rather appealing. You think it's passé, Goldbaum? Well, so it is. But it has happened before, you know. Can you picture,

Boris, an enraged mob invading neighborhoods like Bom Retiro? Or Bom Fim? Beating up your people, setting stores on fire—wrecking your home?''

"I don't live in Bom Fim," says Boris, stubbing out his cigarette.

"Don't you want to do anything to save your finance company?''

"I'm not interested. At least not now."

"You're out of your mind, Boris. Completely off your rocker." Toledo is uneasy and despondent: It looks as if his return trip will be soured by a mission that ended in failure. And he hates failures. As much as he hates such missions. He considers himself a technocrat, not a politician; this kind of scheming strikes him as dishonest, absurd. He is loyal, however, to the Minister of Finance, whose ideas he endorses, particularly the Minister's ideas about the workings of the stock market. As a matter of fact, Toledo's master's thesis— written under the guidance of the Minister himself, who at the time was a professor at the University—dealt with this very subject, the mechanism of the stock markets. However, figuring out the workings, the mechanism, is one thing; shenanigans are something else; just as a financier like Rothschild is one thing and a financial adventurer like this Boris is something else. However, the fact is that Brazilian capitalism, if such a thing really exists, is full of the likes of him. Yes, capitalism thrives in São Paulo, and to a lesser degree in Rio, but here in Porto Alegre—the capital city of a state which is not among the poorest and most backward—things already begin to deteriorate; so, what is to be expected from regions like the North, the Northeast? The hinterland? An economy based on bartering, Indian style: You give me a little mirror, I'll give you brazilwood. Absolutely no accumulation and no investment of capital. And nothing that is calculable: let people sleep to the sound of the war drums. Sighing, he puts the papers back into his attaché case:

"What do I say to the Minister?"

"That I appreciate his concern. But there's nothing I can do. Tell him I'm into something else now. Did you get it, Toledo? I'm into something else!"

"What the fuck are you talking about?" asks Toledo, perplexed. "You're in jail, Boris! You're up to your neck in shit!''

"Maybe," says Boris, smiling. "But I'm now into something else. Rafael here knows about it."

Toledo gives Rafael a look. It's a half-entreating look, as if he were asking for help; he even opens his mouth to say something, then changes his mind:

"All right." Rising to his feet, he makes for the door. Something occurs to him, he turns around, and in one last—and it's definitely *last*—attempt, he says:

"And what about the tree, Goldbaum?"

"What tree?"

"Your tree. The one everybody talks about. The one with the gold nuggets."

Boris makes no reply. He keeps smiling.

"Fake, aren't they?" There is weariness in the voice of the economist Toledo. "They're fake, aren't they? I've always thought they were. Everything about people like you is fake, nothing but a front. Buildings with marble façades and tinted windowpanes, full-page ads in the magazines with nationwide circulation, trips to other countries in chartered jet planes. Everything a façade, everything designed to impress people. Statues with clay feet, that's what the likes of you are. You, Goldbaum, you don't have the slightest notion of what makes for a sound economy, neither you nor people of your ilk. You and your kind creep into the interstices of the economic structure. You are the termites undermining the economy. But the DDT of austerity is in store for you, you can bet on it. We'll squelch you, Goldbaum. We'll ruin you, with or without your Gold Tree. We'll destroy the Pecúnia, just like the wolf destroyed the piglet's house in that fairy tale—with one single puff. We'll seal everything with wax, we'll go through your files with a fine comb. We'll probe your life. We'll interrogate your employees, your friends, your relatives, your lovers. We'll ferret out your international connections, and everything and everyone that is behind you—subversive activities? A possibility, isn't it, Goldbaum? Terrorism, maybe? It wouldn't surprise me in the least. In short, we'll do a complete cleanup, something that will be a lesson to all the Goldbaums of the world."

Panting, he falls silent; with the back of his hand he wipes the froth off his lips. He motions to the guard to open the door. He leaves. His footsteps reverberate in the corridor; there is the sound of another door opening and closing, and then there is silence.

I N SILENCE THEY WATCH T.V. IN SILENCE ONE OF THEM GETS up and turns off the set. In silence they undress and lie down.

Rafael Mendes is unable to sleep. Of what is Rafael the Insomniac thinking? What all insomniacs think of: mother, father. Wife. Daughter. But mostly, this sleepless man, this Rafael Mendes, is thinking of Suzana. Resentment gradually gives way to a nostalgic, melancholy tenderness. He recalls now the good moments; the joyful, tender scenes of his family life: the parties, the picnics, the trips.

Suddenly Boris begins to talk.

It's about himself that he talks. He goes back to his childhood, he tells the story of a poor boy, the son of a communist tailor. He says that this boy was raised in deprivation; he was often absent from school because he had no shoes to wear. And being poor, he had to earn a living at an early age, first peddling clotheshangers, then lottery tickets, and finally books.

"I enjoyed selling books, Rafael. I felt that in this way I was making a contribution to mankind, that I was being faithful to my father's ideas."

But it was a constant source of irritation. Some customers wouldn't pay; others would keep the books for a few days and then return them soiled and damaged (and even with pages ripped out!). And there were also those that would criticize him for selling socialist books at capitalistic prices.

"I grew more and more disillusioned, Rafael. Finally, the pinch of poverty became unbearable and I decided that I would make money. And then . . ."

Boris talks and talks. And suddenly he changes the subject. Now he talks about Suzana. And Rafael doesn't jump out of bed, doesn't strike out at him with punches and kicks; maybe he would like to, but he does nothing. He listens in silence. For many reasons, the main one probably being that Boris now talks about a Suzana that Rafael doesn't—but *wants* to, *has* to—know. "As you know, Rafael, I was like a second father to her," Boris is saying. (It's true: he was a second father.) "She started coming to see me because she was filled with concern; she needed help and I did what I could to help her. I did so not just on her account, or on yours, Rafael, but on my own account too. Helping her made me feel good. Made me feel worthy, do you understand? And it wasn't difficult for me to come up with solutions to her adolescent anxieties.

"Things became complicated when she started university. That's when her political activism began. Up to then she hadn't been interested in politics, but as soon as she became so she turned into a radical. She joined a small but belligerent group of irate leftists, a split group within a dissident group. She began talking about seizing power by violent means, about rivers of blood streaming down the streets. Once she showed me a weapon—a revolver, true, it was old and had no bullets; but I was alarmed and wasn't reassured by the fact that she burst into laughter, saying that she was afraid of weapons and only carried one to impress her friends. But it wasn't just the weapon: She handed out leaflets and edited an underground publication that attacked the multinationals and evoked Tiradentes as the model to be emulated.

"She would often ask me for money—for the cause. Whenever I objected half seriously, half jokingly, that by helping her cause I was in fact digging my own grave, she would reply that my helping out was my only hope, my alibi before the People's Tribunal. 'But will you,' I would then ask, 'testify on my behalf at this Tribunal?' Yes, she would; in fact, she didn't consider me an oppressor, my case being one of opportunism, of speculation, rather than of oppression. 'You're not like the big industrialists or the latifundium owners,' she would say; 'they're the ones who exploit the people directly, and they'll pay with their blood.'

"Just as abruptly as it had started, this political phase ended. Suddenly Tiradentes was a wimp and Trotsky an idiot. She became depressed; she was smoking too much, drinking, doing drugs. And just as suddenly as she had fallen into this pit of depression she came out of it—and joined the sect of the New Essenes. With glittering eyes and a radiant smile, she would say she had found the right road; she took to wearing the long white tunic that was the trademark of the followers of the sect; she became actively engaged in proselytizing, and would approach people on the street. Naturally, I became the favorite target of her tirades. She made me read the leaflets, she tried to prove to me that Jesus was the true Messiah I had been waiting for. 'But I'm not waiting for any Messiah,' I would retort. To which she would say, 'You Jews are full of bitterness, which is only natural, for you haven't tasted the sweetness of the love for Jesus.' One evening she invited me to visit their temple, which was located on the top of a hill, near Belém Novo. We climbed up the hill on foot, as was required by the sect; anyway, there was no road leading to the place. After a two-hour walk—with me on the verge of giving up—we arrived at the temple. A building made of rough stones, with no windows and no furniture, except for a few rustic wooden benches. It was empty; the worship was over.

"Asking me to wait there, she disappeared through a side door. I stood in the stuffy premises, lit only by a single candle. A few minutes later she was back, smiling, with flowers in her hair. Naked."

Boris stops talking. In the ensuing silence his breathing is quite audible; he is panting slightly.

"Naked, Rafael. She walked up to me, embraced me. I returned the embrace. We kissed. And that was all, Rafael. I swear, that was all. Nothing else happened, Rafael. And do you know why not, Rafael? Do you?"

He explains: At that very moment he began to realize that he loved Suzana, just as she too—all of a sudden—was making the same discovery. And what a joy it was to learn that they loved each other! Afterward Suzana left the sect and they became indeed lovers. They were happy, very happy. There were problems, of course: She would fly into a temper, she was jealous even of the secretaries that worked at the Pecúnia. On the other hand, Boris wanted them to get married as soon as possible; he disliked the furtiveness, the dissimulation, especially because of Rafael. She would reply that she didn't want to get married, that marriage was a drag; however, she ended up by agreeing to marry him on condition that they leave for somewhere distant, some peaceful place by the seaside, preferably in another country. There they would lead an idyllic existence—they would stroll about naked, or practically so; they would sleep in the open air or in caves; they would live on wild fruit, and her body would always be adorned with flowers. With the local Indians they would maintain a relationship of amiable respect, expressed only through friendly gestures; they would never speak to the natives, so as to avoid resorting to the corrupting power of words, even of the spoken word. And they would never give those Indians any gifts, little mirrors being particularly perilous. For the moment they did so, or even worse, the moment they accepted something, for example, brazilwood, in return for their gifts, commerce would be introduced, with the resulting loss of the innocence that she and Boris had so painfully regained.

At first such an idea struck Boris as absurd, but gradually he became more and more enthralled by it: a new life, why not? Innocence, why not?

"When things started looking grim at the Pecúnia, Rafael, I felt that the right moment had come. Unfortunately, they caught me—*us*. But I'm going back to Suzana, Rafael, that's a fact, there's no question about it. And I'd like you to accept this fact, Rafael. Nothing is going to keep us apart. Nothing."

He falls silent.

In the darkness, Rafael gets up. He takes a few steps toward Boris's bed. Not many steps; three, to be precise. Considering that the distance between their beds measures two meters and twenty centimeters, and that each of Rafael's steps is sixty centimeters long, it would be possible for him to reach the other man's bed in four steps—but this is not to happen: He suddenly wavers, raises his hand to his forehead, utters a strange sound, a cross between a moan and a grunt, though more like a grunt than a moan, and falls, but not forward, which would allow him to hit his target. Supposing, that is, that Boris's bed *was* the target, supposing that Boris *himself* was the target, which are both—whatever the emotions, hatred or a rush of affection, that prompted this nocturnal wanderer to move—perfectly reasonable suppositions. He falls slightly sideways, more backward than sideways; he falls.

BORIS'S FACE IS THE FIRST THING RAFAEL SEES UPON WAKING up. And Suzana's anxious face—have they sent for her then? is it serious then?—and there's also the face of an old man wearing glasses, a stethoscope dangling from his neck—the doctor.

"Well, then, Senhor Rafael, feeling better?" It's the doctor who asks the question.

With difficulty, Rafael tries to lift himself up.

"Lie back," cautions the doctor. "You mustn't get out of bed. Your blood pressure went way up."

Rafael lets himself collapse on the bed. Suzana kneels by his side:

"Take it easy, Dad. Everything is all right now."

"And your mother, how is she?" Rafael murmurs.

"She's fine," says Suzana, attempting a smile. "She really is, Dad, believe me. She was a bit shaken up at first . . . But she soon rallied, she's taken on the responsibilities of running the house, of looking after your affairs, she's coping well, and she even stopped taking those tranquilizers. The two of us—"

Unable to contain herself, she bursts into tears. And there she is, the girl Suzana, kneeling by her father, who strokes her hair with tremulous fingers. And Boris stands gazing at them, without saying a word.

Boris makes Suzana get to her feet, he helps her to a chair. Then he draws near Rafael, looks him steadily in the eye.

"Rafael, I've got to talk to you. It's important. Are you well enough to listen?"

Rafael closes his eyes; Boris persists: "Open your eyes, listen to me." Oh God, Rafael thinks to himself, why doesn't this accursed man leave me alone? Why doesn't he disappear? Boris is about to speak, hesitates, turns to the doctor:

"Will you excuse us, doctor?"

"Certainly," the man hastens to say. He makes for the door:

291

"I'll be standing just outside. Call me when you're through."
Boris leans over Rafael.

"We'll cut and run, Rafael. Today. In a little while."

Quickly he explains that the doctor will facilitate their
getaway. He needs money: His wife is ill, his son a drug
addict. It was the doctor himself who put the idea to Boris
and Suzana: For ten thousand dollars he will help them
escape. It's simple: Boris will pretend that he, too, doesn't
feel well. Saying that they might be suffering from food
poisoning, the doctor will then have them transferred to a
friend's clinic. From there it will be easy for them to escape,
especially because interest in them is already on the wane
now that the Pecúnia is under intervention. The press doesn't
even mention them anymore; Toledo will only be too glad to
see them gone.

"Well? What do you think?"

"Well, Father?" says Suzana, anxious.

Rafael looks at her: There she is, embracing Boris, just as
at the airport.

"Well?" says Boris again.

Rafael makes no reply; he closes his eyes. With his eyes
closed, he hears Suzana and Boris finalizing the details of
their escape. They'll go first to the state of Paraná, and from
there to Paraguay, where Helena is to join them. Boris then
asks the doctor to come in. They settle on eleven o'clock that
night, when Boris will ask the guard to send for the doctor,
who will be on the alert. The doctor moves closer to Rafael:

"Everything will turn out all right," he murmurs. "Don't
worry, Senhor Rafael."

Rafael stares at him; for a moment, the doctor lowers his
eyes, ashamed of what he is doing—this man, this old Brazilian, is ashamed of lying, of cheating; if he didn't need the
money, he wouldn't be doing it, not even for ten thousand
dollars. However, this embarrassment, this painful embarrassment, is short-lived. A moment later the old man is again
looking Rafael in the eye; and in the expression on his face
there is no longer any constraint; there is sadness, there is
bitterness, there is even—just as in Boris's face a short while
ago—a certain dignity. Pulling up a chair, he sits at the
bedside.

"I know what you're thinking, Senhor Rafael. Strictly
speaking, I shouldn't give a damn about what you think, but
I'd like to tell you something: You know, I'm not doing this

just for the money. Sure, I need the ten thousand dollars, I need them badly, it's something urgent, desperate. But there's another reason why I want to help you. I knew your father, Senhor Rafael. My name is Castellar, Raul Castellar, maybe you've heard about me."

Castellar? Raul? At first the name doesn't ring a bell; but that's because Rafael feels dopey, his mind is sluggish—what kind of drug did this charlatan inject into him? Then it dawns on him: Ah yes, in the *Second Notebook*, he's the doctor who used to work in the Department of Communicable Diseases; the one who only wanted to play snooker.

"Your father was a gentleman of refinement," the old man went on. "As a matter of fact, all the Mendeses were refined people, such an illustrious, traditional family, but Rafael Mendes, my friend Rafael Mendes, he was like a father to me. When he first met me I was going through one of the worst phases of my life: I was a loafer then, interested only in having a good time and in playing snooker; the seven-ball was all that mattered to me. Well, Rafael was very patient and tolerant, he never humiliated me in front of the government employees, unlike the other physician who worked there, a certain Dr. Artêmio, a communist he was. One day Rafael sent for me to announce that he was going to Spain and he asked me to be the acting department head for a while. I was surprised, Senhor Rafael, genuinely surprised, and moved too; nobody trusted me then, nobody believed in me, my wife had just left me after calling me a good-for-nothing, a shameless person, and other such names. And here was your father placing his trust in me! I had never received such an honor before. During my three-month term as department head, I regained my male pride; I was a strict but sensitive boss; dynamic without being chaotic. People liked the way I ran the Department, I can assure you, and they missed me after I was gone. I was replaced for political reasons, and I never held another position of trust, but I achieved something that really mattered to me. I proved to myself that I wasn't a useless creature, a parasite . . . as my wife had claimed. Actually she came back to me, admitted she'd been wrong, and asked me for forgiveness. I was a reformed man, Senhor Rafael. With the small number of patients I had in my neighborhood practice, we were happy and comfortably off until my younger son turned to drugs. This wrecked our lives, Senhor Rafael. I've done everything to get money. Abortions, everything."

Taking a handkerchief out of his pocket, he wipes his eyes; he remains silent for a moment before he continues:

"During all these years I've never forgotten that last talk I had with your father—that was when he told me he was leaving for Spain. I thought it was a beautiful thing to do, Senhor Rafael. Nowadays there's no idealism, everybody wants to do his own thing, it's a rat race, a jungle where the bigger animals devour the smaller ones. But your father was a gentleman who lived in an age of gentlemen, Senhor Rafael, a man capable of dying for a passion."

"By the way," Rafael murmurs in a faint voice, "did he die, Franco?"

"Who?" The old man wonders if he has heard it right.

"Franco. General Franco."

"Ah!" The doctor sounds surprised. "Oh, yes, he died. But why do you ask?"

Then it dawns on him.

"Why, of course, because of your father. It would have been a great moment to him, Senhor Rafael. And it will be a great moment to you, too, when you escape from this place."

The guard puts his head around the door:

"Well, doc? Everything okay?" A warning rather than a question, as if to say: Look, doctor, don't encourage the likes of him to talk. They are important prisoners, yes, but still prisoners, we have to watch out for them. "I'd better be going," says the doctor. He puts the stethoscope into his old, battered valise: "It's a keepsake I've been carrying since my days in the Department," and before rising to his feet he whispers to Rafael: "Don't forget—at eleven o'clock." And turning to Boris: "Complain of pains, Senhor Boris. Moan to your heart's content."

"I'm leaving with you," says Suzana in a firm, assertive voice—now that she's involved in this, she probably wants to make the final arrangements with the doctor and be assured that everything will turn out all right. Before leaving she turns around and throws one final look at her father; a look full of tenderness, naturally; a look of grateful reconciliation. She is about to say something, but at that moment the guard closes the door (without banging it: it's a sickroom now, he can be considerate).

The two of them alone again.

Boris looks at his watch: "Five P.M.," he says. As if talking to himself. He lies down, clasps his hands under his neck. Music from the guard's battery radio filters through the door. A plaintive little waltz in which a pair of country singers bemoan the fact that they've left behind their beloved pampas and their darling mestizas.

In the room the shadows grow denser. Gradually the numbness in Rafael's body recedes and he can move an arm, a leg; he feels better. He sits up on the bed, and right away Boris gets to his feet, concerned:

"No, Rafael, you shouldn't—"

"Leave me alone."

Rafael gets out of bed. Walking with difficulty, he enters the bathroom. He closes the door, turns on the light. The raw brightness of the bulb reveals his face in the mirror. A discomposed face, naturally; but besides being discomposed it looks strange, too. So strange that he is impressed; he has never seen himself looking so *weird* before. It's not just perplexity—or rather, it's perplexity, but of a different kind. A grievous perplexity; what he sees in the mirror is the face of a person undergoing torture. Where does it come from, this startling expression? Could it be caused by something that the doctor injected into him? By the conversation they had before? By everything else? He doesn't know and he doesn't care. What is important now is to react, to not give himself up. *Come on now, Rafael. Make an effort, Rafael.*

It lasts for several minutes, this titanic battle of his will, this conflict of antagonistic muscles; minutes when Rafael sees himself as the loser, defeated by a superior power; but, as he is about to give up, he makes one last effort—and he succeeds. His face undergoes a slow transformation. The corners of his mouth lift, the lips begin to part. The skin beneath his lower eyelids crinkles—he is *smiling,* smiling at his own image. Good, he thinks, relieved, rewarded. Leaning forward, he rests his forehead on the mirror; the coldness of the smooth surface on his damp forehead feels good—and it amuses him, this image he now has of himself, an image distorted by the droll strabismus. He then closes his eyes and remains alone with himself, in peace and quiet. For how long? For a while; when he leaves the bathroom he notices that the guard has already brought their dinner; the tray, untouched, lies on one of the tables. "How are you feeling?" asks Boris. Rafael doesn't make a reply; he lies down. He feels fine; now he feels fine. His head light, his forehead cool; fine. And thus he drifts off into drowsiness; and in this twilight between sleep and wakefulness, it seems to him that all of them are there, standing around the bed—Jonah and Habacuc, Maimonides and Rafael Mendes, all the ones named Rafael Mendes. In silence they look at him. Suddenly he realizes: All of them have the face he saw in the mirror a while ago; all of them are him, he is all of them. Now he understands the *Notebooks of the New Christian;* they are his father's legacy to him—Rafael is no longer beset by doubts. Instead of solutions, fantasies; instead of answers, imaginary possibilities. The perfect message from a perplexed individual, concludes Rafael—and then the figures begin to vanish, and he falls asleep.

He wakes up startled. Boris is shaking him: "It's time," he whispers, "I'll start moaning now."

He lies down, and indeed, he starts moaning. But his performance is so poor and so unconvincing that Rafael can't contain himself; he bursts into laughter, quietly at first, but soon he's roaring with laughter, and a moment later he's laughing his head off, and laughing he rolls on the bed; at times he stops for a moment, his eyes brimming with tears, in order to catch his breath but soon he starts all over again, while Boris, frightened, asks him to stop, for he'll ruin everything, but Rafael, unable to control himself, can't stop laughing, and he laughs and laughs and then Boris begins to laugh too, that's insane, Rafael, we're doomed, this will be the end of us, but he, too, can't control himself, and he laughs and laughs until finally he manages to pull himself together, and he sobers up. Rising to his feet, he draws near Rafael, who has stopped laughing and he, too, gets up. For a moment the two of them stand motionless, their eyes fixed on each other. And then Boris says in a restrained but forceful voice:

"Punch me now, Rafael. Punch me in the belly."

But who are you to be ordering me about?—or so Rafael must be asking himself.

"Come on, punch me," Boris repeats.

"Ah, you dog," moans Rafael. Closing his hand into a fist, he punches Boris in the belly—but not hard enough, Boris barely feels the blow:

"Again. Harder."

Rafael musters all his energy and this time the blow is so heavy that Boris, reeling, steps back and collapses on the bed, moaning. And now he moans properly, and unrestrainedly, as he writhes like a worm—and all of a sudden he winks at Rafael. What a scoundrel, what a royal scoundrel; once again the winner, this crook gets what he wants, and he's now moaning to the letter, thanks to Rafael, thanks to Rafael's fist, and Rafael just stands there, not knowing what to say, what to do.

The door opens; it's the guard.

"What is it, Senhor Boris, what happened?"

"A pain," moans Boris, shrewd Boris. "An unbearable pain."

"You, too?" asks the guard, worried. "Where does it hurt?"

"Here, in my diaphragm," whimpers Boris.

"It couldn't be the food I brought you, could it?" The guard sounds alarmed, afraid that the chief of police will lay the blame on him.

"I don't know," says Boris. "Call the doctor, please, call the doctor."

The guard leaves; a few minutes later Dr. Castellar comes in:

"Wait outside," he tells the guard.

He closes the door behind him.

"Are you ready?" he asks Boris and Rafael, then Rafael and Boris. Boris says he is; but Rafael remains lying motionless.

"I'm not going," he says.

"What?" asks the doctor, surprised.

"I'm not going," Rafael repeats. "I'm staying here."

"But you're going to ruin everything!" The old man is now truly astounded. "What am I going to tell them?"

Boris looks at the doctor; he can't help being amused by the flabbergasted expression on his face. Poor fellow, he is completely floored by what's going on, all he wanted was to make a few dollars and pay a debt of gratitude, or vice-versa, but now he won't be able to do either, in whatever order, the story won't unfold the way he thought it would; it will be a different story, it's already different, and he's unable to make head or tail of it, he doesn't know what's happening, he can't imagine what might happen.

"What are you going to tell the men?" the doctor asks, confused and frightened.

Rafael smiles. He deserves the Gold Tree, this man, this old doctor; instead, what has befallen him is perplexity, the perplexity of generations, from which Rafael has finally freed himself:

"What am I going to tell them?" Rafael shrugs. "Well, my dear fellow. That I was asleep."

"Let's go, doctor," Boris commands. Supported by the doctor, he makes for the door; before leaving, he turns for the last time, gazes at Rafael and it seems that he is about to say something, but refraining, he says nothing. They leave; the door closes.

R AFAEL MENDES LIES DOWN AND CLOSES HIS EYES. HE WAITS for sleep, which will come—and for the dreams . . . Not the eyes of the Prophet, nor the bonfires of the Inquisition, nor the decapitated head of Tiradentes, nor the medieval knight, nor the priestess of Astarte, nor Habacuc, nor Eliezer, nor Naomi, nor any of the Essenes, be they Old or New; nor Maimonides, nor Saladin, nor Bandarra, nor Columbus, nor the Grand-Inquisitor, nor Afonso Sanches; nor the cacique, nor Little Dove, nor the Indians; nor Bento Teixeira, nor Vicente Nunes, nor Joseph de Castro; nor Frans Post; nor Felipe Royz; nor Manoel Beckman, nor João Felipe Betten-dorf, nor Maria de Freitas, nor Grácia Tapanhuna; nor Álvaro Mesquita, nor Zambi, nor M'bonga, nor the people of the *quilombos*; nor Bartolomeu Lourenço de Gusmão, nor Bárbara Santos, nor Pedro Telles; nor Diogo Henriques, nor Isabel Henriques; nor the blind *bandeirante*; nor Garibaldi, nor Anita; nor Dr. Débora, nor Microbe, nor Doutor Saturnino, nor the reporter from the *Alerta*, nor Father João de Buarque, nor Sepé Tiarajú; nor any of the many Rafael Mendeses that lie under the earth, bones and dust, dust and bones; none of them will he see; what he will see is a smiling boy in a sailor suit peering at him from amid the branches of the Tree of Life.

About the Author

Moacyr Scliar lives in Pôrto Alegre, the capital of Rio
Grande do Sul, Brazil, where he has been a practicing
physician in public health since 1969. He was born in
Pôrto Alegre in 1937 and took his degree in 1962 at the
Faculty of Medicine there. His early schooling was at
Pôrto Alegre's "Yiddish" College, the School of Education
and Culture. His secondary studies were in a Catholic
school. He began his literary career in 1968 with the
publication of the story collection, THE CARNIVAL
OF THE ANIMALS. He is also the author of THE
ONE-MAN ARMY (short stories), THE CENTAUR IN
THE GARDEN (a novel), THE BALLAD OF THE
FALSE MESSIAH (short stories), THE GODS OF
RAQUEL (a novel), and THE VOLUNTEERS (a novel).

★ THE BEST FROM THE AVAILABLE PRESS
★